NOT AS PLANNED

The Ladies Who Brunch Book Four

HARLOW JAMES

Paperback ISBN: 9798371805645
Special Edition Paperback: 9798369611234

Cover Designer: Abigail Davies, Pink Elephant Designs
Editor: Melissa Frey

This one is for all the moms—the new moms, the seasoned moms, the bonus moms, and the women who stepped in to any motherly role—being a mom is the hardest job on this earth, whether you have an active partner or not.
But I see you. I hear you. And I'm cheering you on.
Just don't forget to take care of you too.

"Nothing will ever make you as happy, as sad, as tired, or as proud as motherhood. For nothing is as hard as helping a person develop their own individuality, while struggling to keep your own."

Anonymous

Contents

Prologue

Noelle

Age Seventeen

"Oh God. You're not seriously redoing your life plan again, are you?"

Spinning around in the chair at my desk, I shoot my sister a glare. It's the Sunday night before my first day of senior year, and I'm reassessing my goals and schedule for the year. And yes, my life plan. "And what if I am?"

She rolls her eyes while plopping down on my bed, tucking her legs under her. "Having a list isn't going to guarantee that your life works out a certain way, Noelle." Holly, my older sister by only thirteen months who just graduated from high school a few months ago, is leaving for college in San Luis

1

Obispo in two short weeks. "Why don't you just focus on graduating from high school right now? Passing your SAT and completing your college applications. Going to football games and dances. That's what you should be looking forward to, not when you're going to get married."

Growling out in frustration, I drop my pen to my desk.

And before you question yourself, yes—our names are Noelle and Holly. Let's just say my mother is slightly obsessed with Christmas.

"There's nothing wrong with having a plan and setting goals. Knowing what you want and writing it down increases achievement and the likelihood that it will happen. Haven't you ever heard of manifesting success through visualization?"

"Does that mean you're also visualizing a hero from one of those trashy romance novels you're always reading to come in on his white horse and save you?" She waves her hand across the space in front of her like she's setting the scene of a movie. "And let me guess . . . he'll be the perfect man who whisks you off into the sunset and gives you the perfect marriage with a white picket fence and two-point-five kids? Because that's just setting yourself up for disappointment *not* success, Noelle." Reaching over to my nightstand, she picks up my latest read, scanning the blurb on the back. "The girl loses her boyfriend *and* her job and *then* inherits an inn? Sounds like a Hallmark movie gone bad!"

I leap from my chair and snatch the book from her hands. "It's fiction, and it's romantic. She falls for her carpenter, who is grumpy and extremely handsome. That could totally happen!"

Holly throws her head back as she holds her stomach, laughing. "Oh God! That's so cliché!"

"Life and love can surprise you. Serendipity is real and so is love. Just because you don't believe that there are people who genuinely meet in unusual circumstances and spend their entire lives together doesn't mean it doesn't happen. Because it does."

The smirk she gives me makes me want to punch her in the jaw. "And let me guess—a certifiably adorable meet cute like in your books is on your little list there, isn't it?" She motions to the paper on my desk.

"Yes, it is. Because I believe that one day, hopefully when I'm twenty-two and just about to graduate from college, I will stumble upon my future husband in the most romantic way, we'll fall in love, be married by the time I'm twenty-five, have our first child by twenty-seven, buy a house in a community full of other families, and live happily ever after."

It's the perfect timeline, one I know can work if I stick to my plan.

"You know reading that stuff is only going to set you up for disappointment with men, right? Boys don't act like that for sure, and look how many of Mom's friends complain about their husbands all the time."

Our mother hosts a book club each week that is really just an excuse for them to all sit around, drink wine, and catch up on life—while complaining about their husbands.

"Marriage is hard. Look at Mom and Dad. They fight and get annoyed with each other. But that's normal. It doesn't mean they don't love each other." I frown, willing her to understand.

Sighing, Holly stands from my bed and heads toward the door. "Whatever, Noelle. Keep dreaming, I guess, if that's what helps you sleep at night. But just know that while you're so worried about the future, your life is happening right now."

"Do you have a plan, Holly?" My question makes her pause as she's reaching for the doorknob. "Do you have things you want to achieve in life?"

She glances at me over her shoulder. "Yeah. I want to go to college, party my ass off, get as far away as I can from this boring neighborhood, and have the time of my life before I have to get up and go to work every day. If I meet someone, whatever." She shrugs. "And if I don't, that's okay, too. I just want to live without every second of my life being predetermined or feeling like I'm on some sort of time crunch to experience things before a certain age."

"Well, I wish you luck with that. Let me know how it works out for you. But in the meantime, can you just accept that this is how I want to live *my* life?"

Her shoulders fall, but her lips curl in a soft smile. "Yeah, I guess. Dinner's ready, by the way." And then she exits my room, leaving me alone to ponder my future once more.

On the eve of my senior year of high school, it's important to me, now more than ever, to have a plan in place. If I want to become a literary agent and build my family, I don't have time for distractions. My sister may have a cynical outlook on life, but that's not me. I know what I want, and I will do everything in my power to build the future I envision for myself.

Placing my list back in the drawer of my desk, I stare out the window of my room to the street, watching the leaves on the trees in front of our house rustling in the wind. Growing up in a small suburb of LA has shown me what life can be like if you meet the right person. My parents met just after they graduated from high school and have been together ever since, and my grandparents on both sides are still married after forty-plus years. I come from a family of people who have found their soulmates and built the perfect lives, and that's what I want for myself, too. I'm a romantic at heart, always have been, and my obsession with romance novels has definitely contributed to that.

I remember when I picked up my first spicy book. I was sixteen, and one of our neighbors was having a garage sale. I was out riding my bike when I decided to stop by and say hello. Mrs. Yates had five kids who were all grown, and she was cleaning out her house, getting it ready to sell so she could retire up in Santa Barbara with her husband of thirty-five years. Being a bookworm already to my core, I instantly gravitated toward the box of old books, inhaling their scent the moment I stood in front of them. And then I picked up *The Black Lyon* by Jude Deveraux, and my entire world changed.

My mother had a lengthy conversation with me about the book choice but ultimately knew that I was a young woman who loved to read, and as long as I came to her with questions about the content if I had them, she trusted me to make the right choice for me. Thank God I had a mother who was involved and open-minded about the entire situation.

Granted, the book was fairly racy for a sixteen-year-old, and I definitely learned things about sex from that book that I didn't know prior, but I fell in love with the feeling I got while reading it—the push and pull of emotions, the escalation of my heart rate when life kept the hero and heroine apart, the trials and tribulations they faced in the name of love.

I was addicted, completely and utterly consumed by romance novels from that day forward. Because love is the one emotion that everyone can relate to. And no two love stories are the same.

When we discussed potential careers last year in my English class, my teacher suggested trying to get into publishing since books are a huge part of my life. So I decided then and there that I wanted to become a literary agent, help find the next great romance novel that could potentially alter someone's life the way they altered mine.

I walk over to my bed, retrieve my book from the comforter where Holly left it, and flip through the pages, stopping at my bookmark. My eyes scan the words, and before I know it, I've read four more pages, and things are definitely starting to heat up.

Perhaps dinner can wait . . .

Chapter 1

Noelle

Age Thirty

"Holy shit. I'm really doing this." I place the pen down on the desk in front of me, staring at my signature on the client forms I just signed.

"Congratulations, Miss Parker. You are officially a patient of California Cryobank. We look forward to working with you and making your dreams come true."

Exhaling, I lean back in my chair. "Thank you. I'm nervous but excited."

"That's completely normal," Dr. Adams reassures me, clasping her hands together over her desk. "We have several assessments, tests, and exams to go through over the course of the next few months. But hopefully, they will all lead to you starting the family you desire."

Well, this isn't exactly what I had envisioned, but dammit, I was tired of waiting. And I have to say, nowhere in my life plan did I ever write "choose to have a child via sperm donor," yet here I am.

Yeah, if you haven't caught up by now, my future didn't exactly work out the way I imagined. Don't worry, my sister made sure to rub that in my face every chance she got, but her life didn't pan out the way she anticipated, either, so we both got a dose of reality.

And I guess the follow-up question would be: How did I, Noelle Parker, lover of romance and believer in soulmates, end up choosing to have a baby on her own?

Well, that man, the *one* who was supposed to sweep me off my feet and give me the life I always imagined?

He never showed up, and I never found him.

It wasn't for lack of trying, believe me. Hell, after I graduated from college without so much as a blind date to look forward to, I knew I was already behind schedule. So what would any single woman looking for love do? Sign up for dating websites, of course. Dating apps didn't hit the scene until years later, but don't worry, I've tried them, too.

While my closest girlfriends—whom we will introduce later—were busy building their careers and enjoying being single, I was relishing the fact that my internship with Larson Publishing turned into full-time employment right after graduation from UCLA, so I had nothing but time to devote to finding the man in my life. And man, was I determined to find him.

Failed date after failed date, I finally stumbled upon Knox. Knox was an investment banker who looked killer in a three-piece suit. He was tall, blond, and four years older than me. And damn, could the man fuck me sideways. At twenty-three, with only drunk college boys to compare to, he was by far the best sex I had experienced up to that point in my life. He was attractive, confident, and career driven.

On paper, he looked like he was everything I wanted. But sadly, he was only interested in one thing: his job. After six months of dating with no indication of commitment on the horizon and his blatant claim that he never wanted kids, I sadly walked away feeling as if I had wasted time with him. Although, the sex *was* dynamite, so it wasn't a complete waste, if I'm being honest.

A few months later, I met Kellan. Kellan was an HVAC technician and owned his own home. He was a few years older than me as well, but he was kind, thoughtful, and we definitely had physical chemistry. But Kellan had an addiction: collecting Star Wars memorabilia. In fact, the guy would stay up into the wee hours of the morning scouring eBay, spending every hard-earned dime he made and a lot of dimes he didn't have on priceless toys—at least that's what he said. After a few months, I quickly learned that Kellan's collectibles were far more important to him than me or financial security, so I ended things and heard he filed for bankruptcy a year later.

Next to emotionally scar me was John. John was an insurance broker who was tall, handsome, and treated me really well. The chemistry was there, he always bought me gifts, and I genuinely felt adored by him, like I was a priority in his life. We were together for ten months before things went south. One day, he was on my laptop and left himself logged in to his Facebook account. I glanced at the screen as a message popped up and saw something that looked odd, so I delved a little further.

Now, let me preface this by saying that I'm not normally a woman who snoops. I respect my boyfriend's privacy unless I feel a need to question something, but then I try to have a conversation about it—not do detective work because I don't trust them.

Turned out, the comment on the screen warranted my alarm because I saw him share a link to his YouTube channel with a friend of his. I had no idea that John had a YouTube channel after almost a year of dating, so I was curious. But when I clicked on the link, nothing could have prepared me for what I was about to discover—something that rocked my world.

John apparently had a foot fetish and had posted videos of my feet and the feet of other women (probably former girl-friends or hookups) to his channel and shared it with God knows who. When I confronted him about it, he panicked and tried to explain that he liked me for more than my feet. But I felt so violated that I couldn't look at him anymore, so I ended it.

And I think I wore socks every day for a year after that.

Then there was Michael, the one and only bad boy I took a

chance on. I was twenty-six, beginning to feel desperate, and needed to remind myself that there was still a life for me to live, one that didn't involve finding the right man. So one night, the girls and I went to a concert where a local band was playing. The instant I saw Michael on stage, I knew I wanted to get to know him. Covered in tattoos and with several piercings all over his body (and I mean *everywhere*), he was the antithesis of my type, but I was drawn to him unlike anything I had ever experienced before.

When I say there was electricity between us, I'm talking lightning bolts. Being near him made my skin crawl with awareness and my vagina throb with need. He took me on one date, and I slept with him that night, not even worrying that it made me appear easy. In fact, I knew I couldn't have been the only woman who gave it up that quickly to him, but he assured me I was different. After that night, I became a groupie, and Michael and I were inseparable. I followed his band around southern California, cheering them on from backstage and attending every after-party. Michael and I fucked like rabbits in the apartment he shared with his bandmates and spent every moment we could together. For a moment, I wondered if he was the man I was meant to be with and maybe the vision I had in mind needed to be adjusted. He was the complete opposite of what I saw for my future husband and what my life would be like, but maybe that was a good thing, right?

Well, one night, his band was approached by an agent, and they were signed to a record company. Michael was going to be on a six-month-long tour that would most likely extend longer.

I wanted to go with him, but he told me he didn't want me to resent him for chasing his dreams if it meant me leaving mine behind. We decided it was best to part ways, and I was devastated. Honestly, it was the most catastrophic breakup I ever experienced, and it took me a long time to recover. I didn't date for over a year and silently stalked the band as they became the next big thing. The girls nursed me through the breakup, and when I finally found the courage to put myself out there again, I was scared shitless.

And I stayed far away from rock stars—although I did miss the piercings.

Then, at almost twenty-eight, I knew I was way too far behind schedule with my plan. It was time to buckle down and get back on the horse. I did speed dating, went to mixers, found Facebook groups of other singles looking for love, asked everyone I knew if they knew someone they could fix me up with, but I had no luck. There were a few men who seemed promising in the beginning, but I quickly realized that a lot of men my age weren't even thinking about settling down or starting a family yet, and that's what I wanted.

After bad dates and lots of bad sex, I eased up on the pressure but tried to remain optimistic. And then I met Tim. Tim was a high school English teacher, loved to ride his bicycle for miles each day, had a dog, and owned his own place. He had black hair, green eyes, and loved to read. He was perfect, or so I thought. I thought we were headed for the altar.

We chose to wait to have sex until we got to know each other better, something I hadn't tried before so I was hoping that was the key. I remember telling the girls that he was it, he was the man I had been waiting for. And then when we finally decided to do the deed, he said something that shook me to my core.

"You need my pecker, don't you, baby?"

I froze as he lay on top of me. "What?"

"My good girl wants my pecker in her hen house, doesn't she?"

"Tim? Are you talking about your cock?"

"My pecker, baby. That's what you need to call it, and don't worry, I'm dying to give it to you. And then I'm gonna watch you suck my pecker until I shoot my little roosters all over your face."

Yeah, that relationship didn't progress beyond that night in case you were wondering.

So needless to say, I took some time to regroup but never found another man who restored my faith in the idea of love. I didn't stop believing, I just wanted to stop dating, and I did for a while.

Then one night, at the age of thirty, one leg of our foursome, Amelia, said something to me that hit me like a fastball coming right for my face.

I sighed dramatically. "God, I want kids, Amelia. Why on earth do you have to have a man to do that, though?"

"Well, technically, you don't. You just need a few of his best swimmers."

"I just don't know if I could go through with that—picking some guy to be the father of my kid without knowing him."

"Yeah, but look at how disappointing potential men have been recently. I'm not telling you what to do, but I also know that you will be an incredible mother, and you don't need a man in your life to do that."

I stared at her, deep in thought. "You know what, you're right."

And that is how I ended up at California Cryobank, shopping for sperm.

Well, I can't shop yet, but I'm definitely waiting for the store to open so I can sprint inside to get first pick of the bunch, if you catch my drift.

Dr. Adams pulls me from my trip down memory lane. "So we will see you next week to start everything and then go from there. Be patient with the process since it can take a while, and let us know if you have any questions as they arise. You can simply email me, and I will respond as quickly as I can. But remember that you can always change your mind or ask for more time to make a decision if you need it." She offers me her business card, and I accept it eagerly.

"I'm not changing my mind, I assure you. I'm tired of waiting for Mr. Right. I just need some sperm, and I'll be on my way to motherhood like I've always wanted."

Dr. Adams chuckles. "I like your enthusiasm. And this is why we do what we do. Women should have the right to take their reproductive journeys into their own hands. And there are plenty of men who benefit from donating their sperm as well."

"I'm sure the donation process is the best part of the experience for them."

She winks at me. "So I've heard."

I leave the sperm bank, inhaling the fresh air in southern California as I make my way to my car. It's the beginning of fall, and if things go well, I could be a mother sometime next year. Making this decision is scary, but I also feel like I'm doing the right thing. I'm tired of waiting for a man. And if I have a baby with the wrong man, wouldn't that be worse? Having to co-parent, deal with custody battles and child support? Having to explain to my future child that their parents didn't belong together, or worse, that their father didn't want to be in their life?

I know that there are other conversations I'll have to have along those lines, but at least I know my baby will be loved and wanted by *me*, and that's all that matters in the end.

Once safely in my car, I make the short drive back to work.

"Noelle? Regina Thomas is waiting for you." My secretary, Madison, greets me when I walk into Larson Publishing and make my way to my office.

"She's early."

"I know. I told her you'd be back soon, and she didn't seem to mind."

"Okay. Let me run to the ladies' room, and then I'll be right there." After I do my business, I round the corner and see one of the first authors I signed sitting in the waiting room, reading something on her phone. "Regina!"

Her head pops up, and her smile spreads as she stands. "Noelle! How are you, darling?"

"I'm great!" I respond a little too enthusiastically. But hell,

I've had quite the eventful morning, and my blood is pumping with optimism. "Come inside my office, please." She follows me in, and I put my purse on the hook next to my door, making my way to my desk as she sits in the chair on the other side. "How are you doing?"

Brushing her shoulder-length hair off her neck, she says, "Oh, you know. I'm a writer who just made her deadline, so I'm celebrating by actually taking a shower and leaving my house for the first time in weeks."

"Ha. I can imagine. But can I just say, Regina . . . the book . . ." I cover my heart with both hands and shake my head slowly at her. "It's magic. You outdid yourself."

She claps her hands. "Gah! I'm so glad you think so. It felt magical as I was writing it. Those characters spoke to me so clearly that I could never get them to shut up."

I giggle. "I didn't want them to. In fact, I probably could have read about the two of them forever. And the grand gesture? The cupboards and the notes on them? Ugh, so romantic."

"Thank you, Noelle. That means a lot. I'm always afraid that the longer I do this I won't be able to come up with something new and exciting anymore."

Regina found her passion for writing romance novels in her late fifties after she retired from teaching. Now, at sixty-one, the woman has written over twenty novels in the last six years and hit every bestseller's list I know of. When I discovered her, I knew I'd hit gold. And our friendship has been icing on the cake. She reminds me a lot of my mother, which I think makes our bond even more special, but I love the fact that she found a creative outlet and second career later in life. She proves that age does not determine when a person can achieve something, especially women. I know from my own experience that putting an age limit on something can feel stifling.

Why can't we do it all or try it all whenever we want? Why must we feel pressure to have it all by a certain age or do more every second of the day? Why can't we just do what makes us happy without fear of what others may think?

Seems today I'm finally listening to my own thoughts.

"I get that. And I've seen it. But trust me, Regina . . ." I place my hand on the ones she has resting on my desk, reassuring her. "You're talented and meant to be a romance author. And I'll be here for you even when there are bad days."

Smiling while clearly trying to cover up her emotion, she replies, "Thank you. Gosh, I swear, I know you're my agent, but you feel like you could be my daughter as well."

Laughing, I retract my hand and wake up my computer. "I will take that as a compliment."

"We could make it come true, you know? If you would just go out with my son."

Sighing, I flick my eyes back to her. "Regina, we've been over this."

"I know, I know." She waves me off. "But you always tell me how you're dating duds—which, don't get me wrong, has inspired more than one story idea. However, I have a man who I think would be perfect for you in real life, and you just keep shutting me down."

"He's your son. You're my client. It's a conflict of interest, Regina." Like a broken record, I repeat what I always say to her when she brings this up. Ever since we started working together, Regina has mentioned her single son who is "a catch," at least according to her. But I've heard that phrase tossed around a time or two, and it's always only led me to question the people I know and whether they truly know *me* or not.

Don't get me wrong—I'm tempted to take the bait, especially after my luck. But my professionalism wins. "Besides, what if something were to happen between us in a bad way? I would never want that to jeopardize our working relationship."

She sighs and clucks her tongue. "I know, but I'm telling you, you're missing out. My boy is the kind of man women want in real life *and* in their romance novels. If you find yourself longing for some male companionship and you change your mind, just let me know."

"I'm sure he is amazing, especially because *you* raised him and the men in real life suck in general."

Laughing, she tilts her head at me. "Still no Prince Charming then?"

"Nope." For a second, I hesitate telling her what I did today. But I'm chomping at the bit to tell someone, and I know I can trust her. It's Regina. So I do it. "I actually took my future in my own hands today."

She perks up. "Really? How?"

"I signed a contract to be a client-slash-patient with a sperm bank. I've decided I'm going to have a baby on my own."

Her eyes widen, but a soft smile follows. "Oh my gosh.

Congratulations!"

Cheeks burning from smiling, I say, "Thank you. I'm nervous. I know it's a big decision, but I am ready. I've always wanted a family, and I'm tired of waiting on Mr. Right."

"Kids are important to you?"

"Oh, yes. I mean, if I had it my way and things had worked out the way I wanted them to, I'd already have two of them."

She nods, still smiling. "I see. Well, I'm happy that you're making choices to get what you want. Not all men can give that to you."

"I know. And even the ones who I thought wanted those things don't want them right now. So I'm doing it on my own."

She reaches over and places her hand on mine this time. "Then, Noelle, you do what you feel is best for you. You will be a phenomenal mother, and I will be here cheering you on, even on the bad days." I don't miss that her words mirror my own to her earlier.

"Aw, Regina. Thank you so much." Sharing a silent moment between us before we part, I thank God for people like her in my life—women who can cheer you on instead of judge your every decision. "Now, let's get back to the book. I do have a few notes and an idea."

"What's your idea?" she asks as I reach for my notebook.

"What if there's a scene where he thinks there's a spider on him, but it turns out to just be her hair? You know, to mess with him a bit?"

She throws her head back as she laughs. "Oh my God, that's genius! Yes, let's fit that in somewhere."

Chapter 2

Noelle

The Day After Christmas the Following Year

"She's early! She's not supposed to be early!"

"Noelle, just breathe," Dr. Admonsen commands. "Everything is going to be fine. The baby is a good size, you've made it past thirty-seven weeks, which is always the goal, so now you're on your daughter's timetable. And newsflash, honey—now that you're having a child, all plans fly right out the window."

"But . . ."

"No buts, Noelle. Your daughter is coming tonight."

Breathing in short, rapid breaths, I nod my head. "Okay. This is it."

Charlotte bites her lip beside me. "Holy crap, Noelle. You're about to be a mom."

The nurses are moving around the room, setting things up for the delivery. I'm only dilated four centimeters, so we have some time. But the reality is, my baby will be here soon.

"I know. Holy shit. This is really happening."

Penelope walks up to my bed, holding a piece of red licorice, yanking it between her teeth before she chews. I kind of hate her right now for eating in front of me, but she'd better have more once this baby comes out or there will be a price to pay.

"I can't believe you're eating licorice in front of me right now. You know those are my favorite."

Penelope smacks her lips together before she swallows. "Don't worry, I got you, girl. I bought one of those big plastic tubs for you for after the baby is born. I just had to take one for myself. I forgot how good Red Vines are."

"I haven't. But at least you didn't bring Twizzlers. If you had, I may have had to get out of this bed and fight you."

"That won't be necessary," she says, flipping her hair over her shoulder. "You just need to worry about bringing my niece into the world tonight so we can start raising the next generation of Ladies Who Brunch."

When I found out we were having a girl, the four of us joked about how awesome it would be if we all had daughters who could grow up together to be friends like we are. Granted, we all didn't meet until we were freshmen in college, but life-long friendships are rare, and I could only dream of something like that for my Scarlett.

This pregnancy has been a whirlwind, and even though I'm scared to go through childbirth, I can't wait to meet my girl, even if she is early.

The process to get to this moment took longer than I anticipated. Tests, exams, and counseling sessions led me to February until I was able to start choosing my sperm donor. And once I found the man, with the help of my girls, of course, it was time to get pregnant.

My first intrauterine insemination in March was unsuccessful, but the second time was the winner. My due date was supposed to be January fourth, but apparently my daughter is in a hurry to enter this world.

I think I can handle her being the type of person who's early to everything rather than being late. That's who I am, so hopefully that will set us up to avoid future arguments when she's a teenager.

However, my pregnancy was difficult, and not necessarily in the way the average person might think. Sure, there were aches and pains, heartburn, acne, constipation, food cravings and aversions. I carried chicken nuggets around in my bra for six months, for crying out loud. Not sure why I thought that was a good idea, but it just made sense at the time. And it was convenient, I must admit.

No, the difficult part was the fact that the baby's father wasn't there to share it with me. Growing up, and even after as I searched for Mr. Right, I always envisioned having my partner with me at doctor's appointments, choosing nursery décor together, having him there to rub my feet or back when my body was hurting, and listening to him talk to my belly when the baby moved.

I had to mourn those ideas of what I thought my life would look like and learn to embrace the path I chose. Because instead, I had my four best friends with me every step of the way. One of them was at every doctor's appointment. We decorated the nursery together in red and yellow hues and décor that turned out stunningly beautiful. They booked prenatal massages for me when my body ached, brought me food when a craving hit, and I felt the baby kick for the first time at brunch one morning, so they were all there to share that moment with me.

Now, they're all here in the delivery room as well, a policy that I insisted we break since there was no way I was about to go through this without their support.

Amelia comes through the door now with a tray of coffees for her, Penelope, and Charlotte. *And oh my God, it smells amazing.*

I just might have to fight her, too, when this is over.

"How's it going?" she asks as she disperses the drinks.

"She's at a four. Doctor said she's doing great so far and the baby could be born tonight." Charlotte lifts her coffee to her lips.

"I'm gonna bet on the wee hours of the morning tomorrow," Penelope declares.

"Why are you insisting on me being in labor for longer?" I fire off toward her.

"I'm not. I'm just saying that from what I know, first babies usually take longer to come out. That's all." She shrugs. "But it would give me more time to tease Maddox with dirty text messages so he's really randy when I get home after this, too." She bounces her eyebrows.

Penelope fell in love with NFL quarterback Maddox Taylor after her PR firm was hired to represent the Los Angeles Bolts, the team he was traded to last year. They had a one-night stand that turned into a secret relationship, and he was determined to make her his. She had to face a lot of demons from her past to let him in, but thankfully she did, and now they've been together since around the time I found out I was pregnant. I love seeing Penelope in love after she fought the idea for so long in her life. And in true Penelope fashion, she's not afraid to offer up plenty of details about her sex life.

"Please, continue to remind me that you're having sex and I'm not."

She smirks. "I can, if you really want me to."

"No, I'm quite alright. Thank God for battery-operated toys or I may not have survived the second trimester of my pregnancy, ladies. I have never been so horny in my life! And the fact that I had to read romance novels every day as part of my job did not help."

Charlotte chuckles. "So this is what I have to look forward to?"

"Yup. Don't worry, I kept a journal of everything I was feeling so I can fill in the timeline for you pretty well."

Charlotte found out she was pregnant last week and just told her husband, Damien, yesterday, on Christmas morning.

Damien and Charlotte grew up together back in South Carolina and were rivals from a young age, but they both attended college out in California. They ran into each other after twelve years and agreed to fake date to get her mom off her back about not being married yet and for Damien to impress his boss for a promotion. But Amelia, Penelope, and I could all see it—there was an undeniable chemistry between them. What they thought was a childhood enemies relationship quickly turned to lovers and even more when they got married this past June. And now, they're expecting their first child next year.

I must say I'm excited to have another friend who's about to experience motherhood so at least one of them will understand completely what I'm going through and about to go through. And this way, our kids will be close in age, too.

"I hope I don't feel the need to keep chicken nuggets in my bra like you did."

Penelope snickers. "I think that was just an abnormality unique to our girl Noelle."

"Hey. It just made sense at the time. I can't explain it. It's like when women eat pickles and peanut butter while pregnant. Or barbecue potato chips and cranberry juice. You don't understand!"

Penelope places her hand on my shoulder, soothing me.

"It's okay. We hear you. I'm just letting you know that you won't ever live that down, babe. You've scarred us for life."

"Whatever," I mumble.

Amelia steps forward now, grabbing my leg under the sheet over me as a contraction hits, forcing me to breathe through the pain as she speaks to me. "Noelle, I know I've told you this before, but I'm so proud of you. What you've been through the past year has not been easy, but you've shown us how strong you are. In a matter of hours, you're going to be a mother, which is one of the hardest jobs in the world. And even though you won't have a partner in this, remember that you will always have us."

The back of my eyes begin to sting. "Thank you. I couldn't have done this without you girls. I know I have my family's support, too, but you girls are my family as well. We've been through so much, and our lives are changing so fast. I can't wait to hold my baby, but I know that I would never have been able to choose this journey without knowing I've had you girls with me every step of the way."

Charlotte, Penelope, Amelia, and I all lock hands in a circle, smiling at each other as our eyes fill with unshed tears.

Penelope takes a deep breath before declaring, "Alright, ladies. No more tears. Today is a happy day. Let's have a baby!"

"Oh my God! This burns so fucking bad!"

Um, just a public service announcement—doctors and nurses shouldn't advertise epidurals without mentioning there's a window in which you can receive them, and once that window closes, you're about to experience the most excruciating pain you've ever felt in your life. I'm pretty sure someone is holding a match to my vaginal opening right now.

The girls are standing around me—Charlotte and Penelope holding up my legs and Amelia behind me, supporting my back —as I attempt to push my daughter out, beyond pissed that I dilated too quickly to get the good drugs.

"Oh my God! I can't believe I have to do this in nine months!" Charlotte exclaims as her eyes stay glued to the crime scene happening between my legs, a grimace on her lips.

I bet she's second-guessing having unprotected sex right about now, huh?

"Dear Lord! Your vagina is never going to be the same after this!" Penelope adds, pulling my attention to her as I release my breath and rest my head against the bed again.

I turn to her as Amelia wipes sweat from my forehead with a towel. "Why on earth would you say something like that right now?"

Penelope holds her hands up. "I'm sorry! But Jesus Christ, Noelle. This is not making me want to have kids someday!"

"Sorry to kill your dreams, but this is real life, Pen." And then another contraction hits me. "Motherfucker!"

"Now, now," Dr. Admonsen admonishes. "You don't need

to use that kind of language, Noelle. Just push through the pain, and your daughter will be here soon."

Penelope points a finger at my doctor, leaning toward her. "If my friend wants to use the most colorful, vulgar words in the dictionary right now, you're going to let her, you hear me?"

"Penelope," I grate out between clenched teeth.

"No. You swear all you want, Noelle. This baby is destroying your lady garden right now, so you can curse up a freaking storm. You deserve it!"

"I can see the head," Dr. Admonsen announces, flicking her eyes between Penelope and me, wondering if she should call security on my friend, I'm sure.

"Oh my God!" I growl and keep pushing until my doctor tells me to stop. "What? No, I can't. She needs to come out!"

"I need to make sure you don't tear," she replies, moving and putting pressure against my vaginal opening that is already stretched to capacity. "Okay, give me one big one, Noelle. One more push, and you'll meet your daughter."

"Motherfucker!" I shout as Penelope hollers in approval, bearing down as hard as I can and wondering if the doctor is building a campfire between my legs right now. Jesus Christ, this is the worst pain I've ever felt, and I've broken a bone or two in my life.

But then there's an alleviation of pressure, a sigh of relief, and the most amazing sound in the world hits my ears: my baby's cry.

"She's here!" Charlotte shouts as she, Penelope, and Amelia all lean over to see her. "And she's perfect, Noelle. I mean, she's covered in all kinds of nasty shit right now, but she is so freaking cute, too!"

Dr. Admonsen holds her up so I can see her, and I swear, the world stops spinning for a moment as I take in the sight of my child for the very first time.

Oh my God. I created that.

"Let's get her on your chest," the doctor explains, moving forward, pulling down the sheet so my bare skin is exposed and then placing my daughter on my chest. And the wave of pure love that spreads over my body is unlike anything I've ever felt before.

"Oh my God," I whisper, staring down at her as she cries. "Hi, baby girl. Hello, Scarlett."

"She looks like a Scarlett," Amelia adds as the doctor moves back between my legs, doing what she needs to do, but I'm not even paying attention to her anymore.

"She does, doesn't she?" Running my finger down her cheek, she starts to settle, nuzzling into my body more. And then her eyes pop open and find mine, and I burst into tears. "Hi there, sweetheart. Mommy's right here."

Charlotte, Penelope, and Amelia all sniffle around me.

"She's fucking perfect, Noelle," Penelope whispers. "And she looks like you."

"Really? How can you tell?"

"I mean, the goop around her definitely provides a challenge. But she's got your lips and eyes. And looks like brown hair to me, too."

"Well, the donor had brown hair as well, so that's not

surprising." I stroke her back. "It doesn't matter, though. All that matters is she's here and healthy."

Dr. Admonsen clears her throat. "You did great, Noelle. We just need to get the baby cleaned up, check her vitals, and then you can go back to skin-on-skin contact for as long as you want, okay?"

"Okay." I hand Scarlett to the doctor and watch her walk my daughter to the weighing station as Amelia wipes my forehead again.

"You did amazing, Noelle. And now you're a mom."

Crying, I let my tears cloud my vision before closing my eyes, resting my head back against the bed. "I am. I'm a mom."

"And you're going to be the best mom ever," Penelope adds. "And we're going to be the best fucking aunts in the history of aunts. That little girl will have nothing but love surrounding her. That's a fact."

"How are you feeling?" Charlotte asks, reaching for my hand.

"Tired. Sweaty. Sore. You guys, I'm not joking—that burned like my vagina was in hell."

Charlotte winces. "Note to self: Take the epidural as soon as it's offered."

"Yeah, don't wait like I did."

"Seven pounds on the dot!" The nurse exclaims as she wraps Scarlett up in a red blanket, placing a white hat on her head. "And since it's the day after Christmas, we wrapped her up like a present for you." She walks her over, placing the baby back on my chest, and my heart feels whole again.

"Thank you. And red is my favorite color, too. Hence her name."

The nurse smiles. "It's perfect. Congratulations, Mom."

And as my eyes drift down to my sleeping daughter, all I can think about is how I got here and how it was all worth it, how I wouldn't change a thing because it led me to her.

And now, I get to enter this entirely new phase of my life where I get to be the most important person in *her* world—her mother.

It's going to be perfect.

Chapter 3

Noelle

Five Months Later, Present Day

"Come on, Scarlett. I know you're tired." Bouncing my daughter around her nursery, I let my own tears fall as she cries about who knows what in the wee hours of the morning. My guess is her teeth, but I already gave her teething tablets and her crying isn't stopping, so I'm beginning to think it may be something else.

Thank goodness I live in a house and not an apartment, otherwise my neighbors would hate me by now.

I'm just gonna lay it all out there: No one is ready for this. Motherhood, that is—body changes, complete sleep deprivation, and moments of peace only when the baby is sleeping during which you wish you could relax but know you should be getting something done like washing dishes, folding laundry, or showering. And now that Scarlett is on the move, crawling all over the place, I really can't leave her alone for a second or I may get CPS called on me with the shit she loves to get in to.

She's also clingy, teething, and likes to use my breast as a pacifier or chew toy when she eats. Thank goodness she's finally eating some solids, though, because for a minute there, I didn't think my body would be able to keep up with the demand this girl has for food. And even now, I'm supplementing with formula so that her hunger is satisfied.

Motherhood—AKA the hardest 'hood you'll ever go through—is not anything like I thought it would be. Why aren't more women talking about how fucking hard it is?

Like how I love my daughter more than life itself, but I would love nothing more than to be alone for more than an hour.

Or how I don't even recognize my body in the mirror anymore, even though I know I grew and birthed an actual human being. My curves have curves, lumps, and dimples, and none of my clothes fit the same.

Or how I count down the minutes until she goes to sleep but then miss her once she's sleeping. That's some fucked-up shit, is it not?

Don't get me wrong—I don't regret my decision to have a child on my own at all. But I think I was also naïve about how hard it was going to be as a single mom.

I know I have my own parents to lean on, and the girls help

as much as they can, but it's not the same. It's not the same as having a partner who's there with you when you're home to take some of the workload away. And not just the dishes, laundry, and grocery shopping—but the mental load, too.

Like whether Scarlett is hitting the milestones she should be. Or having someone to take over in the middle of the night when you have to be up for work in three hours and the baby just won't sleep, like what I'm going through this instant. Or someone else to just tell me that I'm doing a good job and I'm not alone because that's exactly how I feel right now—alone.

Thank goodness tomorrow is Friday at least.

"Okay, baby. Let's try some more Orajel. It's got to be those teeth trying to break through that has you so upset." I march into the kitchen and reach for the medicine basket, chastising myself for not keeping the gel in her room where it would probably be more convenient. Twisting off the cap, I slather my finger with a good amount and then insert my digit into Scarlett's mouth, rubbing it all over her gums. She gnaws on my finger as I do it, and I let her because she's not crying anymore—finally.

"I know, sweetheart. I know. I wish there was more I could do for you." The last time I was up like this with her, my mother said that she and my father used to rub whiskey on our gums when we were teething. I'm not gonna lie, I contemplated it for a moment, but I'm just not sure I can go through with it yet.

And that's another thing—how come no one tells you that when you become a parent, you constantly second-guess every decision you make? Like you're terrified that making one wrong decision will emotionally scar your child for the rest of their life?

That's a huge weight to carry around!

At least if I had a partner, I know there would be someone else to blame or bounce ideas off of. *Ugh.* Yet another moment where I battle the circumstances that I put myself in but can't regret. It's just hard. The past five months have been harder than I ever imagined they could be.

This has to get easier, right?

Scarlett starts to grow heavy in my arms, resting her head on my chest. I rinse off my finger quietly and then caress the back of her head, smoothing down her beautiful, fine, light-brown baby hairs that are finally starting to grow in, resembling my own. But she got blue-green eyes from her father, whoever he is.

At least she looks like me. It eliminates the commentary about how she must look like her dad. And they say that, in nature, the firstborn child is supposed to come out looking like the father so the dad doesn't disown their offspring—but maybe it worked in my favor this time since the father isn't even in the picture.

Lucky me.

Feeling guilty again for complaining to myself about my situation, I slowly bounce her up and down as I make my way back down the hallway, waiting for her weight to grow heavier so I know that she's asleep. If I'm lucky, I'll get another hour of rest once my mind shuts off, and that should be enough to hold me over throughout my workday.

Gently placing her in her crib, I stare down at this tiny person that I love more than life itself, knowing that I couldn't imagine my world without her in it now. But that doesn't mean that motherhood isn't the hardest thing I have ever done, and that has me sighing, feeling defeated as I walk back to my room, praying she stays asleep for the rest of the night.

I walk into Frankie's Diner Sunday morning carrying Scarlett on my hip with her diaper bag slung over my other shoulder. And before I can say anything, Penelope jumps from her chair and races over to us.

"Gimme my girl," she croons as she takes her from my grasp, tossing her up in the air and then catching her. Scarlett's giggles echo around the restaurant.

"Nice to see you, too," I tease as I find my seat next to Charlotte at our usual table.

Every Sunday, for as long as we've been friends, the four of us have made it a goal to have brunch together. After Maddox coined our official name, The Ladies Who Brunch became more of our identity and a way to cement our friendship. We also all have matching tattoos of our favorite flowers on our shoulders, too, but our brunch dates are what started it all.

Over the past two years, we haven't been able to meet every Sunday, as our lives and obligations have changed, especially for Amelia. Her husband, Ethan, has a seven-year-old son who plays soccer and loves to go camping, so they're busy on the weekends quite often.

When Amelia met Ethan, I knew sparks were flying the moment she mentioned him. She's a marriage and sex therapist and he's a divorce lawyer, and her brother sold him an office in the same complex as hers. Ethan was convinced he'd never get married again, but Amelia showed him that anyone can have a second chance at love, and now they are one happy family.

"Oh, you know I love you, Noelle. But this little girl's smile instantly makes my day better," Penelope replies as she also takes a seat with Scarlett on her lap, tickling her so she giggles again.

I place the cover over the wooden high chair that Frankie always has set up for me as I speak. "And mine doesn't?"

Penelope winces as I fake a smile at her. "Um, not really. You look like a woman who just faked an orgasm and told the guy it was the best sex you ever had."

"Ha. At this point, I'd take it. I can't even remember the last time I had sex."

Charlotte rubs her belly. "I can't get enough right now, so I'm not going to say anything else." Now almost six months pregnant, she's at the cute stage of her pregnancy—where she no longer looks bloated like she ate too much, but she's not swollen like a whale yet, either. I'm okay with it, though; I know it's coming, even if Charlotte is still in denial.

"I'm happy you have someone to satisfy that need, friend,

because I did not, and it was torture. And now, my bed is still empty—except for Scarlett, some nights."

"So why don't you try dating?" Amelia suggests as she fills up three champagne flutes with the bubbly liquid, topping them off with orange juice. It wouldn't be brunch without mimosas, and since Charlotte can't drink one, I have no problem taking her share, especially after the last two nights of minimal sleep. I'll just make sure I pump and dump later.

Frankie comes by to take our order at that very moment. "My beautiful girls! What can I get for you today?"

"I'll have my usual, Frankie," I say, looking forward to the veggie omelet I order almost every time. It may be loaded with veggies, but it's also stuffed full of cheese, and the hash browns are to die for. "And can I have a Coke, too, please?" Coke is one of my vices, and I have to drink it at least once a day. Why not start my morning off with one this time?

"Waffle with strawberries for me, Frankie. You know what I like." Penelope winks up at him while keeping Scarlett occupied.

"I am gonna have the oatmeal and fruit," Amelia adds.

"And I want bacon and eggs this morning with biscuits and gravy instead of toast," Charlotte declares. "Eggs over medium, please."

Frankie takes a mental note of our orders with a head nod, and then he spins. "You got it, girls," he calls as he speeds back toward the kitchen.

"As I was saying, Noelle," Amelia brings us back to our previous conversation. "If you're lonely, why don't you try getting back out there? Going on a few dates? It doesn't have to be anything serious, maybe just about some physical pleasure," she suggests on a shrug.

"Um, okay. When the hell am I supposed to do that? And have we forgotten that the entire reason I chose to have a baby without a man is because I tried the dating thing and had horrible luck?"

"But your vagina must have needs," Penelope interjects.

"Listen. I have plenty of toys, thanks to Amelia, to satisfy that itch."

Amelia winks across the table at me. "You're welcome, and I have some new ones for you to try if you're interested. But that doesn't mean the real thing isn't amazing, too."

"Honestly, I'm a little scared of how sex might feel after having Scarlett. Keep in mind, I didn't have sex for months before I got pregnant, and then I pushed a baby out of the tiniest hole ever and haven't stretched it back out the way a man would since. If I had a man, he would have been more than eager to oblige that request, but there were no six-weeks-after-birth conversations where I got to declare that my vagina was officially back open for business. And thank God, because six weeks in, I could barely hold my eyes open long enough at night to read for ten minutes. I couldn't imagine having to attempt sex at that time, too."

Charlotte's brows draw together. "Noelle? Are you okay? You seem . . . angry."

Sighing, I pinch the bridge of my nose. "Yeah, I'm fine. Just tired. I haven't slept all week. Scarlett has been up teething, and we've barely gotten any rest." I glance over to her as she gnaws on her bib. I grab a rice cracker from the diaper bag and hand it to Penelope to give to her. "She's fine during the day, but as soon as night comes around, it's like my baby becomes possessed. And then she's cranky, and I'm cranky, and it's just been a lot."

"I'm sorry, hun." Charlotte rubs her shoulder. "You sound like you need a break."

"I do, but I don't get those." I shake my head. "And I know I shouldn't be complaining. I chose this, right? And I love her. God, I didn't know I could love someone so much. It's just . . ." Emotion clogs my throat as my eyes well with tears. "It's really fucking hard."

Amelia, our resident therapist, chimes in. "You are allowed to vent. Being a parent is difficult, Noelle. And we're your best friends. We aren't judging you." Penelope and Charlotte nod.

"I know, but I feel guilty if I do. There are a bunch of thoughts that go through my head every day that make me feel guilty. I never realized that I would feel this way. I guess I just thought I would feel this unexplainable love and joy when she was born, which I did. But it's more like little moments of it, not long stretches. And in between them, I contemplate my sanity. I do miss sex. I do miss male companionship, but the last thing I have is energy to date. I miss sex, but I also miss peeing without being interrupted, sleeping through the night, and a schedule that isn't interrupted by a blowout diaper."

Penelope practically jumps in her chair, but thankfully she grips Scarlett so she doesn't catapult across the restaurant. "Oh my gosh! That reminds me. I have to tell you about this story that a coworker told me. Seriously, girls, after I heard it, I was so grateful that I found Maddox. Not only is he a Super Bowl-winning quarterback with the most amazing pierced cock I've ever seen, but he is normal—aside from his obsession with Steve Harvey, that is."

Amelia chuckles. "Thank you for reminding us about your husband, the Super Bowl-winning quarterback with penis jewelry." She winks at me and Charlotte. "So what's the story?"

Penelope and Maddox tied the knot last month at his house in Texas. It was an intimate affair of their close friends, family, and of course, a plethora of NFL players. The boys were dumbstruck the entire weekend.

Penelope adjusts Scarlett so she's standing on her thighs now, looking at all of us, which is one of her favorite ways to be held, facing outward so she can see the world around her. She loves using those strong legs of hers to hold herself up. "I know that was sarcasm, Amelia, but I'm going to let it slide because this story is just too good." She clears her throat and sits up taller. "So one of the interns for the Bolts was telling me about this guy she started dating. Everything seemed normal, right? They were getting along well, they'd slept together, and she was gushing about how great he was, and then he flipped a switch on her that she never saw coming."

"What did he do?" Charlotte asks, leaning forward in her seat. And I'm not gonna lie, I wanna see where this is headed, too.

"One Saturday, they were hanging out at his apartment, and when he came out of the shower, he was wearing an adult diaper and nothing else."

All of us freeze. "No way," I say before reaching for my mimosa, and Amelia follows my lead.

Penelope nods. "Yup. I guess he was waiting until they got serious before he revealed his kink to her, but no shit, this guy likes to pretend he's a baby on the weekends while he's a high-powered corporate lawyer during the week."

Amelia and I both choke on our mimosas. "Oh my God!"

"And that's not even the worst part," Penelope continues. "He would actually pee in the diaper."

"I think I might throw up," Charlotte says, dry heaving in her seat.

I set my glass down and begin wiping the table in front of me where part of my drink spilled from my lips. "First off, you could have warned a person not to drink before you divulged that information. And second, this is exactly why I don't want to even think about dating. Men like that are out there, girls, just waiting to catch us off guard. Remember Tim and his pecker?"

Penelope snorts. "Oh God, I forgot about the chicken dude!"

"And Amelia dated that firefighter for a while who tried to take her to swinger parties because he and his ex-wife did it."

Amelia laughs. "Oh my God, it's been so long since I've thought about that. And let me state for the record, I am not opposed to a couple living their lives that way. But when he kept trying to get me to do the same thing, I was out."

"I don't blame you," I say to her just as Frankie comes by with our food.

"Is there anything else you need from me, my beautiful girls?" He sets down our plates and then reaches for Scarlett's chubby hand and kisses the top of it, making her laugh.

"Do you have any single friends, Frankie?" Penelope asks. "Someone good enough for Noelle?"

"Penelope," I warn her.

Frankie turns to me. "I'm sorry, Noelle. I don't know any men who are good enough for you, my dear. Or Scarlett. And that should be the most important thing to watch for, no? How he treats your little princess?"

My shoulders drop as I smile at my daughter. "You're absolutely right, Frankie."

"So hold out for the right one," he says, blowing a kiss at me before leaving us to enjoy our food.

"Penelope, I swear, if you weren't holding my daughter right now, I would jump over this table and smack you."

"Good thing she's in my hands then, huh?"

Amelia speaks up. "Frankie is right, though. Noelle dating isn't just about her anymore. It's about Scarlett, too."

"Exactly. Even more reason to avoid the feat altogether." I go to pick up my fork but then realize that Penelope probably wants both of her hands to eat. "I can take her now, Pen." I motion for her to hand the baby to me, but she twists away from us, hiding Scarlett from view.

"Nonsense. You eat."

"It's okay . . ."

"Noelle. I've got the baby. Enjoy your freaking meal, woman." She winks at me, and I almost burst into tears.

Thank God for these women. They are my tribe. I never understood that phrase 'It takes a village' until I had Scarlett. And even more, sometimes that village is the one we create rather than the one society tells us should be there. Either way, I have never been more grateful for their souls, their presence, and their love. They may just be better to me than any man I could find, anyway.

"Thank goodness we left a little early today, huh, sweetie?" I kiss the top of Scarlett's head as I hold her to my chest, waiting in line to order my coffee. After another restless night of teething, I knew that some extra caffeine was the only way I would be able to get through my day. Sometimes a coffee that isn't from your house can turn your day around.

Yesterday, after brunch with the girls, I headed home and attempted to catch up on laundry and even snuck in some reading time while Scarlett played in her playpen for a little bit. Remarkably, it made me feel human again for a moment. But as soon as it was time for her to go to sleep, the crying started again.

Now, I'm headed to drop Scarlett off at daycare, but I left early to grab some coffee first. I also owe my assistant a drink after she saved my ass last week when I almost missed a meeting with a client. I was pumping and reading and completely lost track of time.

It will be so nice to have my body back, a reality that I fear may happen sooner rather than later since Scarlett seems to be losing interest in nursing lately.

Speaking of breastfeeding, a familiar burn in my chest lets me know my milk is coming down. *Just great.*

The line moves up by one more person, but Scarlett is growing antsy in my arms. She motions for the floor like she wants to get down and crawl, but obviously this isn't the time or the place.

I spin her around, trying to distract her, and lose my balance, bumping right into the guy in front of me. "Oh my God! I'm so sorry."

For one split second, everything freezes around me as I assess his backside, a rear view that I definitely would have noticed if I hadn't had my child to attend to. Broad shoulders strain against a white cotton dress shirt, the type of shirt that looks like it's part of a uniform with crisp lines and folds in the fabric. His back is massive, but it leads to a narrow waist where expertly ironed navy-blue slacks hang perfectly on his hips, highlighting the beautiful peach that is his ass.

So there are real men who have asses like that?

But then he slowly turns around, and all of the air leaves my lungs. Ice-blue eyes shine behind black-framed glasses, perfect rectangles that provide the ideal shape to highlight his face. A perfect face with a strong jaw covered in dark stubble that boasts flecks of gray and matches the hue of the short hair on his head with gray sprinkled at his temples.

Oh. My. God. That salt-and-pepper look is so underrated, and this man is wearing it like a badge of freaking honor.

For that one split second, I don't know what to say or do because I'm afraid that my tongue has become frozen, but then he smiles and my knees begin to buckle.

"Whoa," he says, catching us before we fall over completely. "Careful there."

"I'm . . . I'm so sorry. I was trying to distract my daughter and lost my balance."

"Not a problem." His lips spread and reveal stunningly white teeth, the kind of smile that melts underwear off women as they're walking down the street. But then his smile falls, his eyes dip down to my shirt, and then he clears his throat, darting his eyes from me. "Um, it looks like you may have *one* kind of problem, though."

"What?"

His eyes flick back down to my chest and then up to mine. "Your shirt."

Dumbfounded, I glance down to my blouse, and my stomach drops. Of course this would happen to me right now in front of Gabe Kapler's doppelgänger. "You've got to be kidding me."

Two round circles of wetness spread across my chest as my milk seeps through my nursing pads and right through my bra, dampening the silk blouse I was brave to wear with a baby in my arms, anyway.

"Wow. Okay. Well, this is embarrassing." Fighting back tears and the redness building in my cheeks as one of the most handsome men I've ever seen in my life saw me in one of my most mortifying situations, I use Scarlett as a shield while I try to figure out what to do.

As my mind reels and the line moves forward, I try to form words to tell Mr. I'm-Too-Sexy-for-My-Shirt that he needs to move up, but he beats me to it and then proceeds to prove that he is, in fact, too sexy for his shirt.

"Here." Without stopping to think, he begins releasing the buttons one by one as I now realize he is definitely dressed in a uniform with insignia on the shoulders and an airplane patch sewn on the pocket. *Is he a pilot?*

"What are you doing?" Scarlett reaches for him as he continues to disrobe in the middle of the coffee shop. I'm sure he's drawing the attention of all the women around us, but I can't even fathom looking anywhere than at the sight of him in front of me, practically giving me a striptease.

"I'm giving you my shirt."

"Wow. Okay. Look, I'm sure you're a nice guy—"

"What's your name?" He cuts me off as he slides his arms out of the sleeves, revealing his torso covered in a practically see-through white tank top and tan skin that is straining against large, muscular arms so beautiful and carved that my mouth and vagina are watering from the sight.

I swallow before I start drooling. "Um, Noelle."

He grins. "And who is this little cutie?" He juts his chin at my daughter.

"Scarlett."

"Well, it's nice to meet you ladies. I'm Grant. And right now, I'm going to give you my shirt to change into so you don't have to walk around like that for the rest of the day."

"But—"

He cuts me off again. "No, buts. And please, don't be embarrassed. You're not the first breastfeeding woman I've been around nor has this never happened in the history of the world." He pulls his shirt from his body and holds it out to me, leaving me even more stunned.

Keep in mind, the line of people waiting for coffee has now completely gone around us as we stand still at the scene of the crime.

"Isn't this your uniform, though?" I hesitate as I reach out and grab the shirt, my hand shaking as I adjust Scarlett on my hip, her giggles pulling my attention to her as Grant starts to play with her, teasing her with his fingers.

"It is, but I have plenty of shirts. Don't even worry about it. Now, go change."

"Um . . ." My eyes dart to the bathroom in the back corner.

"I can hold her until your husband gets here. I promise she's in good hands. I have nieces and nephews. And babies love me." Tickling Scarlett's neck, she squeals and then reaches out for him as I hold her deathly close to me now.

"Well, you'll be holding her for a long time seeing as how I don't have one of those."

"What? A husband?"

"Yes."

"Boyfriend?"

"Nope."

"So you're single?"

"Are you seriously hitting on me right now while I have breastmilk all over my shirt?" I ask through a laugh.

His smirk makes my already wet nipples hard. "Maybe. But let's revisit that conversation in a minute. I swear, I know what I'm doing. I can watch her. Now, go change. We'll be right here."

"I'll watch him, sweetheart," an elderly man sitting at the table next to us assures me, pulling my eyes to him and bringing awareness back to me that we are in a public place as this situation unfolds. "If he tries to get too far, I'll take him out with my cane and then toss my coffee on his crotch so his dick burns off. That'll stop him in his tracks." He taps his cane on the floor in warning.

"See? My manhood has officially been threatened. I think you're good." Grant winks and then reaches for Scarlett. And for reasons unbeknownst to me, I let her go into his arms. She lets out an alarming scream as Grant bounces her up and down, again and again.

"I must be dreaming, because this can't be happening."

Grant nibbles on my daughter's hand, and her giggles even make the old man laugh. "It is, but look at it this way—this sure makes one hell of a story, doesn't it?" He studies me again, kindness reflected in those icy-blue eyes. I haven't felt kindness from a stranger in so long. "Now, go change. I'll take my shirt back if I have to tell you again."

Rolling my eyes outwardly but internally grateful, I take a step toward the bathroom. "Fine. I'll be right back." Pointing a finger at the old man, I warn him as I depart, "Keep an eye on my girl. I'm trusting you."

"I've got you, sweetheart." He taps his cane on the ground again as I scurry away and lock myself inside the single-stalled bathroom.

"Holy shit, this is really happening." I stare at myself in the mirror, flabbergasted at how my morning has been progressing. As I unbutton my own shirt and toss it on the counter, I hold Grant's shirt out in front of me.

This man literally just gave me the shirt off his back. What is going on in the universe today?

And not only was his gesture remarkably kind, but he is also one of the most attractive men I've ever seen in my life. Seriously, if I had met him years ago, it would've been game over. Physically, he's as close to perfect as a man can get.

But I think he was just being nice. I mean, he said himself he's been around women who breastfeed and understands the struggle. I think it was just lucky for me that he happened to be right in front of me in line when my wardrobe malfunction happened.

That's all this is.

My stomach continues to twist as I slide my arms through the sleeves of his shirt, the shirt that is far too large for my tiny frame. The man towered over me, so I'm guessing he's got to be around six foot three or four.

Mmm, come to Mama.

Grateful that I have seen far too many video tutorials about how to make an oversized shirt look cute, I quickly fasten the shirt using one of my favorite methods so that I don't look like someone who wore a Halloween costume out in public. I must say, the patches of stripes on the shoulders *do* add a nice touch against my navy skirt. Once I fix it adequately, I grab two new nursing pads from the diaper bag and replace the soaked ones in my bra.

Remembering that I left my daughter with a complete stranger, I grab my shirt and fling open the door, running out into the coffee shop again, frantically searching for Grant and Scarlett. And when I see them, my heart melts.

At a nearby table, Scarlett is standing on Grant's thighs, facing him as he sits holding her up. She's grabbing at his face, and I see his glasses sitting across the table, presumably so she doesn't crush them. Probably a good call.

She's smiling so big and giggling at him as he makes funny faces and bops her on the nose.

Something twists in my chest, this image of Scarlett interacting with a man like she would have with her father if he had been in the picture, an image that I've mourned multiple times since even before she was born.

But seeing it in real life—granted, Grant isn't her dad, but all the key players are still present—it strikes a chord in me, one that has me swallowing down the consequences of my choice and approaching the two of them in a timely fashion.

"I'm back." Grant looks up at me, his eyes narrowing as he assesses his shirt on my torso now. "What?"

Shaking his head, he stands from the chair, placing Scarlett on his hip, cradled in just one of his giant arms. "Damn. I never thought I'd like the appearance of a woman in my uniform, but I guess I was wrong."

Feeling my cheeks turn red, I huff out a laugh. "Well, I'm sure you never thought you'd hand it over to a stranger, either, because her boobs leaked through her own shirt, yet it happened." I stuff my ruined shirt in the diaper bag I had with me in the bathroom before returning my eyes to his. "Which leads me to the most important words I can say to you right now: *Thank you.* Truly. You're a lifesaver."

"Like I said, not a problem. I get it."

"Most men don't or wouldn't even try."

"Well, I'm not most men."

"That's evident already. But I mean it. Thank you for saving me back there."

"I didn't save you. I just threw you a life jacket—or shirt, if you will."

I smile gently. "Nonetheless, your kindness does not go unappreciated. Please, let me buy you a coffee. It's the least I can do."

He smiles back, still holding my daughter, and the sight is just too much for my ovaries to handle right now. I've completely lost track of time. I'm probably terribly late for work at this point, but I can barely care as some kind of electric current starts to spark between us.

I may just be imagining it, but Grant's eyes have a hint of possession in them, as if he wants to wrap me in his other arm exactly the way he's holding Scarlett right now. And because I'm horny, alone, and eternally indebted to the man, I would definitely let him.

"I would love a coffee," he finally replies, bouncing my daughter up and down.

I try to fight my smile from growing too wide and creepy. "Okay. I'll be right over there in line."

"And we'll be right here again."

Turning on my heel, swinging my hips a little more than necessary as I hope that he's watching me walk away, I step back in the line I vacated what seems like hours ago and wait to place our order. Then I remember I didn't even ask him what he wanted. Spinning around to grab his attention, I'm startled when I find him right behind me, my daughter on his hip, the diaper bag over his other shoulder.

His brows pinch together. "I'm so sorry, Noelle, but I have to go."

"Oh, okay." I take Scarlett from him, and he settles the diaper bag on my free arm. "Is everything okay?"

"Yes. It's work. I lost track of time and have to leave right this moment or I'm going to miss my flight."

"But I have your shirt."

"I know," he says with a lethal grin as he backs away from me. "Keep it."

"And you didn't get coffee."

"It's okay. I got something better out of the trip."

Not sure what else to say but feeling like time is robbing

me of this moment, I call out to him as he heads for the door, "Thank you again."

"Anytime."

And then he's gone, leaving me standing in the exact same spot we met earlier with a different shirt, a thundering heart-beat, a zealous libido, and still no coffee.

Chapter 4

Grant

Throwing open my truck door, I almost slam it into the car next to me. Luckily, that car belongs to Brad, so at least it wouldn't be a total disaster since he is my copilot today and knows I would take care of the damage.

"Easy, Grant. We have time," he says as we both step out of our cars simultaneously. While holding that beautiful baby girl for her equally beautiful mother, I miraculously thought to check the time, confirming my imminent tardiness, and I knew then that if I didn't leave the coffee shop within the next five minutes, I would be late for my flight. Unfortunately, in my haste, I chose not to ask for Noelle's phone number.

I've been kicking myself during my entire drive to LAX for that move—or lack thereof.

Brad's eyes drop down to my torso, and his brows draw together. "Um, where the fuck is your shirt?"

Huffing out a laugh, I open the back door of my truck and reach for one of the spare shirts I keep hanging in the car for emergencies. Guess this little OCD trait of mine finally came in handy. "It's a long story."

"Well, it's a three-hour flight, so you'll have plenty of time to tell me."

Sliding my arms through the sleeves and fastening the buttons, I turn to face him. "Here's the summary. The woman standing behind me in line at the coffee shop leaked breastmilk through her shirt, so I gave her mine."

Brad shoots me a deadpan gaze. "You just . . . gave her your uniform shirt?"

"Yes . . ."

"Was she hot?"

I glare at him as I tuck my shirt into my slacks. "Why does she have to be hot?"

He scratches the side of his head. "Because I'm just having a hard time wrapping my head around this. I mean, good on you for helping out a woman in need, but—"

"But nothing. That's exactly what it was. My sister-in-law used to have that problem sometimes, and I remember her telling us how embarrassing it was. You should have seen the look on this woman's face—it was like she wanted to just give up on her day right then and there."

As soon as I saw that panic in her eyes, pleading for time to rewind so she wasn't standing there in that situation, this overwhelming need to help her slammed into me. I can't explain it, but I knew I had to do something for her. Her green eyes were so round and glittering from the sunlight coming through the windows in the coffee shop that I couldn't look away. And her daughter was so freaking adorable. I remember when my nephews were that little—holding them and experiencing their reactions to the world was the best feeling ever. I guess my actions were partially selfish so I could interact with them both, but I also heard the gratitude in her voice after I gave her my shirt—and that made my chest swell with pride, too.

"I swear, I don't know how you aren't married," Brad says, shaking his head. We both grab our suitcases from our cars, shut the doors, and lock up our vehicles before we start heading into the airport from the employee parking lot reserved for pilots and flight attendants. "Women would be falling at your feet after a move like that. I mean, my wife would probably chastise me if I told her what you just did, asking me why I wouldn't do that for some woman I didn't know."

Our strides eat up the asphalt beneath us. "I didn't even think about it, honestly. I just reacted."

"Please, tell me she offered to thank you in the bathroom or something."

Shoving him to the side, we share a laugh. "You're a pig."

"I know. That was out of line. I'm sorry. But did anything else happen?"

"I held her daughter for her while she changed, and she was about to buy me a coffee in thanks when I realized I'd lost track of time and had to leave."

"Fuck. That sucks."

"I know." My heart lurches a bit. "And she was beautiful, too. Is beautiful . . . you know what I mean."

He shoves me this time. "I fucking knew it. Well, at least you have a story now you can use to pick up other women. You need a woman in your life, man. I'm becoming concerned about your future. You're on your way to becoming a Clint Eastwood doppelgänger. I half expect to find you sitting on your front porch one day, yelling at anyone who passes by your house with a shotgun in your hand."

"You act like I don't have a life. That I don't fish on the weekends, go running, spend time with my family, and travel all over the world thanks to my job. I have a good life."

"Yeah, but don't you get lonely?"

I clear my throat before answering as we make our way into the airport. "Sometimes, but maybe that's how it's supposed to be for me."

"I hardly believe that, but we can drop this for now. This turnaround flight to Chicago will make for a fairly short day, so maybe we can grab a beer once we touch down in LA again?"

"Yeah, sounds like a plan."

As we head for security to gain clearance, I keep replaying my morning in my head. It's been a long time since a woman caught my attention like that, and not just because she had two giant wet spots on her blouse.

No, she was gorgeous in an understated way. I could tell she wasn't one of those women who spent hours on her appearance, and honestly, she didn't need to. With beautiful light-brown hair, bright green eyes, and freckles across the bridge of her nose, she stood out all on her own with her natural beauty, a girl-next-door kind of look that makes any red-blooded male react. She couldn't have been taller than five foot six, but I happen to like women I have a good height difference on. And her curves—*Jesus*, the woman had hips and thighs for days, thick in all the right places. Her body captivated me, especially once I saw her wearing my shirt. *Fuck, what a sight.*

But it wasn't just her looks that garnered my attention—it was her vulnerability. I swear, I could see so much anguish in her eyes over her circumstance. Being able to help her ignited something in me, but I know nothing more could come of it. It's probably good that I left when I did.

But maybe I could find her. I mean, how common is a name like Noelle? Perhaps, after work today, I can spend some time searching through Facebook or Instagram to try to track her down.

But would that make me look a little stalkerish?

And why do you want to, Grant? That's the real question you should be asking yourself.

"You ready?" Brad asks, pulling my attention back to the security line we just went through.

"Oh. Yeah. Let's do this." I grab my suitcase from the conveyor belt, set it down on the ground, and wheel it behind me. "It's a good day to fly."

"You don't look jet-lagged today," my mother says as I step inside her house.

"Uh, thanks, I guess." I lean down to kiss her on the cheek as she shuts the door behind me.

"I'm sorry," she says through a giggle. "It's just that sometimes I can tell you're tired when you're flying between multiple time zones."

"Good to know. But actually, I bid on West Coast flights this last month and won them, so I shouldn't have to deal with too much jet lag for a while."

"Well, that's good. You hungry?" my mother asks as I follow her into the house that I grew up in, heading for the kitchen. The aroma of garlic and tomatoes fills the air along with the scent of home. I don't know how else to describe it, but my parents' house just has this smell that instantly brings me comfort. Of course, seeing my mom after a few weeks makes me feel that way, too.

"Always."

"I thought so. I have some appetizers to hold everyone over until dinner is done. Your brother and the kids are out back, and your dad should be back from golfing any minute."

"Sounds about right." I reach for a handful of chips and a couple of mini corn dogs, which I know my mom put out for my nephews, but sharing is caring, and my nephews need to learn that sooner rather than later. "Does Dad have beer in the garage fridge?"

"Of course. Help yourself."

"Thanks, Mom." I reach across the counter and give her one more kiss on the cheek. "It's good to see you."

After I grab two beers—one for me and one for my younger brother, Gavin—I head into the backyard where screaming assaults my senses as my nephews climb on the playground equipment like monkeys. Our parents take their role as grandparents seriously, so they made sure to purchase a swing set for their backyard as soon as my first nephew could walk.

"Need a refill?"

My brother peeks up at me from his Adirondack chair. "Always." Reaching for the beer I'm handing him, he intercepts it and then drains the rest of his before switching out the empty one in his coozie with the new one. "Thanks." Brushing a hand through his reddish-brown hair, he looks back out at the boys.

"No problem." I take the seat next to him, cracking open my beer as I watch Michael, my oldest nephew, go headfirst down the slide. "How's it going?"

"Oh, you know . . . busy as fuck," Gavin replies. "Work is nuts. We just got a five-million-dollar contract that I'm in charge of, so my workload is stressing me out." My brother is a project manager for a telecommunications company. He used to work in the field, climbing telephone poles and building the networks. Now, he runs the projects from a phone and computer and doesn't have to beat his body up anymore.

"Where's Sarah?"

"Oh, she went inside to use the bathroom, but she's probably in the kitchen helping Mom now."

"We didn't cross paths, so that makes sense," I declare. "Is she happy to be on summer vacation?"

Gavin takes a swig of his beer. "Yes, but that means she's home with the boys all day, and they're already driving her nuts." He laughs. "I love my boys, but they can be a handful."

Gavin's wife is an elementary school teacher, so she's not working at the moment since it's the beginning of June. And at six and eight, my nephews definitely have proven that little boys have an abundance of energy. I love them, but even I need a break from them after a while.

"Well, you remember what we were like—always running around, getting dirty, fighting, riding bikes, throwing some kind of ball around. Just be grateful they have each other." I watch Andrew, the youngest, yell at his brother for cutting him off before he could get to the slide. "You're blessed, though, Gav. You have it all."

I can feel my brother's eyes on me. "You should have had this, too, Grant."

"Yeah, well . . . things didn't work out that way." Still ignoring his gaze, I drain half of my beer.

"You say that like you can't still have it all."

Finally, I turn to him. "I'm thirty-eight, Gav. Hell, I'm practically forty. If I was gonna have a wife and kids, it probably would have happened by now. But you and I know that isn't possible for me, so . . ."

"Says who? Who says that you have to have those things by a certain age? Who says that you can't still have them in an unconventional way? What if you met someone tomorrow? Are you saying you wouldn't pursue her if it felt right?"

Noelle's face flashes through my mind. It's been a week since I met her, and I still can't get her out of my head. The notion is unsettling. "I don't know. I just don't think it's in the cards for me, but I could be wrong, too. Either way, I've made my peace with it. I get to be the fun uncle, and my job kind of makes it hard to have a stable enough life for a family, anyway. I can't offer everything to a woman that she may want, so this is just how my life was supposed to turn out."

"Well, first of all, you *are* a great uncle. Seriously, the best. The boys can't wait to go fishing with you next week, and I know Sarah will be thankful for the break. But two, I don't think you're meant to be alone. I think you'll find the right person. And maybe things won't work out the way you thought they would, but maybe they'll work out exactly the way they were supposed to."

"Did I tell you Mom's been trying to set me up again?"

He laughs. "That will never stop, either, if you don't at least open yourself up to the possibility of finding someone on your own. I mean, when's the last time you went on a date?"

"It's been a while."

Honestly, dating just became frustrating and trivial over the past few years, so I stopped trying about a year ago. It's been a long year of just me and my hand.

"So maybe try again soon. But remember, Mom's just coming from a good place. She wants to see you happy."

"I know. I just feel like maybe I've let her down." That's

the thing that sits like a brick in my chest: this notion that because I'm not married and don't have a family, I never rose to the expectation that I would have those things someday. I mean, I think all parents assume their children will lead a life similar to theirs. Mine hasn't worked out that way, though. "You gave them grandkids and extended our family. I haven't."

"You aren't letting anyone down. You got thrown some curveballs in life, Grant, but you handled them the best way you could. Not all hope is lost for a family of your own. And if Denise wasn't such a bitch and hadn't left you when you were most vulnerable, things could have been different."

Just hearing my ex's name raises my blood pressure. I purchased an engagement ring for her two weeks before she left me. In hindsight, it was a blessing, but in the moment, I was devastated. "I'm glad she left, Gav. She showed her true colors just in time, and it would have ended eventually if she had stayed. She would have resented me because of my issues. And who wants to be with someone who can't support them when they're at their lowest point in life?"

"You're right. I'm just saying, though . . ."

"I know."

"Work going well?" he asks, changing the subject. And I'm grateful, because every time we bring up the previous one, it puts me in a mood.

"Yeah. I'm doing a few round-trip, one-way flights to Chicago, Vegas, and Seattle for the next few months, so I'll be home more than I'm used to. Unless I need to cover someone, which sometimes happens. But hey, it's good money."

"I'm jealous you get to fly all over the country and the world. I'd love to travel more, but between work and the kids, it's nearly impossible."

"I get to see some of the places we go, but when I do these short flights, there's no time to step outside the airport and explore. By the time I get out, I have to go back in to get through security and get the plane prepared."

"That's true."

"But hey, let me know when you and Sarah want to get away, and I can get you a deal on some tickets."

"I knew you were my favorite brother for a reason." He playfully shoves my shoulder.

"I'm your only brother, but I'll take the compliment none-theless."

"Uncle Grant!" Michael shouts when he finally realizes I'm here. He and Andrew dismount the play equipment and run over to where I'm seated with their dad.

"Hey, boys! How's summer vacation?"

"Boring," Andrew says with a roll of his eyes.

"Aw, come on. It can't be that bad. Remember, we're going fishing next week at the lake, so you have that to look forward to."

"But that's so far away!" Andrew whines.

"It will be here before you know it." I pinch his cheek, and he swats me away, but I grab him by the waist, bring him to my lap, and tickle him until he can't breathe.

"Stop, Uncle Grant! Stop!"

"Boys! Dinner is ready!" I hear my mother call from the back sliding glass door.

"Oh, saved by Grandma," I whisper as I release Andrew, and he and Michael run away before I can catch them again.

"I can't believe how big they are," Gavin speaks more to himself than me as we stand and start to head inside.

"I know. I feel like they were just babies. I miss them being that small." Shaking my head, I drain the last of my beer before we arrive at the patio. "I actually got to hold a baby again the other day and forgot how little they are."

Gavin stops me by grabbing my shoulder before I reach for the door handle. "Wait—you held a baby? When?"

I huff out a laugh. "At a coffee shop. I was helping out her mom."

He raises a brow. "How were you helping her?"

Rolling my eyes, I prepare to tell him the same story I told Brad. "I gave her my shirt."

"How very Superman of you. Did you rip all the buttons off when you did?"

"Jesus, no. She was having a wardrobe malfunction, so I helped her out."

"That's all?"

"Yup. I mean, she was gorgeous, but I had to leave."

"You *had* to leave?"

"Yeah, I was gonna be late for my flight."

He shakes his head. "You could have asked her for her number, Grant. It only would have taken another minute."

I narrow my eyes at him. "What are you saying?"

"I'm saying that you chickened out. If you really wanted to get her number, you would have made it happen."

Is my brother right? I mean, even the other night, when I contemplated searching for Noelle online, I ended up talking myself out of it. I know the woman left an impression on me, so why didn't I follow through?

"Don't try to analyze me right now," I argue, opening the door to the house where everyone has gathered in the kitchen to make their plates. "I had to leave."

"Sure, Grant. Whatever you say. But remember that you're not alone just because of your circumstances but because of your choices, too."

Chapter 5

Noelle

Three Weeks Later

Scarlett lets out a wail just as the flight attendant closes the cabin and everyone prepares for takeoff.

"Come on, baby girl. Let's have a good flight. Please?" My daughter grabs at my shirt, pulling herself forward so her face smashes into my chest, crying out again as she begins to suck on the fabric. "Okay, okay. I take it you're hungry, then."

Situating her on my lap, I locate my nursing cover-up from the bag at my feet, and Scarlett wiggles and squirms as her cries grow in volume. Panic sets in as I race to put the cover over my head, lift up my shirt underneath, unclasp my nursing bra, and then carefully bring my daughter under the cover without flashing my boob to the rest of the passengers in first class or the flight attendants scurrying around, preparing for takeoff.

The multi-tasking required when you're a mom is unparalleled and not talked about enough. I'd like to see a man do what I just did in under thirty seconds.

With eagerness, Scarlett latches onto my nipple, suckling with a contented grunt while digging her nails into my flesh. I peek down into the hole of the cover around my neck. "Easy there, girl." Her eyelashes flutter, and then her eyelids slowly close as she takes in her sustenance while the plane starts to taxi down the runway.

Only four more hours of crippling anxiety to suffer through until we land in Chicago.

Normally, a flight halfway across the country wouldn't be such a daunting task, but after having my daughter, everything seems far more complicated and anxiety-inducing than it used to be. I knew what I signed up for being a single mom, but I didn't realize just how lonely and overwhelming it would be at times, how having someone to help would change the mounting stress that takes over during situations that used to be a piece of cake.

The anxiety comes in waves, but for the past three weeks, I feel like I'm starting to gain my footing in this new phase. But then, just when I think I've got my daughter dialed in, she changes things up on me.

My friends help when they can, of course. Charlotte, Amelia, and Penelope love Scarlett as if she's their own. But they're not around all the time, helping with the everyday tasks and giving me a break in those moments where I feel like I'm teetering on the edge of sanity.

And then there are instances like right now, as I make a business trip with my baby because she can't be away from my boobs for more than twelve hours, where I'm questioning whether being a mom is all that it's cracked up to be. I ask myself whether I made the right decision by doing this on my own, and then I feel guilty for even thinking those thoughts because this is what I wanted—*what I chose.*

Scarlett releases my breast with a pop and then pushes herself away from me, forcing me to knock elbows with the man beside me as I retrieve her from under the nursing cover and burp her over my shoulder with my boob still free-ranging it underneath. Luckily, she settles in on my shoulder as the plane gains altitude, giving me the false sense of security that this flight might go smoothly after all—but then my free nipple starts dripping breastmilk all over my thigh.

Ah, the joys of motherhood.

"Shh, it's okay." Evidently pissed off about everything including the confines of our seating arrangement, Scarlett cries while she jumps up and down on my thighs. At seven months old, she's finally reached the stage where moving around is the only thing that matters. And as we close in on the last hour of our flight, my daughter—after being isolated in my lap and declining every baby snack and toy I've offered her—has me on the brink of the breakdown she's already headed toward.

The man sitting behind me taps me on the shoulder. "Can you quiet her down? She's been fussy this entire flight. Even my earbuds aren't drowning her out."

Rage flashes through my chest, but I rein it in as best I can. "I'm trying, okay? I'm sorry—"

"Well, try harder!"

As I prepare to twist around fully and give this man a piece of my mind since I'm teetering *so close* to the edge of snapping I'm bordering on feral right now, I'm cut off by a familiar voice. "I know you're not speaking to this mother that way."

My head spins around so fast that I nearly fall forward out of my seat, clutching my baby to my chest. As my eyes drink in the man standing before me, my jaw drops open and my heart hammers uncontrollably when recognition dawns on both of our faces.

Dressed in his pilot's uniform—one that I still have a part of—Grant flashes me that killer smile before he glares at the man who was just rudely telling me to make my baby stop crying.

"If you had children, you'd know that sometimes there's nothing you can do for a crying baby, and there's sure as hell not much this woman can do while stuck in a metal tube in the sky." He leans down and takes Scarlett from my lap, hoisting her up in his arms, cradling her to his chest as if he's done it a thousand times when he's only done it once. He mouths "Hi" to me before directing his attention back to the asshole behind me.

I swear everyone on the entire flight is just as mesmerized by the sight as I am.

"Well, it's annoying," the disgruntled passenger fires back.

"You're annoying!" Another passenger in first class retorts as more people from the back of the plane murmur their agreement.

Grant bounces Scarlett up and down, and she instantly stops crying, staring at him with wide blue eyes. "If I were you, I'd keep my mouth shut for the rest of the flight, or you just might see what happens when someone insults a mother who's doing the best she can and other people rally behind her."

The asshole rolls his eyes but cowers in his seat. "Whatever."

Grant chuckles. "Yeah, that's what I thought." Then he turns his attention back to me. "Fancy seeing you ladies here."

"Thank you," I whisper as I watch him continue to bounce my daughter in a soothing rhythm, her hands reaching out to grab his face as he does. He smiles at her, nuzzling his nose against hers as she squeals in delight. She reaches for his glasses, but he dodges her chubby hands before she grasps them, pretending to eat her fingers instead. She giggles rambunctiously again.

"My pleasure. In fact, I'd say running into you again here was a pleasant surprise."

"I'll say. Um, aren't you supposed to be flying this plane right now?" I dart my eyes between the cockpit and him.

"I came out for a bathroom break. My copilot is in there. I assure you, you're in good hands." And then he arches a brow. "Well, not as good as mine, but that's just a matter of opinion."

"Or cockiness."

He grins, his lips curling up under that short mustache and beard that frame his face, a face I hate to admit has flashed through my mind more times than I can count in the last three weeks. His eyes twinkle behind his glasses, their irises a blueish gray that is only enhanced by the crisp white shirt of his uniform. "No, just a fact."

Scarlett leans her head on his shoulder and stares down at me, perfectly content being in his arms.

Lucky girl.

"I hate to give her back, but duty calls." Grant smoothes his hand up and down her back as he steps closer.

Sitting up taller in my seat, I reach out for her, and he hands her off. She fusses a bit but eventually settles into my chest. I think the last three hours of unhappiness have finally drained her. "Well, thank you—again. It seems like you keep saving me."

"Be careful, or you're going to give me a savior complex, and who knows what that might do for my ego."

I slowly shake my head at him. "Seriously, Grant. First the coffee shop, now the flight. I don't know how to thank you."

He crouches down in front of my seat, reaching for my hand. "How about this time, you give me your number before we part ways?"

My heart rattles in my chest. "Oh, uh . . ."

"I mean, how else am I supposed to get my shirt back from you?" He winks.

His shirt—the shirt he literally took off his own body to give to me when my breastmilk decided to let down in the middle of the coffee shop that day, soaking my own shirt clear through. The shirt that I still have hanging in my closet and smell shamelessly each morning as I get dressed. The shirt that resembles the one he's wearing right now, part of his uniform as a commercial pilot, which can only be described as one of those jobs that instantly boosts a man's sex appeal—although I don't feel like Grant needs the extra points.

The man looks like Gabe Kapler, the coach for the San Francisco Giants—*enough said.*

"I guess my number would help with that, wouldn't it?"

His smirk becomes lethal. "Wait for me at the end of the Jetway then, after we land. I don't want to leave again without being able to get ahold of you. I think seeing you here was a sign, and we'd both be stupid to ignore it."

"Okay."

He rises and then winks at me again. "Okay. Enjoy the rest of your flight, Noelle." And then he's gone, disappearing into the cockpit and leaving me stunned by how our paths crossed once more.

Excitement builds in my chest chased by fear. Am I really doing this? Am I really entertaining getting involved with someone at this point in my life when I have a child to think about?

Don't get ahead of yourself, Noelle. Nothing may come of

this. You've been let down by men so many times in the past that this will probably turn out to be the same way. Reading too many romance novels has raised your expectations of men to unrealistic levels.

No, they have just made me realize that men could do better, and I deserve that.

And then my mind goes straight to developing the story that's transpired so far, wondering which of my clients I could pitch it to.

Single mom leaks through her nursing pads in a coffee shop, so a handsome stranger, who also happens to be a pilot, literally gives her the shirt off his back but has to leave before they can exchange numbers. Then she runs into him again when, as it turns out, he's the pilot of the flight she's on, and he defends her and her daughter against a disgruntled passenger but asks for her number before she leaves the airplane.

But what happens next? Does he call? Does she agree to see him again?

I guess I'll leave that part up to the author herself . . .

I settle into my seat as Scarlett finally finds sleep, and I try to close my eyes, too, but my pulse is racing as I stare at the cockpit door, wondering what's going to happen when Grant comes out of it again.

Bouncing Scarlett up and down, I wait to the side of the Jetway for Grant to come out. The entire plane has emptied now, and my nerves are running rampant throughout my body. I don't know what he is gonna say or do when he sees us or if he has changed his mind, but waiting is making my anxiety spike even more.

Scarlett squeals, and I turn my head just in time to see Grant stride toward us, looking delectable in his uniform, his long legs carrying him in our direction. His smile and stride are oozing confidence, and his eyes gleam behind his glasses.

"I'm glad you listened," he says when he reaches us.

"What would you have done if I hadn't?" I tease him, more because my nerves are making me want to crawl out of my skin right now, and sarcasm is what comes out of my mouth when that happens.

"I haven't chased anyone through the airport before, but I would have had to hunt you down." He rests his suitcase next to us. "I can't tell you how fortunate I feel to see you today, Noelle. What a small world."

"It was very coincidental."

"It had to be more than that." Taking a deep breath, he stares at me intently. "After the coffee shop, I struggled with not asking for your number. Part of me knows I was on a time crunch, but I could have taken the extra minute for the possibility of seeing you again."

"You wanted to see me again?" I ask, mostly because hearing him say those words has hope building in my chest that I wasn't the only one who felt our connection.

"I did. At first, I was in denial about it," he chuckles, shaking his head. "But seeing you again made me realize I'd be a fool to let you slip through my fingers twice." He digs into his pocket and pulls out his phone. "So before something else interrupts us or pulls either one of us away, can I get your phone number, please?"

On a shaky breath, I reply, "Okay." Smiling, I rattle off my digits. My phone rings in my bag a few seconds later.

"There. Now you have mine, too." And then he turns his attention to my daughter. "And how was your flight, Miss Scarlett?" He tickles her, making her laugh. "Did your pilot do okay?"

"She slept the rest of the flight after you calmed her down. Even the landing didn't wake her up."

He blows on his fingers and then brushes his shoulder off jokingly. "I guess I've still got it."

"That was cheesy."

"You're right. But I can take her if you want?" He reaches for her, and she meets him halfway with her hands. Grant intercepts her, tosses her up in the air, and then catches her as she comes back down. "Hey, beautiful girl!"

"You really do like babies, don't you?"

The way his eyes sparkle as he looks at my daughter nearly takes my breath away. "Yeah, I do." And then he flicks his eyes to me. "I kind of like her mom, too, though."

Heat flames my cheeks. "Jesus. How do you do that?"

He chuckles. "It's a gift. Are you hungry? Do you have time to grab something to eat?"

Realization dawns on me. "Actually, I need to get across

town for a meeting with my client, so I should probably get going."

"Ah. Here for work?"

"Yup. And my breastfed daughter must accompany me because I am her food source." I go to take her back from him, but he twists away from me.

"Let me carry her as I walk you girls out. Give you a break."

I swear, tears threaten to spill over at that very moment. I can count on one hand how many times someone has offered me a break, and it's usually one of my best friends. "If you insist."

"I do." He hoists Scarlett on his hip, grabs the handle of his suitcase to roll it behind him, and then we're off as I grab my bag as well, my free arm feeling empty from the absence of my daughter.

We walk side by side like we're a little family, and I push the notion out of my mind just as quickly as I let it form.

"How long are you in Chicago?" I ask him as we head for the baggage claim.

"I fly back to LA in three hours."

"Wow. That quickly? That means you don't have time to explore."

"It's okay. I've been to the Windy City numerous times."

I scoff. "I imagine you get to go to many different places because of your job."

"I do, but I prefer to fly local. Flights that I can do in one day are nice because then I get to be home at night, like most people with normal nine-to-five jobs."

"I never thought about that. I usually just sit in the plane and count down the minutes until I can get off it."

He laughs. "Yeah, that's pretty normal. I'm not offended." We reach baggage claim and then turn to face each other. "Noelle, I hope you enjoy your trip. How long are you here for?"

"Just the night. I'll be back in LA tomorrow. Will you be the pilot on that flight, too?"

"No, I'm going to Seattle tomorrow and Vegas the day after that. But I have a few days off next week. Would you be willing to give me some of your time?"

"Like a date?"

"Yes. I really would like to spend some time with both of you girls."

I look at my daughter. "Both of us?"

"Yeah. Look, we can work out the details later, but expect a call from me tomorrow, okay?"

I've heard that from a man a time or two before and then nothing. That hope in my chest starts to deflate, but I try to hide it. "Okay. If you say so."

"I do." He plants a kiss on Scarlett's cheek and then passes her back to me. "Be good for your momma, sweet girl."

"Thank you again for your help on the flight."

"It was my pleasure, Noelle. Seriously. We'll talk soon."

"Bye!" I call out to him over my shoulder as I make my

way to the baggage carousel. Grant takes off in a different direction.

My heart is pounding, my mind is reeling, and my eyes are glued to his ass as he walks away from me. Still in disbelief that we crossed paths again, I try to focus on finding my bag so I can hail a cab and meet with my author and then my boss via Zoom later tonight. But I'm not gonna lie, trying to concentrate on anything right now besides Grant is going to be a difficult task.

Chapter 6

Noelle

"I missed you, bitches," Penelope declares as soon as we all get situated with a mimosa. Except for Charlotte, of course.

"How was your honeymoon?" I ask as I spread a few more rice puffs on the high chair in front of Scarlett. We're all at Frankie's for brunch after an almost three-week hiatus. A lot has happened in the last three weeks, that's for sure. Especially in my life.

Penelope and Maddox got married in April but had to wait for a break in the off-season to go on their honeymoon, so they've been in Bora Bora for the past two weeks.

"My vagina might need a week of recovery, ladies. My husband is a sex fiend, but I am definitely not complaining."

Penelope tosses her hair over her shoulders, smiling proudly. "I swear he was trying to knock me up."

"Already?" Amelia asks.

"Even before we got married, all he talked about was having babies."

"And how do you feel about that?" Amelia continues to prod.

Sighing, Penelope looks over at Scarlett. "It's not that I don't want kids with the man. I mean, have you seen him? My ovaries dry hump the air when I'm only looking at him. But I'm not ready. I just want to enjoy this time where it's only the two of us before our lives completely shift."

"Believe me, your life will definitely change once you have a kid," I add as the resident expert.

Charlotte speaks up. "There's nothing wrong with wanting to wait. Damien and I waited for a few months and then just let things happen the way they were supposed to, but we wouldn't have minded waiting a little longer if we had to."

"Ethan and I agreed to wait at least a year after we got married to try," Amelia adds. She and Ethan married last October, so that timeline is definitely coming to an end.

"I know, but I want more than a few months. Everything happened so fast getting engaged and married right away—I feel like we just need some time to be 'us.'"

"That makes perfect sense," I say. "Have you told him that?"

"I mean, sort of. But then he whips out his dick, and I lose all train of thought."

"She's been dickmatized, ladies," Charlotte says through a laugh. "Happens to the best of us."

Amelia nods. "Yeah, I understand that. But one of these days, cover your eyes, and then tell him what you're feeling, okay?" She models holding her hand over her eyes as we all giggle.

"I will. So what else is new, girls?" Penelope turns to us, shifting her eyes between me, Amelia, and Charlotte.

"Still pregnant," Charlotte speaks. "But getting excited for the baby shower next month. Thanks for planning it, by the way, girls."

Amelia reaches over and squeezes Charlotte's hand. "Of course." And then she turns to Penelope. "I'm still working and spending time with my boys," Amelia adds. "Oliver is on summer vacation, so he's spending a lot of time with Ethan's mom right now, and Ethan and I have continued to join forces to encourage couples on the verge of divorce to seek active counseling to try to save their marriages. We have a seventy-five-percent success rate in the last six months." She beams with pride.

"See! I knew you two just needed to combine your super-hero powers for good," Penelope states. And then they all shift their eyes to me. "What about you, Noelle? What's going on with you besides raising the cutest freaking baby on the planet?"

Taking a deep breath, I decide there's no better time than the present to catch my friends up on what's been going on in my world. "Well, I, uh . . . I guess I met someone?" I say as more of a question because I'm still having a hard time wrapping my head around it.

"You *guess* you met someone?" Charlotte asks.

"I did. He, uh . . . he's a pilot."

Penelope bounces in her seat. "Oh, that's sexy. Where did you meet him?"

"At the coffee house on Tenth Street. He, uh . . ."

Amelia arches a brow at me. "Noelle, are you okay?"

Humming with uneasiness, I just decide to rip off the Band-Aid. "I don't know if I'm okay, okay? The entire thing has taken me by surprise, and I don't know what to think. His name is Grant, and he's *so* handsome, like rugged yet clean, distinguished but still playful, and the kind of handsome that makes a woman go stupid and her knees go weak. He gave me his shirt, girls. His freaking shirt! And do you know why?" They sit there in silence with wide eyes waiting for me to continue.

"Because I leaked breastmilk through mine. He noticed and saw that I was embarrassed, so he stripped in the middle of the coffee shop, held my daughter while I changed, and then had to rush to work before I could buy him a cup of coffee to thank him. But then last week, on my flight to Chicago, he came out of the cockpit to use the bathroom, surprising us both, and then defended me against a disgruntled passenger who was angry because Scarlett wouldn't stop crying during the flight. After he swooped in and saved me *again*, he asked me to wait for him at the end of the Jetway so he could get my number. Then he called Friday and wants to take me on a date with Scarlett this week. This is nuts, right?"

All three of my friends are staring at me, but Charlotte is the first to speak. "Holy shit. I wish I could have a drink after that verbal diarrhea."

"I've never dealt with breastfeeding issues, but that is by far one of the most chivalrous and arousing acts I think I've ever heard of a man doing for a woman," Amelia states while shaking her head.

"When you guys finally have sex, make sure you role-play the sexy pilot and stewardess doing it in the cockpit," Penelope proclaims. "Now *that* is sexy. But also, *hot damn* to that man for saving you like that. Where the hell did he come from?"

I throw my hands up in the air. "I have no idea. And now I'm supposed to go on a date with him?"

"Why do you sound conflicted about this, Noelle?" Amelia questions. "You were just talking a few weeks ago about how you missed male companionship and how awful dating can be. Well, this guy seems pretty damn fantastic, so why wouldn't you give this a shot?"

"Because I don't know if I should," I reply honestly.

Amelia's brows draw together. "Why?"

Glancing down at my daughter, I stroke the top of her head. "Because my focus should be on Scarlett now, not me and dating."

Silence grows between the four of us, but I keep staring at my baby, this tiny human who I'm responsible for now. And I can't help but feel selfish when I consider doing something for myself, even though I haven't been able to stop thinking about

Grant since I met him and he handed me his shirt without a second thought.

Can I really do this? Before my daughter, I would have been cautious, but I would have taken the risk for love. Now? I have *her* to think about, *her* getting attached, *her* getting her heart broken.

But she's not the only one who runs that risk, either, is she, Noelle?

I saw the way Grant was with her, the way Scarlett reacted to him. If things didn't work out, it would definitely break us both. I know she's young, but babies are perceptive. She feels safe with him, but could I feel that way, too? And by taking that risk, am I jeopardizing being the mother I feel that I need to be and should be?

"What's going through your head right now, Noelle?" Charlotte asks as she rubs her belly.

And for some reason, a scene from my favorite television show pops into my head at that very moment. "I feel like I'm Monica from *Friends* right now, having a breakdown over not being the mom who makes the world's best chocolate chip cookies! And that is a legit fear of mine." I point at my chest. "What if my daughter never has a memory like that because I was too busy working or dating to bother with making her chocolate chip cookies in the first place?"

"I'll save you the hassle—the secret is Crisco. Best cookies ever," Penelope declares proudly.

"Okay . . ." Amelia starts, refilling our mimosas. "I'm trying to follow you here, Noelle, but you need to elaborate."

"I'm serious, you guys. I guess I just feel like there's so much pressure—to have it all, be it all, and want it all as a mom. But society is telling me that I should be ashamed to want it all because that means my kid isn't my top priority. You know, I was a person before I became a mom, and she still matters, too. But I also don't want Scarlett to grow up emotionally scarred. I don't want to miss some critical moment because I was off dating random guy after random guy. Because then one day, when she's thirty, she'll be sitting in a therapist's office, processing the childhood trauma inflicted by her mother unknowingly."

"It's not going to be you who traumatizes her—it's going to be Penelope," Charlotte teases.

"Hey!" Penelope snaps back.

"Newsflash, Noelle." Amelia slides a full champagne flute over to me. "Everyone has childhood trauma, and most of the time, people don't blame their parents for it. Rather, they find it's important for them to process the reason why what happened affected them the way it did. They don't necessarily see it as a bad thing."

"Listen to the therapist here, Noelle," Penelope says, jutting her thumb over at Amelia. "And I will not traumatize her. I'll be the fun aunt she comes to talk to about sex and asks if she should be scared of penises." She glares over at Charlotte.

Charlotte ignores her and raises her hand. "Sorry, I'm gonna pipe in here with the motherly trauma, because it is a thing. But I also know that you would never do something like that to Scarlett, Noelle. Plus, it probably would have done me and my mother some good if she'd had a life of her own and wasn't so involved in mine."

I nod from side to side, appreciative of that perspective. But then I sigh, slouching down in my seat. "I just feel overwhelmed, like I was entirely unprepared for what this would all entail, especially since I'm doing it on my own. And then I still have these desires that I did before I had her, and they're not going away."

"Because you're still a woman—and a human," Amelia interjects. "We aren't meant to sacrifice our entire lives and happiness to take care of our offspring because they eventually leave home and then what are you left with?" I don't answer her. "Trust me. I see this in older couples all the time. They spend so many years in their marriage taking care of their kids but not investing in their marriage, and when the kids leave, suddenly they don't know their partner anymore. Before you know it, they're filing for divorce. Having your *own* life, your *own* relationship, isn't going to make you a terrible mother. It's going to make you a better one. Often, when I speak with married women with small kids, they feel like they've lost their identity. They don't have anything for themselves anymore, and then they grow resentful. Not only that, everywhere they turn, someone needs something from them. They never get a chance to relax without being stimulated by someone's needs or questions. And do you know what I recommend to them?"

"What?"

"To find a hobby, something they love that allows them to feel human again, like a version of themselves before they had kids. Something that brings them joy. And one of the first things I recommend is reading romance novels."

I smile proudly. "Really?"

Amelia nods. "Yes. One, because I know what they can do for a woman's sex drive, which, in turn, helps her relationship with her partner. But second, they offer an escape for her mind so that, for the small glimpse of time she gets to read, she's not a mom, she's not a wife—she's just a woman living vicariously through the love stories of perfectly flawed humans like herself. And she gets to just *be*."

With tears in my eyes, I sit there, stunned. "Wow. That's exactly how reading makes me feel."

"I know. It's amazing what the genre has done for women, and most of that I know because of you, Noelle. It's wonderful that you have that, but you also deserve someone in your life to share all of the ups and downs with. You deserve to still find love. You jumped the obstacle to have a child, and you and I both know that Scarlett is the best part of your world now." I nod. "But you deserve *all* the good parts, Noelle, and that includes companionship."

Charlotte sniffles in her seat, reaching for a napkin. "Damn hormones. Why do you have to get all sentimental, Amelia?"

"Uh, that's her job, Charlotte—duh. That's what makes her the best therapist ever," Penelope fires back, winking across the table at Amelia.

Amelia rolls her eyes. "Yes, I might know a thing or two. But what I know more than anything is that the fear you have inside right now is a good thing. Embrace it, but let it build like the excitement you feel while reading a romance novel, knowing the rollercoaster you're about to ride has to have a happy ending."

"I know that's how it's supposed to end, but it's scary to jump on when you've never had that ending before," I reply, running my hand over Scarlett's head again.

"Didn't you say he wanted to have a date with both of you girls?" Penelope asks.

"Yeah. He didn't want me to have to worry about finding a babysitter, and he wanted to spend time with her, too."

"That's a pretty strong statement, Noelle." Amelia smiles at me. "So take a chance. Spend some time with him. And worry about the chocolate chip cookies later when Scarlett is old enough to appreciate them."

"And if you need a babysitter in the future, let me and Maddox do it."

I turn to Penelope. "Seriously?"

"Yeah. It will be a good way to get Maddox off my back about having kids if he spends some time with a real one." But then she pauses, concern etching the lines in her face. "Wait. This girl is still attached to the boob, right? Would you be opposed to me sticking my nipple in her mouth if I can't get her to stop crying?"

"What?!"

"I just mean, she may not know it's not your nipple. A nipple is a nipple, right?"

"Penelope!" I squeal.

She waves me off like what she said is no big deal. "It's

fine. I'm not gonna do it. I just need to know I have your permission just in case."

"Great. Now on top of dating, I have to worry about babysitters, too." Slapping a palm to my head, I sigh. "This is too much."

"No, it's not. You'll be fine. Scarlett will be fine. Penelope will *not* put her nipple in your child's mouth, and before you know it, this will just be some funny memory we reminisce about in the nursing home," Charlotte says.

"Oh. I'd better call them and make sure we have room for the boys now," Penelope declares as she jokingly reaches for her phone. "And I'll be sure to hold a spot for Noelle's sexy pilot. Although by then, his plane may not be able to take off anymore on its own, but that's what those blue pills are for, am I right, ladies?"

Amelia shakes her head, Charlotte rolls her eyes, and all I can do is laugh.

What would I do without these girls?

"There's my granddaughter!" my mother coos as we walk through her front door. It's a Tuesday evening, and my mother offered to watch Scarlett for a few hours so I could go to a Pilates class and run a few errands by myself. I just picked her up from daycare and feel like I should be eager to spend the evening with her, but I really just need some alone time right now.

"Are you sure you're okay with taking her?" I ask as I hand her off.

"I wouldn't have offered if I wasn't sure, Noelle." She tosses me a glare. "Now go. Go spend some time alone. Go take care of yourself. You'll feel better after you do."

Relief washes over me as my mother's words set in, and then I repeat to myself the words Amelia told me to say when I feel guilty: *I am not a bad mother because I want to be alone. I am not a bad mother for wanting something for me. I am not a bad mother for wanting to live my life for me.*

At that moment, my sister comes around the corner from the kitchen. "Hey. I didn't know you were stopping by." She tosses the rest of her cookie in her mouth as she stares at me.

"Mom's watching Scarlett for me for a few hours so I can get some alone time."

Her eyes narrow. "How convenient for you."

"Well, hello to you, too, Holly. And Jesus. What's that supposed to mean?" I fire back as my mother steps further into the living room and sits down on the couch, holding my daughter and making her laugh.

"I just find it funny how you chose to have a baby on your own and then expect everyone to help you."

My sister might as well have thrown a knife at my chest. "Wow. Is that what you think?"

"Girls . . ." my mother warns, but we continue to glare at each other as the tension rises in the room. The last thing I thought I'd have to handle this evening was defending myself against my sister, but apparently she's in one of her moods, and I'm tonight's punching bag.

"No, seriously, Holly. Is that how you feel?" I look around the house. "Wait. I don't see your kids here. Where are they?"

"They're at home with Seth."

"Wow. How convenient for *you*," I fire back, using her own words against her.

"No, not convenient. He's my husband. That's the beauty of marriage. I can ask my husband to watch my kids for me."

"Really?" I plant my hands on my hips, ready to lash out because now all of the guilt I was feeling a few moments ago has manifested into anger. "You have to *ask* him? And how long did he give you this time? Or better yet, how many times has he already called you, asking you to come home? And when's the last time he changed a diaper, Holly? Or woke up in the middle of the night to feed a baby?"

My sister and her husband have three kids, ages ten, six, and one-and-a-half. Yeah, if you do the math, she had a baby in college. My carefree sister got knocked up and married the guy, but she's far from living in a fairytale world. She got the family I always wanted, but I would never want the relationship they have.

Sure, they got married and are still, but her husband never helps. He thinks because he works and pays the bills, he shouldn't have to. They constantly fight, I can't remember the last time they went on a date, and as a father, he's barely lifted a finger to help. Honestly, I'm beyond surprised that he's home alone with all three of the kids right now.

"Seth helps."

I roll my eyes. "Okay, sure. Whatever you say. But most importantly, why don't you stop and think before you just start spewing judgment in my direction for the way I've chosen to live my life? I swear, every time you're around me, you have to take some sort of jab at me, and I'm getting sick of it!"

"Girls!" my mother shouts, pulling our attention her direction. "That's enough." Shaking her head, she stands and walks toward us, holding my daughter. "I can't believe you two. First, Holly? Why the hell did you just decide to attack Noelle the second you saw her when *you* ran out of the house to come here for a moment of peace, huh? You should know more than anyone what Noelle is going through with a new baby, and instead of trying to support her, you're tearing her down." And then she turns to me. "And Noelle? Your sister's marriage is none of your concern. How they choose to raise their kids is their decision." Bouncing Scarlett on her hip, she sighs. "Now, both of you get out of here. Do what you need to do, and I don't want to hear you attack each other like that again in my house, got it?"

"Yes, ma'am."

"Yeah, Mom. I'm sorry," I say, reaching out for Scarlett's hand and kissing the top of it.

"Now go. Go do what you need to do to feel human again, and I'll see you in a few hours. And Holly?"

My sister turns to her. "Yeah?"

"Don't answer Seth's texts again. He is a father, and he can handle those kids on his own. And if not, then maybe it'll be his wakeup call to be more hands-on."

Fighting my smile, I head for the front door and feel my sister walking right behind me.

"I'm sorry, Noelle. I just—"

"You're angry," I cut her off. "But I don't think I'm the one you're angry at."

She brushes a hand through her hair. "You're right. It's not you, not exactly. I just . . . I had to get out of my house. I just needed a break."

"I get that. I do. But why can't you just admit that instead of attacking me?"

My relationship with my sister has always been a little strained, but ever since I decided to have Scarlett on my own, she's been nasty toward me, making backhanded comments and judging me for the choice I made. I've tried not to let it bother me, but when my nerves are already on thin ice, hearing her say shit just tips me over the edge.

"I guess . . ." She stares off across the yard as a few cars go down the street. "I guess part of me is jealous."

"What?" My mouth drops open. "Why?"

"You're alone."

"Yeah. Rub it in some more, why don't you?"

"No, you don't understand." I watch her swallow, and then she barely whispers, "Sometimes I wish *I* were alone."

"Holly . . ."

"Sometimes I think it would be easier to do this on my own, without Seth. You're right. He doesn't help. I do everything, and I'm so resentful about it. Tonight, when he got home, I literally grabbed my keys and ran out the door. I didn't even tell him where I was going, but I just knew that I had to get away."

Realization floods my chest. "Being a mom is really hard."

Tears fill her eyes. "It is. And I'm sorry that I've taken out my own shit on you. I know you're doing it all on your own, and I guess I'm resentful of that, too. Because you're doing an amazing job, and here I am with a husband who should be helping me, but I feel like I'm drowning."

Holy shit. This is so eye-opening. "Holly . . . I'm barely surviving right now. Seriously. That's why Mom offered to take Scarlett for me. I didn't ask, she insisted, but it's like she knew I needed a break."

"I feel so guilty for wanting to run away, though." She wipes the tears from under her eyes.

"I do, too," I whisper back, "especially since I chose this."

"You were so brave to do that, Noelle." She grabs my hand. "I don't know if I've ever told you how much I admire what you did. You made that decision all on your own, and you're doing so great."

We both stand there and stare at each other, tears sliding down our cheeks. "I think this is the most honest we've ever been with each other, Holly."

She laughs. "Yeah."

"And in the name of honesty, I'll tell you that I have never felt more alone in my life."

"Me, too."

"See? It doesn't matter if you have a partner or not, being a mother is just—"

"—hard," she finishes for me.

"Yup. And I wish I had someone to lean on, but the whole reason I had Scarlett on my own is because I didn't want to settle. I want a real man in my life, someone who wants to help and support me."

"You deserve that. Every woman does." And then she sighs. "Seth definitely doesn't live up to that expectation. And lately, I just keep thinking that I never should have married him."

"That's a pretty bold statement. Have you tried talking to him about how you're feeling?"

"I mean, yeah, a little. But he goes back to how my role is to stay home and take care of the kids . . ."

"Says who? This isn't the 1950s anymore, Holly. You deserve a husband who helps you since he's also living in that house and helped create those kids."

"I know. You're right."

"You know, if you wanted to talk to someone, I have a friend who's a kick-ass therapist."

Holly chuckles as she wipes under her eyes. "Yeah, I know that, too." Then she takes a deep breath and blows it out. "I'll figure it out."

"You will. We both will."

She pulls me in for a hug. "I'm sorry for what I said."

"Thank you. I'm sorry, too."

"Enjoy your night," she tells me.

"Same to you. I'll see you in a few weeks?"

"Maybe sooner if I run away to your house next time," she says as she winks and then heads toward her car.

As I drive to my Pilates class, I think about what just happened and the things that my sister said to me. You can be alone and also be with someone and feel alone as well. And even though I know the idea of dating again is scary, I know that I won't allow myself to end up like my sister with a man like her husband. I've waited this long to find the right person, so I can continue to wait. And if I never find him, I know I'll be alright.

But Grant . . .

That man intrigued me from the get-go, and I know that if I don't at least take the chance to get to know him, I'll regret it. He could end up being the man I've been waiting for or just another man who proves he doesn't deserve me or my daughter.

And so with renewed confidence in my decision and after an eye-opening conversation with my sister, I pull into the parking lot of the Pilates studio, shift my car into park, grab my cell phone, and text him to make plans for our date.

Chapter 7

Grant

S tanding outside the Los Angeles Zoo, I can't help but bounce on my feet as I wait for Noelle and her daughter to arrive. Nerves crawl over my skin while I accept the fact that I'm truly putting myself out there as I attempt to date a woman, hoping this time it's worthwhile.

My brother was right. It was my own choice not to get Noelle's number the first time I saw her. I could have very easily taken one extra minute to secure a way to contact her. And after he called me on it, I wrestled with how to find her.

Some internet research did little good without a last name to go off of. And surprisingly, Noelle is a far more popular name than I thought. There were no traces of her on Facebook and Instagram, and I figured if she wasn't using those two platforms, the chances of her using Twitter, TikTok, or something else were probably pretty slim.

But then fate stepped in.

Three weeks after our run-in at the coffee shop, I saw her on one of my flights. I had to blink several times to make sure the woman I was staring at was her. And when it hit me, I knew I'd be a fool to let her slip away twice.

I heard the message from the man upstairs loud and clear, and I listened.

Now, one week after our second encounter, I'm waiting for the woman who has captivated me to show up for our date with her daughter in tow. I know there are things I'll have to discuss with Noelle at some point, but for right now, I'm going to ride this high I feel when I'm around her and Scarlett and hope that will help quell the fears that lurk in the back of my mind.

It's been a long time since a woman has intrigued me like she has. Honestly, in the past few months, I'd begun to accept the fact that I may just be alone for the rest of my life. Dating became such a hassle and never ended well. But something about this woman—along with a little dash of serendipity—told me to take the chance. So that's what I've decided to do.

"Grant!" a voice calls out, pulling my head in the direction of the parking lot. And that's when I see Noelle hustling toward me, pushing Scarlett in a stroller, her hair pulled up in a ponytail that's swaying as she walks.

God, she's so beautiful.

"I'm so sorry we're late," she says, out of breath as she arrives right next to me.

"Don't worry about it. I haven't been waiting long."

She brushes a few hairs from her face and then lifts her sunglasses so I can see her stunning green eyes. "I swear, before I had Scarlett, I was early to everything. But now—"

I hold my hand up to cut her off. "Noelle, it's fine. I'm in no rush, and neither should you be. Take a deep breath. It's okay."

She inhales and blows it out slowly. "Okay. Thank you." And then her eyes drop from mine down my body, taking me all in.

I dressed casually for a day at the zoo in khaki shorts, a simple navy-blue shirt, and comfortable sneakers. I brought a hat as well to ward off the sun. But as Noelle takes in my more than casual appearance compared to how she's seen me before, I take this opportunity to do the same to her.

In a red sundress with thin straps, she stands slightly shorter than I remember. But as I take in the flat white sneakers she's wearing today, I realize she was in heels the last two times I'd seen her. Her hair is pulled back in her ponytail, highlighting the slightly red tint to her light brown hair as it shimmers in the sun, and her vibrant green eyes are highlighted by natural makeup while her lips shine with a simple pink gloss.

I wonder what those lips taste like.

"Are we done checking each other out now?" I ask, pulling her back to the present as her cheeks turn pink from my words.

"Sorry," she says through a laugh. "I just haven't seen you out of your pilot's uniform yet and was trying to decide which look I liked better."

"Hmm. And what's the verdict?"

She reaches up and taps the bill of my baseball cap, which has the Los Angeles Bolts logo on it. "I have a thing for men in hats. And glasses, apparently."

"Really?" I lift my hat off my head, spin it around so the bill is facing backward now, and then put it back in place. "What about now?"

She bites her lip. "You're definitely not playing fair."

Chuckling, I motion for us to start walking. "All's fair in love and war, right?"

"Are we already fighting?"

"Absolutely not. Although I will fight you if you don't let me push the stroller for a bit."

She slowly moves to the side. "If you insist."

"I do." Pulling the shade canopy back so I can see Scarlett, I bend over the stroller to look down at her. "How're you doing, sweetheart?" The squeal she lets out when she tilts her head back and connects her eyes with mine is enough to make my ego swell to twice its size. "That good, huh?"

"She actually got some solid sleep last night, which means I did, too, so we're both in decent moods today."

I push the stroller forward, headed for the front gate. "Lots of sleepless nights lately?"

"Oh, yeah. Teething is the worst."

"I remember my nephews at that age. My brother and his wife were going crazy."

"That's a nice way of putting it," she says as she glances

over to the ticket windows. "Aren't we going to buy tickets?" She points in that direction.

I hold up my phone. "I already got them."

"Oh. Well, thank you."

"Of course. This was my idea, so I feel it's only natural that I pay."

"We appreciate that. I'll have to repay you somehow."

I stop walking and reach out for her chin as she freezes beside me, tilting her head up so our eyes meet. "You don't owe me anything, Noelle. Just getting to spend today with you and Scarlett is enough, okay?"

Her bottom lip trembles, and she releases the breath she was holding. "Okay."

"Attagirl. Now, let's go see some animals."

As we make our way through the gates, gift shops line the walkway on either side of us. I can see Scarlett looking in every direction, so I know I'll have to purchase something for her later.

"Where to first?"

"Honestly, wherever you want. Let's just start at the first exhibit and work our way around."

"Sounds like a plan." Stopping by one of the counters, I scan the QR code for the map and pull it up on my phone so we can see where everything is.

I push the stroller to the left where we find the first exhibit filled with California sea lions. "Look at that, Scarlett," I say as we get closer to the glass. The zoo just opened, so luckily the crowds aren't too bad yet.

"I love sea lions. Their bark reminds me of a dog I used to have growing up."

"Really? What kind of dog?" I ask.

"His name was Oakley, and he was a Puggle, a pug and beagle mix. They barked and howled at the same time, so it always sounded like there was a sea lion in our backyard," Noelle says, smiling as she looks at the animals.

"I bet your neighbors loved your family."

"Oh, we warned anyone who moved into the neighborhood. It felt like the right thing to do so they knew a helpless animal wasn't being murdered in our yard."

I chuckle. "Where did you grow up?"

"I've lived in Los Angeles my entire life. My parents bought a house here in the '80s and fixed it up. It was just me and my sister, but we had a good childhood, and my parents are still married." She turns to face me now. "What about you?"

"I was born in Nevada, actually. My parents divorced, and my mom brought us down to southern California when I was about ten to be closer to her family. It was me and my younger brother, Gavin, and we lived in Laguna Hills for a while. Now I live pretty close to LAX because—"

"—of your job."

I nod. "Yup."

"Laguna Beach, huh? I bet when that television show came out on MTV, anyone who met you had a field day."

"Oh, that was while I was in high school, so everyone was obsessed with it. I actually knew Stephen, but he was always very hush-hush about the show. Now, of course, we know the thing was scripted heavily, but back then, that's all anyone from the city could talk about."

"I bet." Scarlett screeches from her seat. "I think she's ready to move on."

"As you wish, Princess."

We walk along the path, headed to the next exhibit. "I wonder if they have polar bears here?" Noelle asks.

"I don't think so." I show her the map on my phone as her face twists with disappointment. "You like polar bears?"

She grins as she glances at me. "Yeah, they're my favorite animal."

"That's a unique one you don't hear that often. Why polar bears?"

"Well, it's kind of silly, but because of the Coca-Cola commercials growing up."

"Oh, those were the best!"

She laughs. "Right? And my grandmother collected Coca-Cola memorabilia, so when all of the polar bear stuff came out, she always bought extra for me. I still have some of her collectibles."

"That's pretty amazing."

"Especially because she's passed away since then. But I guess that's why I still drink the soda, too. It reminds me of her."

I reach down and grab her hand, shocking us both, but it just felt like the right thing to do at that moment. "Thank you for sharing that with me."

Her eyes bounce back and forth between mine. "I'm sorry. I

probably shouldn't be telling you my entire life story already, down to details about my dead grandmother, but you make me nervous."

"Is that a bad thing?"

She shrugs, but there's a slight smile on her lips. "I don't know yet." Shaking her head, she pulls away slightly.

"If it helps, I'm nervous, too. But I want to know about you, Noelle. That's the entire reason I asked you out. Don't be afraid to share your thoughts and memories. Those are what make you you."

"I never used to be this anxious going on dates. I would be antsy with anticipation but not in a bad way. But now . . ." She turns her head toward Scarlett.

"Now you're not just thinking about you." She nods, still not meeting my eyes. "I get that. But I want you to know I understand that, too." Finally, she locks gazes with me again. "I wouldn't have asked for your number if I wasn't serious about this. I know you don't know me very well, but I hope we can change that. I like you. You intrigue me, and I hope you'll allow yourself to relax enough to explore whatever this is right alongside me." *Please, meet me halfway here so I don't freak out as well.*

I watch her shoulders fall and her eyes soften. "Thank you."

Laughing, I release her hand and use both of my arms to push the stroller up a hill, surprised by what a workout this is turning out to be, especially after I put in a few hours at the gym this morning trying to burn off my nervous energy. "You're welcome. Now in the meantime, you can keep telling me all about you, if you want. I mean, that is kind of the point of a date, right?"

"Right." We head toward the reptile exhibit, but Noelle stops me with a hand on my forearm. "Can we bypass the snakes and reptiles, please?"

"Sure. Is everything okay?"

"I just really hate reptiles. Snakes, lizards, alligators . . ." She visibly shutters. "They give me the creeps."

Chuckling, I nod my head. "Okay. No reptiles. The elephants are up ahead. How about that?"

"Totally on board with elephants."

We make our way to the outside of the massive elephant exhibit. Scarlett grows fussy in the stroller when we pull up to the fence, so I reach down to take her out. "Hey, sweet girl. You want out of this thing?"

"I can get her," Noelle chimes in, reaching for her daughter as I hoist her to my hip.

"Nonsense. I've got her." Scarlett instantly calms in my arms, a feeling that gets stronger every time I hold her. I don't know what it is, but ever since that day in the coffee shop, I get this warm fuzzy feeling when I hold this little girl.

"Are you sure?"

"Yes, Noelle. I'm sure."

She shakes her head. "I'm sorry. I'm just not used to having help."

Her bringing that up reminds me of something I wanted to ask her. "I can imagine, but there's no need to apologize. You said in the coffee shop that you didn't have a husband or boyfriend, which I'm grateful for, considering we're on a date right now." She laughs. "But if you don't mind me asking, where is Scarlett's father then?"

She veers her eyes off to the side. "He's . . . he's not in the picture."

"I'm sorry."

She turns back to me, clarity in her eyes. "It's okay. Truly. It was better this way." I get the feeling she wants to say more, but she startles me by asking me a question instead. "Do you mind me asking how old you are?"

"Are you afraid I'm too old for you?"

Her eyes widen. "Oh gosh, no! I was just curious."

Smirking, I reply, "I'm thirty-eight."

"Wow."

"Wow? Does that surprise you?"

"Yes, but not in a bad way." She reaches for Scarlett's hand, kissing it. "I just don't understand how you're still single." Her eyes dart around us. "I don't think you understand how women look at you and how perfect you seem."

I take a step closer to her, closing the gap between us. "Why would I care about them when I'm looking at the only woman I care about seeing right next to me?"

"Jesus." She laughs. "I don't know how to feel about you."

The corner of my mouth turns up in a grin. "I'm just being honest."

"I appreciate that, but I'm not used to it, I guess."

"Listen, Noelle. I'm not going to beat around the bush with you, okay? I like you. A lot. And it's been a long time since I put myself out there because I've been burned. It was devastating, and since then, I've kept my guard up and haven't really tried to get serious with anyone. I'd just ask you to be honest, too, okay? And be confident about it."

Her eyes widen, but she nods and swallows. "Okay. I will. I like you, Grant. A lot. Probably more than I should this early on, but I feel something here. How's that for honesty?"

I can't fight my smile. "That's pretty freaking amazing. And just so you know," I say, looking between Noelle and Scarlett, "I was drawn to you the second I turned around in that coffee shop."

"So where does that leave us right now?" she asks as she peers up at me.

"At the Los Angeles Zoo, enjoying a beautiful day together." Movement from my left catches my attention as an elephant walks toward us. Scarlett screams, reaching for the metal pole in the fence to get closer.

"You like elephants, baby girl?" Noelle asks, smiling so brightly at her daughter before reaching for her phone and snapping a picture of me holding her as Scarlett reaches for the animal. "Is this okay?"

"Absolutely. Here." I motion her closer, pulling her into my side. "Take one of all three of us."

She flips the camera around to selfie mode, and we all crowd together, the baby smell of Scarlett assaulting my nose just as Noelle's scent hits me, too. It's sugary and sweet with a slight floral smell. The woman fits so perfectly against me. Hell, they both do.

Some sort of twinge flashes across my chest, and as Noelle snaps the picture, the image of the three of us is burned into my mind. Before I can analyze how I'm feeling too thoroughly, I focus back on the baby in my arms and the woman beside me, happy with the decision I made to pursue whatever this is.

"Sorry," Noelle says as she sits down on a bench and nestles Scarlett under her cover-up to nurse her.

I take a seat next to her, crossing my ankle over my knee. "Stop apologizing. Your daughter has to eat, Noelle."

"I know. I guess you probably didn't imagine being on a date and having to rest because your date had to nurse her baby, did you?"

Tilting her chin toward me, I stare intently into her eyes. "If I cared that much about it, I wouldn't have made an effort to include her."

She swallows roughly. "I'm still surprised that you wanted to."

"Why does that surprise you? She's an angel."

Noelle snorts as she peeks under the cover to check on her daughter. "Yeah, around you. She saves her witching hour behavior for me at night." Chuckling, she turns her eyes back to me. "I just never thought I'd be taking my daughter on a date . . . like, *ever*."

"Well, one, I didn't want you to have to worry about finding a babysitter when I genuinely wanted to hold her again.

Two, I didn't want you to use *not* being able to find a babysitter as an excuse *not* to go out with me." I wink at her, her lips finally curving up into a smile. "And three, you're a package deal. I was raised by a single mom. I know what that struggle is like. And I don't ever want you to feel like I want you any less because you have a child. I mean, it *is* her necessity to eat that brought us together, remember?" I flick my eyes down to her completely covered chest, but I'm trying to make a point.

Releasing her chin, I watch her cheeks turn pink. "Then I guess I should just stop trying to tell myself that you're too good to be true."

"You should. I'm human, like anyone else. I have my faults. But we're here together because that's the way things worked out. Trust me, I have no problem taking a rest. These old knees are already starting to throb."

She giggles. "You're not that old."

"Really?" I take my hat off, running my hands through the short strands of my hair. "Have you seen this gray?"

She licks her lips. "I have. And I have to tell you, Grant: Gray hair is rather sexy on men."

That little piece of information has me grinning as I place my hat back on my head. "Really?"

"Oh, yeah. I don't know what it is. Maybe it makes you look more distinguished, wiser, or like you have life experience? But ask any grown woman—gray hair just does something to us."

"I'll cancel my Rogaine and hair dye order tomorrow, then."

Laughing, she brings Scarlett out from under the cover-up, the girl's smile beyond adorable from her milk-drunk appearance. "All done, sweet girl?"

"Here. Let me take her while you get cleaned up."

Noelle hands me the baby and a receiving blanket to place over my shoulder as I stand and begin to burp her, remembering all too well how important that was from when my nephews were little.

"Thank you," Noelle says as she situates her dress again and removes the cover from around her shoulders.

"My pleasure. Now, are we ready to see some gorillas?" Scarlett lets out a belch that would make a grown man proud. "I think that's supposed to mean yes." Noelle laughs and pushes the stroller beside me as I hold Scarlett to my chest. "So what else do you girls have planned for this weekend?"

"Well, Sundays, I usually have brunch with my three girlfriends at Frankie's Diner."

"I've heard of the place. Good food?"

"The best, plus bottomless mimosas," she says as she smirks at me.

"Nothing wrong with that on a Sunday."

"It's a tradition my friends and I started back in college. We don't get to do it as often now that my friends are all married and starting families of their own, but we try to keep the standing date as often as we can."

"I love it. True friendship is hard to come by."

"Don't I know it. Those girls are like my second family."

"Tell me about them." We continue to walk aimlessly,

trying to stay in the shade as much as possible. It's the end of June, so it's hot and a bit humid outside. I lead Noelle to the side of the path so we can take advantage of the shade while we have it.

"Well, Charlotte is the career driven one of the bunch. She's a senior advertising executive for Revision Magazine. When I hear that song by Beyoncé about who runs the world, I think of her." I laugh. "Now, she is married to Damien, who happened to be her childhood nemesis."

"Interesting."

"Oh, it was an interesting turn of events that led them to each other. They fake dated to appease her parents and for Damien to try to secure a promotion at work. They hadn't seen each other in twelve years, and then upon crossing paths again, they realized the sparks between them weren't just full of hatred. It was quite entertaining to watch."

"Sounds like it. Who else is part of the group?"

"Amelia is the quieter, more reserved one, but don't let that fool you. She's a sex and marriage therapist, and the girl has no shortage of confidence in that arena. She's damn good at her job and always keeps the four of us in tune with our emotions. She's married to Ethan, who ironically is a divorce attorney who opened his practice in the same complex as hers."

"Oh, that sounds like a recipe for disaster. How did they manage not to kill each other?"

Noelle laughs this time. "Oh, it almost came to that, but Amelia stood her ground against him, and he ultimately realized he was in love with her. They balance each other out so well, you can't help but admire their relationship."

"And last but not least is . . ."

"Penelope." Noelle shakes her head with an amused smile. "Penelope is one of the sassiest and most outspoken women you'll ever meet, but that's what we love about her. She's bold, unapologetically honest, and loves hard. But she fought love for so long because of a loss she had in her past, and we just found out last year about it."

"Wow."

"Yeah. But then she fell for Maddox Taylor—"

I reach out to grab her arm, halting our steps. "Wait . . . *the* Maddox Taylor? Of the Los Angeles Bolts?"

"Yup." Noelle nods and then keeps walking. "Penelope was hired to do the PR for the team when Maddox was traded, and they fell in love. He's one heck of a man but the perfect man for her."

"Damn. Your friends sound like some incredible women, and apparently they have good taste in men, too," I joke.

Noelle stands taller, more proud. "They are my second family. I wouldn't be who I am today without them. It's so rare to find friends like them. I know I'm blessed to know them and have them in my corner as I navigate life."

"Well, I hope someday you feel I'm worthy of meeting them." She tries to keep her smile small, but I see her fighting it. "So what do you do Monday through Friday then, when you're not at brunch with the girls?" I ask, changing the subject since Noelle seems to be relaxing and there's so much more I want to know about her. "I never got a chance to ask you what you were in Chicago for that day. I was too busy trying to get your phone number before I missed my chance again."

She smiles. "I'm a literary agent. I discover authors and sign them to my publishing house in hopes of making their dreams of being a full-time writer come true."

Damn. I don't know what is so sexy about a woman who reads, but Noelle also helps publish books. Visions of her sitting behind a desk, wearing a skintight skirt and blouse like she was the day I met her, biting on the end of a pen with a pinch in her brow during a meeting has me getting half hard. *Didn't see that coming.* "That's incredible. You were probably a big reader when you were younger then, huh?"

She straightens her spine. "Absolutely. It's been a dream come true to take my love of reading and make a career out of it."

"Any particular genre?"

Casting me a side-eye glance and a smirk, she says, "Romance."

"Romance?"

"Yes. And before you say anything, I'll have you know that romance books are a billion-dollar industry . . . that's *billion* with a *b*. Women know what they want to read, and I help give them the stories I know they'll fall in love with."

Hoisting Scarlett up higher on my hip, we continue to walk. "Hey, I'm not knocking the genre, if that's what you think. I am completely aware of how powerful those books are."

"Really? How?"

"The women in my family are big readers, too," I reply, casting her a wink. "I'm pretty sure my brother became a father after his wife read something a little too hot."

Noelle laughs. "Wouldn't be the first time that's happened. Many authors get letters from fans announcing the births of their babies thanks to one of their books. Think of it as women helping women in an unconventional way." Then she turns to me. "Okay, enough about me. What about you, Grant? What do you do when you're not flying around the world? Obviously, I know what *you* do for a living."

"Well, tomorrow, I'm actually taking my nephews fishing."

"That's sweet."

"It's a hobby I picked up from my stepdad in my early teen years. My brother and I got hooked on it, no pun intended, but he works so much that we don't get to go nearly as often as we used to. Plus, the boys are on summer vacation right now, so it's a good excuse to get them out of the house and for me to spend some time with them."

"I'm sure your brother and his wife appreciate that."

"Oh, they do. They tell me often how much they need a break sometimes."

Noelle lets out a sigh. "Being a parent is exhausting. It's amazing but exhausting."

"I know. I mean, I don't completely, but I've seen what they've gone through. Can't say I don't envy them sometimes, because I do. I mean, I'd love to have my own family, but . . ."

Noelle gasps. "Oh God. I'm sorry. Complaining must just make me sound—"

"—normal, Noelle. You sound like a normal parent," I reply, cutting her off. "I've heard it all from my brother and his wife. Besides, today, you have my help. And this little girl looks like she wants to watch some gorillas."

Ending the conversation, we approach the glass surrounding the gorilla exhibit, getting close enough that I can point out the animals to Scarlett as we stand there and watch.

"So you fly planes and fish. Any other talents I should know about?" Noelle asks as we watch a gorilla swing from a tree.

"I'm not ready to divulge all of my talents just yet." I smile at her, making her blush.

"Well, I guess there should be some surprises for next time, shouldn't there?"

"Are you already agreeing to a second date with me?"

"Are you asking me out on one?"

"I planned on it before we said our goodbyes later."

"Well, I guess I just wrecked your plan, didn't I?" she replies playfully.

Reaching out to tuck a strand of loose hair that fell from her ponytail, I say, "Yeah, you definitely did. But I'm not mad about it at all."

With a stuffed elephant in the stroller next to a sleeping Scarlett, we head for the parking lot as I walk Noelle and her daughter to their car. Noelle starts the engine to get the air conditioning on so the car can cool off before gently placing Scarlett in her car seat. The little thing is so tuckered out, she doesn't even stir.

Once Noelle secures her and gently shuts the door, she turns to face me, biting her lip.

"You're going to need to stop doing that around me."

"What?"

"Biting your lip." I reach forward to curve my hand around her hip, loving the way she feels in my palm.

"Why?" she whispers breathlessly.

"Because it's making it hard for me to be a gentleman right now."

"You sure have a way with words, Grant," she says teasingly. "And just so you know, I don't think I'd mind if you flipped that switch and let me see that side of you."

Leaning forward so I can line up my lips to her ear, I pull her closer and lower my voice. "I want to show you that other side, Noelle. But not yet. I wanna take things slow with you so we're both sure of what's happening here. I don't want you to keep second-guessing how you're feeling and whether or not you can trust me." Inhaling her scent, I blow out my breath against her neck, watching her skin pebble as I do. "But when we do cross that line, I won't hold back, sweetheart. That I can promise."

I lean back so I can see her eyes again, and bright green orbs are staring back at me, pupils dilated. "Thank you."

"You keep saying that to me," I joke.

Her face and gaze softens. "I know, but I don't think you

understand how difficult this has been for me. It's been so long since I've dated. Well before I had Scarlett. And now with her in the picture, everything is different. I just want you to know that I appreciate your patience and understanding."

"That's the very least I could give you. So when can I see you again?"

"What does your schedule look like?"

"I have some availability in the middle of next week. Do you think you can manage a date on a Wednesday?"

"Am I bringing my daughter this time?"

"That's up to you. I'm good with either option."

She bites her lip again. "I think maybe a night with just the two of us would be a good stepping stone next."

Cupping the side of her face, I nod. "Then that's what we'll do."

Her eyes dart to my lips, and I know she is waiting for me to kiss her. But as we stand outside of her car in the parking lot of the LA Zoo, I know that this isn't how I want to kiss her for the first time. I can tell how uncertain she's been all day with her feelings, which is totally understandable given the circumstances.

But when I kiss her, kiss her the way I truly want to, I don't want her to second-guess a moment of it. I want her to be all in and absorb every sensation that will crackle between us.

Pressing my lips to her forehead, I stay there for a moment, soaking up the heat of her skin beneath my mouth. I can tell the movement caught her off guard, but I know it was the right move to make.

She clings to my shoulders, breathing deeply as we stay like that for a moment before I reluctantly pull away.

"I'll call you."

Looking slightly disappointed, she recovers quickly and flashes me that beautiful smile of hers. "Okay. Bye, Grant."

"Bye, Noelle."

I watch her get inside her car and pull away before I make it over to my own. And as I start the engine, I think back to how perfect today felt with the two of them, an indication that maybe taking the risk of putting myself out there again is actually worth it this time. Maybe dating a woman who already has a kid is helping take some of the pressure off me and the inadequacy that my past likes to remind me of at times.

And maybe that's exactly what I need right now.

"You two ready to go fishing?" Standing in my brother's living room, I stare down at my nephews who are barely awake and lying on the couch in their pajamas.

Andrew lets out a groan as he pulls his security blanket over his head. "It's so early."

"Yeah, but if we don't go early, we miss the fish. They're early risers."

Sarah comes around the corner and steps into the living room holding her cup of coffee. "I tried to tell them you were going to be here before six, but they didn't believe me."

I hold up a pink box in my hands. "I guess no one wants

donuts then, do they?" That has both of them perking up. "Go get dressed, brush your teeth, and then we can eat them in the truck."

The two of them race off just as my brother comes down the hallway, scratching his stomach and yawning. "Good morning."

"Morning. Sorry to wake you."

"It's okay. Sarah and I are gonna take advantage of no kids today, and I didn't want to waste any time." He winks over at his wife. "Right, babe?"

She rolls her eyes but smiles nonetheless. "So what time do you plan on bringing them back?" she asks, turning to me and ignoring Gavin completely.

"Whenever. I can keep them for the day if you want the time."

Gavin slides up behind his wife. "I always want time with this woman."

A spark of envy strikes my chest, but I shove it away. "Glad I can help. Say, I have a question for you two . . ."

"Shoot." Gavin releases Sarah and moves to the cupboard to grab a coffee cup.

"If you had a chance to go somewhere without the kids, where would you go?"

"Um, we're planning to stay home and fuck all day if I hadn't made myself clear," my brother replies just before Sarah reaches out and slaps him. "What?"

"Jesus, Gav. This is your brother."

"Yeah, and?"

Sarah shakes her head, clenching her teeth together. I'm sure she'll find some way to get back at him for that comment. "Why do you ask, Grant?"

"Well, I've got a date this week, and I'm looking for ideas."

My brother inserts himself back into the conversation. "A date? Are you serious?"

Scratching my face through my beard, I stare down at the floor. "Yeah. It's actually the woman from the coffee shop."

His grin grows in a flash. "Holy shit. You tracked her down?"

"Ha. Not exactly. She actually appeared before my eyes."

Sarah's eyes dart back and forth between us. "Who is the coffee shop girl?"

I spend the next few minutes filling them in on how Noelle and I met and when I saw her again on one of my flights. Within that span of time, Sarah has to go break up a fight between Andrew and Michael as they brush their teeth next to each other in the bathroom, but once that's settled, I finish my story, arriving back at my original question.

"Well, first of all, I'm freaking proud of you, Grant," my brother declares.

I huff out a laugh. "Thanks."

"And secondly, a single mom? I don't think that could be any more perfect for you."

Sarah interrupts. "Well, I agree, but at the same time, you know how sacred dating a single mom is. Remember *Jerry Maguire*? Cuba Gooding Jr., aka Rod Tidwell, said it best."

"Hey. It's not like that. I . . . ." Staring off into space, I pause to gather my thoughts. "There's something there, Sarah. The fact that she already has a kid does alleviate some pressure on my end, but it's more than that. Her daughter is a little slice of sunshine, and she lights up every time she sees me. It makes me feel like Superman. But Noelle is also . . ."

"Okay, okay. I can tell by your googly eyes that you like her. So what was your question again?"

"Yesterday, I took her and the baby to the zoo because I wanted her to know I understand that her daughter is the biggest part of her life and I accept that they are a package deal. But this week, I'm taking her out, just the two of us. And I guess what I need to know is: Where would you want to go if you had a night out, away from your kids?"

My sister-in-law clutches her hands to her chest. "Oh my God. I don't know if you even realize how perfect you just sounded."

Gavin swats at her playfully. "Hey! Your husband is right here."

She bats him away. "I'm aware. But seriously, Grant. What you just asked is like asking a mom what her deepest, darkest fantasies are."

"I thought all of your fantasies involved me, babe?" my brother questions, his brow drawn together.

She shoves him this time before answering me. "Here's what moms really want—or at least the things that come immediately to my mind. I would want to go to the movies where the film is rated over PG and there are no kids to share my snacks with or no kids I have to get up to take to the bathroom." She looks up at the ceiling, resting her chin in her hands as if she's daydreaming. "A wine bar or a concert where I can have a few drinks and not have to worry about mothering someone while I'm there or after. A massage or pedicure where no one talked to me during it. The grocery store, alone . . . basically anywhere kids aren't allowed."

"The grocery store?" Gavin asks.

She turns to him. "Hell yes. Why do you think I leave you and the boys home most of the time when I go? Not only do I spend more money when the three of you are there, but going alone is legitimately peaceful. And now, I actually like the music they play in the grocery store because those are the songs I spent my youth dancing to."

Amused by the two of them right now, especially by the look of bewilderment on my brother's face as he learns new facts about his wife, I ponder what Sarah just divulged. "I'm sure the movies would be good, but I kind of want to go somewhere with her where we can talk more, so that won't work. A concert would be hard to find on such short notice, and a massage and pedicure won't work for a date." And then a light-bulb illuminates in my mind. "But I think I might know of a place we can go."

"I'm sure she'll be happy wherever you plan on taking her."

"I hope so."

Gavin narrows his eyes at me. "You seem nervous about this date."

Ripping my hat off, I toss it on the counter. "I am. I mean, come on . . . you guys know what I've been through. But this is the first time in a long time that I actually want to put myself out there."

Sarah grabs my hand. "We know. And we also know that you deserve happiness, Grant. Don't stress about the what-ifs right now. Just enjoy getting to know her. And then let us know when we get to meet her."

I squeeze her hand and let it go. "I will, but I kind of want to wait this out for a bit before we get to that point, okay?" Grabbing my hat, I place it back on my head. But then I point a finger at my brother and his wife, and their eyes widen comically at the same time. "But don't you dare say anything to Mom yet, you hear me? The last thing I want is to get her hopes up." Getting that look from my mom time and time again is one of the reasons I eventually gave up on dating. It wasn't necessarily pity but sadness and remorse for circumstances in my life that I had no control over, circumstances she could do absolutely nothing about. And I can only imagine as a mother how helpless she felt knowing she couldn't prevent the chaos of my life unfolding.

Sarah marks an X over her chest. "Promise."

"Yeah, your secret's safe with us—for now, that is," my brother says, bouncing his eyebrows at me.

"What secret?" Andrew asks as he and Michael enter the kitchen.

I turn to face him, smiling when I see the two of them dressed with hats on their heads like mine. Gotta love the Los Angeles Bolts, especially now that Maddox Taylor is their quarterback. "I figured out a new bait for us to use to catch fish."

Michael's eyes widen. "Really?"

"Yup. I'll tell you all about it in the truck. Say goodbye to your parents." The boys rush their mom and dad, hugging them both. "You two have fun today," I say, eyeing my brother while bouncing my eyebrows.

"Don't worry. We will."

"Yup. Lots of cleaning to do before any fun gets had," Sarah bites back.

I lead the boys out to the truck, make sure they're buckled in, give them each a donut and napkin, and then head for the lake.

"Are we gonna catch any fish today, Uncle Grant?" Andrew asks.

"I don't know, buddy. It all depends on our luck and if we can woo them more than the others."

"I think we can. We are Thomas boys after all," Michael states proudly.

"Yeah, I think you're right. But sometimes, it's important to remember that we have no control over what happens. The only thing we have control over is how we react to it."

Chapter 8

Noelle

Fiddling with my outfit for the thousandth time, I stare at myself in the full-length mirror by my front door. I've got on my most comfortable pair of mom jeans that are high-waisted enough I can tuck in all of my motherly curves, a sleeveless black tank that gives just the right amount of cleavage while being non-restrictive, and a pair of sensible wedges since Grant told me we were going out tonight to have some fun. "Sexy but comfortable" were the words he used when I asked him how I should dress, so I hope I followed directions.

I pumped before I got dressed so I didn't have to worry about leaking through my bra and shirt again, I've shaved every spot on my body that hasn't seen a man's eye in over two years (even though I'm not ready to sleep with him yet), and got my hair freshly dyed and cut last night. I'm as ready as I'm going to be for this date in all the physical ways. Now, if only my mind would catch up.

"Why am I so nervous?" I ask Charlotte as she holds Scarlett to the side of her growing belly. She and Damien offered to babysit Scarlett tonight while I go on my date with Grant alone, and I suggested they come to my house since all of Scarlett's things are here.

I'm beyond grateful for my friends, especially since they're about to be parents and will soon understand all of the struggles that come along with that.

"Because you like him."

"I'm just excited that I get to meet him," Damien says as he carries a bowl of popcorn from my kitchen and takes a seat on the couch. "Gotta make sure he's good enough for you."

Charlotte smiles proudly at her husband. "See? You not only have us girls but also our men eager to protect you if something goes wrong."

"I don't think anything is going to go wrong. I'm just unsure of the speed at which to approach this. Dating after having a child is a lot different than it was before she was born." I cup the side of my daughter's face. "It's just scary."

"I know, but it's gotta feel exciting, too, right? I mean, I've known you for a long time, Noelle. And just because you decided to have a child on your own doesn't mean that the romantic side of you is gone. The girl who loves romance novels and always believed in love is still in there," Charlotte says softly.

"Yeah, she is. She's also a lot more cautious than she was before, which I think is causing most of my nerves."

"Just try to relax. Have fun. You get a night out with a gorgeous man—your words, not mine—a free meal and drinks, and hopefully some stimulating adult conversation."

"Ha. The only time I get that is with you girls, and mostly the conversation consists of sex, me oversharing about mother-hood, and more sex."

Charlotte laughs. "Yeah, sounds about right."

"I don't know if I'm even capable of talking about anything besides my kid anymore."

"Is this what we have to look forward to?" Damien asks around a mouthful of popcorn.

I turn to him, planting a hand on my hip. "Yup. Don't worry, the day is coming where you will be legitimately obsessed with your child's poop schedule, and then you'll look at yourself in the mirror and wonder how this is where you ended up in life."

He stops chewing. "Dear God."

But then I smile and kiss my daughter's cheek. "Yeah, but then you'll also ask yourself how you ever lived without this tiny person in your life before or how life ever had true meaning until they existed." Nuzzling Scarlett's nose, she giggles and dives for my face, covering me in her slobber as Charlotte holds her tightly. "Parenthood is quite the roller-coaster, just to warn you."

Damien stands and moves to grab Scarlett from Charlotte, tossing her up in the air as she squeals. "I can't fucking wait. And our little Ivy Grace is gonna have a built-in best friend in Scarlett, isn't she?" he asks my daughter.

"I know you're struggling a bit with all of this, Noelle," Charlotte says, pulling my attention back to her. "But I'm honestly so grateful that we have you to lean on through this journey. Knowing that one of my closest friends truly understands how much our life is about to change is a level of comfort I didn't know I needed." Her words make my eyes fill with tears. "I mean, it's not like I can rely on my own mother for support or advice."

"Come here." I pull her into me, hugging her as tightly as I can with her belly between us. "I will always be here, Char. Always," I whisper in her ear. "You are going to be an incredible mother. You're going to question everything you do, but in the end, your daughter will be loved on a level you never received. And I will be here beside you for every bump in the road and small success along the way."

"I love you, Noelle. I just want you to be happy." Charlotte's tears hit my shoulder, but I don't even care because I remember what it was like to surrender to all of the emotions pregnancy brought. "Please, promise me that you'll try to enjoy this with as little pressure as you can muster on yourself."

"I love you." We part and both swipe under our eyes to clean off the tears, hers worse than mine because I really am trying not to completely ruin my makeup. "I will try to relax, okay? And thank you for watching my girl."

Damien clears his throat after letting us have our moment. "Anytime, Noelle. At least until our little bundle arrives."

"Then we can just have girls' nights, and you two can come over in your pajamas so you can help me lather my nipples in udder balm so they don't crack and bleed," Charlotte jokes.

"I can help with that, babe," Damien says, winking at her.

"And we can commiserate about how our vaginas and breasts will never be the same," I add through a laugh.

"I'll still never get enough of your pussy or boobs, Char," Damien adds, smirking.

"You're one lucky girl, Charlotte Montgomery," I tell one of my best friends, kissing her on the cheek before walking down the hall. "Now, I'm gonna fix my makeup before Grant gets here."

"Sounds good. And just so you know, you deserve a man like Damien, too."

"Thank you."

Staring at my reflection once more in the mirror after I clean up my face, I take a deep breath and try to convince myself that if each of my friends can find happiness with a man, so can I.

I like Grant. *A lot.* He makes me feel sexy, which is something I didn't know was possible after having my daughter and battling the way my body doesn't even feel like mine anymore. He genuinely wants to know me, which is comforting. And he accepts and interacts with my child so easily—what more could I ask for?

So what's holding me back?

Honesty.

I've wondered how I would manage to deal with this situation numerous times when I thought about the possibility of dating after I had my daughter. But now I know I need to be honest with Grant and myself.

I know that if I want to give this a real shot, I need to tell him everything about Scarlett so I never feel like there's a wedge between us. I want him to understand that while I genuinely intend to get to know him and would love to have him be a part of my life if that's the road we're headed down, I don't need him.

I didn't need a man to have my daughter, and I sure as hell don't need a man who doesn't accept how she came to be. I don't need someone who's going to judge me for my choices or throw them in my face down the line.

I don't think Grant's that type of man from the parts of him I've gotten to know thus far, but I want to be sure that all of my cards are out on the table.

It's still nerve-wracking knowing that I have to have this conversation with him tonight.

"Noelle!" Charlotte calls from the living room just as the doorbell rings.

Shaking out my hands to the side, I take one more deep inhale and then exit my room, headed for the living room just as I hear a familiar voice that has goosebumps pebbling across my skin.

"Grant. It's nice to meet you."

As I enter the room, Damien reciprocates Grant's hand-shake while Charlotte holds my daughter.

"Damien Shaw. And this is my wife, Charlotte."

"Are you one of the brunch friends?" Grant asks, a twinkle in his eye.

Charlotte bounces Scarlett. "Oh, yes. I see Noelle told you about us."

"A little. It's nice to meet you both, though."

Charlotte's eyes bounce up and down Grant. "Likewise. I can definitely see what Noelle sees in you."

"And what exactly is that?" Damien questions, playfully curious about Charlotte's response.

Knowing I should probably break the tension building between my babysitters, I finally clear my throat, drawing everyone's attention toward me. "Hi there."

Grant's lips spread into a wide smile as he takes me in. "Noelle. Damn, you look . . ."

I hum appreciatively at the sight of him as well. "So do you."

In dark-wash jeans, an olive-green shirt, and brown boots, Grant looks more like a cowboy right now than a sexy pilot. And I'm not sure which look I like more. His hair is freshly cut, his beard is neatly trimmed, and those glasses are still probably my favorite accessory of his besides the ball cap he was wearing at the zoo.

Damien and Charlotte stand there, watching us admire each other, but in that moment, I don't even care. My libido is stretching her arms, waking up from her beauty nap, and launching herself out of bed with eagerness to do all kinds of filthy things to this man.

Jesus, it's been so long since I've seen a real penis that I feel like a cat in heat. Well, at least I know my pretty kitty is primed and ready to pounce.

The click of a phone camera pulls us both from our blatant staring.

"There. Now we have proof you two were last seen together in case Noelle goes missing," Damien says smugly. "This picture also shows that the two of you have a bad case of eye-fucking you should definitely get checked out."

Chuckling, I pull my attention back to my daughter. "Thanks for looking after her."

"Of course. You two have fun." Charlotte turns to Grant. "This girl is a catch, Grant. She's one of the best people on the planet. If you mess this up, you have no one to blame but yourself."

He nods his head. "I appreciate the warning and concern of a good friend, but I'm aware. You have a good night, too, sweet girl." He reaches for Scarlett's hand and kisses the top of it as she moves toward him. "Aw, what the heck? Can I get some baby love before I go?" Charlotte nods as I watch my daughter practically jump out of Charlotte's arms and into Grant's. "How's my girl doing?" Scarlett screams and then smacks Grant in the face, but he just closes his eyes and takes it.

"I'm sorry," I finally speak up.

"She's just excited, Noelle." He blows a raspberry on her cheek, and her giggles make us all laugh. "Be good, sweet girl." Handing her off to Charlotte again, he turns to me. "Ready to go?"

"Yup." I give my daughter one last kiss and then grab my purse before waving to Charlotte and Damien. I exit my house with Grant right beside me, his hand on my lower back, heating up my entire body from his touch. He opens the door to his truck and helps me up. "Thank you."

"My pleasure." Shutting my door first, I watch him round the front of the vehicle and then he takes his seat, cranking the engine and pulling out onto my street, heading for our night out with just the two of us.

"**O**h my gosh! I've heard of this place but never thought I'd get a chance to go here!" My eyes soak in the adult arcade, bar, and restaurant around us. The Social, as it's named, is like a more sophisticated Dave & Busters but with multiple stories and a full-sized bowling alley underneath.

"Well, tonight, you get to." Grant gives the hostess his name, and she promptly takes us to a booth in the restaurant. I slide in one side and watch as Grant folds himself into the opposite seat—a challenge, it seems, given how tall he is. And I have to say, his height is just another turn-on for me.

"You okay over there?"

He chuckles. "Yeah, I'll manage." A waitress comes by almost immediately asking for our drink order, and I don't miss the way she appreciatively eats him up with her eyes. *Welcome to the club, girl.* "I'll have a Stone IPA, please," he says to her and then turns to me. "What would you like to drink, babe?"

I don't miss the term of endearment he throws out there nor how our waitress reacts to it. "Um, I'll have a whiskey and Coke, please."

Grant's eyebrows shoot up as our waitress walks away. "A whiskey girl, huh?"

"More of a Coke girl, remember?" I smirk at him. "But yes. That was my preferred drink back in college. Now I enjoy wine and champagne more often, but every once in a while, I like to go back to my roots, like on special occasions."

"Like a date with a man who hasn't stopped thinking about you since he met you?" he says, nearly taking my breath away as he reaches for my hand across the table.

"That seems like a good enough reason." Tucking a strand of my hair behind my ear, I bite my lip and watch his eyes drop to the sight.

"Already wanting to play with fire tonight, Noelle?"

"I don't mind a little heat." This playful flirting and banter is exactly what I wanted tonight, to see the other side of the man who has already demonstrated the size and capacity of his heart. But I want to know he has a switch that can flip as well, the kind that promises pleasure and need in a more visceral way.

The waitress comes by with our drinks, and we pause our conversation to give her our food order before diving back into the conversation.

"Thank you for spending the evening with me. I know

Wednesday nights aren't usually a date night, but it's one of the hazards of being a pilot—a wonky schedule."

"I'm happy to be here. I must say, it's kind of nice to be out of my house on a Wednesday night. By now, I'd be heating up leftovers, shoveling them in my mouth while feeding Scarlett some sort of puree of which half would end up in her hair, then rushing her to the bath before she can touch anything. And then my night would have ended with my Kindle in hand as I fought to keep my eyes open to read for ten minutes before I passed out."

"That sounds like a pretty incredible night to me."

I sigh. "It is, but this is definitely an exciting change of pace," I reply, trying to lighten the mood before I bring up my child again. "I'll try not to talk about Scarlett all night, but it's hard."

"I never said I didn't want to hear about her. She's your life, Noelle. I understand that."

"Thank you." Squeezing his hand, I release it and then reach for my drink, sucking down some liquid courage. "So how was fishing with your nephews?"

Grant takes a sip of his beer as well. "It went well. Everyone caught at least one fish, which always makes for a successful trip."

"I bet they loved that."

"They like it when we catch fish. The time between that happening is a lot like keeping monkeys from climbing the walls, though."

"I can imagine. When do you go back to work?"

"Saturday. I'm flying all weekend. I have one overnight flight to Chicago Monday night, but then I'll be back on the ground during the middle of next week."

Biting my straw, I lean forward in my seat. "What's it like flying a plane? I'm sure you get asked that question a lot."

He chuckles. "I do. It's actually quite boring once you're in the air. Thank God for my co-pilots, or I might fall asleep. On long flights, we take turns catching a little shut-eye, but once the plane is in the air, I hit a few buttons, and that's where we stay. I do a few things here and there when there's turbulence, but taking off and landing is where I actually get to use my skills. I will say, the view from the cockpit never gets old."

I feel like Penelope would insert a dirty joke right here.

"What made you want to become a pilot?"

Grant cracks a smile. "What little boy doesn't want to fly planes for a living?" Adjusting himself in his seat, he takes another drink of his beer before continuing. "It was one of those jobs like fighting fires that gives you an adrenaline rush without being as dangerous."

"Tell that to the millions of people who are legitimately afraid of flying," I counter.

He laughs. "I know, but your chances of dying in a car accident are much higher than in a plane."

"That's reassuring, I guess."

The waitress comes by with a plate of spinach and artichoke dip with chips. "Thank you," Grant tells her as she drops off two glasses of water as well.

"I'm so glad you ordered this without me having to ask.

Out of all the appetizers, this one is my favorite." I reach for a chip, don't think twice when I cover more than half of it with the cheesy concoction, and then pop it in my mouth.

"Mine, too."

"So what are we gonna do after this?"

Grant finishes chewing before he answers me. "Care to go bowling? There's a full bowling alley beneath us. Or we can play some games. Part of me wants to see if you're hiding a competitive side beneath that soft feminine exterior."

"I'm not sure you're going to be able to handle my competitive side, Grant." He laughs. "Gosh, I can't remember the last time I went bowling, though. It was probably high school."

"Same, but I thought tonight would be a good excuse to reminisce and take advantage of you having the use of both your hands."

"What do you mean?"

He drains his beer. "Scarlett isn't here, which means you can do more. I want you to enjoy yourself tonight. Just have fun with me. Show me Noelle—not the mom, not the literary agent, but the woman who is loving, loyal, smart, and sexy." His eyes dip down to my cleavage for a moment before popping back up. "So damn sexy."

My stomach does a flip. "Alright, Grant. I think I can do that." I shove another chip in my mouth, chew frantically, and then reach for another.

"Hey. Slow down there, tiger. I'm not going to eat it all."

Eyes wide, I lean back in my side of the booth. "Oh God. Jesus. I'm sorry."

Grant arches a brow at me. "Stop freaking apologizing, Noelle." He blows out a breath and then leans forward. "I'm not gonna run for the hills every time you do or say something you think you should be sorry for, okay?"

A little stunned, I nod. "Okay."

"Good girl. Now, why on earth are you acting like the chips and dip are about to grow legs and run away?"

"I'm used to having to inhale my food," I admit. "If I don't eat in a hurry, Scarlett will almost always interrupt me or finish before me, and then I'm scrounging for crumbs or the rest of my meal later when it's cold."

"I see." Before he says another word, he stands from his side of the booth, moves around the table toward mine, and motions for me to scoot over. I obey his command so fast that I feel my feminist agenda leave my body while I wait for his next move. "I hope you don't mind me joining you over here. You were a little too far away from me for my liking, anyway."

"Uh, sure. Yeah, this is nice."

He rests his arm along the back of the booth, curling his hand down to graze my shoulder with his fingertips as his leg rubs up against mine under the table. "Now, here's what we're going to do. I'm gonna feed you for the rest of this meal, and you're going to relax." My eyes bug out, but he keeps talking. "I'm not gonna do anything you won't like. I'm not trying to control you either, okay, sweetheart?" he says, his voice softening up again, even though the command in his tone was seriously doing things for me. "But you need to relax, slow down, and enjoy tonight. And it's my responsibility to make sure that happens."

"Grant, I—"

"Shh," he whispers, placing a finger over my lips. "Just do this for me, okay?" I don't speak. I just nod and then watch him slide a chip in the dip and bring it to my lips, his eyes fixated on my mouth the entire time. "Open for me."

Letting my mouth fall open, I stick out my tongue as he gives me the chip. I close my lips around his thumb as I take it all in, and I swear I hear a low groan crawl up his throat.

"Jesus," he growls, dragging his thumb along my bottom lip as I watch him watching my mouth. The temperature in this restaurant just reached surface-of-the-sun levels, and my libido is rattling against her cage right now, fighting to get free.

After I finish chewing and swallow, we simply lock gazes, processing the extremely erotic moment that just happened between us.

"Um, thank you."

The corner of his mouth lifts. "You're welcome."

"I don't know that anyone has ever fed me before, but I can't say that I hated it."

"Yeah, neither did I." He moves to discreetly adjust himself beneath the table, but I don't miss the movement nor the outline of his erection through his jeans.

Holy shit. Is that a baseball bat in his pants?

"You ready for another?" he asks.

Taking a sip of my whiskey and Coke, I place my glass

back on the table, stare up at him, bite my lip, and nod. "Absolutely."

The pleased grin he gives me makes me think of all the other ways I could make him smile at me like that, but before I get ahead of myself, he grabs another chip, commands me to open for him, and feeds me while my panties combust beneath me.

"Is there such a thing as a bowling shark? Because that's what you are!"

Grant smirks as he carries himself back to our station after throwing yet another strike. "Don't get petty because you're losing, Noelle."

Playful Grant is back, which is both necessary and disappointing. The tension during dinner was so thick, flashes of me mounting him at our table were playing on repeat in my head. I also contemplated sinking to my knees below the table and sucking on his cock like a lollipop one too many times, so it's best that we left that situation behind for something a little more lighthearted.

But Grant came to play, and apparently his competitive side is just as strong as mine. He's also one hell of a bowler.

"I call bullshit. You totally have bowled since high school."

"I mean, I may have gone a few times with the nephews, but the last time I was competitive about it was back then."

"Wait! You bowled competitively?"

His smile is full of delight. "You're looking at the bowling league champion back in 2003."

"I knew it!" I shout, pointing a finger at him as he holds his stomach in laughter.

"Sorry, babe. But you definitely are giving me a run for my money if it makes you feel better."

"Oh, I see how it is. This is an entirely different side of you I'm seeing now. I thought the commanding man who fed me chips and dip earlier was it, but now . . ."

Grant leans down in front of me where I'm seated, cupping the side of my face and staring intently into my eyes. "You liked when I fed you. Don't deny it."

Licking my lips, I stare back at him. "I mean, it was kinda hot."

"And now that you've seen my bowling skills? And know that I was a master back in the day? Am I not hot anymore?" he chides.

"Nope. Still hot. But I am glad to know you didn't always have this swagger you possess now."

"Um, you never saw me back then. I made bowling shoes and bleached tips look good, Noelle."

I throw my head back in laughter. "Of course you did."

"Now, now . . . don't go bruising my ego too much." With a drag of his thumb over my bottom lip again, he pulls away, reaching for my hand to help me up, spinning me around so his chest is to my back, our eyes pointed in the direction of our lane. "Don't make this easy on me, Noelle. Show me what you've got." He lands a playful smack on my ass, and I yelp, twist to face him, and find him smugly grinning at me.

"Oh, don't worry, Grant. You may have me beat here, but I'll be sure to get my revenge later." Spinning on my heels, I sway my hips emphatically for his pleasure, grab my ball, and take my last two turns, ultimately losing at bowling but feeling like I'm winning with this man nonetheless.

After kicking Grant's ass in air hockey, redeeming myself and my competitive side, we left The Social and head out to get something sweet before Grant takes me home.

"So what's your flavor, Noelle?" he asks me as we stare into the freezers, waiting for our turn to order our ice cream.

"Salted caramel, hands down. It's the best of both worlds."

"Salty and sweet?"

"Exactly. Too bad it doesn't pair well with Red Vines, though."

"The licorice?"

"Yup. That's my favorite candy in the world. Call me old-fashioned, but there's just something pure and nostalgic about a Red Vine. Pair it with a Coke, and I'm one happy girl."

"I haven't had licorice in ages."

"You're missing out."

He tucks his fingers under my chin, forcing me to face him. "The only thing I've been missing out on is you, apparently."

With a deep breath, he continues. "I've had the best fucking time tonight."

"Me, too." As butterflies swarm around my belly, so do nerves. I was so busy having fun and trying to relax earlier that I forgot all about telling Grant about Scarlett and how I became a mother. And now, after the amazing night we've shared, I'm not sure I want to anymore.

This guy is quickly checking all of my boxes, bringing me closer to a place where I remember the high of dating someone new and being hopeful that the connection we share is one that we can build on.

So maybe I can hold off a little longer? Live in this bubble we're existing in and explore this playful and exciting side of our relationship before we get to the really serious stuff . . . ?

After we order our ice cream, Grant and I walk slowly back to his truck, savoring the cool night air and the last little bit of our date. And ladies—he walked on the outside of the sidewalk, securing me safely away from the edge. *Cue the swooning.*

"So how did I do for a second date?" he asks as I take my first bite.

"You set the bar pretty high. But beating you at air hockey was definitely the highlight of the evening."

I feel his laugh all the way down to the tip of my toes. "Don't worry. I'm sure we'll find all kinds of games to play where we can take turns winning." His words are laced with promises of dirty games, and I am so here for it.

"I'm gonna hold you to that."

"So how was your night away from motherhood?"

Guilt crashes into me so hard, I almost fall over. "Oh my gosh. For a moment there, I kind of forgot I have a baby to go home to."

Grant catches my reaction and pauses us in our steps. "Hey, it's okay. That's what we wanted, right? To relinquish that responsibility a little tonight?"

"Yeah, but I wasn't prepared for when it slammed back into me." Suddenly, it feels hard to breathe.

"You okay?"

"I guess I just wasn't prepared for how easy it was to step out of that world for a minute. And God, it felt good, Grant. So good."

He smiles. "That's what I wanted for you, Noelle. There's no shame in that. When's the last time you let loose?"

"I . . . I can't even remember." Looking to the side, I try to find an answer to the question but come up empty. "I don't really think I have. I never got to be wild. Even in college, I played it safe, always intent on dating the right guy, the one I could see myself marrying, the one who wasn't a bad boy, the one who wouldn't hurt me. The only exception was the lead singer of a band. I dated him for almost a year after college. That boy broke my heart."

"Let me guess . . . he got a record deal and chose that over you."

"Kind of. We mutually decided to part ways. Now I can look back on it and realize it was the right decision. That's not what I wanted for my life, but it still hurt."

"It's not for everyone."

"I know, but that was about as reckless as I ever got. So I mended my broken heart and kept dating. And instead, I found men who were boring or didn't know a clit from a belly button —true story."

His face fills with genuine concern. "Just so you're aware, I definitely know where the clit is, so you don't have to worry about that."

I huff out a laugh. "That's good to know. But I guess I just look back with a hint of regret that I never did something spontaneous or dangerous. I never lived on the wild side. And now, I'm on a date with a man who's trying to help me let loose, and when I actually do in the most PG-rated way ever, I freak out." Slapping a hand to my head, I groan. "God, I'm pathetic."

Grant grabs my ice cream that I'm practically done with anyway and tosses it in the trash with his. And before I can say anything, he takes me by the hand, leads me over to his truck, spins me around, and presses me up against the side of it, crowding me in.

"You are *not* pathetic, Noelle. You are an incredible woman who is doing one of the most selfless things on the planet— raising a child on her own. You are stunning, funny, sexy, and full of life. You don't have to take big risks and live dangerously in order to live a full life. We don't leave impressions on this planet by what we do but by our relationships with other people. And right now, the relationship that we're building is one I want to see through more than I've wanted anything in a very long time."

Stunned, I stare up at him, watching his intense eyes behind the lenses of his glasses. "Thank you."

"Do you regret having your daughter?" he asks, and I sway on the balls of my feet at his question.

But I don't even hesitate with my answer. "Absolutely not. But becoming a mom alerted me to the fact that there are parts of my life before I had her that I've taken for granted and experiences that I wished I'd had before she became my whole world."

"I can see that. But what about all of the experiences you get with her now? Things you never would have experienced if she wasn't in your world?" He arches a brow. "Seeing her smile for the first time? Her first words? Learning to crawl or walk? There are so many moments yet to come that you will get but that others never get to experience with children of their own." I move to speak, but he silences me with his finger over my lips. "And I'm not saying you're taking those things for granted. I'm just saying that you get to have both sides of that coin, sweetheart. Embrace it. Love every high and low. And let me show you that you can have it all."

My heart hammers, my breathing starts to feel shallow, and before I can talk myself out of it, I do what feels right in the moment.

"Kiss me," I whisper, desperate to feel his lips on mine after that little speech.

"I was already planning on it."

Before I can take a proper breath, Grant's lips are on mine, his hands are in my hair, and his pelvis is pinning me to the side of his truck, giving me a glimpse of how badly he wants me. If I had a penis, I'm sure it'd be rock hard in this moment as well.

God, I want to melt into a puddle for this man.

Surrendering to his control, I let Grant's tongue into my mouth, and it swirls with my own as every nerve in my body comes alive. I grip his shoulders, wrapping my arms around his neck to pull him closer, and let him own me with his kiss.

And oh God, does he ever.

His movements are smooth yet intense. Bold yet soft. His passion is evident in every nip of my lips, lash of his tongue, and moan that travels up his throat.

I let him devour me, make me feel like a woman—not the same woman I was before I had my daughter, but this new version who is more secure in what she wants and able to admit that her life is nothing as it was before. But I don't want that life back, anyway.

The woman he makes me feel like is ready to take a leap of faith with her heart again. She's ready to explore a relationship with a man seven years older than her, a man that seemingly accepts her for who she is and the life she is living right now.

And I'm ready to let her do that.

Grant slows down the kiss before we part, and my eyes are still closed as his lips leave mine. Slowly, I open them and find him smiling down at me, his pupils dilated and his erection still making its presence known between us.

"I don't want you to ever feel like you can't be honest with me, Noelle—about how you're feeling, what you're thinking, or any of your fears. Do you understand me?"

"Yes."

"Good girl." He dips his head again to press our lips together, and this time, the kiss is much more lazy and exploratory than before—but equally as hot. The physical chemistry is there. The emotional connection is building.

And maybe, just maybe, a future is forming, too.

Chapter 9

"Oh my God! It's a Bolts onesie!" Charlotte exclaims as she holds it up for the room full of people to see. The opening of presents has finally commenced at her baby shower, and I watch my friend fondly, thinking how this was me about ten months ago.

"Fuck, yeah! Ivy is gonna be rocking that outfit every game day," Damien adds, high-fiving Jeffrey.

"I need to have a kid just so I can buy one of those for myself." He reaches over and grabs the stuffed teddy bear who is also wearing a Bolts jersey. "Or maybe I'll just snag this."

Damien snatches the bear from Jeffrey. "Back off, man."

I lean over and whisper out of the side of my mouth to

Penelope. "How much longer do you think this is going to go on?"

"Not sure. I bet Charlotte is regretting having a coed baby shower right about now, though, huh?" she replies through a laugh.

The crowd starts to pick sides as Damien and Jeffrey battle it out over all of the baby paraphernalia that has the football team's logo on it.

"Boys! I will throw you out of this shower!" Charlotte finally exclaims, and they both freeze. Damien lets go of the bear, Jeffrey steps back, and Penelope and I snicker under our breath.

"I'm sorry, babe. You know the side he brings out in me," Damien says, moving over to sit next to his very pregnant wife. He hands her another gift, and they proceed to open the rest of the gifts together as Amelia snaps pictures with her camera.

"You sure she'll want to remember this part?" Penelope asks Amelia as the click of her lens goes off again.

"Of course. Who wouldn't want to remember almost murdering your husband at your baby shower because he was fighting with his best friend over a bear?" She giggles. "Remind me when it's my turn to just have girls only."

"Gladly," I interject. "Mine was perfect in that respect, because then we could talk about feminine things and not feel like we were walking on eggshells around the men as we did."

"Some of the birth stories those women shared at your shower still make me queasy," Penelope says, visibly shuddering.

"How do you think it made me feel hearing all that just months before I had Scarlett?" I ask, pointing a finger at my chest. "It was terrifying. Let's just say, I'm glad it's not me this time."

"Yeah, but would you do it again?" Amelia asks.

My eyes find my daughter, who's playing with Oliver, Amelia's son. "Absolutely. I want Scarlett to have a sibling some day."

Penelope nudges me with her shoulder. "And who knows . . . maybe Grant will be the one to give you a baby the old-fashioned way." She bounces her eyebrows.

"Um, that would require us having sex, so probably not."

Amelia and Penelope both turn to me. "I thought things were going well?" Amelia inquires.

I sigh wistfully. "They are. Really well. Like, it's scary how fast I can see a future with him."

"So what's stopping you from getting back on the horse?" Penelope asks.

I take a moment to watch Charlotte open up another gift, a beautiful circus-themed bedding set in creams and greens. "Gosh, where do I begin?"

The three of us step down the hallway of Amelia and Ethan's home, eager for some privacy. We enter a guest bedroom, and Penelope plops herself down on the bed, bouncing a few times. "Talk to us, Noelle. What's going on?"

"Do I really need to spell it out for you? Sleeping with Grant will be the first time I've had sex in over two years."

Amelia nods. "Okay, and we've already established that you miss sex and like him, so what's the problem?"

After Grant and I went out on our date last week, I told the girls all about it at brunch the following Sunday. And since then, I've relived that kiss and everything about that night multiple times a day. This week, Grant has been busy flying nonstop and even had to cover a few flights, so we haven't seen each other since our date. We have talked, though. He even sent me a video of him in the cockpit and the view of the clouds from way up in the sky. It was amazing.

"Maybe my vibrator will just be my best friend from now on," I mutter, feeling uneasy when I think about having sex again. And I shouldn't. If the way he kissed was any indication, I'm sure the man is damn good at the other stuff, too.

"Has your battery-operated toy collection been getting a little workout lately?" Penelope snickers.

"Um, yes, it has. In fact, I left my vibrator out to charge, completely forgot about it, and my cleaning lady came that day. I'm sure she thinks very highly of me now."

"Don't be ashamed. At least your cleaning lady now knows that you pleasure yourself and don't feel embarrassed about it."

"I guess. But now that Grant is in the picture, I'm wrestling with whether I'm ready to bring a man back into my bedroom, especially now that my body has changed so much, too. Plus, I think it's time to wean Scarlett. She's losing interest in nursing anyway, and if Grant and I decide to get naked, I would love to not have to worry about leaking breastmilk all over him while I'm turned on."

Amelia pipes up. "There are millions of breastfeeding mothers that still have a sex life. I'm sure there are ways to work around that."

"I know, but it's yet another thing I feel like I have to worry about." I sigh. "I just want my body back. But then I feel guilty."

"Don't. You're doing what's best for you and Scarlett, whether that's continuing to breastfeed her, pump, or give her formula. The best avenue for everyone is just the one where your baby is being fed."

"You're right."

"So we've established we're worried about leaky boobs. Are you also worried that your coochie is loose?" Penelope asks.

"What? My coochie is not loose!" But then I retract. "I mean, okay, I might pee a little now when I laugh or sneeze or cough or do a jumping jack . . . but I'm not loose. I just had a baby!"

"Of course, Noelle. I'm sure your coochie is in prime condition. That's why I brought it up. It would be silly to worry about that. I mean, Maddox has done some wicked things to my pussy, and he still tells me how tight I am, so I imagine a child's head coming out of there wouldn't alter it too much, if at all."

My stomach drops. "Oh my God! What if I'm *loose*? What if he can tell? I haven't had sex in so long, and I'm sure things have changed down there. What if I'm damaged goods now?" Suddenly, I feel the need to throw up.

Amelia walks over to me, resting her hands on my shoulders as I practically hyperventilate. "Breathe, Noelle. Let me ask you this. Have you ever had a guy turn you down once you got naked? Has he ever seen your belly, stretch marks, or cellulite and was like, 'Nope. Sorry. I'm out,' even before you had a baby?"

I huff out a laugh. "No."

"That's because there's a naked woman in front of him." She smirks knowingly. "Men honestly don't care about that shit. And if they do, they are just shallow, self-absorbed members of the teeny weenie committee."

"Amen, sister!" Penelope exclaims.

"Grant is not going to care about those things because he cares about *you*. He's not with you just for the physical connection. He's proven he's invested, wants to get to know you and your daughter, and listens to you. Sex with him will be incredible because you two share a connection, and all the other stuff won't even matter if you focus on that."

Penelope chimes in again. "Listen to the shrink, Noelle. And honestly? I know I was anti-sex-with-feelings, but it really does make it a thousand times better. And if you need a babysitter, remember Maddox and I are willing. He gets back from training camp next week. Me and my vagina can't wait, but that means we will be free."

Commotion rings out from the living room. "We'd better get back out there. But thanks, girls."

"Of course, Noelle. We're always here for you. You know that."

I exhale heavily. "I know. This dating thing is just a lot. I'm so up in my head about it. I'm trying not to be, but my analytical side is working overtime right now."

The three of us head back out to the shower where I see Jeffrey with his head buried in a diaper.

"Oh. My. God! Jeffrey!" I shout, drawing his and everyone else's attention. "You're not supposed to eat the candy bars in the diapers! That's cheating!"

Apparently, the "melt candy bars in clean diapers and then try to identify which ones are in each diaper" game has started. But it appears that someone didn't explain the rules correctly.

"No one's going to eat these, right?" He licks his lips. "Can't let them go to waste."

Slapping a palm to my forehead, I walk over to where Scarlett is still with Oliver. "I can't with you today." Bending down in front of my daughter, I grab her chubby little hand and kiss the top of it. "How's my girl doing?"

You'd think I was chopped liver right now with the way she looks around me. I glance over my shoulder to see one of the *Despicable Me* movies on the screen.

"We're watching *Despicable Me 2*," Oliver explains. "Scarlett is in love with the minions."

"You don't say?"

"Oh, Oliver loves this movie, too," Amelia explains as she comes up behind him, ruffling his hair.

"Well, now it's Scarlett's favorite, too," he says.

My baby squeals with delight as the minions do something silly on the television. "You like the movie, baby girl?" She smacks her hands together as if she's clapping, something she picked up recently, and Amelia and I share a laugh. "I guess so."

"See? Even Gru took a chance on love." Penelope gestures to the television.

I stand up from my crouched position. "I'm taking a chance. I'm just nervous about getting naked in front of the man."

Jeffrey walks over at that exact moment, shoving a cupcake in his mouth. "Don't be."

Rolling my eyes, I smooth my shirt over my stomach. "Thanks, but—"

"No, seriously, Noelle. You have nothing to be worried about." His eyes bounce up and down my body. "Hell, if I knew you were dating again, I would have thrown my hat in the ring."

Tilting my head at him, I smile. "Aw, Jeffrey . . ."

"Does that mean I missed my chance?" He smirks.

"There never was a chance, Jeffrey."

His shoulders drop. "Yeah, I know. I just like to fantasize about what it would have been like to end up with one of the three of you."

"There are four of us—you know that, right?" Penelope corrects him.

"Duh. I can count. Sometimes. But come on. You girls and I know that once Damien started fake-dating Charlotte, she was automatically eliminated."

"This is true," I agree.

"Seriously, though, Noelle. If the guy is interested in you, he's not going to care about all of the silly things you're worried about like stretch marks and cellulite. The only thing on his mind will be teasing and pleasing the fuck out of you." With a wink, he saunters off, leaving the three of us open-mouthed.

Penelope turns to me. "Well, there you have it. Jeffrey just dropped some wisdom, and I'm not sure how to feel about it."

"Same." Shaking my head, I look back at my daughter. "I guess I'll just take it one day at a time and see how I feel. Hopefully, there will come a moment when I throw caution to the wind and get out of my head."

"Yeah, and hopefully it's because your lady garden will be so primed and ready from the man who's making you horny like a dog that hasn't been neutered yet that you won't even think twice about getting naked with him." Penelope bounces her eyebrows.

"Oh, that's not the problem. The man is walking sex."

"Speaking of, when do we get to meet him?"

"Let me worry about meeting his dick first, and then we'll work on the other part."

I finally lay Scarlett down in her crib after a long afternoon at the shower, eager to call Grant. He texted me earlier to tell me he was tucked into his hotel room for the night and would eagerly be waiting for my call.

I haven't stopped smiling since.

"Hey, Noelle." The deep rasp of his voice fills the line when he answers after one ring.

"Hey, you."

"God, it's good to hear your voice."

"You just heard my voice a few days ago."

He chuckles. "Yeah, but it's been too long. How are my girls doing? How was the shower?"

My girls. I don't know if I'll ever get used to hearing that term of endearment from him. "We're doing well. I just put Scarlett to bed, and now I'm about to relax in mine." I turn down the covers and wrestle underneath.

"I miss my bed."

"I bet. I don't know how you sleep in hotel rooms as often as you do. I hate any bed that isn't my own."

"Agreed. And I don't know if it's just because I'm getting older or the beds really suck that much, but it takes a few days for my body to readjust once I get back to my own bed."

I giggle. "I totally know what you mean."

"So the shower?"

"Oh, yeah. It was fun. I'm not sure Charlotte was happy with her decision to make it coed, but everyone had a good time, especially Scarlett."

"My brother and sister-in-law had a coed one for their first son. I didn't know so many people could get drunk at a baby shower, but apparently that's a thing. Also, adults like to drink at a one-year-old's birthday party as well, just an FYI."

"I will keep that in mind."

"So Scarlett partied hard, huh?"

I laugh. "She did. Oliver, Ethan and Amelia's son, watched her quite a bit for me, but he introduced her to the *Despicable Me* movies. She was entranced. It was the cutest thing."

"Well, she's the cutest thing, so I have no doubt." He goes quiet for a minute. "I can't wait to see both of you. This leg of overnight flights couldn't have come at a worse time."

"It's okay. It's your job."

"I know." He blows out a breath. "But I feel like you and I just started dating, and I want to explore that so much, but my stupid job is getting in the way."

My cheeks start to burn from smiling. "We're still exploring that."

"Yeah, but it's not the same. I promise, once I get back, I'm taking you out as much as I can. I want to see Scarlett, too. I—" He clears his throat. "I feel like I'm already growing attached to you two."

My heart starts to beat wildly. "Wow."

"I like you, Noelle. A lot. Like, fucking *a lot*. I don't want you to question otherwise, okay? I know space can do weird things to our minds. I know not talking every day can make you think that I've lost interest. But I haven't. If anything, being away has helped me gain perspective. I'm all in, Noelle. I really want to see where this goes."

Holy shit. My chest feels like it's about to explode. This man is laying out all of his cards just like that, so I guess I can, too. "I like you, too, Grant. *A lot*. I can't wait until you return. You make me nervous but hopeful. It's been such a long time since I've felt that . . . and it scares me even more now, but hearing where you're at is helping ease those nerves."

"Fuck, I wish I could kiss you right now."

"Me, too." I rub my thighs together to quell the ache that's starting to throb between my legs. How I think I'm going to be able to resist this man—despite my reservations about getting naked with him—is beyond me.

"The next time I see you, you aren't going to be able to pry my lips from yours."

"That's a pretty big promise."

"I don't like to make promises I can't keep. But that's one I am confident I will see through." He groans. "I'll be home Tuesday night, and I'd love to take you and Scarlett to dinner if you're free?"

"We'd love that."

"Perfect. And can you get a babysitter for next Friday? There's somewhere I want to take you, but it's not quite kid-friendly."

"I should be able to." I make a mental note to text Penelope to take her up on her offer to babysit.

"Okay. Save the date for me, babe."

Biting my bottom lip, I hide my squeal. "I will." Grant lets out a yawn that reminds me he's two hours ahead of me right now in Chicago. "Oh, gosh. You're probably exhausted. I'll let you go."

"I am tired, but I'm not ready to hang up just yet."

"It's okay, Grant. I know you need rest."

He chuckles. "I do have an early flight. But hearing your voice just made my day."

"I like talking to you, too," I whisper.

"I'll let you go, I guess. But promise me that we'll talk again tomorrow."

"I'll be around. Just errands and laundry on the agenda tomorrow. Oh, and reading."

"Sounds like a fun day."

For the first time in a while, I smile at that statement. "It's my life now."

"And you're blessed to have it, Noelle." His words slam into me. "Goodnight, gorgeous."

"Goodnight, Grant."

I wait for him to hang up before I throw myself down on the bed, spread out like a starfish, focusing on how hard my heart is beating right now.

The way this man makes me feel is unlike any of my other relationships in the past. I've been in love before. I've felt butterflies and envisioned futures with men who I've dated previously. But something about where I'm at in my life, the confidence that Grant has about our connection, and how differently my future looks now with my daughter makes the possibility of what can happen here more monumental.

I just hope it's worth putting my heart on the line.

"Hayden!" Standing from my desk, I greet one of the players from the Los Angeles Bolts who also happens to be a good friend of Maddox.

"Noelle. You look gorgeous, girl. How have you been?"

"Oh, busy being a mom and literary agent . . . you know." I shrug. "Just trying to keep my head from spinning."

"I get it. Moms are superheroes. As I got older, I wondered how my mom handled it all. My dad was working all the time, so she was the one who took me to and from football practices, was there at all my games cheering me on, and even made sure I had a home-cooked meal every night." He shakes his head. "And she always did it with a smile on her face."

I think about Scarlett playing a sport in the future or being involved in an extra-curricular activity that would require me to do the same thing. I'm instantly exhausted at the idea but also looking forward to those days. "Moms will do anything for their kids. I know I'd take a bullet to protect Scarlett in a heartbeat."

Hayden chuckles. "My mom used to say the same thing. That Momma Bear mentality is strong."

"Yes, it is."

"That's quite the display of red roses you've got there." Hayden points to the vase of fresh flowers that was delivered earlier this morning, flowers from Grant that instantly propelled my heart into a sprint. The card simply said, *Can't wait for our date*, and all I can think about is how his flower selection is so damn perfect that it makes me think he is perfect, too.

"Oh, yes, it is."

"You got a secret admirer I don't know about?" he teases.

"There is a special someone in my life at the moment, if you must know." I move around my desk to take my seat again, gesturing for Hayden to sit in one of the empty chairs across from me.

He follows my command. "Good for you. Judging by your smile, I'd say he's making you happy so far."

"He is." Feeling my cheeks grow hot, I choose to change the subject. "Well, let's get to the meeting, shall we?"

"Absolutely. I'm so fucking pumped for this."

"So am I. Thank you for agreeing to do this. I know it's going to be huge for my client and for you. Women will eat it up."

He rubs his palms together. "You know I like the ladies."

"I'm well aware."

A knock on my office door stops our conversation as my secretary, Madison, pops her head in. "Noelle? Regina is here."

"Fantastic. Send her in." A few seconds later, one of my favorite authors walks through the door. "Regina!"

"Noelle!" She rushes toward me, pulling me into a hug. "It feels like it's been forever."

"Well, our last few meetings have been video calls, so it has been a while since I've seen you in person."

She releases me but keeps her hands firmly planted on my upper arms. "You look different." Her eyes assess me. "Happy? Balanced? I don't know, but something has changed." Then her eyes shift to the same flowers Hayden noticed, and the corner of her mouth tips up. "Well, I definitely know those roses weren't there before."

Tucking a strand of hair behind my ear, we part and take our seats. "I mean, not much has changed. Well, I *am* seeing someone now, but—"

She smirks. "Oh, that has to be it. There's a light in your eyes, your cheeks are rosy . . . you look like a woman in love."

"Not love." *Not yet.* "Just extreme like."

Hayden chimes in. "I think I need to meet this guy to make sure he's good enough for you."

Regina turns to Hayden, her eyes widening. "Oh, dear. You are quite handsome."

Hayden flashes his killer smile at her. "Why, thank you. And you must be Regina . . ."

"Regina Emerson," she finishes for him, reaching out to shake his hand and then taking a seat next to him on the opposite side of my desk.

"Yes, Regina is the author I would like to feature on the podcast you're associated with, Hayden," I explain, steering this meeting to the point of why we're here.

"I'd love to. The podcast has taken off tremendously in the last six months, and we're always looking for new authors to feature."

When Penelope started dating Maddox and introduced me to Hayden, I knew we'd become fast friends. The boy was a little too young and rambunctious for me to date, which I made sure to tell him when he hit on me the first time, but I heard from Maddox that Hayden listened to a romance podcast in his spare time. One evening, I sat down and talked to him about it since romance books are my specialty and suggested he start his own podcast. He ended up reaching out to the one he listened to avidly and became a guest host who would pop in to episodes when his schedule allowed. The podcast blew up in popularity, and since then, I've been working with him to feature authors in the name of exposure.

It's been a marketing dream come true.

And Regina deserves this opportunity immensely, especially since her next series will be focused on siblings where one of the brothers plays in the NFL, like Hayden. It's a win-win.

"Well, Regina is eager to participate."

My client chimes in. "I mean, at my age, I have very little experience with podcasts and all of that, but I'm willing to do whatever Noelle suggests."

I smile at her. "That's a smart move."

"Noelle knows what she's doing," he reassures Regina. "And she said your series you want to promote is related to football, so it's perfect. I can't wait to read it. Honestly. And I do know a thing or two about the sport." He winks at her. "Also, if you have any questions, I'd be happy to answer them as well."

"I appreciate that so much."

Hayden pulls out his phone as it chimes. "Damn. It's my brother. I need to take this."

"Of course."

He launches himself from his chair as he answers the phone and then quietly exits my office.

"He is so handsome." Regina fans her face.

I laugh. "He is, and he's such a sweetheart under the surface. But he's young."

"So he's not the man who has you glowing over there?"

"Nope. I actually found me a slightly older man." I bounce my eyebrows, which makes Regina laugh. "But it's still new."

"Well, I'm happy for you, Noelle. I know how arduous finding love has been for you."

"It's definitely been a roller coaster. But I feel very optimistic about this one. It's not every day that a man literally gives you the shirt off his back and genuinely adores your daughter."

"He sounds dreamy."

"I swear, the way we met and then crossed paths again was something out of a romance novel, Regina."

"I guess this means you're never going to give my son a chance, are you?"

Shaking my head at her, I reach for my mouse to wake up my computer. "You know that can't happen."

She snaps her fingers. "I mean, it's worth a shot asking. My son has so much to offer someone—I just don't want to see him end up alone."

"I know the feeling. That's how I felt most of my twenties and then more so right before I decided to have Scarlett. But I guess timing really is everything, because now I feel hopeful for the first time in years."

"Sometimes life doesn't work out the way we plan. I never thought I'd get divorced or be a single mom at one time. Luckily, I met Franklin later, and he accepted my boys and me into his life as if we'd always been there. And trust me, as a single mom, that's all you can really ask for."

I place my hand over my heart. "It's so true. I never imagined how dating would feel after having Scarlett, but it's so different. I'm questioning everything and analyzing every conversation."

She nods. "I used to do the same thing. The biggest piece of advice I can give you is this: If you don't see a future there or there's a red flag at any moment, run. Don't waste time, don't risk your heart and the heart of your daughter if you see and feel your intuition talking to you. I was seeing one man and saw something that rubbed me the wrong way, and I didn't realize until it was too late that he was actually showing me his true colors. The split was nasty, and my boys were devastated for the second time since me and their dad split up."

"I appreciate that. Thank you."

"Of course. And as I said, if it goes sour, please, let me set you up with my boy." She clasps her hands together in front of her chest, jutting her bottom lip out.

Rolling my eyes, I huff out a laugh. "Fine. If things go wrong with him, I will."

A squeal leaves her lips. "Seriously?"

"I mean, what the hell? I honestly don't feel like things won't work out, which is the only reason I'm agreeing." She purses her lips as she glares at me. "But if they don't, I might as well see what your son has to offer since you speak so highly of him."

"Oh my God! I'm so excited!" And then her shoulders deflate. "Well, damn. Now I'm almost hoping things with this guy don't work out so you can date my son instead."

Laughing, I pull over the paperwork for the book deal we're working on next. "Don't jinx me, Regina. I'd hate to have to hold that over your head in our working relationship, and I really don't want to do that."

She mimes zipping her lips. "I will keep all ill thoughts to myself then."

"Sounds fair. Now, let's talk books. Tell me all about this football series."

"Well, I'm thinking it might be siblings, actually. Like, one of the brothers is a football player, but then his siblings are the main characters in the other books, but football still plays a big role . . ."

"Oh, yes. Tell me more."

Chapter 10

Grant

I'm standing on Noelle's doorstep, my body buzzing with adrenaline. Even though I just saw her and Scarlett on Tuesday for dinner, tonight I'm a little nervous for our date. It can either go extremely well or backfire enormously. I'm hoping on the first option, but either way, I think the risk is worth the reward.

Being away for work on and off for two weeks has been torture, and last week, it finally hit me just how invested I am in this woman. I'm still surprised that I was so hellbent on being alone, waving off the thought that I'd actually find someone intriguing enough to put myself out in the dating world again, and then I met Noelle just as I was starting to accept my fate.

But I was a goner the second her green eyes met mine. And when I saw Scarlett beam up at me, I fell even harder.

There's something so sexy about a woman who is a mom. Call it protective instinct or maybe it's because I watched my own mother be strong even when she felt like she would crumble from the pressure, but Noelle's energy, her vulnerability and poise, has me wanting more. She's got the allure of a woman to whom I can't help but want to give everything. And tonight, I'm going to give her something she feels she's been missing.

I just hope she appreciates the gesture instead of questioning my sanity.

"Hey." Noelle answers the door, her smile soft but bright.

"Hi, beautiful." I step through the door, wrap my hand around the back of her neck, and pull her into my chest, pressing my lips to hers without a second thought. She hums and then opens up her mouth for me, tangling her tongue with mine. We get lost in our kiss for minutes until I finally force myself to release her lips.

"Well, that's one way to greet me."

"It's the most PG-rated way to greet you," I counter. "Is Scarlett already gone?"

"She is. I dropped her off with Penelope and Maddox about an hour ago."

"I still can't believe you know Maddox Taylor." Shutting the door, I follow Noelle further into her house. I didn't get a good look around the first night I was here because her friends, Charlotte and Damien, were introducing themselves the second

I walked through the door. Plus, I was nervous meeting them and picking Noelle up for our date. But now, as I battle between looking around and staring at Noelle's ass in her jeans, her ass wins, and yet again, I don't care what the room looks like around me. All I know is that the house smells like home, like she's burning a candle that instantly makes you comfortable. It's something vanilla and citrusy, and I find myself inhaling deeply as she takes a sip from a glass of water.

"It's even weirder that one of my best friends is married to him. But he is seriously the best guy."

"Better than me?"

She smirks. "You jealous?"

"No, he's married. I just want to know where I stack up next to Maddox Taylor."

Walking toward me, she clenches my shirt in her hand, drawing me closer to her. "Maddox is the best guy for my best friend. And you? You're turning out to be the best guy for me." She presses her lips to mine gently, only staying there for a second before she leans back again, staring up into my eyes.

Reminding myself that we're on a time crunch, I battle between mauling this woman right here in her kitchen or following through with my plans for the evening. And even though I'm dying to explore Noelle's body, I know that she's the one who has to make that decision. She's the one who needs to take the lead and bring us to that moment when she's ready. The last thing I want is for her to feel like I can't be patient in that respect. I mean, it's been a while for me, but I know that being with Noelle physically will be worth the wait.

"We'd better get going, or we're going to miss the show."

"Show?"

"Yup." With a wink, I grab her hand. "Let's go, beautiful."

As my truck jostles down the bumpy dirt road, I cast a glance at Noelle in the passenger seat. She's holding on to the handle above the window for support.

"You okay over there?"

"Um, sure. I'm a little lost right now but trying to trust you."

"You sure that's a good idea?" I tease her, but she darts her eyes to me with lightning speed, worry etched in every line of her face.

"Are you saying I shouldn't?"

"No." I laugh. "You're perfectly safe with me." Reaching over, I grab her free hand and bring it to my lips, kissing the back of it.

"But what about law-abiding? Because I'm pretty sure I saw a 'no trespassing' sign about a mile ago."

"Don't worry. I have a connection. We're fine." At least for an hour or so, that is.

When I find the spot I'm looking for, I shift the truck into park and shut off the engine but then crank it back so the radio stays on for background noise. "We're here."

Noelle casts her gaze all around us, and then the roar of a plane sounds overhead. "Are we at the airport?"

"We're right next to it. Come on." I jump down from my side of the truck, looking behind me to make sure that Noelle follows my lead. With reluctance, she opens her door and steps down into the dirt, searching the area around us.

She won't find much. We're in the middle of an empty field save some weeds and a few critters, but the lights of the runway in front of us light up the area and cast a glow over the sky. The 1 Freeway also runs behind us, so the sound of cars filters around us, too, but that should die down as the night goes on.

It is a little louder than I thought it would be, but we'll roll with it.

I head toward the back of my truck, bring the tailgate down, and then hop up inside, listening to my knees crack as I do.

"You okay?" Noelle asks.

Searching for her over my shoulder, I reply, "You heard that?"

She giggles. "Yup. Getting old there, huh, Grant?"

I stand up tall now and stare down at her, my hands on my hips. "Weren't you the one who said I wasn't that old?"

"Yes, but that was before I just heard the sound that came from your knees." She continues to laugh as I shake my head and turn back to the rear window, sliding it open and reaching inside for what I need.

"You can come up here."

"Not sure I can make it without ripping a hole in my jeans."

I drop what I'm doing, walk over to the tailgate, reach for both of her hands, and hoist her up inside, catching her against my chest. "We can't have that happening. I don't have an extra pair of pants for you to wear, and mine will definitely not be fitting you. My shirt? That I can make work. But I draw the line at handing you my pants, Noelle. We need to work on limiting your wardrobe malfunctions."

She slaps my chest playfully. "I'll try my best."

Laughing, I go back to the window and pull through the air mattress and pump, turning it on and spreading out the rubber material so it can fill up as "Before You" by David J filters from the speakers inside. My chest tightens as I listen to the words that have so much more meaning to them than they did a few weeks ago. Then I grab the blankets and pillow and bag of snacks I packed for us to watch the planes take off and land tonight.

"I know we aren't stargazing, but I wanted us to be comfortable," I tell her as I start to arrange everything.

"I appreciate comfort." She glances up at the sky. "I wish we could see the stars, though. I can't think of the last time I was able to. There are far too many lights in LA. I feel like on a clear night when they're visible, there's nothing better than that view. It just reminds us of how small we are in this universe. But like stars, we are all unique, too."

"I know and agree. Maybe one of these dates we can head for the mountains, get out of the city, and I can show you the stars like you've never seen them before." I fluff a few pillows and then rest my knees on the mattress, patting the spot next to me. "Come here."

Crawling across the mattress while trying to keep her balance, Noelle makes her way over to me, flipping onto her back and staring up at me when she's settled. "This is amazing. Thank you. I hope I don't fall asleep."

"Don't worry. I have plenty of tricks up my sleeve to keep you awake," I reply, lacing my words with many unspoken innuendos.

"Is that so?"

"Yes." I grab the bottle of wine, pop the cork, and reach for the plastic cups I brought. "Care for a drink?"

"Absolutely."

"I brought red wine and Coke. What would you like right now?"

Noelle reaches over and intertwines her fingers with mine for a few seconds. "You brought me Coke?"

"Yes, beautiful. I also brought these." I hold up the package of Red Vines and watch her eyes light up. "Now, would you like to save that for later and have some wine now? Or forgo the wine?"

"What are you gonna have?"

"Wine right now. Just a little to set the mood."

"Then I'll have some, too, please. Thank you. And a Red Vine, of course." I pour a small amount of wine in both of our glasses and then hand one to Noelle, moving to open the package of licorice next and handing her a piece. She takes a sip of the wine and then moans. "Oh my God. That's good."

"I'm glad you like it. It's one of my mom's favorites, so I knew it wouldn't disappoint."

"She has great taste." Noelle tears off a piece of the licorice, chewing slowly.

"Yes, she does. And perhaps one day, you'll get to tell her that in person." I grab the container full of charcuterie and pop the lid, setting it between us. Noelle sits up carefully, trying to avoid spilling her wine, and then begins to sample the cheese, meats, nuts, and fruit as I join her.

"You want me to meet your mom?"

"Yeah. I thought that was a given. I told you, I'm in this, Noelle."

Her eyes sparkle from the lights around us. "I would love to meet her, Grant."

"We can decide on a time later." The roar of a plane engine pulls our attention toward the runway, so I point over there. "Here we go. Here's the first one."

"I can't believe you took me to see planes on our date." She giggles.

"Why not?"

"It's just such a unique idea, but it fits you, obviously." She glances around my truck bed then focuses back on me. "This is amazing. I've never done anything like this. I feel like we shouldn't be here."

"Well, we shouldn't."

"Really?"

"Yeah, but we should be fine." I take a sip of my wine, avoiding her eyes just as the plane picks up speed and starts careening into the sky. "Look! Fuck, that sight and feeling never gets old." I watch the plane take off, caught up in the memory of why I wanted to be a pilot in the first place: solitude in a world so big where I felt so small for a large part of my life.

"How fast does the plane have to go before you can ascend?" Noelle asks, pulling my eyes back to her.

"It depends on the plane. A 747 has to get up to about 200 miles per hour in order to get off the ground."

Noelle finishes chewing her cheese and cracker. "That's insane. I bet it's an adrenaline rush, isn't it?"

"Oh, absolutely. It always gives me a high."

"Do you enjoy doing other things that get your blood pumping like that?"

"There was a time I didn't. But then I started to seek it out." *About ten years ago, actually.*

"Like what?"

"Skydiving, race cars, and cliff jumping. I like to fly smaller planes for fun sometimes, too. It makes me feel alive."

She assesses me with her gaze, but I avoid it. I don't want to dampen the evening's mood by diving into that topic just yet. I know I need to tell her about my past, but not tonight.

"I don't know if I could ever make myself do something like that," she says, thankfully not reading into my shift in mood.

"Why not? You only live once."

"I know, but I think I would let my fear win. Also, the idea of something happening and not being able to get back to Scarlett would be reason enough for me to keep my feet firmly planted on the ground."

I reach out and cup her face, stroking her cheek with my

thumb. "I get that, but there are other ways to get your adrenaline pumping, beautiful."

She bites her bottom lip, teasing me with that move again. "Like what?"

"Don't worry. I'll show you when the time is right." I check my watch and note we have about thirty minutes before my surprise commences.

Noelle tips her head back and looks up at the sky as another plane takes off. "You know, I've been meaning to ask you something."

I pop a slice of gouda in my mouth as the song "Hurricane" by Luke Combs ends. "Shoot."

"I heard pilots aren't allowed to have beards. Is that just a myth?"

"Generally speaking, most airlines don't allow facial hair. But the rule is changing slowly, and my airline is one that has allowed facial hair up to a certain length." I reach up and scratch my jaw. "That's why you're only going to see this scruff short and neatly trimmed. But I prefer to have facial hair, so that was a huge deciding factor when I chose my airline."

Noelle leans over and caresses my jaw now. "Well, I'm glad you're able to keep it. It's very sexy."

"You like my beard?"

Her eyes twinkle again. "I like everything about you, Grant." She leans forward and kisses me, holding my jaw in her palm as our lips tenderly meet. "So why are you still single? I mean, I know you told me about being in a relationship once upon a time, but I'm still baffled that you were available. And don't take this the wrong way, but you're kind of too perfect to not be attached to somcone."

Wondering how to explain things without divulging too much, I pause before I speak. "Life has thrown me some curveballs that kind of put me behind or didn't make dating feasible at the time. I was almost engaged once when I was twenty-five. It ended because I realized the person I thought I loved wasn't the person I thought she was. And then timing was off in other instances, a woman and I wanted different things or they couldn't handle my job. I dated one woman who was convinced I was having sex with every flight attendant during my flights. I asked her how she thought that was possible when I was supposed to be flying a plane. It didn't end well, as you can imagine."

"I'm sorry."

"It's okay. Things worked out the way they did. I have a full life. I have an amazing family. I just never found that person I was meant to be with, and after a while, like you, I stopped looking. Then you appeared with wet spots on your shirt, and I was a goner."

She laughs, and I can almost guarantee that her cheeks have turned pink, but it's too dark to tell.

"But I like everything about you, too, Noelle. I still think it's crazy that I'm here with a woman I gave my shirt to." I grab her cup from her hand, place both hers and mine on the edge of the bed of the truck, move the charcuterie out of the way, and then lead her to lie down next to me on the air mattress so that we're face-to-face, the cool summer breeze wafting around us.

"Iris" by the Goo Goo Dolls comes on, and suddenly the entire mood shifts.

"What are you doing?" she whispers as I stroke her face.

"Showing you everything that I like about you." I run my fingertip along the bridge of her nose. "I love these freckles right here. They're dainty but bring out the brown hues in your otherwise unworldly green eyes. They give you a hint of youth without taking away from the fact that you're a sophisticated woman."

I move my hand down her arms to her waist. "I love these curves. Your body is full, voluptuous, and womanly. You're so incredibly sexy, and I don't think you realize just how much."

And then I move my hand back up to her face and tap her temple. "But most of all, I love getting inside your mind, learning about you and what makes you tick—what makes you Noelle. Not just this incredible, strong mother, but this woman who is captivating me. I want to know everything about you."

Her eyes well with tears, but she holds strong and doesn't let them fall. "You are unlike any man I've ever met. You're so selfless and listen to me, which is beyond refreshing. You have this energy about you that is contagious and lively, but I also feel like there are layers to you that I can't wait to discover." She runs her fingernails through the hair at my temples. "I know you poke fun about it, but your gray hair is so freaking sexy to me, and so are these." Her hand moves down my shoulder to my bicep, and she squeezes. "These big, strong arms that have me fighting to take things slowly with you, but also, when they're holding my daughter, they make me fall for you even more." She lowers her voice. "I can't believe I'm here with you right now. It's still so shocking to me." And then she takes a deep breath. "But before this goes any further, I need to tell you something."

My heart rate spikes, but I keep a calm composure. Those are words that can change a person's life in an instant. Trust me, I know. "Okay . . ."

"I'm just afraid of the way it may make you feel about me."

"I doubt it." Stroking her arm, I try to help her relax. "You can tell me anything, Noelle." Suddenly, I feel like it's a thousand degrees outside. Sweat trickles down my back, and my mind is running a hundred miles per hour as I wait to hear what she has to say.

"I told myself that I needed to tell you this before things go further because, while I'm not ashamed, this detail about me is important, especially if we're going to move forward."

"I'm listening."

She takes a deep breath and licks her lips, taking the time to deliver her revelation. "I don't know Scarlett's dad," she finally says with conviction that has me drawing my eyebrows together. And then the words sink in.

She doesn't know Scarlett's father. But what exactly does that mean? Did she sleep with multiple guys within the same time frame? If so, why not have paternity tested? "Okay . . ."

"I told you he wasn't in the picture, and that's true. I mean, I know his age, ethnicity, and what he does for a living. But I never met him," she says, providing more information that still has me perplexed.

"And how does that work?"

With a tremble in her bottom lip, she says, "Scarlett was conceived via intrauterine transfer. I used a sperm donor to have my daughter, Grant."

My head rears back in shock. "Wow. That's—"

"I know. There are probably a million thoughts going through your mind right now, but I have to say this—if that information is a problem, you need to tell me right now because then this can't go any further." Her eyes drop from mine as she fiddles with her fingers, and I let her words soak in. "I felt bad not telling you at the zoo, but it just didn't seem like the time or place. It was still early in our relationship. But now, sitting here with you? I realize I can't keep this from you any longer. But if you can't handle the truth and accept it, then it's better we part ways now before I—"

"Noelle," I cut her off, reaching forward and placing a finger over her lips to silence her. "Take a deep breath, okay? Relax for a minute." She exhales, our eyes darting back and forth between each other's. "First of all, thank you for trusting me enough to tell me something like that. And secondly . . ." I can feel my hand shaking as I realize her confession does change everything, but not in a bad way. It means I need to tell her my truth, too. "Would you mind me asking why you chose that path?"

She nods, and I remove my finger from her lip. "I was tired of waiting for Mr. Right, Grant. I spent so much time trying to find the man I was supposed to be with, but he never came along. I wanted children. I wanted to start my life, so I took matters into my own hands."

"You are so brave . . ."

"Brave or selfish?" she asks, a joking lilt to her voice.

"Fuck, Noelle. You're not selfish, not in a bad way like you're insinuating, at least. Hell, it takes guts and strength to do what you did. It was selfish in the respect that you took your life into your own hands without worrying about what anyone else would think. In fact, it just solidifies in my mind the woman I know you are- -headstrong, dedicated, independent, and passionate. You knew what you wanted and went after it. Why on earth would that make me feel differently about you?"

"I don't know. I've received so many different reactions from people when they find out that I wasn't sure what to expect from the man I'm dating." She drags her nails through my beard as I hold her. "I have always wanted to be a mom, ever since I was a little girl. I was always carrying around a baby doll or pretending to be the mom when we played house. Having kids was just a given, but the older I got, the further off that dream appeared to be. I was tired of waiting, and now I have the most incredible little girl who I love more than life itself but also makes me question my sanity." She lets out a small laugh.

I pull her closer to me so our bodies align, my hard edges pressing up against her soft curves. I hold her face in my palm and tilt her chin up toward mine. "Thank you for telling me that. Your daughter is a miracle, and she is yours. She was wanted and is loved. There is nothing wrong with that."

"You always know what to say," she murmurs before our lips meet and we get lost in our kiss.

This woman. Her soul knew she was meant to be a mother, so she went after that and made it happen for herself. And hell, it should be a relief for me. It helps diminish the pressure I feel hovering over me much more than I thought. But what if she wants more kids?

I feel like I'm running out of time to tell her about my past, but with every second our mouths are connected, the notion gets pushed further toward the back of my mind.

Noelle groans as our kiss grows more intense, our limbs searching and pulling each other close. I reach for her hip, squeezing the flesh there as I make sure that she feels exactly what she's doing to me.

I'm unraveling with every pass of her tongue over mine. As we continue to kiss, I think of how easy it would be to rip her jeans down her legs and fuck her right here in the bed of my truck. I want her so badly. Every moment I spend with her only confirms that I was powerless to resist her.

But then red-and-blue lights flash around us, reflecting on the bed of the truck, alerting me to the second act of the evening that I almost forgot about because of the woman in my arms.

"Grant. Is that . . . ?"

"Fuck," I mutter, sitting up and trying to keep my game face on.

"That's the police, isn't it?" Noelle asks, her eyes wide.

"Yes, it is."

She twists toward me, clenching my bicep now. "Oh my God. This can't be happening. You said we'd be fine . . ."

"Well, I guess I was wrong."

"Grant!" she shrieks, looking around us as if she's contemplating jumping from the bed of my truck and running through the field. I don't blame her, but she won't get very far.

The door to the Ford Explorer slams shut, and I squint to try to see if Colton is the officer approaching us. When his smirk comes into view, as well as the other officer that's with him, I know everything will be all right.

"Good evening, Officer," Noelle says next to me, her voice rising a few octaves, making her sound innocent.

"Are you two aware this is private property? That there is no trespassing allowed?"

"Sorry, Officer," I mutter. "I was just trying to take my girl out for a nice night to watch the planes take off and land."

"Well, this isn't the place to do it. I'm afraid we're going to have to take you in." Then he eyes the red Solo cups of wine that we've barely touched. "And you've been drinking as well?"

"We only had one sip!" Noelle shouts, moving to stand up but almost falling over because of the uneven surface of the air mattress.

"Doesn't matter. Now you're drinking on private property." Colton reaches for his gun at his hip. "You both need to come down from the bed of the truck now."

Noelle turns to me, tears in her eyes, and I almost blow it right there and tell her this is all staged. When the idea came to me, I almost talked myself out of it. But after our last date when she spoke about never being reckless, never experiencing that part of her life before she became a mom, I knew I wanted to give her that adrenaline rush more than anything.

Is this a little over the top? Faking our arrest?

Maybe a little.

But I want to see this through.

"Officer, we're sorry. I tried to tell him we shouldn't be here, but you know men." Noelle crawls to the tailgate and hops down.

"Are you selling me out?"

She spins to face me, her eyes wild. "This is your fault! This was your decision! I was just along for the ride!"

"You were enjoying yourself up until a minute ago."

"Well, a minute ago, we were making out, not talking to police officers." The blue-and-red lights are shining around her, lighting up the fear and anger on her face.

Fuck, maybe this is too much. I probably shouldn't egg her on any more.

"So you two were about to be naked out here, too?" Colton turns to his partner. "Add public indecency to the list of offenses."

Jesus, he's having too much fun with this.

"No!" Noelle shouts. "Officers, I have a baby girl. I have to get home to her." She clasps her hands in front of her. "Please."

"Ma'am, I'm gonna need to detain you until we decide how to proceed." He motions toward the back door of his SUV and pulls it open as I hop down from the truck bed.

"I have to go in there?"

"Yes. If you go easily, I won't have to cuff you. But if you put up a fight, well . . ." He shrugs, and I suck in my lips to keep from laughing.

Noelle spins to me, her eyes brimming with tears. "Grant?"

"Let's just do as he says." I motion for her to go in and then slide along the seat beside her as Colton slams the door shut and turns to his partner, pretending to discuss the situation.

"I can't believe this . . ."

"I'm sorry, Noelle."

She shakes her head. "I've never been arrested in my life. I've only had one speeding ticket, for crying out loud. I'm a good, law-abiding citizen, but now . . ." She sucks in a trembling breath. "And Jesus. Penelope has Scarlett. She's going to shove her nipple into my daughter's mouth out of desperation. Scarlett is going to wonder where I'm at . . . I don't even have a will or guardianship papers drawn up . . ."

I reach for her hand. "Hey, it's going to be okay."

A tear streams down her cheek. "How can you say that? This is so bad."

"It's reckless of us, huh?" I ask, leading her where I want her to go.

"Yes. And irresponsible."

"Is your pulse hammering?"

"I feel like my heart is about to break free from my chest and my skin is about to break out in hives." She places her palm over the center of her body.

"And you're sweaty, too, huh?"

"Yes, Grant! I'm freaking the fuck out."

Leaning closer to her so I can make out the color of her eyes even though we're in a dark car, I ask her, "What if I told you this was all fake?"

Her eyes bug out, but then she narrows her gaze at me. "What are you talking about?"

"What if I told you that I set all of this up so you could feel what being reckless is like?"

"Why on earth would you do that?"

"Because you told me you regret never getting to experience something like that, so I figured I'd help you knock that off your list."

Her eyes are wild, and she's silent for so long that I'm scared to know just exactly what she's thinking. But then she finally puts me out of my misery. "I don't think I like this feeling very much."

"It's not for everyone."

"This is really fake?" She begs for my answer.

"Yes, sweetheart. The officer out there is a buddy of mine."

"This was a risky move, Grant."

I chuckle. "I know, but how do you feel?"

She ponders her answer. "I can't believe I thought I was missing something."

"You feel like you aren't?"

She shakes her head. "No. This is terrifying. I don't know why anyone would want to feel this multiple times." Her gaze shifts to the window outside. "So they aren't real cops?"

"No, they are. But Colton is someone I've known since I was a kid."

She turns back to me, her breathing evening out and the corner of her lips lifting. "You really set all this up?"

"I did. Do you hate me?"

"I am debating between wanting to karate chop you in the junk or straddle your lap and fuck you in the back of this cop car."

Jesus Christ, I think I just fell in love.

"How about no karate chopping and I fuck you somewhere else besides this car? Because if we do that here, we might actually get arrested."

Noelle launches herself across the seat, straddling me anyway and smashing her lips to mine. Our moans fill the cab as we clutch at each other.

"I kinda hate you right now," she mumbles against my lips between kisses.

"I was beginning to severely regret my choice when I saw the tears in your eyes."

"This was so scary."

"I know, but what a rush, right?"

"My adrenaline is still flowing. But now, I just want to take out my aggression on you."

"I am totally fine with that."

We stop talking and continue to maul each other until a tap on the window breaks us apart.

"I take it you told her?" Colton's voice is muffled through the window, but I can make it out.

"Yeah, she knows."

He opens the door and finds us in a compromising position as Noelle scrambles to get off of me. "Do you want me to tase him, Noelle? I'd be more than happy to get him back for making me do this to you."

Noelle smiles but shakes her head. "No, I'm okay. I'm glad he told me sooner rather than later, because otherwise, I might have taken you up on that offer."

Colton laughs. He steps aside so I can get out of the car, holding my hand out for Noelle to follow.

"He's lucky his intentions were good," Noelle chimes in behind me. "Otherwise, I'm sure we could have come up with some reason for you guys to arrest him and let me go scot-free, right?"

"Of course," Colton replies. "Now, I will say that you two should probably get out of here sooner rather than later, because if another patrol car drives by, you won't be so lucky."

I reach out to shake Colton's hand and then his partner's. "Thanks again for doing this."

Colton darts his eyes between me and Noelle. "Yeah, seems the night isn't over yet for you two. Enjoy the rest of your evening." With a nod of his head, the two officers settle back into their car and then slowly drive off, killing the red-and-blue lights as they do.

Turning to Noelle, I stare down at the woman who still looks like she's plotting my death. But then she surprises me by jumping into my arms and attacking my lips with hers again.

Leaning against the tailgate, I hold her up in my arms as we make out, groaning as the kiss turns more frantic.

"We need to get out of here," I mumble against her lips.

"Yes, we do. Take me home, Grant."

"Okay . . ."

"Take me home, and make love to me."

I separate my lips from hers and stare into those green eyes that I can't get enough of. "Are you sure?"

She nods. "Yes. I want you. I need you. I'm ready to take that step with you."

"Fuck, Noelle. I want that, too."

With lightning speed, I clean up the back of my truck, fire up the engine, and slowly make our way out of the field and back onto the highway toward Noelle's house. I'm bouncing with nervous energy as I think about what's to come and everything I want to do to this woman.

"What are you thinking?" I ask Noelle as I get closer to her house.

"I'm nervous, but I know I want this."

"What's making you nervous?"

She sighs, squeezing my fingers that are intertwined with hers. "I . . . I haven't had sex in a long time."

Fuck. Knowing that instantly makes my dick harder. "How long?"

"Over two years."

"Jesus."

She huffs out a laugh. "I know. But I've had a kid since then. My body is—"

"Hey," I cut her off. "I don't want you to worry about that at all, do you hear me?" She doesn't say anything, so I continue. "I know exactly what you must be thinking right now, and I'm telling you, you are *so fucking sexy*, Noelle. You have the body that only a grown man knows how to worship, and that's exactly what I intend to do." I punctuate every word for effect. "I don't give a shit about all of the imperfections you *think* your body has now that you've birthed a human. I'm about to fucking devour you, make you scream my name, and make you come so hard you won't even worry about any of that shit, do you hear me?"

Casting a glance in her direction, I watch her fight her smile. "Holy shit."

"I'm trying not to break the law and get a fucking speeding ticket right now because I can't wait to get you naked, do you understand?"

"Yes."

"So don't worry, sweetheart. Tonight is all about pleasure, and no stretch marks, loose skin, or cellulite is going to get in the way of that."

Chapter 11

Noelle

I'm really doing this. Every tremor of fear racing through my body is chased by a shot of anticipation. Grant did something incredible for me tonight- -he orchestrated a risky situation to give me an experience I feel that I missed out on. Luckily, it was fake, because I'm not sure I could live through that type of fear again without losing a few years of my life from the spike in my blood pressure.

But it was the thought, the time, the energy he dedicated to me and my desires that has me wanting to fulfill the physical ones with him, too. And even though I'm vibrating from my nerves, I know that I want this more than my next breath.

As soon as we pull into my driveway, I feel my adrenaline

spike. Grant hops down from the truck, strides purposefully to my side to open my door for me, and then takes me by the hand so I can hop down as well.

It takes me a few minutes to find my keys because my hands are so shaky. Grant smoothes his hands over my shoulders, kissing my exposed skin at my collar and up the column of my neck from behind me as I struggle to put the key in the lock.

"Relax, sweetheart." Another pass of his lips behind my ear. "I'm not going anywhere."

"I'm just nervous."

"I am, too, if that makes you feel any better."

Spinning around once I get the door open, I stare up into his blue eyes, eyes that look darker as the blackness of night surrounds us on my porch. "Why are *you* nervous?"

Grant sighs, brushing my hair from my face. "Because I want this to be good for you. I want to make you feel good, but I'm afraid I might lose control. It's been a while for me, too, Noelle. And I want this night to be perfect for both of us."

Throwing caution to the wind, I rise up on my toes and wrap my arms around his neck. "It already has been . . . so let's make it stellar."

Grant growls and then smashes his lips to mine, encircling my lower half with his arms as he lifts me and I wrap my legs around his waist. His legs carry us into my house, but he stops to kick the front door shut behind him. Light coming through the window from outside casts a soft glow in the room, illuminating it just enough so we can find our way as Grant leads me to the couch, sitting down with me still wrapped around him.

He grabs a handful of my ass while I grind on him, moaning as I feel his hardness beneath me. He's so *big*—strong, powerful arms, thick legs, massive shoulders, and height that towers over me. Being in his arms makes me feel safe. I'm so small compared to him, but somehow we fit together perfectly—and I hope that also extends to him fitting inside of me as well.

"God, your curves," he mumbles against my lips, squeezing the flesh of my ass and hips so hard he might leave a bruise.

"I'm glad you appreciate them."

"I love them. Gives me something to hold on to."

I run my hands down his arms, squeezing his biceps. "That's how I feel about these."

He chuckles as we break apart. "Glad to know there's some reciprocation here." His hands travel under my shirt, stroking the soft skin of my belly, and I suck in on instinct. I know that I want this, but the last thing I want is for him to be turned off by my body.

I internally repeat his words from earlier, reminding myself that he said he doesn't care. And I want to believe him, but sometimes as a woman, we can't believe someone else's words or appreciation of our body. It's not until we accept it on our own that we can absorb another person's praise, and I'm still trying to get used to my new skin.

"Relax, Noelle," Grant whispers, slowly peeling my shirt up my torso.

"I'm trying."

"I hate that you're questioning my desire for you right now." The shirt comes up over my bra, and I lift my arms so he can extract it completely. He tosses it to the side as my hands move to my stomach, covering my rolls. But he rips them away and looks me straight in the eye. "I know that I can tell you until I'm blue in the face that I don't care about the physical reminders that you've had a child, but ultimately, it's up to you to believe me. But I will say this . . ." He kisses me chastely and then pulls back, taking my hand between us so I can feel the steel rod in his pants. "I have been like this all night. And in a moment, you're going to feel every inch of me inside of you. The last thing you'll be thinking about is what you look like, and the only thing I'm going to be concerned with is making you come all over my cock—do you understand me?"

A rush of arousal travels through me. "Yes."

"Good girl." He leans forward and licks the swell of my breasts, teasing me with his hot, wet tongue and a nip of his teeth, and I throw my head back in pleasure until I feel him reach behind me to unclasp my bra.

I put my hand on top of his arm. "Let's leave my bra on."

"Okay . . ."

"I'm still nursing, and I, uh, I don't want to leak."

Understanding registers in his eyes. "Gotcha. No worries, babe. There's plenty more of you to explore." With a jut of his chin, he says, "Go ahead and stand up for me, and take your pants off."

I slide off his lap, standing before him as we watch each

other undress. Grant removes his glasses from his face, setting them to the side, before he rips his shirt off by reaching behind him, one of those ridiculously sexy moves men do that make a woman turn feral. And when I see his chest, his abs, and his entire cut torso on display in front of me, the smatter of short chest hair all over his pecs, and a happy trail that I desperately want to travel, drool nearly slips from my mouth. This man is carved and beautiful, mountains of muscle I can tell he's dedicated time to building. His strong hands—hands that I become more fond of every time I feel them or see them- -reach down to unbutton his jeans, exposing the band of his black briefs, which he also pushes down in one move as he kicks off his boots and pulls his pants down his legs.

And then I see it, his massive cock—long, proud, and dripping at the tip with pre-cum. He's huge, the biggest I've ever been with, and suddenly, my vagina clenches in protest and need simultaneously.

Grant reaches down to stroke himself a couple of times as I step out of my jeans, revealing my body to him as well, and the way his eyes darken gives me a boost of confidence that I need to see this through. Even though I still have my bra on, I'm glad it's black and trimmed with lace so I still feel sexy.

He slides off the couch, landing on the floor so his back is resting against it. And then he crooks a finger at me with the hand that is not yanking on his length, commanding me forward. "Come here, Noelle."

I move to sit on his lap, but he shakes his head, dropping it back so it rests on the cushion, and then points to his mouth. "Nope. You're sitting here."

"What?"

"Sit on my face, sweetheart. Come over here so I can taste you and make you writhe on my tongue."

Oh, Jesus.

Following his order, I place my knees on either side of his face, hovering over him. But then he reaches up, grabs my hips, and pulls me down on his mouth, letting out a groan of approval when my sex connects with his tongue.

And oh God—I forgot how good this feels.

Grabbing the back of the couch for support, I finally start to relax while Grant's mouth explores every inch of me. I moan in approval when his tongue hits my clit, swirling around the bud, applying the perfect amount of pressure and teasing me relentlessly.

"Fuck, you taste incredible, sweetheart," he murmurs against me before spearing his tongue in my entrance, circling the opening and making me cry out with pleasure.

"Fuck, yes. Give me all of your sounds, Noelle. Don't hold back." He squeezes my hips again and pulls me even closer to him as he finds my clit again, sucking that bundle of nerves between his lips this time, lighting up my entire body.

"Oh God, Grant . . ."

"Ride my face, sweetheart. Fuck yourself with my tongue."

Without even thinking, I start swiveling my hips, using the couch as leverage, circling and grinding on his mouth. I'm probably suffocating the poor man, but his grunts and groans of approval keep me moving and trying to block out all of my reservations at the moment.

And then I feel his fingers broaching my core, slowly pushing inside, filling me up, and the spark of my orgasm grows exponentially.

"Oh, fuck yes!" I cry out, feeling that burst of pleasure rush through me, ready to explode.

Grant doesn't let up, sliding his fingers in and out of me faster, smacking my ass a few times to spur me on, and attacking my clit in the most amazing way. Suddenly, my orgasm detonates, and I'm crying out in ecstasy.

"Oh God! Oh God, yes . . ."

He doesn't let up, wringing every last ounce of pleasure from my body until I finally collapse against the back of the couch and he slides out from under me.

I turn over, staring down at him between my legs with a proud smile on his face, his entire mouth and beard covered in my arousal.

"Fuck, that was even hotter than I thought it could be."

"That was amazing," I say on an exhale, still trying to get control of my breathing, my limbs spread out like he just drained every last ounce of energy from my body.

"Oh, we're not done yet." He leans forward and drags his tongue through my sensitive flesh, making me shudder. But then he stands, searches for his pants, extracts a condom from his wallet, and sheathes himself in front of me. "Lie down, Noelle."

I crawl up the couch and then turn around, lying on my

back, more than ready to feel this man inside of me.

"Nice tattoo, by the way."

Recollection dawns on me. "Oh, yeah. Sometimes I forget it's there." I reach back to my shoulder, drawing my fingers over my rose tattoo that I got with the girls back in college.

"You'll have to tell me about it later, because right now, I need to be inside you."

"I need that, too."

Grant crawls over me, and at this moment, I've never been so grateful that I purchased a large sectional for my living room. I know we could move to my bed, but I don't think either of us wants to waste another second moving.

"You ready?"

I nod. "Yes."

He looks between us, watching himself drag his cock through my wetness while teasing my clit with the head. I'm gasping from the feeling. And then he slowly pushes in, stealing both of our breaths.

I wince as he stretches me open, a slight burn making me aware of how long it's been since I've been with a man, but as he pulls back and pushes in further each time, the other sensation takes over—the one where indescribable pleasure resides —and I focus on the fact that I'm letting this man inside me in more ways than one.

Grant drops his head to my shoulder once he's fully seated. "Fuck, I need a minute."

Giggling, I drag my nails over his back as I feel him twitch inside of me. He shifts his hips, sparking pleasure throughout my core. "God, I'm so full right now, Grant."

"You feel so fucking good, Noelle. Jesus Christ, woman. I think I've died and gone to heaven."

"Take us both there, please."

Lifting his head, he locks his eyes with mine and then he rears back, sliding back in slowly as we both moan. He picks up his pace as our hips move on instinct, bumping and grinding against each other in a rhythm that is all our own.

I cling to his shoulders as he moves, and he holds my hip in one hand and my face in the other. We barely speak as we race toward the precipice. I feel like time stands still as this man shows me how much he desires me with his body, how insane I make him feel. And the feeling is mutual. This experience is raw and carnal and so intense that my body is priming for another release faster than I anticipated.

"Fuck, Noelle," he finally grates out. "Do you feel me? Do you feel how hard I am for you? That's what you do to me."

"Yes, I feel you. I feel all of you, Grant." He hits that spot inside that I know will set me off in no time as he tilts my hips up more. "Oh God, right there. Don't stop."

"I can't stop. Jesus, I want to do this all night."

"Grant . . ." I whisper with each thrust he gives me. He's making me wetter by the second, my body is tensing in preparation for my release, and his pace increases as he reads my reaction.

"Fuck, Noelle. I'm gonna come."

"Yes—I'm coming!" I scream as my orgasm slams into me,

rushing through me with an intensity that steals my breath. Grant curses as he thrusts a few more times and then stills, finding his release as well.

"Holy shit," he says, collapsing on top of me as we both catch our breaths. And it's then that I realize he was right—I wasn't worried about what I looked like or what he saw. All that mattered right then was our connection, our pleasure, and the moment between the two of us that was better than I could have imagined.

"So tell me about your tattoo."

We've moved to my bed and have just finished round two as Grant holds me, my back to his front, his fingers brushing over the red rose that means so much to me.

"Roses are my favorite flower. Red ones, to be exact."

"Then it must be luck that I sent you those already without knowing that." He presses a kiss to the ink in my skin and waits for me to continue.

"Or maybe you know me pretty well already."

"I like that reasoning better."

I continue with the story. "The girls and I decided to get matching tattoos back in college, but we wanted them to be unique as well. Charlotte suggested our favorite flowers, so that's what we did. She got a sunflower, Amelia got an orchid, Penelope got a calla lily, and I got a rose."

"It suits you. Classic. Timeless. Beautiful."

"Thank you."

"For some reason, it reminds me of *Beauty and the Beast*."

"Well, Belle was my favorite Disney Princess. I related to her love of reading, for sure."

"It's a pretty bold statement for you girls to do something like that."

"They're my second family. Even if something in life changed, I know I'd want to cement that moment in time where we felt so connected that nothing could break that bond."

"You're lucky to have them."

"I know." I glance at the clock on my nightstand as the hour approaches one in the morning. "We should probably get some sleep," I say, wiggling my ass against Grant. He instantly hardens against me.

"That sounds like a terrible idea. I think my dick needs to be buried inside of you again at least one more time." Rubbing his length between my ass cheeks, my body warms up to his words just as quickly as he rose to the idea.

"I have to pick up Scarlett from Penelope and Maddox's kind of early."

Grant nibbles on my ear lobe as he reaches around my hip and finds my clit, circling it softly with the tip of his finger. "I can be quick."

"What if I don't want you to?" Moaning in appreciation, I open my legs wider to grant him better access.

He slides a finger inside me. "I'll do whatever you want me to, Noelle. And I don't see that changing any time soon."

"Make love to me again then, please."

"Let me go get a condom."

He leaps from the bed, hurries down the hall, and returns just as fast already covered. "This is my last one anyway, so we'd better make it count." Returning to his position behind me, he lifts my leg and rests my foot on his calf. "Open up for me, sweetheart. Let me inside that beautiful pussy."

I wait with bated breath as he toys with my entrance but never fully slips in. "Grant, please . . ."

"God, I love the way my name sounds coming from your lips." Without wasting another second, he lines up and slides in, the pressure and sensation more intense from this angle. We move around to get more comfortable, which allows him to slide in fully. "Fuck, Noelle."

"So good . . ."

Holding me close to him with my head turned back toward his face and my legs open, Grant begins to pump his hips, locking his eyes on mine before bringing our mouths together.

We lie there, soaking up each other's gasps, breathing heavily as our bodies writhe and connect, maintaining eye contact when our lips aren't together. Soon I feel my release building, but I almost don't want it to end.

Grant reaches down to where we're joined, and my eyes follow his hand. "Do you like watching my cock slide in and out of you?"

God, this man and his dirty mouth. I never knew I could like those words so much. I've never been with a man so vocal before, but I am not complaining.

"Yes, I like to watch." My arousal coats him as he

continues to thrust in and out of me, building me up even faster.

"I like it, too. It's so sexy watching you take all of me." He thrusts harder, making me gasp. "We fit together so perfectly, Noelle. It's so fucking crazy but so fucking right."

"I know." I reach behind me and bring his lips to mine again, kissing him as he picks up his pace. I pull away to catch my breath. "Grant . . ."

"You there, babe?"

I nod against his head, our foreheads pressed together. Grant reaches down to circle my clit again, bringing me over the edge as I cry out when he finds that perfect spot and pressure. He continues to pound into me through my release, and just as mine ebbs, he finds his own.

"Fuck."

I mumble something, but I'm not even sure what it is. All I hear is Grant's chuckle before he stands from the bed to deal with the condom as my body slips into a comatose state. By the time he returns, I've already grabbed the comforter and wrapped myself in it like a cocoon.

"You gonna let me in there?"

"You're staying?" I ask, half asleep.

"Hell yes, Noelle. I'm not going anywhere." The bed dips, I feel him move in behind me, and the last thing I register is his lips over my tattoo again as I drift off to sleep.

"Oh, hallelujah! You look freshly fucked!" Penelope shouts the second she opens her front door and takes one look at me. "Maddox! Come here, and tell Noelle she looks freshly fucked!"

"Not sure that's a good idea," Maddox calls out from deeper in the house but suddenly appears holding my daughter, who is also holding the stuffed elephant Grant bought her from the zoo a few months ago now. And I couldn't care less about giving Penelope shit for her comment as I reach for my girl and hold her tightly to my chest, kissing her head and fighting off tears.

"Oh, hello, baby girl. Mommy missed you so much." I kiss all over her face as she giggles. "Were you a good girl for Uncle Maddox and Aunt Penelope?"

"She was. She only woke up once, but we gave her a bottle, and she drifted right back off," Maddox replies.

"Yeah, I tried to wake up for that, but Maddox fucked me into a coma about an hour before that happened, so . . ." Penelope shrugs but has an unapologetic grin on her face as she does.

"Yeah, I got put to sleep last night, too." I smirk at her while still hugging Scarlett.

"I knew it! Oh, girl, you need to tell me everything." She waves Maddox off. "Shoo, you. It's time for girl talk."

"Noted. Glad you had a good night, Noelle. You deserve it." He winks at me and then leaves us alone.

"How was it?"

"Amazing. Incredible." My cheeks start to burn from smiling. "It has been so long, and it was just—"

"—perfect?" she finishes for me.

"Yes."

"Gah! I'm so glad. So when can we meet him?"

"Soon, I promise." I kiss the top of Scarlett's head as she rests hers on my chest. "But thank you again for taking her. Grant planned this whole thing, and it was so thoughtful, and I . . ." I stare off into space, trying to articulate what I'm feeling.

"You're at a loss for words. That rarely happens to you, Noelle."

"I know. I'm falling for him, Pen. So fast. It's scary."

"You're preaching to the choir, Noelle. You don't have to explain it to me. I get it."

"I know you do. I just—"

"Take it one step at a time right now, okay? I know you're battling with yourself so hard about all of this, but that smile on your face?" The corner of her mouth lifts as her eyebrow accompanies it. "I haven't seen you smile like that in ages."

Letting out a long breath, I nod. "I know. Thank you."

"Of course. And thank you for letting us watch Scarlett. She was an angel, and I think I finally got through to Maddox about the whole baby thing."

"I'm glad."

"Now, enjoy the rest of your day. When are you seeing Grant again?"

"Well, he was still in bed when I left to come here."

Her eyes widen. "Then why the hell are you still standing here with me? Go home to your man. We can catch up next week at brunch."

"We will, definitely." Amelia couldn't make brunch tomorrow, so we pushed it for the following weekend.

After I gather Scarlett's things and put her in the car, I make my way back to my house, wondering if Grant is still going to be there. I didn't wake him up when I left because he was sleeping so peacefully and I knew I needed to get my daughter. Even though last night was incredible, I definitely missed her, and the mom guilt was setting in. So I snuck out despite not knowing if he'd still be there when I returned.

I know we said a lot of things last night, but it's a new day, and the hormones have subsided. Who knows what today will bring, and now I'm nervous again as I close in on my home. For some reason, every incredible moment with this man brings me back down to earth as I simultaneously wait for the other shoe to drop—because in every relationship I've ever had, it does.

When I pull into the garage, I gather Scarlett and her bag and head into the house, only to be stopped by the smell of bacon cooking. As I enter the house through the garage, the sight in front of me almost makes me drop everything in my hands, including my kid.

Grant is standing at the stove, shirtless and in nothing but his briefs, cooking bacon and whistling to himself with his back to me. Said back is rippling as he moves, taking strips of cooked bacon from the pan to a plate with a napkin on it and then depositing more pieces in the skillet to cook. He's moving effortlessly around my kitchen, making me question if I'm dreaming or if this is really happening.

"I can feel you watching me," he says before finally casting his gaze over his shoulder, grinning at me.

"You're still here?"

He turns to face me completely this time. "Yeah. Where else would I be?" And then his face falls. "Shit. Do you want me to leave? I don't want to overstay my welcome, it's just that I wanted to see Scarlett, and I figured you'd be hungry, so . . ."

Setting her bag down on the floor and then walking toward him, I shake my head. "No, not at all. I'm glad you're here, and thank you for cooking. That's really sweet."

He leans forward once I'm close enough and gives me a soft kiss. "Of course." But then his face lights up as he turns to Scarlett and takes her from my hands. "Well, hello, sweetheart." Scarlett drops her stuffed elephant as he tosses her in the air, and she screams in delight. "How are you?"

"She did great, at least that's what Pen and Maddox said."

"I'm sure she did. She's independent and tough like her mama." He dips down to pick up her elephant. "You like this guy, huh?" Scarlett grabs the elephant from him and shoves it toward her mouth.

"She never lets go of it."

Grant smiles adoringly at my daughter before turning back to me. "You hungry?"

"Starving," I say, casting my eyes down his torso only to look back up and see him smirking at me.

"You should have stayed in bed longer if you wanted some more of that."

"Maybe you'll just have to make it up to me later."

"It would be my pleasure." He turns back to the stove with Scarlett on his hip. "You have time to take a shower if you want. I've got the girl and the food."

My heart nearly skips a beat.

This.

This is what I've been missing—a partner, someone to carry the load, someone to let me take a shower without worrying about my daughter.

I almost burst into tears.

Grant turns to me. "Get that beautiful ass in the shower so I can feed my girls."

Before I break down in front of him, I scurry off, sending a thanks to the man upstairs for bringing me the man who's currently shirtless in my kitchen, a man I wouldn't mind finding there every day looking just like that from here on out.

The sound of the doorbell ringing startles me as I glance across the carpet at Grant. He's been here all day since he stayed the night last night, and I'm definitely not ready for him to leave. When he offered to pay for dinner to be delivered, I guessed he planned on staying another night as well—or it could have been the dirty words he's been whispering in my ears all day, describing in detail how he wants to touch me later. I've been a pile of horniness and limp limbs all day waiting for night to fall and Scarlett to go to sleep.

"That must be the food," he says, moving to stand up. "I'll get it."

"Thank you."

He kisses the top of my head as he passes me. "Of course."

I roll the ball back across the carpet toward Scarlett, continuing the game we were just playing. She screams in excitement and crawls after it since it veered off to the right. Smiling from ear to ear, I watch her until the voice at the door pulls my eyes in that direction.

"Who are you?"

Oh, shit.

"Grant Thomas. Can I help you?"

Scrambling off the floor, I nearly trip on the end table by my couch trying to get over to greet my sister. "Holly? What are you doing here?" I brush my hair from my face as I stand next to Grant, reading her expression. And from the look on her face, I can tell she's both caught off guard and curious about the man in my home.

Holly arches a brow at me. "I came by to visit."

"You ran away from your house, you mean."

She shrugs. "I told Seth I was going out. Apparently that meant to bug *you*. I miss my niece. But much to my surprise, a man answered your door." Her eyes scan up and down Grant, assessing him. "A very *large* man, that is."

Grant casts a curious glance over at me, pushing his glasses up his nose with a small smile on his lips, but I'm still staring at my sister. "Holly, this is Grant. My—"

Grant cuts me off. "'Boyfriend' sounds sort of juvenile, but we can go with that for now." He extends his hand to her. "Nice to meet you."

"You have a boyfriend?" Her eyebrows meet her hairline. "When the hell did you start dating?"

"I'm not going to discuss that now," I hiss. "Are you coming in or not?"

She huffs out a laugh. "Oh, I definitely am coming in. You've got a lot of explaining to do." Scarlett crosses the carpet at record speed, army crawling toward us. "There's my little girl." Holly hoists her up, kissing her chubby cheeks. "Auntie missed you."

Grant closes the door behind her and then turns to me. "Guess that wasn't our food."

"I know. I'm so sorry. I had no idea my sister was going to show up here, but this is what she does."

He leans down and kisses my cheek. "It's okay. I would have met her eventually, right?"

"Yes."

"Then I guess it's happening now."

"So how long has this been going on?" Holly asks, twisting to face us now with Scarlett on her hip. My daughter grows antsy in her arms, though, reaching for Grant. He steps in and retrieves her, sending a message to my sister loud and clear without any words. I guess it's good to know where her loyalty lies.

"For a few months."

"*Months?*"

"I'm a commercial pilot, so we see each other when we can, but things are getting serious." Grant stares down at me as his arm wraps possessively around my waist. And my insides melt while simultaneously heating up for him, too. Isn't it everyone's bedtime yet? I need to get this man alone again.

"Does Mom know?"

"Yes, she does. She hasn't met him yet either, though, if that makes you feel any better." I move around her, headed toward the kitchen.

Holly follows after me. "Not sure it does."

Grant clears his throat. "I'm gonna go change her diaper, babe. Food should be here soon." He tosses a thumb over his shoulder. "I left cash on the table by the door."

"Okay. Thank you."

"No problem."

We both watch him take Scarlett to her room, and then Holly's eyes bug out. "He's changing her diaper?"

"Yes."

"And ordering you guys food?"

"Uh-huh. And he spent the night last night after taking me on a date." I don't elaborate on the details of that date, but I hope she gets the message. "Why all of the questions?"

Crossing her arms over her chest, she shakes her head at me. "I guess you found your diamond in the rough then, huh?"

"Excuse me?"

"Your perfect man. The one you used to make lists about."

Glancing down the hallway where I hear Scarlett laughing and the deep rumble of Grant's voice as he talks to her, I smile. "Yeah, I think I did."

"God, you *would* find a man like that." She groans but then fixes her eyes on me again. "But I'm happy that you have. Believe me, hang on to that one, Noelle. A man that changes diapers *and* looks like that? That's like finding a four-leaf clover in the wild."

Laughing, I nod. "I know."

"Are you happy?"

"I am, Holly. I'm sorry I didn't tell you, but I'm still feeling things out. And like you said, he's amazing, almost too amazing. I guess I'm still doubtful that it's real, if I'm being honest."

"That's okay. I guess part of me is jealous, too."

I tilt my head at her. "Things not better with Seth?"

"I mean, yes and no. I've talked to him more about what I need, especially after you and I talked last. But part of me just feels like I'm not a priority anymore. The kids get his attention, but then there's none left for me. So I leave." She shrugs. "I'd rather be alone than watch him ignore me."

"Holly, I'm sorry. That's no way to live in a marriage."

"I know. I just don't know what to do."

"Amelia knows other therapists she can recommend," I suggest yet again. The bottom line is, though, Holly has to make the first step and call them.

"Yeah, I might take you up on that." Scarlett's squeal from the back of the house breaks the conversation. "My niece seems to like him."

"Oh, she does. She's the reason we even met in the first place."

"Really? I'd love to hear about it."

"And I'd love to tell you more, but our dinner is about to arrive, and Grant has something planned for me later." I won't mention that it involves me on all fours, but I'm dying to experience it. The man is a walking sex ad, and after seeing him naked, I don't think I ever want him to wear clothing again. "Let's do dinner one night this week. Grant will be out of town for a few days for work, so it will be perfect."

"Aw, listen to you coordinating your life around your boyfriend now." She sighs. "I miss those days, but yeah, that sounds great."

"It's a date."

"Okay, I'll leave you to it then." Holly jingles her keys in her hand just as Grant returns with Scarlett. "I'm gonna take off and let you two enjoy the rest of your evening." She kisses Scarlett on the cheek. "Grant, be good to my sister."

"I never planned on doing anything but that."

"Good. See you all later."

"We'll make it happen."

Holly nods and waves at us, opening the door just as the delivery guy appears with our food. Grant pays the man, takes the bags into the kitchen, and deposits Scarlett in her high chair.

"So everything okay?"

"Yeah. My relationship with my sister is complicated. And

she's not too happy at home right now, so sometimes she just takes off and shows up unannounced. It's her M.O."

His brow furrows. "That doesn't sound good."

"It's not. I hope she chooses to work through it, though. She deserves to be happy, even though her life didn't turn out the way she wanted it to. In all honesty, I think she holds on to some resentment about that."

Grant focuses on the plates he's loading with Chinese. "That's understandable."

"Yeah, but it's her choice to feel that way. She needs to work for the marriage and life that she wants or else she's never going to be happy. I just hate to see her this way, and I wish there was more I could do."

He brings the plates to the table and a small bowl of rice for Scarlett, taking his seat beside me. "It's not your job to fix that for her, Noelle. You know that, right?"

"Yeah. It still sucks, though."

He leans over in his seat, planting his lips on mine. "You have the biggest heart of anyone I know, you know that?"

"Not sure if that's true."

"I do. It's one of the things I like most about you."

"Oh, yeah? And what else do you like about me?"

"Your ass," he replies, our noses touching.

"Hmm. I like your ass, too."

"Good to know. And tonight, I'm going to make your ass turn red under my palm. Are you ready for that?"

Wetness pools between my legs. "I am."

"Good. Now, eat up. You're going to need all of the energy

you can get." He smiles around his fork as we stare at each other while we eat, counting down the minutes until we can tuck Scarlett in her crib. All I can think about is how a man who is so nurturing with my daughter can be so downright possessive with me.

And I am not complaining about that at all.

Chapter 12

Grant

"Aw, you got laid."

"Well, good morning to you, too," I reply to Brad, my copilot for my flight to Seattle today. After an amazing weekend with Noelle and Scarlett, it's back to flying over the clouds.

"Tell me I'm wrong."

"I'm not telling you shit." We walk through the automatic sliding doors, entering the airport and heading to our terminal to check in for the flight.

"Fine. But answer me this: Is this woman a one-time deal, or is she more?"

"Why do you care?"

"Because I'm your friend, and I know that men are *not* better off alone."

I sigh, relenting to his inquisition, because he's right—being alone is for the birds. "She's a forever type of woman, one I just might keep for that long."

Brad puts his hand on my bicep, stopping us in the middle of the walkway. Luckily, it's early, so there aren't a ton of people milling around us. "Holy shit. You're serious?"

"Yeah. It's the woman from the coffee shop."

"The mom you gave your shirt to?"

I laugh at the memory. "Yup."

He fist-pumps the air. "Dude. Hell yes!"

I smack his arm down. "Jesus, will you calm down?"

We grab our suitcases and begin walking again. "I can't. You nabbed yourself a single mom. They have the best snacks."

"How the fuck would you know?"

He holds his hands up. "Obviously, I don't. But come on, moms always have snacks on them. It's like a rule. Where there are kids, there are moms with snacks. They basically leave a Hansel and Gretel breadcrumb trail leading you to them."

"You have issues."

"That's what my wife says, but she still loves me, and she always has snacks, so my assessment checks out. So . . . things are going well then, I take it?"

Thinking back to this weekend and how it felt being in Noelle's home with her and Scarlett—the sex, making them breakfast, fixing a loose step on her porch, hanging lights in her backyard for her, watching cartoons and playing with Scarlett, ordering in dinner, the sex after—I think I'm invested more than I thought I was.

"Yeah, things are definitely going well."

"Well, hot damn, Grant. Congrats. Let me know when the wedding is and what snacks you'll be serving. I personally can always go for some goldfish or a granola bar."

Laughing, we swipe our badges and head into the pilot's lounge. "You'll be the first to get the invite and list of what we're serving."

"Uncle Grant!" Two miniature versions of my brother attack me as I step into his house.

"How are my favorite boys?"

"Do you want to come see what we've built on Minecraft?" Andrew asks.

"Of course. Let me say hello to your mom and dad really quick though, okay?"

"Okay." They race back to the television and pick up their controllers, jumping right back into their game. I round the corner and find Sarah in the kitchen, stirring something at the stove.

"Hey, Sis."

Sarah spins around to greet me. "Hey, there. How's it going?"

There's no containing my smile. "Good. Actually, really freaking good."

Setting the spoon down on the counter, she turns to give me her full attention. "I take it things with Noelle are going well then?"

"Yeah, they are. I want you guys to meet her."

"Wow. That's a big step. Hell, I don't think we've met a woman since Denise."

"For good reason. But this one's different, Sarah. Everything about it feels different."

"And the baby?"

"She's just the icing on the cake."

My brother walks into the house from the garage at that moment. "Hey, Grant."

"Hey." He kisses his wife on the cheek and then reaches into the fridge to grab a beer for me and himself, handing it to me. "Thanks."

"Of course."

"Grant was just telling me that he's falling in love," Sarah teases as she goes back to the pot of food she's stirring.

My brother's eyebrows shoot up. "Holy shit! Already?"

"I did not use the L-word, but there are definitely some strong feelings brewing."

Gavin slaps me on the back. "Then when do we get to meet her?"

"I was actually discussing that with Sarah. I want you guys to meet her, but there are a few things to consider first."

Gavin looks between me and Sarah. "Wanna talk outside?"

"Yeah." I follow him out onto his back porch as the sun descends in the sky in front of us, blinding me, so I turn my back to it and lean up against the railing. Gavin follows my lead.

"So what's on your mind?"

"Well, for starters, I feel like things are happening quickly."

"What things?"

"My feelings. I mean, hell, Gavin—the woman has dug herself into my heart, and I feel like it's too soon."

"Says who? The only people who think there's a timeline for love are ones who have never experienced the overwhelming kind themselves. Hell, with Sarah? I knew within two months she was the woman I was gonna marry."

"I remember that. And Noelle and I have been seeing each other for about that long now when our schedules have allowed."

"So what's the problem?"

I run my hand through my hair and then drain half my beer. "I've been avoiding conversations with her because I'm afraid of how she'll react."

He tilts his head to the side. "I totally understand where you're coming from, but the longer you push out those talks, the worse they may be."

"What if what I have to tell her is a deal breaker? What if I can never give her kids of our own?"

"Wow. Two months in, and you're already thinking about kids? I'd say you are pretty serious about her."

"I am, but that idea is always in the back of my head with any woman I date. It's been a while since I've had to worry about it, of course, but now, with Noelle . . . I can see that future."

"Then you need to talk to her about it. And maybe see your doctor, too?"

Nodding, I take another swig of my beer. "I was thinking about that. I mean, I know that after my treatment, my chances of conceiving the natural way were low, but I wonder if things have changed in that respect."

"Only one way to find out."

"Fuck. This is what I've been avoiding, Gav. This is what I haven't wanted to face." Every time I think back to the cancer diagnosis that changed not only my health but my outlook on love, I've wondered how I would broach this subject with the right woman if I ever found her. Being told at twenty-five that you have testicular cancer, that you may never have children of your own, was a hard pill to swallow. Add on an almost fiancée who walked out on me before I ever started my treatment for cancer as I fought for my life, and well, you can't really blame me for the reaction I had toward women after that.

Lucky for me, I survived, went into remission, and have been cancer-free for over ten years now. But the scars on the inside, the ones no one can see? Those never truly faded. And now, with Noelle, I feel like old wounds are being opened up again, and that pain is back—but this time, it's being chased by hope, too.

"I know you've been pushing aside dating because you

didn't want to face your reality, but what I guess I want you to ask yourself is this: Is she worth it? Is she worth the risk? Is she worth telling your story to in hopes that you can find happiness in an unorthodox way?"

Staring at the house in front of me, I nod slowly. "I think she is."

"Then start by going to see your doctor. Have all the information in front of you so that you can be upfront and honest with her. Show her that you care about her but want her to know the reality of your future. And if she cares about you the same way you do for her, she'll stay. She'll love you regardless. She'll approach the subject with tenderness and a willingness to work with you instead of against you in deciding how you might create a family of your own. I mean, she already has a kid. Maybe she doesn't want more."

"Maybe, although watching her with Scarlett and knowing how much she loves her, that woman was meant to be a mom." I smile at the mental images I have of the two of them together. I know Noelle feels overwhelmed in her new role, but she's so nurturing and loving to that little girl that my heart thaws every time I see them together.

"And there are plenty of ways to do that. You still have your sperm you froze before chemo, right?"

"Yeah."

"Then you have IVF and surrogacy as options, too. Try not to focus on only the bad outcomes that can happen when you tell her. Focus on all of the options you have and, most importantly, how you feel about her. But she needs to know, especially if you're struggling with it. You care about her; otherwise, this wouldn't matter so much to you."

"I do, Gav. She's everything I wasn't looking for—passionate, funny, beautiful, and smart, and she has the biggest heart."

"Then what the hell is she doing with you?" he teases.

I shove him, and he stumbles back. "Hey!"

"Thanks for the pep talk and then ruining it right at the end."

"What are brothers for?"

Pulling him into me, I hug him tightly. "Thanks, Gav."

"Anytime, Grant. It's going to be okay. I have a good feeling about this one."

"God, I hope you're right." *Because if not, I don't know if I'll ever be the same.*

"Grant. It's good to see you." Shutting the door behind him, Dr. Anivan walks further into the room, standing at the end of the table I'm currently sitting on.

"You, too, Doc."

"Is everything okay? You aren't due for an exam for another year."

I clear my throat. "Oh, yeah. I'm good. No concerns . . . well, except for one." After seeing my brother earlier this week, I called my urologist and was able to slide into a cancellation appointment two days later.

Dr. Anivan takes a seat in his chair, spinning around the

floor until he's right in front of me. "Okay. What can I help you with?"

"I kind of wanted to test my count."

His eyebrows pop up. "Oh?"

"There's a woman I'm seeing . . ." Taking a deep breath, I look to the side of the room. "And I can see a future there, Doc. But I . . . I want to know what kind of future I can offer her."

He smiles. "I see."

"I know the last time we did the test, the count was low but not horrible. But I know you also said that it can decrease over time."

He flips through the chart in his lap. "Yes, I recall. It's been a few years since you've inquired about this, so I definitely agree a test is in order. I want to remind you, though, that you may not get the results you want."

I inhale deeply again. "I know, but I need to know for sure so I can have that conversation with her if need be."

"You must be enamored with this woman if you're considering the implications your history can have on your future."

"I am," I answer honestly. "So where do we go from here?"

"Well, I can have you make a deposit today. Although, I have to ask, when's the last time you had sex?"

"Last night," I reply, remembering what Noelle looked like on all fours in front of me, and now I'm fighting my dick from getting hard. Not being able to touch her for days will be a test of my control, for sure.

"Then today might not be the best time. We need a few

days for volume to build up, and then, ideally, I would like you to come in a few days after that to collect a second sample. Sperm counts can vary from day to day, and we want the most accurate analysis, especially given your history."

Fuck. That means I won't be able to connect with Noelle like that for a while. I know I won't get to see her Thursday because of my work schedule, but this weekend, I had planned on worshiping her as much as possible. I can still do that, I suppose. I just won't be able to let her reciprocate.

"So Friday and Monday might be our best bets for accurate collection. Does that sound doable to you?" Dr. Anivan pulls me from my thoughts.

"Yeah, I can make that happen."

"Great." He scribbles a note in my chart. "I'll put in the order, and then we can get you some answers. But like I said, prepare yourself, Grant."

A rush of fear races through me. "I'll try."

"Remember, if you get a result you're not happy with, we still have the deposit you froze after your diagnosis."

"I know. But even that's not guaranteed, Doc." Shaking my head, I lock my eyes on his. "I just need to know everything. I need to know what options I have, because this woman deserves the truth. But I want to know just exactly what that is."

He nods. "I get it. Given your history, I understand your concerns. We will get you some answers. I promise."

"Hey, gorgeous." I walk through the front door of Noelle's house on Friday night, eager to see her after a few days apart. I just came from the doctor's office where I made my first deposit and stopped to pick up dinner on my way here. The aroma of chicken tacos from a little hole-in-the-wall restaurant I love fills the house the second I step inside.

"Hey," she replies with a loud sigh.

"Everything all right?"

She shuts the door behind me and then kisses me chastely. "Yeah, it's just been a busy week. I'm exhausted."

I hold up the bag in my hand. "Well, I brought dinner, so there's one thing off your plate. What else do you need me to do?" I set the food down on her kitchen counter and scan the house. A pile of laundry sits on the chair in the corner, Scarlett is tossing toys out of her toy box in the living room while *Minions* is playing on the television, and there's a sink full of dirty dishes.

Her eyes dance around the house as well. "I . . . I don't even know where to begin." She places a palm on her forehead. "My mind is swimming. Earlier, Penelope asked me what I want to do for my birthday in four weeks." She lifts her head, and her eyes finally connect with mine. "I didn't even realize my birthday was coming up, Grant. My own birthday!"

"Hey, it's okay." I pull her into me, kissing the top of her head. "You have a lot on your plate."

"I do. Work is insane right now. I have a book I need to finish reading by Monday, and I'm not sure I'll be able to finish it in time. My house is a wreck, and I think . . ." Her lip trembles, and her eyes brim with tears. "I think I'm going to stop nursing Scarlett, and it's hitting me harder than I thought it would."

Aw, that's probably the catalyst for all of this.

Lifting her chin so she is forced to look at me, I say, "You are human, sweetheart, so stop beating yourself up. Scarlett will be fine. I know the idea of not nursing is worse for you right now, but if you feel it's time, listen to that."

"I'm ready to have my body back, too, but that doesn't make it any easier for me."

"It's the mom guilt," I say on a chuckle. "My sister-in-law talks about it all the time."

She groans. "It's the worst."

"Other than that, all of the other things can wait, or I can help you with the house. And as far as your birthday is concerned, what if you and I did something together?"

"That sounds nice." She wraps her arms around my neck but rests her head on my chest, taking a few deep breaths.

"It does." Running my hands down her back, I breathe her in as that overwhelming need to make her smile takes over. All I want is to be here for this woman. I've never felt that before, and it's as exhilarating as it is terrifying. "Now, why don't you get in the shower? I'll watch Scarlett and take care of a few things, and then we can sit down and eat together."

A loud crash comes from the living room, startling us both, and Noelle takes off in that direction. Luckily, it was just the sound of a toy being thrown at the TV stand by the little girl in question, but Noelle scoops her up and holds her to her chest. "See? I can't even turn my head for two minutes because she can hurt herself or worse."

"I know. Once babies start moving, you can give up on trying to multitask. But that's what you have me for." Intercepting Scarlett, I hold her on my hip. "Now, go relax. Take a bath if you want with your Kindle. Just don't come out for an hour."

"An hour?" she practically shrieks. "But Grant—"

I press a finger to her lips to quiet her. "Go, or I'll punish you later."

Her eyes instantly twinkle, and a grin appears on her lips. "Well, now I might want to disobey you just to find out what my punishment may be."

Chuckling, I remove my finger and then press a kiss to her lips. "There will be pleasure either way for you tonight, I assure you."

"Thank you," she says softly before kissing Scarlett on the cheek and then sashaying down the hallway, giving me one hell of a view as she does. "I won't be long."

"Take your time. I'd better not see you for an hour!" I call after her. Turning to the munchkin in my arms, I bop her on the nose. "You've got to be a good girl for Mommy. No throwing toys, you hear me?" Scarlett smacks my chest with her hand and then leans her head on my shoulder. "Aw, I missed you, too, little girl." A wave of endearment and a protective instinct runs through me. I know it was this little girl I fell head over heels for first, but her mom is also carving an imprint on my heart, and I feel as if letting them in has opened this side of me I've kept locked away for so many years.

That's why I went to my doctor. Why I'm following through with my tests.

Because every moment with these girls shows me a future I thought I'd never have, but now it's right in my hands, and I don't want to fuck it up. If anything, the thought is helping me latch on to the tiny sliver of hope that I may have found the person I'm meant to be with, and her daughter feels more like mine every time I hold her.

But does that mean I'm not destined to have a child of my own?

For the longest time, I just assumed it would never happen. But now that I found Noelle, I want to know: Is there still a possibility? Or will I have to let down yet another woman? And will she stay when she knows?

Shaking off that thought until my test results come in, I grab Scarlett's carrier, strap her to my chest, and get started on the dishes, trying to focus on what I can control in this very moment—and that's making Noelle's life easier. Part of me wants to go check on her, but part of me also doesn't want to disturb her. She needs to relax, so I'm going to do everything in my power to help her do that.

"Hey."

I peer up at Noelle standing before me, freshly bathed and in a matching pajama set of soft black cotton. She looks fucking beautiful—her face clear of makeup, her skin glowing and soft—and much more at ease than she was earlier.

I place my finger over my lips, though, before I startle the baby in my arms as I sit on the couch with my feet up. "Shh. She just passed out."

"Thank you for bringing me dinner." While Noelle was in the tub, I put her dinner on a tray and delivered it to her to eat when she was done in the bath.

"You're welcome."

Noelle stares down at her daughter adoringly. "Did you give her a bottle?"

I hold up the empty one next to me. "Yup. She drank it all like a champ."

Her face turns to the television where one of the minion movies is playing. It was the same one that was already playing before. I can't remember which one it is, but I'm pretty sure I've watched all of them with my nephews. "And you put on the movie?"

"The girl is obsessed with the minions, right? I mean, I just hit play again once it ended. Is that okay?"

"It is, I just . . ." She clutches her hands over her chest, tears filling her eyes.

Carefully, I stand from the couch, holding Scarlett in my arms as she grows even heavier. "Let me put her down—then we can talk."

Noelle nods and then follows me down the hallway to Scarlett's nursery. Gently, I lay her down in her crib, and Noelle situates her perfectly. She presses a gentle kiss to her forehead, and then we leave, closing the door softly behind us. I grab her hand and lead her to her room, which is just two doors away, also closing us in with a gentle press of her door.

"Grant, you are . . . you make me . . ."

Before she can say anymore, I wrap my arms around her and bring my lips to hers, reciprocating the feelings I know she's trying to articulate. I feel like she's about to crumble and all I want to do is hold her up, be her rock—and I haven't wanted to do that for someone in a long time.

We stand there, getting lost in our physical connection before finally parting.

"Thank you. I just—I can't thank you enough. It's like you showed up and gave me exactly what I needed at that moment."

"I'm glad I could, Noelle. I want to be there for you and Scarlett in any way I can."

She shakes her head. "I'm just not used to it. I accepted a long time ago, when I decided to have my daughter, that I would be doing this alone—and it's so hard. So much more difficult than I thought it would be. But having you around has opened my eyes to what this would have been like with a partner, and I . . . I'm so grateful for you. I just want you to know that."

"Aw, babe. I'm grateful for you, too. Fuck, Noelle, you've been like a night light guiding me in the dark. I crave you and your company. I love spending time with you and Scarlett. And

I want to help you. I know you can do everything on your own, but you don't have to anymore. I'm here."

One more kiss, and then she leads me to the bed, the covers already turned down. I tear off my shirt, chuck my pants, and get comfortable next to her in nothing but my briefs. With a sigh, she says, "All I keep thinking about lately is how tired I am and wondering how people manage this with more than one kid. I can't imagine."

My heart rate instantly picks up. "Well, good thing you only have the one right now, huh?"

She chuckles and bobs her head up and down. "Yeah. I mean, I would like another someday, but the thought is just exhausting at this point."

Lying down next to her so we're facing each other, I broach a subject I've been avoiding. "What if you never have another one? Would you be okay with that?"

Her brow furrows. "Yes. There are a lot of people in the world who never have children but want them. I consider myself lucky in that respect, but I also envisioned myself with at least two kids and a family." Then she huffs out a laugh. "Although, look how that turned out. Nothing in my life has gone according to plan." She runs her fingers through my chest hair. "I made a list when I was younger, you know?"

"Seems like something you'd do."

She chuckles again. "Yeah. I thought that by writing down my hopes and dreams, I would manifest them somehow. I think I still have that list somewhere, actually. But anyway, I know now that I was naïve. It took a long time for me to realize that my life was really in my own hands, but when I did, I felt like I finally started living. And now, even though I'm so exhausted I can barely keep my eyes open, I wouldn't trade where I'm at for anything." She reaches up to smooth my hair from my forehead. "Especially this recent development of having you in my life." Her lips find mine, and my body awakens.

"I know the feeling."

"I know I already said it, but thank you again for what you did for me tonight."

"All I did was fold laundry, wash dishes, and hold the most adorable baby girl in the world."

"It may seem trivial to you, but to me, those were *huge* things, monumental things—the type of things that matter to a woman and mother. You saw I was struggling and stepped in. I—I've never had someone do that for me before besides my friends."

"I want to be here for you in that way." Reaching down, I gently run my finger through her slit covered by her pajama shorts. "But I want to be here in this way, too."

"I want that as well."

Scooting closer to her, something hard digs into my side. "Crap. What is this?"

She reaches under me and extracts a small tablet. "Oh, that's my Kindle. Sorry."

"Did you finish your book?"

"No. I got close, though. Unfortunately, I had to stop at a sex scene, because I didn't want to get myself all worked up in the bath."

I press the button to awaken the screen. "Well, why don't we read it together?"

She stares at me, perplexed. "You want to read my book with me?"

"Why not? I feel like doing so gives me a little glimpse into what you like." I waggle my eyebrows at her.

"Fictional kinks are not necessarily real-life kinks, Grant. What may sound hot in our imagination does not necessarily translate with a partner, although this story is making me question if I truly want to try this."

"That's fine, but now you have me intrigued. What were you reading, you dirty girl?"

She giggles. "It's the first book in a new series. The hot, broody boss falls for his assistant, but he has rough tastes, and they've been experimenting to find out if those are her tastes, too."

"Damn." I reach down and adjust myself before pulling the Kindle up above our heads as we both lay on our backs. "This is where you left off then?"

"Yup. Do you want to read or me?"

"Whatever you want."

"You can read. I think I might like the scene even more in your voice," she murmurs as her lips find my neck. My skin pebbles from her touch.

Clearing my throat, I begin reading the scene in the boss's office. He takes his tie from around his neck and ties it over the woman's eyes, taking away her sense of sight. Then he pushes up her skirt so all of her is exposed to him. And Jesus, the description is so vivid and full of the emotion the man is feeling, I can tell why women enjoy this.

He begins to play with her pussy, blowing cold air on her clit and then slapping it.

"Slapping the clit, huh? Interesting."

Noelle giggles beside me as she rubs her thighs together. "Yeah . . ."

"Is that what you've never done?"

"Uh-huh."

"What about the blindfold?"

"Never done that, either."

"Fuck, Noelle." I reach down and adjust the dick that is trying to escape my briefs. "Do you want me to keep going?"

"Yes."

I continue reading out loud as the words describe how the man touches her with his mouth, tongue, and fingers. He bites the inside of her thighs, leaving marks, smacks her ass when she's on all fours in front of him, and pinches her clit, leading her to orgasm. And right as I finish reading her release, Noelle reaches over and strokes my cock through my underwear.

"Grant . . ."

I chuck her Kindle to the side and scoop her up in my arms, kissing her with a passion that feels like it's trying to escape my body. "Do you want to experience that?" I ask against her lips in between diving my tongue into her mouth and coming up for air.

"Yes, please."

"Fuck, I want to do all of that to you and then some." She

moans in approval. "Hold on." With one more quick kiss, I leap from the bed and head to her closet to find something to use as a blindfold. A satin strap catches my eye, so I pull it from a hanger and walk back out to Noelle, who's trembling with anticipation on the bed. "This will work."

"That's a belt from one of my blouses."

"Is that okay?"

She nods. "Yes."

"Then sit up for me, beautiful." She does as I ask so I can tie the sash around her eyes, the dark-blue color of the fabric likely helping block out the light. "Can you see anything?"

"No. This is weird," she laughs.

"It's about to feel good. Now, lie back." Following my orders again, Noelle slowly descends until she's flat on the bed. "Do you trust me?"

"Yes," she replies with no hesitation, and the word makes me want to beat my fists against my chest like a caveman.

I start by teasing her, trailing my fingers up and down her arms, watching her skin break out in goosebumps that I then decide to trace with my tongue. As I move my mouth over her exposed skin, my hands reach down and start to remove her shorts, pulling them down her legs. Her skin smells like strawberries and cream, which must be her lotion, because I catch this scent every time I'm around her and it makes me hungry for dessert and Noelle.

But then I smell her pussy, too, her arousal that's calling to me when I look down and see the wet spot against her panties. Trailing my finger over the dampness, she jolts. "Fuck,

Noelle. You're soaked. Does this happen every time you read?"

"Yes."

"So you just walk around turned on?"

"Sometimes, but most of the time, I'm home, so I take care of myself and relieve the pressure."

"Jesus, that's hot."

"But tonight, it was so much better because your voice read the words to me. I swear, I'm never this soaked."

"You're about to be even wetter." Nibbling on the inside of her thigh, I lick the sensitive skin and press my lips everywhere around where she wants me, but I don't want to touch just yet.

"Grant, please."

"Patience, baby. You trust me, remember?"

"I'm so horny. I need to come."

"And you will, multiple times."

"Oh God, please . . ."

I drag my nose up her slit, hooking my thumbs in the waist of her underwear and slowly dragging them down, revealing her pussy to me that's been neatly trimmed. And fuck, do I love that she's not completely bare down there. There's something about a little pubic hair that reminds a man he's with a woman, and Noelle is the sexiest woman I've been with, without a doubt.

Running my finger through her now, I groan as I find her slick and ready, even wetter than I could tell through her underwear.

"Grant . . ."

I use my thumbs to part her lips, opening her up so I can blow all over her clit as was described in the book. I can see her clit throb as I alternate between cold breaths and short flicks of my tongue.

Noelle is panting, writhing, and pressing her hips up to meet my mouth, begging for more with her body. But there's one other thing I need to try to make the fantasy come to life. As she rears up again, I slap her pussy, shocking her for a moment before she moans. "Oh God . . ."

"You like that?"

"Yes. It stung, but it felt so good. God, Grant, I'm so close."

"I know, baby. I'll give you what you want soon." Dropping my mouth back to her pussy, I work her up more, spearing her with my tongue, circling her clit, sucking on the nub and then blowing air on it again, only to end with a smack that has her crying out. I bite the inside of her thigh, marking her even though I already know in my gut this woman is mine. And as that word registers in my brain, I know I've traveled down a path I have no desire to go back up.

I dive in with purpose now, flicking her clit and sliding two fingers inside of her, working her up and up, curling inside to reach that magical spot, and without much more effort, she explodes, screaming and squirting all over my fingers, which is one of the sexiest things I've ever seen. The sight of this woman coming undone as I continue to play with her clit and fuck her with my fingers is bringing me to the brink of my own orgasm, but I hold off as best I can. I don't want to jeopardize my test results, but I can't *not* touch this woman for a week. That's a ridiculous notion that I refuse to fight.

As Noelle comes down from her orgasm, I flip her over on all fours and go back to attacking her core with my mouth.

"Oh my God, Grant!"

"Shh, don't wake up the baby."

"I can't take anymore."

Pressing two fingers back into her soaked pussy, I groan. "Yes, you can." I smack her ass playfully, which grants me a moan of approval. "You like that, don't you?"

"Oh God, yes. I like everything you do to me."

"Fuck, that's what I like to hear."

She turns her head over her shoulder to look back at me. "Please, fuck me, Grant. I need it. I need you."

Groaning in frustration, I shake my head. "Not tonight, Noelle. Tonight is about your pleasure, not mine."

"Why?"

"Because you need it, and I want to please you, baby. I want to see you squirt all over my hand and mouth again. I want you so overcome with pleasure that you never forget who's giving it to you."

She sucks in a breath. "I never will forget, Grant. No one has ever made me feel like this."

Maintaining the strokes of my fingers, I put my mouth back on her and bring her over the edge two more times before she finally collapses on the bed. While practically asleep, I take a warm washcloth and clean her up before pulling the covers over us.

For a minute, I wonder if she's conscious. But then soft snores fill the room, and I know I literally made her pass out from pleasure. Despite my dick being painfully hard, I fall asleep with a smile on my face, knowing that even if I couldn't come with her, at least she came long and hard enough for the both of us.

Chapter 13

Noelle

With tears in my eyes, I stare down at my daughter nursing for the very last time. After talking with Grant last night, I knew in my heart that this part of parenting was over. Even now, as I lock on to the blue eyes of my baby, she's playing with my nipple, sucking for a few seconds at a time before releasing me and smiling up at me.

I know this transition will be harder on me than her, but honestly, I'm ready to have my body back, especially now that there's a handsome man in my bed some nights.

"I love you, baby girl," I whisper, trailing my finger down the side of her face. "Momma has loved feeding you like this, but you're growing up." She gives me a high-pitched squeal in response. Through a giggle, I say, "Yeah. Time is moving too fast and so slow all at the same time." I reach down to the floor by the rocker, pick up the bottle I made and took in here with me, and hand it to her. The eagerness in which she shoves the bottle into her mouth and closes her eyes tells me I'm making the right decision, even though my heart is breaking and simultaneously jumping for joy at this very second.

I continue to rock her as her eyes grow heavy and she fights sleep, and I remind myself that motherhood is full of ups and downs, and this phase is one I won't soon forget.

"Good morning," Amelia greets me as I hand her Scarlett so I can situate her high chair. Scarlett has the stuffed elephant Grant bought her from the zoo in one arm and a stuffed minion in the other. I wrestle them from her grip and plant them in the high chair beside her after I get her in the seat.

"Hey."

"Everything all right?"

With a heavy sigh, I reply, "Yeah. I just . . . I nursed Scarlett for the last time last night, and I'm still a little up in my feelings about it."

"Is that why your breasts look lumpy?" Penelope asks, drawing my eyes down to my shirt.

"Those are cabbage leaves."

Her face grows even more confused. "I'm sorry, did you just say *cabbage leaves*? As in, you are walking around with cabbage leaves in your bra?"

"Yes, I did. They help dry up my milk. One of the women at work told me about it. She said to give it a couple of days, and I'll be as dry as the Sahara Desert."

Charlotte pipes up. "Just another thing to look forward to, I guess." She rubs her very pregnant belly, wincing a bit. "Like these damn Braxton Hicks contractions. I swear, I don't know which is worse: period cramps or these."

"I'm never having kids," Penelope mutters under her breath as I take my seat and grab some snacks from my diaper bag for Scarlett, who's already slapping the high chair in demand of food. "I think I'm going to draw the line at vegetables in my bra, thank you very much."

"You say that now, but I'm telling you—every pain and weird symptom is totally worth it." Leaning down to kiss the top of Scarlett's head, I place a few rice puffs in front of her, and her chubby hands reach for them instantly.

"That's why babies are so freaking cute, huh? To hypnotize you after the traumatic experience that is childbirth in the hopes that you'll decide to go through it again? That has to be the only explanation why women are willing to do that more than once."

Huffing out a laugh, I nod. "I have to say I agree."

Frankie comes by at that moment, delivering our champagne, orange juice, and menus. "How are we doing today, ladies?"

"Great, Frankie. How about you?" Amelia replies.

"Counting my blessings, Amelia, as always. Are you all ready to order?"

Amelia looks around the table, and we all nod. "Yup."

We rattle off our choices to Frankie, and then he slips away just as quickly as he came. Penelope starts filling three glasses with champagne.

"God, I can't wait until I can drink again," Charlotte whines.

"I remember that feeling. And now that I'm done nursing, I can really enjoy it." Clinking my glass with Amelia's and Penelope's, I take a large gulp before setting it down. "So girls, how's it going?"

Amelia speaks first. "Well, now that school is back in session for Oliver and the soccer season has started, life is back to craziness. Ethan finally agreed to take on fewer clients through the end of the year since he burned himself out last year during this time by trying to do it all."

"You got him to listen to you, huh?" Penelope smirks at her.

"Yes. I might have also reminded him that our anniversary is coming up, and that's when we agreed to start trying for a baby, so he's going to need his energy for that." Amelia smiles. "It was a pretty easy conversation after I explained that rationale."

Charlotte laughs. "I bet. I'm so excited you guys are going to try for kids. I want our children to be close together." She turns to Penelope. "Not that I'm trying to pressure you." She winks. "But did you and Maddox talk any more about kids?"

"We did. And we agreed to wait at least a year. The season just started anyway, so we're both crazy busy. But we did talk, and he finally listened to my concerns, so we're in agreement now."

"Good. I'm glad you guys worked through that," Amelia adds, turning to our pregnant friend now. "How's maternity leave going, Char?"

Charlotte is due in less than three weeks, so she's finally off work. I suggested she take time off before the baby arrives, even though she wanted to work up until she delivers. But having a moment of peace before her entire life changes is something I strongly advised her to do, and I'm glad she listened.

"Well, Damien calls me eighty times a day to check up on me, so that's fun. He's a little nervous ball of energy right now, but I know he's just anxious about the birth. Other than that, there's only so much cleaning and organizing I can do. I completely understand the term 'nesting' now." We all laugh. "I'm just really ready to meet her and to be able to breathe normally again and to not have to pee every five minutes."

"The end is the worst. Don't worry, she'll be here soon enough, and then you'll just complain about sleep deprivation and postpartum sweats."

"Again, you're not making pregnancy sound too appealing, ladies," Penelope mutters before taking a drink of her mimosa.

"Noelle? I believe that leaves you to catch up with," Amelia declares. "How are things going with Grant?"

My lips take on a mind of their own as I smile and don't even try to fight it. "Good. *Really* good."

"Ladies, you should have seen her face when she picked up

Scarlett after their overnight date. I think the man is redefining the phrase 'good dick' for Noelle," Penelope teases.

"Um, yes, he is. And I am happy to report, I didn't realize it could be this good."

"It is with the right person," Amelia explains. "But other than the physical, how is everything else? How is he treating you? Have you guys talked about the future yet or where this is headed?"

Frankie arrives with our food at that moment, putting a pause on the conversation. I refill Scarlett's tray with snacks, and then we all dig into our meals.

"He wants to introduce me to his family."

Saturday morning, before he left my house, he told me that he wants to take that next step. He wants me to meet his mom, stepdad, brother and sister-in-law, and their kids. I was surprised in the moment but otherwise elated that he felt so strongly about the idea. Of course I agreed, and he told me he would work on scheduling a time and place.

"That's a big step," Charlotte says around a mouthful of her omelet.

"I know. But you guys, I'm falling for him, hard. I feel like it's really fast, but I can't help it."

Charlotte lets out a little noise that can only be described as a squeal. "Oh my God!"

"You okay over there?" Penelope asks her.

"Yes!" She wipes her mouth with her napkin before leaning forward in her seat. "I'm telling you girls, when he picked her up for their date, the one we watched Scarlett for, I saw fireworks between them. He looked at her as if the world only spun when she was near."

"You saw that from him that night?" I ask on a whisper.

"Oh, yeah. And I didn't want to say anything because I didn't want to jinx it, but even Damien mentioned it."

Sighing, I lean back in my chair. "I feel it, too. He's so thoughtful, attentive, and sexy. My God, the man is so freaking hot." The girls laugh as I jokingly fan my face. "And he listens, cares, and genuinely shows up when I need him. I was so exhausted this week between work and just life in general. I felt like I was on the verge of tears all day, but then he came to my house Friday night with dinner for me, demanded I take a bath so I could relax and read my book that I had to have finished before Monday, folded my laundry that was sitting on the couch, washed dishes left in my sink, and watched a movie with Scarlett before putting her to sleep."

"Damn. Are you sure he's not really Superman and that whole pilot thing is a cover?" Penelope jokes.

Amelia rests her hand on mine, drawing my attention to her. "He's invested in you, Noelle. Those actions are ones of someone who deeply cares for another person. He sounds like an incredible partner."

"He really is. And Scarlett just adores him. Every time he holds her, she's like putty in his hands. She smiles so big when she sees him for the first time, and he's a natural with her. I mean, she carries this elephant around with her everywhere we go, and he's the one who got it for her. There's obviously adoration there."

"See? Your daughter has good taste in men. You should be proud." Penelope winks.

I laugh. "Yeah, I guess. But after he did all of those things for me, he also read a spicy part of my romance novel out loud to me when we were alone, reenacted part of it, and then made me come until I passed out."

"Praise the Lord! He's a keeper then!" Penelope declares.

"He is, it's just . . ." The nagging fragment of doubt in the back of my mind runs right up to the edge of letting myself be happy and questioning reality, even though I've been fighting it for the past week.

"What?" Amelia asks. "You know you can tell us anything, Noelle."

Blowing out a breath, I say what's on my mind to my three best friends. "I guess I just feel like he's perfect, like *too* perfect. There has to be something wrong with him or something I'm missing. I don't want to be one of those women who misses the red flags that are waving right in front of my face, but part of me isn't sure there are any, and that's even more terrifying."

"Why?"

"Because where has he been?" I toss my hands up in the air, letting the frustration out. "Why on earth didn't I meet him five years ago? Why all of a sudden did he just pop up out of nowhere and put most of my book boyfriends to shame? And why can't I just let myself be happy that I found this man *now* instead of wondering if I'm just setting myself and my daughter up for heartbreak?"

Amelia places a hand on my shoulder as I drop my arms down. "Noelle, just breathe." I take a deep breath and blow it out, staring into her honey-colored eyes. "I know you're scared. It's fear that's running your mind right now, but I want to ask you this: Why can't you just accept that you met him *now*, he loves your daughter, and that timing truly is everything?"

Dropping my voice down to almost a whisper, I say, "Because what if he's not the one, either? Every man I've dated up until now has disappointed me in one way or another." I shake my head, fighting off tears. "I want the white picket fence. It's all I've ever wanted, but I guess I just never thought I'd get it like this."

Amelia softens her voice and tilts her head at me. "What if the fence is brown? Or green and vinyl? Or chain link?" She shrugs. "What if it's unique and different but is exactly what you need, Noelle? Not every fence looks the same, but they all serve a purpose."

"God, I love when she slips into therapist mode," Penelope snickers as she sips her mimosa.

Amelia keeps her eyes on me, holding my hand now. "You need to allow yourself to feel your fear but not let it run your mind. And if you're really feeling as though something is off, just ask him. If he's hiding something, that will be the perfect time to tell you. Has he talked about his past at all? Or why he's still single?"

"He did mention that he dated someone for a long time, but he saw her true colors and realized she wasn't who he thought she was."

Amelia nods. "Okay, so he's been hurt and disappointed. So maybe he's being cautious with his feelings, too. By the way he's behaving, I'd say he's feeling strongly for you as well, but perhaps he's battling his own fear. And the only way for you to find that out is if you talk to him about it."

I sigh. "You're right."

"I know. It's a gift." She winks at me.

"But also remember that even if this doesn't work out, you have us and Scarlett, and everything will be okay."

Squeezing her hand, I lean in to hug her. "Thank you. This is just very overwhelming for me right now."

"I understand, but I'd hate to see you sabotage a good thing because you're afraid. And secondly, when do we get to meet him? If you're meeting his family, we should get to meet him, too."

Penelope raises her glass in the air. "I second that."

Charlotte sits there, smiling smugly. "I already got to meet him."

"Yeah, but not really," Penelope argues. "It was only for a few minutes."

"Still. I saw the sparks, remember?"

"Okay, enough," I chime in before they claw each other's eyes out. "I'll talk to him about it, and we will set up a time for you all to interrogate him."

Penelope rubs her hands together. "I can't fucking wait."

Chapter 14

Noelle

"Go, Oliver! Run!" Amelia screams as Oliver takes the ball on a breakaway to the goal, trying to score in this tied game with only ten minutes left.

I never was a nail-biter before this, but I think watching a kid's soccer game might turn me into one. "I never thought you'd be *that* parent at the soccer field," I say to her as she jumps up and down, still shouting as Oliver passes the ball to another player on his team.

"What parent?"

"The one who yells. You're usually so levelheaded and calm."

Ethan comes up to my side. "I was shocked, too, but I can't deny, it's kind of hot."

"Shoot! Shoot the ball!" Amelia screams as the kid sends the ball flying past the goalie and into the net. "Yes!!!"

"Good job, boys!" Ethan claps beside me as Amelia takes a sip of her water and then turns to us.

"What were you saying? Sorry, I wasn't listening." Brushing the wild blonde curls away from her face that fell out of her ponytail, probably from all the jumping, she stares at me and her husband.

"Never mind." The corner of my mouth tips up as I watch my friend go right back to cheering on her son.

"She's in her zone. Once the game is over, she'll be back to normal." Ethan stares after her.

"Let's hope."

"Thanks again for coming out to cheer on Oliver. He loves it when you girls show up." Ethan wraps his arm around my shoulder.

"Well, he's one of my nephews as far as I'm concerned, so of course I'll be here to support him." Scarlett lets out a shriek, one that's new this week, although on second thought, she might have picked it up from Amelia after watching her. "Say, 'Go, Oliver, go!'" I tell her, rubbing her hair as she sits in the stroller next to me, watching the game in front of her while eating her stuffed elephant.

"It seems like a lifetime ago when Oliver was that small."

"I can imagine."

Staring at Scarlett longingly, he says, "I can't wait to do that again with Amelia this time. It's going to be so different." Ethan's first wife was not interested in motherhood. They got pregnant young, and ultimately, Monica realized she didn't want to be a parent, leaving Ethan and Oliver when he was just two.

"I'm excited for you both." As I say the words, my mind drifts to an image of Grant in the hospital with me, having a baby of our own. I try to push it aside, but the swell of hope that builds in my chest makes it very hard.

Suddenly, I know exactly what Ethan must be feeling. It's different to experience something as beautiful as having a child in life with someone who's as invested in the moment as you. And after the conversation at brunch last week with the girls, I'm allowing myself to hope and plan a future with Grant just a little bit more.

In fact, I'm supposed to meet his family tonight. We spoke briefly last night but then agreed he would pick me up tonight and drive us over to his mother's house. I'm nervous but also really eager to learn more about him, see him with family in his element. And I hope it will help alleviate some of the apprehension I've been having about my feelings for him.

"Yes! Way to go, boys!" Amelia shouts as the referee blows the whistle, ending the game.

"I'd better go over there," Ethan says to me, squeezing my shoulder. "Thanks again for being here."

"Anytime." I lean down to check on Scarlett, but when I pop my head back up, I have to do a double take at the image I'm seeing.

On the field in front of ours is Grant, standing next to a woman with his arm around her shoulder, much like Ethan was just embracing me. He leans over, presses a kiss to her temple, and begins clapping his hands as my stomach drops. Two little boys who have to be about Oliver's age run up to him, intercepting his high fives and listening to him speak.

This is it, huh? This is what he's been hiding. A family? The man has a family of his own?

Oh my God! What if he's married? What if I've been dating a married man this entire time?

How on earth do you keep something like this a secret? An entirely different life? I've always wondered how women will say they found out their husband had another family and that they had no idea. And now I think I might be one of them. I'm questioning my sanity at this very moment.

Suddenly, I feel like I'm about to throw up.

"What's going on?" Penelope and Charlotte walk up to us from their trip to the bathroom and apparently the snack bar as Charlotte rips off a piece of her churro with her teeth.

"Um, well . . ."

Penelope stands in front of me, blocking my view of Grant. "Noelle, you're practically white as a ghost. Are you okay?"

"I just saw Grant."

She twists around. "Where?" Pointing, I guide her eyes in his direction. "Standing next to the two boys and their parents?"

"Wait. What?"

Penelope nods and then points at him again. "The man standing next to him—who honestly looks just like Grant but shorter—is kissing his wife. Must be his brother."

Relief floods through my veins, and my body sags. "Oh my God, it's his *brother*. And those must be his nephews." His *nephews*. Oh my God, I can't believe I just assumed—

Charlotte places her hand on my shoulder. "Did you just think . . . ?"

"I did." I nod, completely embarrassed but still so relieved. "My mind went to the worst possible scenario."

"Noelle, honey. If any man was dumb enough to cheat on you, you know we'd all kick his ass, right?" Penelope asks.

I huff out a laugh. "Yes."

"Okay, but do you honestly think Grant would do that?"

"No. It's just—"

"That fear again," Amelia says, coming up to my other side, holding her water bottle. "Have you talked to him about it yet?"

"No, because I'm meeting his family tonight and thought that maybe after I'd feel better."

"I understand your reasoning, but look at what just happened because you're scared."

"I know." At that moment, Grant spins around as if he's looking for something, and then his eyes land on me. And his smile—it could light up this entire soccer field in the dark. That smile makes my worry dissipate, too.

"Um, sorry, but a man who smiles like that at you is *not* cheating on you." Charlotte gleams with excitement.

"I second that," Penelope interjects. "But hey! At least now we can meet him," she says just as Grant starts crossing the field Oliver's team was just playing on, heading straight toward us.

Scarlett screams when she sees him, kicking in her chair, beginning to fuss as he gets closer. Seems I'm not the only one thrilled about him coming over here. But I'm also anxious. Him meeting the girls is a big step but one I know it's time for.

"Okay, okay," I say to my daughter as I unbuckle her and hoist her to my hip. "Calm down. He's almost here."

Just a few seconds later, Grant appears right in front of us, and I can only imagine what he sees—four women and a baby staring up at him as he towers over us.

"He's tall," Penelope says as if he can't hear her. "Taller than Maddox, for sure. And built. You did good, Noelle."

Grant laughs and then extends his hand toward her. "You must be Penelope. Nice to meet you."

"Likewise."

"I'm a big fan of your husband."

"I like you even more now."

He smiles at her before landing his eyes on mine. "Hey, sweetheart."

"Hi. Fancy seeing you here."

"My nephew, Michael, had a game, and Andrew has one next. I didn't know you'd be here, otherwise I would have come over to say hello sooner. But I felt like someone was watching me, and then there you were."

"Here I am." Scarlett tries to launch herself out of my arms, and luckily Grant notices and intercepts her, tossing her into the air as she giggles and comes back down to his chest.

"Hello, sweet girl." He kisses her cheek and nuzzles her nose. "I missed you, too."

"Oh my God," Charlotte croons beside me. "This is just too sweet." She begins to fan her face, fighting back tears. "I'm too pregnant to handle this right now."

"I told you she adores him." We all stare as Grant speaks to my daughter, asking her all kinds of questions, and I swear, I can hear all of the ovaries in the vicinity squeal with approval.

"I'm Amelia," my curly blonde-haired friend interjects, introducing herself since I'm still trying to wrap my head around Grant being here in front of me, meeting my friends like this.

"It's so great to meet you." He shakes her hand then turns to Charlotte. "Good to see you again, Charlotte."

But before she can reply, Penelope steps forward. "So what are your intentions with our Noelle?" She goes straight for the jugular with that question, crossing her arms over her chest and tapping her foot on the ground.

I smack her arm. "Penelope!"

Grant laughs. "It's okay, babe. I got it." Turning to Penelope, he adjusts Scarlett on his hip. "I adore her and this little girl right here." He bops Scarlett on the nose. "I'm all in, and the more time I spend with them, the more I see a future with them. Noelle has taken me by surprise, but she's enriched my life in a way I didn't know I was missing, and I care for her deeply." He reaches out to cup my jaw, smoothing his thumb over my skin while my heart grows wings and tries to fly out of my chest. "How's that for an answer?" he asks, turning back to Penelope now.

My knees threaten to buckle, and I bite my lip to keep from smiling like a fool in love.

"Still doubting him?" Amelia whispers in my ear. But I don't answer. I can't. I'm too busy handing over my heart to him without him knowing it.

"Eh. It'll do," Penelope replies mockingly as Grant drops his hand from my face, pulling me into his embrace this time and kissing the top of my head reassuringly. "Just know that if you hurt her, you'll be answering to us and Maddox. You may be a fan, but I can still ask him to kick your ass."

Grant laughs, shaking his head at Penelope. "Noted. I promise, I never intend to hurt these girls." He stares down at me again. "I kinda like them."

"We kinda like you, too." I press up on my toes to give him a kiss, a kiss I soak in even though I can hear my friends snicker behind us. But the next voice I hear startles me from our kiss.

"Grant? Honey, the next game is about to start."

And there goes my stomach dropping again, but this time for a very different reason.

Grant releases me and turns to face the woman who just about gave me a heart attack. "Be right there, Mom."

"That's . . . that's your mom?" I ask, almost out of breath.

"Yeah." He steps aside, and that's when our eyes connect.

"Noelle?" Regina asks, freezing in her steps as she gets closer to us.

"Regina?"

Grant shifts his head back and forth between us. "You two know each other?"

"Noelle? This is the man you've been seeing?"

"Yes."

"Oh my God," she whispers, smiling but shaking her head.

"Noelle, what's going on?" Grant asks me, but my eyes are still trained on Regina—my client who has been trying to set me up with her son for years, the same son who I'm currently dating and falling in love with.

And there is the shoe that I felt was waiting to drop, one I did not see coming at all.

"**H**oly crap." I release Regina from our hug and stare down at her. She's a tiny little thing, something I never paid much attention to until now, especially as I look back at her son who towers over both of us.

"I must say, I was not expecting this." She turns to her son. "Noelle is my agent."

Grant's eyes go wide. "Holy shit."

"I don't really discuss my books with my boys," Regina says, tucking a strand of hair behind her ear. "So it's not Grant's fault that he didn't put two and two together. But I have to say, I'm extremely pleased with this turn of events."

I stand there laughing and then realize the girls are still standing behind me. Turning to them, I say, "Girls, this is

Regina. She is one of my clients and writes under the pen name R. Nelson."

Amelia's eyes go wide. "Oh my God! I love your books!"

Regina blushes. "Thank you."

"I have so many questions," Grant mutters, tossing his eyes between me and his mother. His mom. Regina is *his mom*.

Regina lays a hand on his shoulder. "I know you do, but we can discuss this more at dinner tonight, right? You still plan on coming by?" she asks me.

"Oh. Yes, we'll be there." My heart is still hammering but for an entirely different reason now. The woman who has been trying to set me up with her son is my client, which is the main reason I never took her up on her offer. But now? Well, I'm afraid I'm in too deep with him to disengage. Yes, we definitely need to talk later.

"Okay. I'm going back to the game. See you there in a minute, Grant?"

"Yeah, Mom. I'll be right there."

"Perfect. Nice to meet you, ladies," Regina says to my friends before turning around and heading back in the direction she came.

Grant runs a hand through his hair. "I'm still trying to process what just happened."

"Uh, you and me both." I look to Scarlett who is happy as a clam in his arms. "We can talk more when you come pick me up, okay?"

"Yeah, okay." He leans down to kiss me, and I let myself

get lost in his lips for a moment before he pulls away. "I'll see you in a few hours."

"See you then." I take Scarlett from him, who fusses when he walks away, and turn back to my friends, who are all standing there with wide eyes.

"Well, that was interesting."

Placing a hand over my heart, I say, "I can't believe it. This has to be a joke."

"It didn't look like anyone was laughing," Charlotte declares.

"You didn't know they were related?" Amelia asks.

"No. Not at all. He never mentioned his mother's name, and I'm guessing he didn't mention mine to her, either. Noelle isn't a particularly common name, so I feel like she would have put the pieces together if he had."

"Well, that's concerning if he didn't tell her about you."

Pursing my lips in thought, I nod. "Yes, but there has to be another explanation. I swear, this entire situation just blindsided me."

Amelia steps forward. "Don't think too much about it. Just go to dinner tonight, meet his family, and talk it all out. But at least now you know that little inkling in the back of your mind was right. There was something you weren't seeing."

I teeter my head back and forth. "Yes, but I don't know if that's a good thing or a bad thing."

Penelope chimes in. "Only one way to find out."

"So did you talk to your mom more during the game?" I ask Grant as we drive to his mother and stepdad's house. He swung by and picked us up, but we decided to just drive my car so we didn't have to move Scarlett's car seat.

"I did. First of all, I swear, babe, I had no idea who you are to her. And my mother thought I said the woman I'm seeing is named Elle, not Noelle. I had to tell her that maybe she needs to get her hearing checked, which she didn't appreciate at all."

"I can imagine."

"Also, you should know that my mother doesn't really discuss her author life with us. I know she writes, but she calls them love stories, so I always just thought she wrote stuff like *The Notebook*, you know?"

I roll my eyes. "Men can be so dense about romance novels. They are not all like *The Notebook*, Grant."

Grant stops at a red light. "I know that now." And then his face opens up, his eyes bugging out as he reaches over and places his hand on my arm. "Oh my God, Noelle. Please tell me that the scene I read to you the other night and then reenacted was not from one of my mother's books."

I can't help it. I burst into laughter. "Oh my God, Grant." Placing my hand over his as the light turns green, he casts his gaze back to the road. "No, it wasn't," I manage to say when I get control of my giggles. "I promise."

"Thank God, because I think that's something that just might scar a man for life."

"You're okay." I rub his arm as we continue to drive. "But I have to ask, are you okay with this development?"

"What do you mean?"

"I mean, I work with your mom. Did you know she's been trying to set us up for years?"

He smirks, shaking his head and sniffing the air. "Doesn't surprise me. She's always trying to set me up."

That admission doesn't make me feel so great. "Oh."

He reads my reaction well. "Hey, not like that. I mean, my mother has always kind of worried about me ending up alone, but she wouldn't just push me to date anyone. She knew if a woman was worth my time. I just never followed through with her request."

His words bring me a little comfort. "Why?"

I watch his face harden as he turns onto a residential street. "I told you. I've been burned and kind of resigned myself to being alone."

I run my fingernails through the hair at his temples. "Then why did you change your mind about me?"

Reaching for my hand, he brings it to his lips and presses them against my skin. "Because I figured fate was stepping in when I ran into you a second time. You and Scarlett made an impression on me that day in the coffee shop, so I knew I'd be a fool to let you go twice. And now look." He turns to me briefly. "Talk about fate again. You work with my mom. She's been trying to set us up for years. I'd say there's a reason we're here together now."

He pulls into the driveway of a renovated home in a quaint neighborhood of Los Angeles that's been here for years, shifting the car into park.

"I sure hope so." Leaning over the console, I let my lips do the talking as my heart catches up. His kiss is gentle, tender, and when he reaches up to cup the side of my face, I melt into it even more.

Knowing that he believes this was all meant to be makes it easier for me to accept. I still need to talk to Regina, but there's no way I'm walking away from Grant now. She and I will just have to find a way to make our professional relationship work.

When our lips release, Grant whiffs the air again and then winces. "Not to ruin the mood, but do you smell that?"

I take a deep inhale and pick up something sour. "It smells . . ."

"Rotten, right?"

Nodding, I peek around the car. "Yes. Naturally, I would blame it on the girl in the car seat who can blow out a diaper better than the rest of them, but that doesn't smell like shit. It smells like . . ."

"Something sour." Grant kills the engine, opens the door, and then rounds the hood, smelling above it. "It's not the engine."

"I should hope so." I follow his lead, stepping from the car and then sniffing the air. "It's not outside."

"Then it has to be inside the car, Noelle." He heads for the rear door on the driver's side, opening it and finding Scarlett passed out in her seat. Carefully, he unlocks it from its base and takes her outside, setting her in the shade provided by a huge mulberry tree in the front yard.

I open the other back door and begin sniffing around, the

smell growing stronger as we search the entire backseat. Grant leans down and starts running his hand under the bench seat, his smile growing as he locates something and pulls it up.

And when he does, I almost lose my lunch.

Curdled formula sloshes in the bottle in his hands, reeking of that sour smell we caught a whiff of earlier that sent us on this discovery mission. And thanks to the scorching California heat, my car has been the victim of a science experiment gone bad.

"Oh my God," I say as I dry heave and Grant does the same, tossing the bottle to the concrete outside the car.

"Blech," he says, holding his stomach as he hunches over, his gags growing more frequent.

The smell is lingering even though we're in the open air now. "Blech," I return his heave with one of my own, trying not to throw up outside of his childhood home. My stomach is lurching every time the smell hits my nose.

"How long has that been in there, Noelle?" he asks, holding a fist over his mouth.

"I have no idea. Scarlett must have tossed it out of her seat one day when she was done, and it rolled under the bench."

Grant holds in his heave this time, but his cheeks puff out as he docs. "Oh my God, that's vile."

"I know. I'm sorry!" Shaking my head, I feel like a failure of a parent right now.

"Hey! Is everything okay?" A man calls out from the front porch, the man I recognize as Grant's brother from the soccer field today.

Grant spins to face him. "Yeah. We just found an old bottle full of formula in the car."

Gavin laughs and then descends the few steps, making his way across the yard to us. "Oh, we've been there. It's the worst."

Taking a deep breath and making sure I'm not going to throw up, I shut the back door to my SUV, round the front of the car, and then hold my hand out to Gavin. "Hi, I'm Noelle."

His smile is just as charming as Grant's. "It's nice to finally meet you, Noelle. I'm Gavin."

"I've heard so much about you. Sorry to be meeting you like this."

He chuckles. "No worries. I know this feeling, only for us, it was a bottle we found in the windowsill of my son's room. He put it up there behind the blinds and curtains. It was probably there for a week before we realized where the smell was coming from."

I stare at the bottle in question on the ground, thinking back to the day I gave her that one with that colored top on it. "This was at least a few days, I'd say. But that smell. I feel like I'm going to have to light my car on fire to get rid of it now."

Gavin grabs his stomach as he laughs. "Just some Febreze and leaving the doors open should help."

Grant picks up Scarlett in her carrier and hustles up the driveway to meet us. "That smell is what I imagine evil must smell like."

"I don't think I can take any more surprises today." I race

over to grab the bottle off the ground, plugging my nose as I do, before taking it to the trash can.

"Well, get ready for a night of answering every question known to mankind," Gavin says, opening the front door. "My wife especially is a nosy one."

"So let me get this straight," Gavin says around a mouthful of food. "Our mom has been writing porn for six years, and we never knew about it?"

Introductions were made between me, Franklin, their step-dad, and Sarah, Gavin's wife, and then they all went gaga over my daughter, especially as she held herself up on the coffee table and tried to escape Grant as he playfully chased her. Scarlett has been all about pulling herself up on anything she can lately, which makes me think walking is in our near future.

"Mommy porn is the colloquial term, I believe, right, Noelle?" Sarah asks, smirking around her fork as she shovels a bite of mashed potatoes into her mouth. "It's funny, though. Gavin doesn't complain at all when I read it, do you, babe?"

Gavin nearly chokes on his food. "Are you seriously going to bring that up at the dinner table with my parents?"

"Why not? Your mom writes some steamy books, Gav. You should be thanking her," I add as Grant chuckles beside me. Thankfully, his reaction hasn't been as childish as Gavin's, but I can tell he's still on the fence about this new knowledge. He didn't seem bothered when we discussed it on the drive over, but now that we're with his family, he's been quiet on the topic.

Rolling my eyes, I cut another piece of my tri-tip. "I've heard it all, Sarah, and I've been reading for a long time. But what matters is that your mom"—I point my fork at Grant and Gavin—"is a talented writer and loves what she does. Maybe she didn't give you the whole truth, but it's not because she was ashamed. It's because she feared you would react exactly the way you're reacting right now."

"Couldn't have said it better myself. Thank you, Noelle." Regina raises her glass at me.

Gavin turns back to Sarah. "Do you really read my mom's books?"

There's a gleam in Sarah's eyes. "Wouldn't you like to know?"

Gavin dry heaves. "I can't."

"Oh, stop it," Franklin finally interjects. "You're being immature. I'll have you know that your mother makes more money writing steamy romance novels than she did teaching. How's that for you?"

Grant finally chimes in. "It is a billion-dollar-a-year business."

I shove his shoulder playfully. "And who told you that?"

"You." He leans over and kisses my cheek. "I'm not gonna lie, the whole thing is still processing in my brain, but I'm glad she has you in her corner. You've helped her dreams come true, and I can't thank you enough for that."

Smiling and fighting my eyes from welling, I lean in and

kiss him on the lips in front of his family, a group of people I feel extremely comfortable around considering I just met them an hour ago. But they're good people, just like Grant—kind, thoughtful, and not afraid to give each other shit. They're exactly the type of people I could see being my in-laws, especially Sarah—she'd fit right in with the girls, too.

"Noelle has been incredible, Grant," Regina speaks up. "I am eternally grateful to her, and now even more so that she's made you smile like that." Clasping her hands together under her chin, she continues, "That's why I always wanted you two to meet. My gut told me that you'd hit it off."

Grant turns back to her. "Guess I should have listened to you, huh, Mom?"

I giggle. "You're not the only one who pushed back on the idea. I mean, Regina is my client." My eyes find hers again. "But right now, in this moment, I'm really kicking myself for not taking you up on your offer to date your son sooner."

The entire table laughs. "Well, we're honored to have you here," Franklin says, raising his glass. "Here's to many more dinners with you girls."

Scarlett smacks the high chair at that moment, flinging mashed potatoes across the room, making everyone laugh again. I cover my mouth with my hands. "Oh my God, I'm so sorry."

"Nonsense. It wouldn't be the first time food has been thrown in this house." Regina stands from her seat, moving to the kitchen. "Just be glad you had a daughter. Boys are messy and ruthless."

"I second that notion," Sarah agrees before turning to her husband. "Now, are you gonna man up and act your age, or am I going to have to make you hang out with the kids for the rest of the evening?"

"Please, tell me you don't write from real-life experience, Mom," Gavin pleads.

Regina places her hands on her hips as Grant takes the towel from her, wiping up the mashed potatoes my daughter just tossed around like confetti. "Are you ever going to pick up one of my books?" she asks him.

"Hell no."

"Then yes, Gav. I do. All the more reason to leave the reading to your wife and women who appreciate them."

"Grant?" He turns to his brother for support. "How are you not freaking out right now?"

Grant pushes up from his seat, staring down at his brother. "Because I guess it takes a real man to admit that we all benefit from those books, so what's the problem? Are you saying that you can't support Mom? Or Noelle? Noelle literally helps authors like our mother get published. Who cares what the books are about? If she was writing murder mysteries about serial killers, would you be reacting this way?"

"No, but—"

"Sex is natural, Gav. And guess what? You have two kids, so we all know you have it. Why does it matter if Mom writes about it?" He finishes cleaning Scarlett's mess and then heads toward the laundry room off the kitchen.

Sarah comes up beside me as Grant walks away. "Are you swooning so hard for that man right now?"

"Um, yeah." I swallow hard, trying to conceal my nipples that I know are poking through my bra right now. God, I can't wait to show him later just how riled up that little speech got me.

"I can't wait to tease Gavin about this for months. It's going to be epic."

"Noelle?" I twist in my seat to find Regina standing with two glasses of wine. "Care to join me outside while Grant helps Gavin through his meltdown?"

Laughing, I stand from my chair but then glance down at Scarlett.

"Go, babe. I've got her," Grant declares when he returns as he picks her up from the chair. "I think I might give her a bath in the sink, if that's okay? She's covered in food."

"Yeah, that's fine. There's an extra outfit and shampoo in the diaper bag."

"Perfect." He kisses me on the cheek. "Go ahead, then. I'll be right here."

"Thank you." I turn to Regina. "I just need to run to the bathroom really quick."

She nods. "I'll be outside."

As I walk down the hallway lined with photos, I soak up the home that Grant lived in the latter part of his childhood. Franklin seems like an incredible male role model, one I'm sure was pivotal in shaping Grant into the man he is today. Like he said, he was raised by a single mom for a while. I know from speaking with Regina about Franklin that she met him almost five years after she divorced the boys' dad. When he signed on to date her, he signed on to care for her boys, too. It takes a strong, honest man to take responsibility for nurturing and raising children who aren't his own, and I know that Grant is also that type of man, thanks to the precedent that Franklin set.

Snapshots of Grant's childhood line the walls from elementary school through college as I make my way to the bathroom. A picture of him on the bowling team makes me laugh when I think about his little revelation on our date to The Social that night. Photos from Gavin and Sarah's wedding fill a collage frame, and my word, Grant sure does look fine in a tux.

But then a picture next to that one catches my eye. Grant is sitting in a chair in what looks like a hospital, and he's bald. There's not one hair on his head. Standing around him are a group of men I don't recognize besides Gavin, and Regina sits next to him, holding his hand. There are tubes connected to his arm, but he's smiling despite looking far less muscular and solid as I know him to be now.

The questions just start rolling in, but the need to pee reminds me why I'm venturing down this hallway in the first place, so I lock myself in the bathroom while my mind is still wondering about the story behind that picture.

Once I finish up and wash my hands, I hurry out to the patio in the backyard where I know Regina is still waiting. A cool breeze wafts through the air on this early September night, granting us some relief from the heat still holding strong, offering no reprieve from an intense summer. By the end of the month, southern California will finally grant us a few weeks of fall before turning cold.

"Sorry to keep you waiting," I say to her as I take the seat beside her and intercept the glass of wine she hands me.

"Nonsense. I'm just glad to have a moment so we can talk."

I let out a long breath. "This is crazy, Regina. I mean, what are the odds?"

She chuckles. "I know. I guess it was just meant to be."

Turning in my seat to face her, I offer up the truth. "I'm crazy about your son. He's incredible. He's been nothing but supportive and invested in me and Scarlett. He listens and nurtures and is so amazing that I'm not sure I deserve him."

"Oh, but you do, Noelle. Every woman deserves that kind of love."

"We haven't used that word yet."

"But you're feeling it, aren't you?" She looks at me knowingly, so all I do is nod. I don't want Grant's mom to hear those words from me before he does. "So what's the problem?"

"Well, first off, our working relationship. It's the reason I've always turned down the idea of dating your son in the first place."

"I know, but it doesn't have to change anything, Noelle."

"But what if something happens between us?"

"You're breaking up with him already?" she teases.

"No, I'm just saying—"

"We can cross that bridge if we get there, but if it would make you feel more comfortable, we could always assign me to another agent. I'd hate to stop working with you, but I'd understand if it made things less awkward."

"I love working with you, Regina, and would love to continue if you'll still have me."

She reaches for my hand. "I want that, too."

"Now, I have to ask: You really didn't tell your sons what you write?"

Her laughter echoes around us. "I told them I write love stories, just not the dirty kind."

"I see."

"I just didn't want them to think differently of me, I guess. I mean, I am their mom. I'm not ashamed at all of what I write, but it's different when your grown sons realize their mother writes dirty, raunchy sex scenes."

"You do write some good ones."

She smirks and then takes a sip of her wine. "I try. And thank you."

"And you've raised one hell of a man," I add.

"Thank you for that, too." She sighs, staring out across the yard as a breeze whips through and rustles the leaves. "I worry about Grant so much. He hasn't had the easiest time in life. He's had his heart broken and battled obstacles you couldn't imagine."

"I-I saw the picture in the hallway of him in the hospital. Was he sick at some point?"

She holds her hand up, stopping me. "It's his story to tell, Noelle, and I want to respect that. If he hasn't told you already, I'm sure he will soon. But I almost lost my son, and so part of me will always be protective of him. I think I already know the answer to this, but if you're not sure you see a future with him, please don't string him along. He comes with baggage that I'm sure he'll let you see soon, but until then, please, be gentle with his heart."

"I will. Like I said, Regina, I'm crazy about him. He's made me feel things I didn't know I could. It's not that I've never been in a relationship before, but I've never been with someone who makes me feel like I have a partner, a friend, and a lover all wrapped into one." She smiles softly. "Grant told me you were a single mom for a while, too, so you know that it's not easy to open up your heart to someone."

"Oh, I know, Noelle. I guarded mine for years, especially when the father of my children felt nothing when we walked away from him. I knew that if I ever let a man into my life again, he would have to love my boys first. And Franklin battled every one of my reservations to prove he wasn't going anywhere, even with two preteen boys in the mix."

"I can tell he's had an influence on Grant in that respect. Grant adores my daughter. In fact, I think he was enamored with her first."

Regina chuckles. "It doesn't surprise me. He's always loved kids. It's a shame he doesn't have any of his own." She clears her throat. "But he will love that girl like she's his own if you let him."

"I want to. I'm just scared."

"I understand that more than anyone, Noelle. But trust what you feel. Let yourself fall if you're there. You won't regret it, but you might regret pushing away something incredible because of fear, and no one wants to live with that, even my own son. I think you're the first person in a long time he's contemplated letting in. Don't make him regret that, either."

"I won't."

Regina smiles, squeezing my hand. "I still can't believe you're here. But I mean, now that you are, do you want to hear about my new story idea that I just plotted out?"

"Yes!" I take another sip of wine and listen to Regina tell me about a small-town series that she wants to write in between her sibling series, the first book starting with a big city woman who inherits a house in a small coastal town but ends up falling in love with a grumpy bar owner.

I can already imagine how much her readers will love it, and just like that, we get lost in the fantasy of love while in reality, love is all around me tonight, too.

Chapter 15

Grant

Kissing the top of Scarlett's head, I lay her down in her crib as Noelle stands beside me. We just returned to her place after dinner with my family, and this little girl barely lasted two minutes in her car seat before she was fast asleep.

"She's out," Noelle murmurs.

"I know."

"Mommy loves you, baby girl," she says before leaning down and kissing Scarlett's cheek. And in that moment, watching her do that, I wish I could say those words out loud, too.

I love these girls.

Tonight only solidified it for me, watching them interact

with my family, seeing how Noelle fit right in and how she was with my mom.

Shit. That little plot twist still has me scratching my head.

All this time, the woman who I feel ready to let in has been under my fingertips. She's had a connection to me for years. Perhaps that's why I felt something different when I met her, but honestly, who knows?

I don't want to play the what-if game, because it won't change where we are now. Although, Noelle was awfully quiet on the ride home, so I can't help but wonder where her head is at or how this night is affecting her, too.

I close the door to Scarlett's nursery after we both exit and follow Noelle into her room.

"Are you ever going to show me where you live?" she asks, spinning on her heels to face me, her voice shaky.

"What?"

"Your home. We've been dating for months now, and I don't even know where you live. It dawned on me earlier, and I'm not sure why it never crossed my mind before. Maybe it's my mom-brain, juggling life and raising my daughter while falling for this incredible man, but I don't know where you live."

"Okay . . ."

"There's a lot I don't know about you, Grant." Her eyes grow more narrow, and suddenly my heart starts racing.

"Noelle, are you okay?"

She shakes her head, clenching her hands into fists. "Yes

and no. Tonight was amazing, truly. I love your family, and you already know how I feel about your mom. I'm glad that she and I got to talk after that bomb was dropped about you being her son, but then I saw something at your parents' house tonight that has me scared. It makes me question if I'm being blinded by my attraction to you, by the way you've inserted yourself into my life so seamlessly. And I've just let you."

"Come here." I reach for her hand, but she pulls away, and that racing heartbeat I felt before just multiplies.

"No. I want to know why you've never taken me to your place." Standing before me, she crosses her arms over her chest, and I feel like she's forming a shield against me. I'm not sure what's making her act this way, this determination to drill me with questions, but I can answer this one with very little effort.

"I've never taken you to my place because all of Scarlett's things are here, and I was just trying to make things easier on you. I figured if we were in your domain, you would have one less thing to worry about, because you had everything you needed for her." I shrug. Her jaw unhinges, her mouth pops open slightly, but she still keeps her arms crossed. "But baby, if you want to see my place, I'll take you right now." Standing from the bed, I walk over to her, uncrossing her arms and holding her hands in mine. "I'll take you to my home, lay you down in my bed, and make love to you there so my sheets smell like you. Believe me, it's something I really want, I just didn't want it to be a burden to you."

"Grant . . ."

"Where is this coming from, Noelle?" Searching her eyes for answers, I continue. "I thought tonight was amazing, but you seem angry. A little hostile, even. Did I do something? Say something? Did my mom mention something to you? She can be a little overbearing, but she means well. Was it my brother? I know he was acting like an ass, but I tried to defend you and my mom—"

"No, Grant. You didn't do anything," she replies, cutting me off. "I just . . ."

"What? Tell me."

She takes a deep breath and then looks me dead in the eye. "There was a picture in the hallway. I saw it on the way to the bathroom, and I . . ."

My stomach drops. I know exactly what picture she's talking about, one that I forgot was even there. "Oh."

She lowers her voice. "For weeks, I've felt like I was missing something, that there's a piece of you that you haven't shared with me, and then I see something like that, and I . . ." Tears fill her eyes. "Are you sick? Am I going to lose you? Because I don't think I can handle that."

"Fuck." Pulling her into my chest, an ounce of the anxiety I was just feeling dissipates when I realize Noelle's demeanor right now is fear, fear that I've been keeping something from her—which I have, but not in the way she thinks. I knew this conversation was inevitable, and it looks like there's no reason not to get everything out in the open tonight. "Come here. Sit with me."

She wipes her eyes as we sit on the edge of her bed. "I'm sorry. I just feel blindsided right now, and then I kept thinking about what else you could be hiding, which then made me realize you've never taken me to your home, which made me think maybe you were a serial killer or something, you know? It's always the ones who seem so perfect and charming and then, bam! You're frozen in the bottom of a deep freezer."

"Okay, maybe you should cool it on the crime documentaries." That gets a little chuckle from her. "I'm not a serial killer, Noelle. And I already told you I'll take you to my house this instant if you want, but I think we can both agree that waking Scarlett up would be a terrible idea."

She nods. "Agreed. But that picture, Grant. I-I need to know what that's about. My mind is racing with the worst possible scenarios, and I'm freaking out."

Inhaling deeply, I run a hand through my hair. "Noelle, my past is complicated. And unfortunately, it has affected my future."

"What happened, Grant? Please, just talk to me. Tell me that it's going to be okay, that you're okay."

"Aw, baby." I cup the side of her face. "I'm fine. I've been fine for ten years. I had cancer, Noelle, at twenty-five. But I beat it, baby, and it hasn't been back since."

Her bottom lip trembles. "Cancer?"

Relief washes through me from just saying the words out loud to her. "Yeah. It was terrifying, but I conquered it. I had an amazing support system. The men in that photo with me, Gavin, and my mom were buddies of mine from college. They would take turns sitting with me through chemo and radiation treatment. I think my mother took it the hardest, but I promised her I would fight, and I did. It was only Stage 2 when they found it, so I was lucky we caught it in time, but it was a rough time in my life I don't like revisiting." Clearing my throat, I connect a few dots for her. "The woman I was with at the time is the one I was planning to propose to. After my diagnosis, she decided she didn't want to stand by me and left. It was like rubbing salt in the wound."

Noelle covers her mouth with her hands. "Oh my God, Grant. That's awful."

"It was pretty shitty, yeah. But I learned from it. I learned that people aren't always who you think they are. It's part of the reason I haven't dated seriously since then. And then you changed all that." Stroking her cheek, I say, "When you stared up at me with these green eyes, I was powerless to stop the pull I felt toward you."

"I'm so sorry that happened to you."

"It's okay. I'm okay."

Noelle's eyes drop, and I release her. "What kind of cancer did you have, Grant? Is it something that can come back?"

"Fuck, Noelle. I really didn't want to talk about this tonight." I launch myself from the bed, starting to pace.

"Why?"

"Because I'm afraid once I tell you, it's going to change things for us."

She places her hand over her chest. "It won't. Please, just tell me, Grant. I can handle it."

"Testicular," I say on a low groan. "I had testicular cancer, Noelle."

Her eyes widen instantly. "Oh."

"You might not have even noticed, but I had a testicle removed. One of mine is . . ." I gesture to my crotch, hoping she understands what I'm alluding to. Thank God for reconstructive surgery so I at least feel normal on the outside as a man, but it just doesn't change the reality of what I went through.

"Oh," she says again.

"Yeah. There you go." I throw my hands up in the air. "Now you know, Noelle." Turning away from her, I place my hands on the back of my neck, pulling my head down as I close my eyes, not wanting to see her face right now.

I can't look at her. I can't wonder what she's thinking as the silence between us grows to an uncharacteristic volume.

My mind swirls with what she's going to say, how this is going to affect everything we've been building. Is this going to come back and bite me in the ass because I waited too long to tell her? Or can she possibly understand why I didn't until now?

"Grant, look at me." I shake my head. "Grant, please."

The desperation in her voice has me turning, peeling my eyes open to see hers filled with moisture, her hands clasped in her lap.

"God, don't look at me like that, Noelle. I can't take your pity. It's why I haven't told you yet—I didn't want to get this look from you." Shaking my head, I tilt it to the side, clenching my jaw, trying to hold my composure.

"Grant, I don't pity you." She stands from the bed, walking slowly toward me. With my hands clenched into fists at my side, I brace myself for what she's about to say. Does she understand the implications here? Does she realize that I might not be able to offer her everything she could want for her future?

"Grant." Her hands find my chest, and I flinch. I watch her eyes bounce back and forth between mine before she surprises me with her words. "Make love to me."

"What?"

"I need you," she says, running her fingers down my abs before she begins unbuttoning my jeans.

"Noelle."

"I want to feel you inside me." Pulling the zipper down, she shoves my jeans and briefs down my ass and then drops to her knees in front of me. And Jesus, the sight has me hard in seconds.

"Noelle, you don't have to—"

She doesn't let me finish before she takes my length into her mouth, sucking me in and swirling her tongue around the head. She reaches up to cup my balls, and for a moment, I almost let myself fixate on the gesture and ruin the mood, but she's too busy showing me her desire as she takes my cock as deep as she can in her throat, cradling my balls and swirling them gently with her fingers.

"Fuck, Noelle."

"Mmm," she moans as she keeps working me over with her mouth. I latch onto the back of her head, holding her steady as she pulls my cock in and out of her lips, flicking her tongue across the slit and then taking me deep again.

"Jesus." I yank her up and crush my mouth to hers, realizing that this conversation took a turn I wasn't anticipating, but I am not about to stop in the middle of this to continue it. "Take your clothes off."

Noelle strips before me, keeping her eyes locked on mine, baring herself to me with no reservations. Her chest rises and falls as she waits for me to finish getting naked as well, and I stroke my cock in front of her once we're both void of clothes.

"You want this?"

"Yes. Nothing between us."

"You're sure?"

"Grant, please, fuck me. Make me yours."

"You are mine, Noelle." In two seconds flat, I crash into her, molding her lips to mine, seeking out every inch of her body as we fall to the bed and grind against one another. She's already soaked, which I discover as I part her slit and slide my fingers through her arousal. I hook her leg around my hip as we lay on our sides, keeping her lips attached to mine, line myself up to her, and sink into her heat as hard as I can, stealing the breath from her lungs.

"Oh God."

"Fuck, baby. You feel incredible." I've never been bare

with a woman. Even though I knew the chance of having a child was low, I never tempted fate. I didn't want to run that risk with someone I didn't see a future with. But Noelle is it for me. She's the woman I want to give a child to more than anything. I just hope I can.

"Grant. Harder, please."

I spin her onto her back and thrust forward, causing her to shriek when I bottom out and pound into her as hard as I can. I can't describe how this woman makes me feel. She doesn't make me question my virility or wonder if I can please her. Even before she knew about my cancer, it was different with her. This visceral need I feel when she's in my arms is incomparable to what I've felt with any other woman.

And now that she knows, it's as if she knew we needed this connection so that my truth wouldn't affect that.

"Yes. Fuck," Noelle moans as I latch onto one of her nipples with my mouth, sucking the bud between my lips. She stopped breastfeeding last week, and I've yet to truly enjoy putting my mouth all over her tits and making her wild from playing with them. "Oh God. More, Grant."

Cupping her breast in my hand, I suck harder, biting her gently as I feel her clench around me while I smack my hips against her ass, fucking her hard and deep like she asked for. Swirling my tongue around her nipple, I listen for her cues that she's about to come, and then I release her and find her clit, stroking her between us as her wetness covers us both.

"Fuck, baby. Come all over my cock."

"I'm coming," she shouts, digging her head into my neck as I do the same and we find our release together. I come long and hard, not even questioning what the consequences of it might be, tempting fate with the action itself.

"Grant, look at me," she whispers as we catch our breaths, my face still buried in her neck. Slowly, I lift my head and find her eyes. She brushes the hair from my face and says, "I'm not going anywhere."

"Noelle . . ."

With a press of her finger to my lips, I stop talking. "Listen to me. I want you, all of you, and that includes your past and your future. Part of me is relieved that you talked to me tonight, and I also know we need to talk more. But right now, I just want to stay here with you, entangled in your arms so I can feel you." She conceals her face in my chest, and her next question is a little muffled. "You're really going to be okay?"

Sighing, I kiss the top of her head, still buried inside her. "I'm okay, Noelle. I go for routine checkups and scans. I'm as healthy as a horse."

She squeezes my biceps. "Strong like one, too."

Chuckling, I force her to meet my eyes again. "I'm sorry I didn't tell you sooner. I just didn't want it to change things between us."

"But it did." On a shaky breath, she says, "I'm falling in love with you, Grant."

The 747 full of baggage that I've been hanging on to takes flight in my chest. "Fuck. I'm so in love with *you*, Noelle. And

Scarlett," I reply, releasing tension in my body before gently pressing my lips to hers. "I want a future with you, I just don't know what that may look like."

She nods. "I know. We can talk about that later, but for right now, I just want you to know that I'm here. I'm not leaving, and I want you in my life. I love you."

"I want that, too, baby." Kissing her deeply, we stay connected for so long that I grow hard again while still inside of her. Slowly, I start to swivel my hips as I feel hers thrust up to meet mine. "Care to go another round?"

"God, yes . . ."

So we do. We make love two more times before finally succumbing to sleep, all of our truths out in the open. And she stayed. The woman I love stayed, and my heart can barely absorb the feeling.

I found her. Now the question is: Can I give her everything she deserves?

The second I open the door, I steal Scarlett from Noelle's arms and kiss the top of her head. "God, I missed you girls."

"We missed you, too." Noelle presses up on her toes to land her lips on mine, and I wrap my arm around her waist to pull her closer to me.

"Three days felt like five years."

"It did."

"Come in. Let me check on dinner, and then I can show you around."

After last weekend and the emotional turmoil it put us through, I promised Noelle that I would have her and Scarlett over once I returned from my three days of back-to-back flights out of town. These little sprints used to be something I looked forward to as a change of pace, but now that I have these girls in my life, they just keep me away from them, so I've started to resent my job, a feeling I haven't felt before.

"It smells amazing." Noelle follows me through the entry-way, past the living room on my left and into the kitchen on my right. My place is small, but it's just me. This house was a steal I snatched up when the market dipped years ago, so it keeps my cost of living down and is perfect for a single guy like me—at least, the single guy I was.

Now, I'm proud to say I'm taken and loving every minute of it.

"I made chicken parmesan," I reply as Scarlett fusses for me to let her down. Carefully, I sit her on the kitchen floor and give her a basket of Tupperware lids to play with. My sister used to do this with my nephews all the time, and I was always amazed at how fascinated they were by them.

"Tupperware lids?"

"Yup. Got that trick from Sarah."

Scarlett bangs the plastic against the tile, giggling as she makes her own version of music. "Good to know."

"You hungry?" I ask her, casting a glance at her over my shoulder. Noelle is peering around my house, taking it all in.

"Yes." Spinning around again, she says, "Your house is beautiful, Grant. Did you do the renovations yourself?"

"A little. The kitchen was already updated, thank God, because I don't know if I would have had patience for that. But I did do the flooring, crown molding, and painting. I changed out all of the light fixtures, too, just to update the whole place."

Looking out over the dark gray walls, white crown moldings, and navy-blue couch in my living room, pride fills my chest. I'm proud of my home, of what I've created by myself. But I'm quickly realizing that it's far more meaningful to share it with someone else.

"I love it." She spins to face me again. "Thank you for having us here."

After plating our dinner, I walk over to the table and set down our meals. "Like I said, I would have done it sooner, but I was just trying to accommodate you."

Noelle moves to pick up Scarlett, taking her over to the table. "Well, I'm glad we're finally here. You even got a high chair." I smile. I'd never regret that purchase. "Obviously, I needed one if you girls are going to be here more often."

Smiling, Noelle buckles Scarlett in, and then I put a small pile of cut-up noodles on her tray, letting her feed herself. If there's one thing this little girl knows how to do, it's eat.

While we eat dinner, we catch up on our weeks. We hadn't had a chance to speak much because of my flight schedule.

Noelle scrolls through the calendar in her phone after she finishes her dinner. "So we have the Bolts game in two weeks and then dinner with my family for my birthday."

"Right. You sure you still want me to meet them?" I tease her.

"Yes. I'm just afraid they might scare you off."

"Why do you say that? Do you think they won't approve of us?"

"It's mostly my sister I'm worried about. She can be very opinionated and has no filter. Just don't take anything she says too seriously, especially because I'm sure she's going to grill you with questions. You know, since she didn't get the chance when you two met the first time."

"There's nothing she could say or ask that will change the way I feel about you." I reach over and grab her hand as she continues to scroll.

Sighing heavily, she turns her phone off. "God, I can't look at that right now. My work schedule is insane for the next month or so, and it's overwhelming me." She shakes her head. "I don't want to be thinking about that when I'm with you."

"I'm sorry you're stressed."

"It's not stress, per se, I'm just really busy. And my mind never stops moving. Sometimes I'll wake up in the middle of the night, and as soon as I do, my brain turns on. Suddenly, I'm thinking about all the things I have to do, and my mind wanders from thoughts about work to worries about Scarlett to things I want to do with you."

"Oh, yeah?" I bounce my eyebrows. "What kind of things?"

Giggling, she waves me off. "Not dirty things, Grant. More like places I'd love to travel with you, things I'd like to see, maybe one night staying in and having a date on the couch after Scarlett goes to sleep."

"We can do all of that."

"I know, but then sometimes I wonder what it would be like to just escape it all for one night, you know? Not be Noelle but some other person who doesn't carry around these thoughts and worries. Sometimes, I wish I could turn it off and just be someone else." She closes her eyes and shakes off the thought. "Sorry, I know that may sound ungrateful for my life, but right now, like I said, I'm just overwhelmed."

I rub the top of her hand with my thumb. "Hey. I told you, I never want you to feel like you can't be honest with me. That's what I'm here for, to be your sounding board. That's what we're supposed to be for each other. I know you have the girls, but I need to hear these things, too. I'm not a mind reader." But what I won't say is that she just gave me an idea for her birthday three weeks away.

"You're right. I just feel guilty for feeling that way some-times, like I want to run away. It's not that I'm unhappy. It's that I feel so consumed with doing things for everyone else that I feel like I forget to do things for myself. I believe the unoffi-cial term they call it these days is 'self-care.'" She uses quota-tions around the word.

"I'd prefer if you'd let me take care of you," I reply suggestively.

She laughs, standing from the table to clear our plates. "You do that just fine, thank you very much."

"I get it, though. Responsibility can take a toll on a person."

"Yes, it does." She stands at the kitchen sink and starts washing the dishes.

I grab Scarlett from her high chair and take her straight back to the bathroom to clean her up. "I'm gonna give her a bath."

The endearing smile Noelle gives me makes me want to make her smile like that for the rest of our lives. "Thank you. She loves when you do that."

Holding Scarlett above my head like Simba in *The Lion King*, I say, "I know. I think it's our thing now, huh, baby girl?"

The shriek of excitement and kick of her legs has me laughing and bringing this sweet baby to my chest, kissing her cheeks and squeezing her tightly to me, soaking her all in.

I take my time talking to Scarlett as I bathe her, watching her splash around in the tub. I got a bath seat like the one Noelle has at her house so she has room to play but she's still sitting up and safe in the water.

By the time Noelle finishes the dishes, I'm in one of the rooms in my house I couldn't wait to show her this evening.

"Grant?" she calls out to me.

"We're in the first bedroom." Finishing the buttons on Scarlett's pajamas, my back is turned to the door, but I hear Noelle's gasp when she enters.

"Oh my God . . . what is this, Grant?"

I pull Scarlett into my arms and then turn to face her. "This is Scarlett's room."

"What?" she whispers.

"I know it's not much, but I wanted to have a space for her

when you girls stay here." I look around the room that my mother helped me put together yesterday after I got home from my last flight. She painted the walls a soft pink while I was gone and found a few pieces of artwork for the walls, but I hung everything up and built a changing table this morning. Pictures of elephants grace the walls, and there's even a giant stuffed minion in the corner. That was a find by my brother. He owed me one after the way he behaved at dinner last weekend.

Noelle's eyes fill with tears as she walks toward me, wrapping her arms around my neck. "This is the sweetest thing I think you could have done for us."

"I love you, Noelle. And I love this little girl, too." I press a kiss to both of their cheeks as Scarlett lays her head on my shoulder. "You're part of my life now, the biggest part, and I'm making space for you both."

Noelle sniffles and then looks around the room again. "What do you think, baby girl?" Scarlett babbles something completely incoherent, but it makes us laugh. "I think she likes it."

"I hope so." Placing her on the ground, I let her explore. She instantly crawls to the mirrored closet doors and pulls herself up, pressing her hands into the glass before smushing her face into the mirror. Slobber covers the surface, but she just giggles and does it again.

Noelle takes a seat in the rocking chair in the corner, and I get down on the floor with my little girl—the sweet baby who feels more like mine with each passing day.

Scarlett drops down to her knees again, crawling over to the changing table and then pulling herself up against it. But then she lets go, standing there all on her own.

"Oh my God, Grant!" Noelle whisper-shouts. "She's standing!"

"I know. Do you have your phone?"

Noelle scrambles to retrieve it from her pocket. "Yes, I do."

"Get your camera ready, Noelle."

"It's too soon. She's only ten months old."

"If she's ready, she's going to do this, babe." I look at Scarlett. "Can you come to me, big girl?"

Scarlett lets out a squeal before falling down on her butt.

"It's okay, baby girl," Noelle croons as Scarlett pulls herself up again and holds onto the table until she feels ready to release it. And when she does, she finds her balance and takes a step toward me.

My entire body seizes up.

"Da!" she shouts as she takes another step and then falls to the ground.

"Holy shit! She just took her first steps, Grant!"

"I know, babe. I know." Crawling across the floor to her, I pick her up, tossing her in the air before smothering her with kisses. "You did it, Scarlett. You walked!"

Noelle drops to the ground beside us, tears falling from her eyes. "I'm so proud of you, sweetheart."

Scarlett just babbles and kisses us back as we celebrate the milestone in her life we just witnessed together. But then all of the oxygen leaves my lungs at what she shouts next.

"Da-da!"

Noelle gasps, and I hold my breath as Scarlett says the word again. "Da-da!"

"Grant," Noelle whispers, looking at me.

And as I stare back at her, all I can say in response is "I love you."

"I love you, too."

Chapter 16

Noelle

Two Weeks Later

"**D**amn. What a view."

Standing next to Grant in a private box at the Los Angeles Bolts stadium waiting for the game to start, I stare out at the field. Bright lights illuminate the enclosed stadium, and the field is crawling with people preparing it for the battle between Los Angeles's and Denver's teams. Fans are slowly starting to trickle into the stadium to find their seats as well.

"I guess it is all about who you know, isn't it?"

He chuckles. "Apparently so." Turning to me, he draws me into him by my waist. "You know I love you regardless, but the fact that one of your best friends is married to Maddox Taylor is pretty damn sweet."

"Oh, I'm aware."

Ethan comes up beside us. "This view never gets old."

"I was just telling Noelle how fucking amazing this is," Grant replies.

"I remember the first time Penelope hooked us up with these seats. I was nearly in tears."

Grant laughs. "Totally understandable."

Rolling my eyes, I say, "Men and football. Probably one of the only sports that can bring a grown man to tears."

"Hey, party people!" Penelope announces as she walks through the door with Maddox, Hayden Palomar, and Vince Dayton trailing closely behind. It's still an hour before the game, so I imagine she was able to pull a few of the players away after she sweet-talked the coach. Of course, Penelope also works for the team now, so I'm sure that helps. "The talent of the evening has arrived, and no, I'm not talking about the men in spandex."

Amelia comes over, chomping on one of the hors d'oeuvres that are supplied in excess in this box suite. "And what talent would that be?"

"Sarcasm and PR pizazz." She flashes us spirit fingers. "Seriously, though, the boys wanted to say hi and meet Grant."

Grant walks over to shake all of their hands, and I'm pretty sure I see his entire arm shaking. "Holy shit. So nice to meet you guys. I'm a big fan."

"Thanks, man. Happy to have your support." Maddox

shakes his hand first, followed by Vince then Hayden. "I've heard a lot about you, so it's great to put a face to a name."

"Absolutely. My brother and his sons are huge fans, too."

"Pen, can we get some jerseys up here to sign for him and his family?" Maddox asks his wife.

She instantly starts tapping on her phone. "You've got it, babe." But then she looks up to him. "Did you forget what else you're supposed to do?"

"You were serious about that, Pen?"

She stares at him as if he's grown two heads. "Um, fuck yes, Maddox. Noelle is one of my best friends."

Groaning, Maddox turns to Grant. "Pen said I'm supposed to threaten you with bodily harm if you hurt Noelle, but I personally don't want a harassment suit on my hands, so I'll just say: Treat her well or else. I imagine since you're here, she cares about you, so just don't make her regret it. You feel me?"

"That was not nearly threatening enough, Maddox."

"You're lucky you got that out of me, woman." He gestures toward me. "Obviously, the woman is happy or else Grant wouldn't be here. So leave them be."

She arches a brow at him. "You know damn well that's not my style. I protect my girls at all costs, and since you're my husband now, that duty extends to you, too."

Smirking, Maddox pulls Penelope into his arms. "I know, baby. It's one of the things I love most about you." He kisses her, and not in a way that's appropriate in front of other people.

"All right, you two," Vince interrupts. "We get it. You'll take out your aggression on each other later." Rolling his eyes, he turns to us. "Noelle, sweetheart, it's so good to see you. And I, for one, am pumped you found a man who not only loves football but also cheers for the Bolts."

Laughing, I launch myself at him, hugging him tightly. "Me, too." I release him and turn to Hayden. "And you . . . did you know that Regina is Grant's mom?"

"No shit?" Hayden looks back at Grant. "Your mom writes some steamy books, bro."

Grant groans. "So I've heard."

"Hayden is part of a podcast that talks about romance books, and they recently filmed an episode featuring your mother. It's going to be a huge hit," I explain.

"Well, thanks for supporting my mother then." Grant pats him on the shoulder.

"My pleasure. I'm telling you, men should truly read some of these books. It's like getting a glimpse inside a woman's head, which we all know we could use from time to time." The men in the room nod in agreement and snicker. "I keep trying to tell my QB and center here that we should start a book club, but no one's taking me seriously."

"I'm in!" Jeffrey declares, popping up out of nowhere. I know I would have heard him if he were here earlier, so I guess he just arrived.

"Yeah, you need all the help you can get with women," Ethan teases him under his breath.

"If Damien were here, he'd corroborate that I do experience success with the female population from time to time, but I feel like there's always something to be learned as well."

"See? That's what I'm saying!" Hayden exclaims. "Jeffrey, I think you and I need to make this happen."

"Just let me know when and where, my man." He pops a chip in his mouth and then turns to me and Grant. "And you must be Noelle's new man?"

"I'm Grant. Nice to meet you."

"This is Jeffrey," I explain. "You'll get used to him."

Jeffrey's brows draw together. "What's that supposed to mean?"

I rest my hand on his shoulder. "Nothing, honey. You're just unique in your very own way."

He narrows his eyes at me. "I feel like I'm being insulted, but there's free food and booze, so I'm going to let it slide." Brushing me off, he crosses the room to the table with all the food and begins filling up a plate.

Penelope claps her hands together. "Okay, boys. I'd better get you back to the locker room before Coach Williams puts out a missing person's report on all three of you."

"Yeah, I need to talk to the offensive coordinator again before the game starts." Maddox turns back to us. "It was really nice to meet you. We'll have to all get together when I'm not working so we can get a chance to actually hang out."

"I'd fucking love that," Grant replies. "Good luck, guys."

"Good luck, boys!" Amelia and I say simultaneously as Pen leads them out the door and back to the locker room.

"I'll be back in a bit, bitches!" she says as the door shuts behind her, and we all refill our drinks, fill our plates with food, and get ready to watch the Bolts win their third game of the season.

"Hell, yeah!" Grant and Ethan high-five each other in front of the glass as the Bolts make a fourth-down conversion just before halftime.

"Nice fucking play!" Ethan declares.

"Hayden was right where he needed to be on that one," Grant agrees.

"Yes, he was."

Amelia, Penelope, and I stand off to the side at the back of the suite, sipping our champagne while leaning against the counter, watching the men concentrate on the football game in front of them. There are only thirty seconds left on the clock, and the Bolts are trying to tie it.

"This feels wrong without Charlotte and Damien here," Amelia says.

"I know, but they've had a rough first week at home, and Ivy isn't sleeping well. I don't blame them for wanting to stay in."

Charlotte and Damien's daughter was born last Tuesday after being five days late. Charlotte was in labor for eighteen hours before their baby girl entered the world, but she did beautifully, and little Ivy Grace was perfect and already has a set of lungs on her. We knew there was a slim chance that they'd be attending this game anyway, given how close it was to her due date, but it still feels like we're missing a piece of our puzzle tonight.

"I went over last night to bring them dinner, and Charlotte seemed happy, just tired," Amelia explains. "Damien was running around like crazy trying to keep his girls happy, though. It was so sweet."

"Sounds about right. Those first few weeks home are a blur. They go by so fast and are so overwhelming." I take another sip of my champagne. "Once they get a routine down, that will help a lot."

"Do you remember that time we came by after you had Scarlett, and you had baby poop in your hair and didn't even realize it?" Penelope asks through a laugh.

"Thanks for reminding me."

"You were like a zombie, just walking around completely oblivious. You smelled so bad, I don't know how you didn't realize."

"Because I was covered in puke *and* shit. Who the hell knew what I was smelling at that point?"

Amelia giggles. "Are you still planning on seeing them tomorrow, Noelle?"

"Yes. I'm gonna make something in the Crock-Pot so they can have a home-cooked meal."

"They'll enjoy that."

"I have Tuesday night dinner duty and will probably make some enchiladas," Penelope interjects.

"That sounds good, too."

Ethan, Jeffrey, and Grant all cheer again as a play is made on the field, pulling our attention over to them.

"I'm so glad he's getting along with the boys—at least the ones who are here," I say. "I didn't doubt that he would, but it's like he was meant to be a part of our group the entire time. I love him so much—I didn't know I could be this lucky, you guys."

"Oh, definitely." Amelia smiles at me. "And you look blissful, Noelle. I know we haven't caught up much since the soccer game a few weeks ago, but how are things going? Did you talk to him about how you were feeling?"

The emotions of that weekend come back to me. I was able to tell the girls through text that the dinner with his family was successful, but I haven't really been able to share all of the details of what happened that night, the revelations that were made and how they made me feel.

"I did, but a lot of stuff sort of came up. You know how I felt like I was missing something about him? Like there was a piece of him I couldn't see?" They nod. "Well, it turns out his past was a lot more complicated than I realized. Grant had cancer at twenty-five. Testicular cancer," I whisper, not wanting the guys to overhear our conversation. I explain how I saw the picture in his mom's house and how I kind of went off on him when we got home that night until he told me what it was about.

"Oh my God," Amelia says. "But he's okay now, right?"

"Yes, that was my first concern. But he's been cancer-free for over ten years now. However . . ."

"What?" Penelope questions, waiting for me to continue.

"He made a comment about how he doesn't know what our future may look like in terms of kids, and we never got around to talking about it."

"Why not?"

"Because after he confessed that to me, I could tell he was struggling with how that would make me look at him. The last thing I wanted him to think was that I saw him differently. We expressed our feelings in other ways, if you know what I mean, and ultimately told each other that we love each other, which I've already known for a while."

"But you haven't brought it up since?" Amelia prods.

I shake my head. "No. It's like we're avoiding talking about it." I let out the breath I was holding, relieved to be able to discuss this with my girlfriends. I wish Charlotte was here, too, but I can talk to her when I go to her house tomorrow.

"That's not good."

"I know, but at the same time, it's not like we have to make a decision about it right now, right? We know we're serious about each other. We know we're committed, so when that time comes, we can discuss how to navigate that obstacle."

Penelope lowers her voice. "So can he *not* have kids? Is that what you're saying?"

"I-I don't know," I reply honestly. "From what I've read, each case is different. It depends on what treatment he had, if he froze sperm or not, or if he still produces sperm on his own. He did mention that he had to have surgery, but he didn't elaborate beyond that."

"Holy shit. That's a lot to unpack."

"I know. And I'm scared that if I bring it up, he'll just shut down. I mean, when he finally confessed it to me, it was like the light in his eyes vanished. He was angry. You could tell that it still affects him."

"With good reason," Amelia says. "But you deserve to be able to ask questions, too, Noelle. If he's your partner, you two need to talk about this."

I look back over at him, so grateful that I found him and yet equally terrified to lose him. I can't imagine what that period of his life was like, but it clearly still lingers under the surface like a virus that only shows itself when you scratch too hard and it spreads. I just don't want it to affect *us*, and there are questions I need answers to so that I know what our future will look like. Grant has allowed me to dream about tomorrows again, but now I wonder if we're on the same page about what our tomorrows may bring.

"She is so precious, Char." Staring down at the sleeping baby in my arms, my mind drifts back to when Scarlett was this little, just ten months ago. It seems like a lifetime ago —and also just yesterday. "You did good, my friend."

"Thank you. Although, I carried her for nine months, but she came out looking like her dad, so that kind of feels like a slap in the face."

I laugh, readjusting Ivy in my arms.

"Nothing wrong with that, babe," Damien says, handing both of us a mug of hot tea before sitting on the floor and playing with Scarlett, who's currently tearing apart her diaper bag. The girl is on the move now, and there's no stopping her. After the few steps she took at Grant's place, she's pushed her boundaries by teetering all over the place. She's not fully walking, but she's definitely eager to get there. Part of me is impressed that she's determined to walk so early, but it also has changed my ability to keep an eye on her yet again.

"How are you guys doing, though? Honestly." I cast a knowing glance at Charlotte as she takes a sip of her tea.

"Well, Ivy decided to scream for four hours straight last night, so there's that. When she finally went to sleep at four this morning, I was so dazed, I think I was sleeping with my eyes open. We tried everything to calm her down, but nothing seemed to help."

"Scarlett did something similar. It will pass. But if it doesn't, consider asking your pediatrician about her having colic. It's pretty common."

She nods. "Okay."

"Have you been crying? Feeling blue or sad for no reason?"

"Not really. I cry from exhaustion, but that's about it."

"I've been keeping an eye on her for signs of postpartum depression, Noelle. It's one of my fears, so believe me, I'm on it," Damien says, bouncing Scarlett in his lap as she hangs onto his shoulders.

"Good. I think I had a little bit of it around month three, but nothing too crazy. It was more just feeling overwhelmed or bouts of rage. They don't talk about how it can present like that, too."

"Well, when your life completely changes, and suddenly you're responsible for another human being's care, that's to be expected." Charlotte winks at me. "The good thing is, nursing is going well. That's what I was concerned about most, so I think that's alleviated some of my worries."

"Let me know if you need any nursing pads, bags for milk, or a spare pump. Now that I'm done nursing, I have extra stuff left over."

"Thank you."

Damien blows out a breath. "Oh God! Scarlett! You are one stinky lady!" Scarlett giggles as the scent of a freshly blown out diaper hits my nose. "Holy hell, what are you feeding this girl, Noelle?"

"She eats anything she can get her hands on these days, Damien. But I can change her. Hold on." I move to get up from the couch, but Damien puts his hand out.

"Don't worry, Noelle. I've got it." He stands up, keeping Scarlett in his arms. "I'm a professional diaper changer now. In fact, Ivy has already projectile shitted on me, so I've earned that parenting badge. Now, I'm in the process of collecting them all."

Laughing, I nod at him. "Okay. Thank you."

Damien grabs one of Scarlett's diapers and then marches down the hall to change her in the nursery.

Charlotte turns to me. "So how was the game?"

"Oh, it was a blast, as usual. Grant was just beside himself with the experience."

She smiles. "I bet. I was sad we missed it, but honestly, I don't think I could have survived that even if I wanted to. Being home is safe. I'm afraid for when we go somewhere or worse, when Damien goes back to work. I'm not sure how I'm going to handle it."

"It gets better. You'll find what works for you. Just try to be patient about it. The worst thing for me is that I'm a planner, and you can only plan so much when you have a child."

She tilts her head at me. "I know I've said this before, but I'm so glad I have you, that you've gone through this already so I have someone else to tell me I'm not crazy. I already feel so different, Noelle—like I'm an entirely different person in an entirely different body. I'm trying to remind myself I just grew a human, but my mind is already at war with this new suit of armor I'm wearing and this new identity."

I sigh as Ivy shifts in my arms. "Gosh, I remember feeling the exact same way. In fact, I think on some level, I still do. Motherhood is this life-altering experience. The entire world becomes a different place when you bring another person into it. And something that I'm learning, slowly but surely, is to remember that *you* are a person, too. Amelia said something to me a few months ago that really helped me let go of some of the guilt of wanting a break from motherhood sometimes."

"What did she say?"

"She said to remember that even though I'm a mom, I'm a whole human, too, and that person deserves not to be lost."

"Wow," Charlotte replies with tears in her eyes.

"I think she said that to me about a week before I met Grant, and I had to remind myself that it was okay to go after something I wanted, even though I wasn't completely sure it was the right decision at the time. But my point is, you can't be responsible for Ivy all the time. And as much as it kills me to leave Scarlett some days, I'm glad I have people I trust enough to watch her, especially because I didn't have a partner right after she was born. So don't be afraid to lean on Damien or us girls. Take time for yourself. Damien loves you and isn't going to understand everything that you're feeling, but try to let him. I wish I had Grant with me back then. Who knows how differently I would have felt if I wasn't all alone."

"But you have him now, right?"

I smile, staring down at Ivy again. "Yes, I do. But . . ."

"But what?" Charlotte sits up straighter on her side of the couch. "Did something happen between you two?"

"Oh, no. Nothing bad, that is. Just . . ." I take a deep breath and relay the same information to her that I did to the girls at the game. By the time I'm done, Charlotte's eyes are so big that I think they might fall out of her head.

"Wow. That's a lot to think about."

"I know." Clearing my throat, I look down at the sleeping baby in my arms again. "Let me ask you this: If you knew that you might never be able to have another baby, how would that make you feel?" It's the one question I haven't been able to wrap my head around, the one question that I don't want to answer out of fear of what that answer may be.

"Well, my vagina is currently recovering from having the first one, so I think it's too soon to ask me that question," Charlotte jokes, making us both chuckle.

"Understandable. But seriously. If Ivy was it, if you and Damien couldn't have any more kids, would you be okay?"

She stares at her daughter as her lips move into a soft smile. "I think so. I mean, Damien is my husband, he's who I chose to live my life with. We created this beautiful girl, and by God's grace, if she's the only one we're meant to have, then so be it. I would be okay with being everything for them, even though I always imagined myself having more kids."

Her answer resonates with me, but I still want to press this further. "I totally agree. I love Scarlett with all of my heart, but I chose to have her on my own. Grant isn't her father, even though that's the role he's slowly taking on. So for me, I want more than anything to create a family with him, create a person who shares our DNA. That's what I always envisioned when I thought about my future, having a baby with the man that I love."

Charlotte smirks at me. "Noelle, you and I both know that family doesn't have to share DNA." She reaches for my hand. "You girls are proof of that. We're family no matter what biology says."

Her declaration makes my eyes sting. I look into hers and see tears forming as well. "I know."

"So if you can't have a kid with Grant, who's to say that you aren't a family? You could adopt. You could try IVF if he has frozen sperm. You could go the sperm donor route again if you want. There are other ways to have children, but there's only one of him."

And that right there solidifies it for me.

"You're right. You're absolutely right. It doesn't matter what it looks like as long as it's with him."

She squeezes my hand. "Exactly. Family is the people we choose to have in our lives. That's how you know you're truly rich, when the people around you are the ones who are meant to be there."

"I love you so much, Char. Thank you. I needed to hear this." On a shaky breath, I wipe under my eyes. For the past few weeks, I've been internally processing the what-ifs of Grant's revelation. But now I know that it doesn't matter what happens down the road. As long as I'm with him, that's all that matters.

Chapter 17

Noelle

"Grant?" I close the door to my house, partly out of breath because I'm running late for our date this evening. Today is my birthday, and Grant has something planned. I assumed he would be here to pick me up, but as I look around my house, I don't hear his usual noises.

I rushed from work to daycare to pick up Scarlett and then brought her to my mom right after that. She was eager for some granddaughter time when I called and asked her to watch my daughter for the night last week. She practically shoved me out of her house once I dropped her off, only wishing me a happy birthday and a good night before slamming the door in my face.

Grant met my family two days ago, and they fell in love with him just as fast as I did. My mother, particularly, was thrilled, which is probably why she was so eager to watch my daughter tonight.

My phone rings in my purse as if on cue, and I pick it up to see his name and the picture of the three of us from our first date at the zoo on the screen. "Hello?"

"Hello, beautiful."

"Babe, where are you? I thought you were picking me up?"

"I never said that."

I stare at the ground. "Oh. I guess you didn't. But where are you?"

"I'm where you're going to meet me in about an hour."

I glance at the clock, noting it's already a quarter to six. "Okay . . ."

"I have a surprise for you on your bed. Go take a look. It will explain everything. And Noelle?"

"Yes?"

"I know this may be a little strange, but try to have fun with it. I just wanted you to escape for a night."

"What?" I ask, but he ends the call before I can get an answer out of him. Wasting no time, I traipse down the hallway to my room and open the door, gasping as I take in the scene before me. Red roses cover every surface, the same flower tattooed on my shoulder that Grant always kisses every time he can get his lips on it. Electric tea light candles are sprinkled on the furniture, and in the center of the bed is a red lingerie set and gorgeous black cocktail dress along with a note.

I pull the cardstock out of the envelope and speedily scan the paper.

. . .

Noelle,

Tonight, for your birthday, I want to give you an experience that you'll never forget. You should know by now that I'm a good listener, and weeks ago you made a comment about wanting to escape this life for a night. Personally, I love our life. I look forward to every day that we're together and all of the memories we're making. I love spending my nights with you and Scarlett and making love to you after dark. But I also understand that sometimes, it's fun to be free, to feel like the weight of responsibility isn't holding you down. So that's what I want to give you to embark on this new year of your life, a year that I can't wait to spend with you.

Meet me at the Morgan Hotel downtown at seven sharp. I want you to go to the bar, order yourself a drink, and pretend that you're someone else when I come up to you. Not a mom, not a literary agent, but a beautiful woman who's enjoying her own company because every woman should be able to do that. So when you see me, I want you to pretend you don't know me. We're strangers, and tonight, we get to be whoever we want to be.

I love you, and I will see you soon.
Grant

"Oh my God." Clasping a hand over my mouth, I reread his words just to make sure that I understood him correctly. And suddenly, a thrilling excitement builds in my veins.

This man.

I can't even begin to describe how he makes me feel, and actions like this only solidify what I know deep in the marrow of my bones—he's the one man who was made for me, and I don't think I would have appreciated him and cherished him if I hadn't met him when I did. He makes me feel seen, not just as a mom but as a woman. He knows every part of me, every title that I wear—he acknowledges them and doesn't make me feel ashamed for wanting every facet of my life to be rich.

I drag my fingertips over the red lace knowing that Grant picked this out, that this is what he wanted to see me in. The dress lying next to the lingerie is low cut in the front to offer a view of my cleavage—or what I have left of it—with thin, delicate straps that will show off plenty of skin. The waist is accentuated, but the skirt is free-flowing and cascades down to the floor, and the slit up the side will surely hit me mid-thigh. It's sexy, and I can't wait to put it on.

I waste no time hopping in the shower, only cleansing my body and keeping my hair dry so it won't take as long to style. I reapply my makeup with a smoky eye, pull my hair up in an elegant twist with a few loose tendrils down to frame my face, slip my sexy underwear and dress on, and hop into the Uber that Grant ordered to arrive at my house to take me to the hotel.

Opulence surrounds me when my heels click against the tile floors of the Morgan Hotel in downtown LA. White marble floors with flecks of gold shine under my shoes, cream-colored walls with black accents frame the open lobby, and crystal chandeliers hang from the ceilings. I've always heard that Wesley Morgan, the current CEO of the Morgan Hotel empire, spares no expense on his family's legacy, and apparently the rumors are true.

A bar to the right calls to me, the place where Grant said to meet him, so I slowly make my way over, my skin vibrating with anticipation and my heart trying to break free from my ribcage. While I was getting ready, I tried to decide who I wanted to be for the night, and so many ideas popped into my head that I had the hardest time choosing. Ultimately, I decided that I'll know who I want to pretend to be when I see Grant. The thought is more thrilling to me than I care to admit.

Deep, rich wood gleams under the dim lighting of the bar. Stepping into this area is like stepping into an entirely different building than the clean and crisp hotel lobby I was just in. A bartender behind the bar, dressed in a full tux and bowtie, wipes the counter in front of him. The room is giving off speakeasy vibes with red velvet booths and bottles of whiskey displayed on glass shelves along one of the walls.

The air smells of alcohol, bad decisions, and sex—sex I'm sure will be so spectacular with the man I'm waiting to surprise me at any moment that I can barely stand the suspense.

But he doesn't approach me right away. I keep checking the time on my phone, lighting up the screen to see if I've missed a notification from him. But there's nothing. And that excitement from before begins to turn to apprehension.

Did I go to the wrong bar? Did something happen to him?

"Waiting on someone?" the bartender asks, topping off a drink order for one of the waiters and pulling me from my thoughts.

I almost say yes but then remember I'm not supposed to be me tonight. So I lie. "No. Just checking the time."

"It's almost seven thirty. It's still early."

"Well, it's also kind of late. Today is my birthday, and that means it's almost over." I figure telling that truth isn't against the rules for the night, and part of me is having a hard time slipping into another persona.

He flashes me a kind smile. "Well, happy birthday."

"Thank you."

"No woman should be alone on her birthday." A deep, familiar voice rings out next to me, alerting all of my senses. Goosebumps rush over my skin as I turn to my left and find Grant standing there in a tux—and dear Lord, he looks good enough to eat. He looks like he could be the next James Bond with his Armani glasses, crisp white shirt, perfectly pressed black tux, and barely there scruff on his face. If he was hiding a gun in his pants, he would be that much hotter.

Fortunately for me, I know he is packing some serious heat in there, just not the lethal kind.

Saliva pools in my mouth, so I rush to swallow before it spills out. This man is gorgeous, and he's all mine.

But for tonight, he's someone else.

And so am I.

"Can I buy you a drink to celebrate?" he asks, trailing a finger down my bare arm.

"Yes, thank you."

He takes the seat next to me, spreading his legs so his thigh rubs against mine and gestures to the bartender with his chin. "Whiskey neat for the lady," he declares and then shifts his eyes to mine. "Are you waiting on anyone?"

I shake my head, slightly nervous about how this is all going to play out. "No."

"I guess that's good for me then." He turns in his chair to face me.

"And why is that?"

"I won't have to tell any other man that his date has been taken for the evening."

"You would steal me away from a date with another man?" Oxygen enters and leaves my lungs quickly as I try to stay in character.

"In a heartbeat." His eyes dance all over my face, my upper body, and down my legs before trailing back up to meet mine. "You're the type of woman wars are declared over."

Warmth travels down my spine and rests right between my legs. "What if I don't want to be fought over? What if I just wanted to be alone tonight?"

"I don't believe you."

"No?"

He shakes his head, smirking. "Not at all. Not with the way your eyes were eating me up a few moments ago when I came over."

Oh, so that's how he wants to play this? Bold and to the point? Well, perhaps he needs to work for this a little more.

"I was just admiring your tux," I say, shifting to lift my glass and take a sip, diverting my eyes from him. "It's designer, and I have a flair for fashion."

"Is that so?"

I nod. "Yes. In fact, tonight is my last night in Los Angeles. I'm leaving for Paris tomorrow for a year. It's my gift to myself for my birthday: starting over in a new country. I'm a writer and am hoping that the French landscape will inspire my next novel."

"A writer, huh?"

"Yes. It's always been a dream of mine." That part is not a lie, but one day I will make it a reality.

"And so you're leaving tomorrow?"

"I am."

"Care to make your last night in LA one you won't soon forget?"

I turn to face him again now, fighting to hide the smile on my lips. "And how would I make that happen?"

"By spending the night in my bed."

My breath catches, but I recover quickly. "That's a little forward, don't you think?" My mind is reeling with how Grant is talking to me right now, this commanding and possessive tone in his voice. I only hear it from him when we're in bed, and it does insane things to my libido every time. I think the feeling's exaggerated right now because we're pretending to be strangers, and I'll be the first to admit that if Grant had approached me like this one night at a bar and told me boldly that he wanted me in his bed, I would have agreed pretty damn quickly.

"And what might I find in there?" I ask teasingly, taking another sip of my drink.

"Pleasure, and plenty of it."

"You haven't even asked for my name," I counter.

"Do I need to? Names are just a formality, and I know you won't be needing mine, either. The only thing you're going to be calling me is 'God' in a few minutes, so what's the point in trading useless information?"

My thighs clench together. "One night? No names?"

"One night, a night we'll both remember forever, because I have a feeling I'll never forget this face." He reaches out and cups my jaw, drawing my bottom lip down with his thumb, making my breath hitch.

And that's when I know I'm done playing this game. I just want to be as close to this man as I can get.

"Then I guess you'd better take me to bed before I change my mind."

Grant stands, slaps a hundred-dollar bill on the counter, grabs my hand, and leads me out of the bar without a second glance at the bartender or anyone else watching us.

We stand in front of the elevator, waiting for one to arrive, and the entire time, I'm trembling with anticipation and also trying really hard not to laugh.

When the doors open, Grant pulls me into the small space, presses the button for the doors to close so no one else can join us, and then pins me to the wall, caging me in.

"Goddamn, you look so sexy tonight. I can't wait to defile you."

I grab the lapels of his jacket and pull him closer. "Why don't you start now?"

Without any hesitation, Grant crashes his lips to mine, thrusting his tongue deeply in my mouth and stealing the breath from my lungs. He hikes one of my legs up around his waist and grinds his erection into me, making me wetter than I already was.

"Grant," I moan out of habit, which makes him stop.

"I'm not Grant tonight, remember?"

And that's when it hits me—it's nice to pretend, to think about what it would be like to be someone else for a night, but ultimately, I just want to be us—because us together is a place I've fought to get to for a very long time, and Grant is who I want to spend my birthday with.

"No." I shake my head. "I want it to be you."

"Are you sure?"

"Yes. I want to be us. You are the man I want to sleep with tonight. You're the one I want to celebrate my birthday with."

"Fuck, thank God." He rests his forehead on mine, breathing heavily. "I was trying so hard back there to be someone else, but when I saw you, all I saw was Noelle, the woman I fell in love with."

"You did a good job at being demanding, though. That was sexy, and I'm not going to complain if you still want to defile me."

His lips twist in a smirk. "Oh, baby. That I plan on doing no matter what, especially now that I have you alone and in that dress." He takes a step back, wiping the corner of his mouth with his thumb as he looks me up and down. "Fuck, Noelle. You're so damn beautiful. And this dress highlights every part of your body that I love."

"I can't decide whether I like you better in a tux or naked," I retort.

Grant chuckles. "As long as you'll take me either way, I'm okay with that."

Reaching out, I grab his jacket and pull him against me again. "I want you any way I can have you."

"The feeling is mutual, baby."

When the elevator dings on the eleventh floor, Grant grabs my hand and drags me down the hall toward our room. The entire floor is quiet, which I'm hoping means there aren't a ton of people near us, because I'm about to be the opposite of quiet.

When we reach the door, Grant takes the key card out of his pocket, holds it up to the sensor, and the unit lights up green, letting us inside. And as soon as the door shuts behind us, he pins me against the wall, holding my hands above my head. Dragging his nose up the column of my throat until he reaches my ear, he whispers, "Did you wear the lingerie?"

"Yes."

"Then it's time to strip, baby. I want to see it."

He releases my hands and then steps back before moving further into the room. I stand there waiting for his next move until he takes a seat in the chair in the corner, unfastening his tie and tossing it to the side, spreading his legs wide and adjusting his cock as he beckons me to him.

On shaky heels, I stride across the floor, waiting until I'm right in front of him to step out of my shoes, depriving myself of the extra three inches they provided me.

"Slowly," he commands, jutting his chin toward me.

And now that it's really him in front of me—the man that I love who can also command my body in an instant—I truly feel like this is the celebration I wanted tonight.

I reach up and push one strap of my dress off my shoulder, letting it fall down my arm. Then I repeat the process on the other side before slowly forcing the dress down my chest and stomach, stretching it over my hips before it pools on the floor beneath me, leaving me standing there in the red lace that Grant chose for me.

"Fuck me, Noelle." He licks his lips. "Turn around, baby."

I do, slowly like I know he wants, casting a glance at him over my shoulder when he sees my entire back side. The underwear he chose wasn't a thong but is definitely a high-cut, cheeky brief that lets most of my ass cheeks show. Which, in my opinion, is even sexier.

And even though I still struggle with my body and the new appearance and scars that it bears, Grant never makes me feel undesirable. In fact, I can hear his heavy breathing behind me, his movement as he takes off his jacket and tosses it somewhere else in the room.

"Come here, Noelle."

I spin around and start toward him again, reaching his chair as he directs me to straddle his lap. He runs his hands all over my ass and hips and then up my back until they bury into my hair to pull my head toward him so our lips can meet.

"I love you," he whispers, placing a chaste kiss on my lips.

"I love you, too."

"Tonight, I want to show you how much."

"You show me every day."

He lets out a groan. "I try, but sometimes I feel like it's not enough." He runs his hands up and down my body again before I can interject and argue with him about that. "I want to go slow, but I also want to fuck you into next week tonight."

"That sounds perfect."

His low chuckle vibrates all over my skin. "Let's start with making you come on my tongue." My vagina twitches at the thought. "Stand up."

I move to step off the chair, but he stops me. "No, on the chair. I want that pussy in my face." He looks above us. "You can put your hands on the wall so you won't fall. I'm gonna eat you right here so you can see me under you and watch my tongue dance all over your clit."

"Grant," I gasp as he helps me stand on the uneven cushion, settling into a position where I feel like I'm not going to fall.

He removes his glasses, sets them on the table next to us, and then bites his bottom lip. "As much as I love these under-wear on you, they need to go." He hooks his fingers in the sides and pulls them down my legs, helping me step out of them as I support myself with my hands against the wall in front of me. "Fuck, that's better." Slowly, he drags a finger through my slit and groans when he feels how wet I already am. "You're drenched, baby."

"I've been this way since I got your note."

"Good. Now let me taste you."

He puts his hands on my ass and guides me forward so my pussy lines up with his mouth. I have to bend my knees slightly to get to the right height, but Grant helps support me with his hands just as his tongue finds my clit and draws a lazy circle around the nub.

I throw my head back and close my eyes. "Oh God."

"Told you you'd be calling me God," he mumbles against me as he gets to work, flicking and sucking every part of me he can reach.

I keep one hand on the wall and bury the other in his hair as his touch sets my body on fire. Grant looks up at me between my legs, his blue eyes trained on my green ones as he devours me, dragging his tongue slowly through me, hands full of my ass so he can keep me right where he wants me.

"Yes," I moan, feeling my orgasm start to build. Grant runs a finger through me from behind and unhurriedly pushes it in, filling me slowly while keeping his tongue moving between my legs. "Oh God, yes."

"Come on my tongue, Noelle." I feel him start to rub that magical spot inside of me, and then I'm seeing stars, struggling to keep myself upright and not smother his face with my body. Grant draws out every last tremor before he brings me down to his lap and holds me close. "Damn."

"Best birthday ever."

"Oh, I'm not done giving you gifts yet, babe." He moves for me to stand and kisses me hard the second we're both on our feet. I feel his fingers pinch the clasp of my bra, and then he rips it from my body, baring me completely to him. He cups my breast and pinches my nipples, which sends an electric current through my body straight between my legs.

"Grant, you need to be naked."

"Help me," he mumbles against my lips as I reach for his shirt and undo his buttons as fast as I can while our mouths continue to move against each other's. Grant begins to pull his dress shirt down his arms and tosses it to the floor as I unbutton his pants and pull down the zipper. He makes quick work of shoving those down his legs as well, kicking off his shoes before he can fully remove them, and then his cock hits my stomach as we collide again.

I reach down and wrap my fingers around his length, stroking him, and then drop to my knees to taste him.

"Fuck, Noelle."

I draw him in, suck him hard, and lick him from root to tip on my knees as my body heats up again, knowing what his dick feels like inside of me. And that's all I want right now, more than anything.

Grant must feel the same way, because he hoists me to my feet before I can work him up too much and directs me to the bed.

"Get on your hands and knees." I follow his orders, pushing my ass out toward him, which he playfully smacks, simultaneously shocking me and turning me on even more. "Fuck, I love your ass."

"I love your cock. Now, give it to me, please. Make me come again, Grant."

"Oh, I plan on it."

He runs the head of his dick through my wetness before slowly pushing in, stretching me out and filling me up. And it's exquisite. Nothing compares to the moment we join each and every time.

"Oh, yes."

"Fuck, baby. Your pussy takes me so well."

His dirty words always spark arousal within me. "Grant . . ."

He finds a pace that spurs us both on and then fucks me— hard, fast, deep, and with such force that each thrust has me crying out. I feel him rip the clip from my hair, letting it fall around my face, and then he grabs a handful of it, pulling me back to him so his chest is pressed up against my spine.

"You are so fucking sexy, Noelle. I don't ever want you to doubt that I want you." He smacks my ass with his other hand before smoothing his palm over my still stinging skin. "You drive me wild. You're the most incredible woman I've ever met. And I plan on making you come over and over for the rest of our lives. Do you hear me?" I feel his fingers drift across my hip to my pubic bone and then down to circle my clit.

"Yes."

"I love you," he whispers in my ear as he picks up the pace

with his cock and his fingers, driving me closer and closer to the edge of indescribable ecstasy.

"I love you, too."

"Come with me?"

"Yes, I'm there," I breathe.

And with a few more thrusts, we shatter together, my screams echoing in the room, Grant's groans vibrating against my ear and his lips hitting my neck as we come down. He turns my head further to the side as he releases my hair and kisses me. And my body finally melts when our tongues touch.

Once we clean up, we lie next to each other in bed, face-to-face. I draw lazy circles across his chest through the short hair there, still in awe that this incredibly handsome, selfless man chose me.

"Do you remember the day we met?" I ask him, feeling nostalgic in this moment.

"I think about that day all the time."

"Really?" My eyes find his.

"Yes. Why does that surprise you?"

A soft chuckle leaves my lips. "Because sometimes I still can't believe that you gave me the shirt off your back."

"Honestly? Me, too," he replies, smiling.

"Really?"

"It was just an instinct that I couldn't ignore. I had to help you."

"You've helped me so much since then. Seriously, Grant. You've changed my life."

He runs a finger down the side of my face. "You've changed mine, too, baby."

My fingers continue to dance across his chest, the mountains of solid muscle that I love so much. "I don't know why this is coming to mind right now, but I remember calling you Mr. I'm-too-sexy-for-my-shirt in my head that day."

He laughs. "Is that so?"

"Yes, and the next thing I knew, you were handing me yours." I kiss his chest this time. "I'm happy to report that my assessment was accurate. You shouldn't wear shirts, like, ever." Running my palm over his skin now, I sigh. "But then again, I like being the only one to see you like this. I just love your body."

He rolls me onto my back and begins trailing a finger across my stomach, tracing my stretch marks and instantly making me self-conscious. "I love your body, too."

"Are you sure?"

"Yes, Noelle. I told you, I don't care about these marks like you do." He leans over and kisses my stomach. "These are your tiger stripes, baby. You made a human. There's nothing more beautiful than that." His eyes find mine again, and then he's cupping my face. "But more importantly, the things I love about you aren't physical. I think we fixate so much on our outward appearance that we forget that it's our souls that matter most, the type of people we are and how we make others feel. And you make me feel ten feet tall. You make me feel like I have a purpose when I didn't for so long."

Whispering, I reach for the back of his neck, drawing his

lips to mine. "I love you. Thank you for one of the best birthdays I've ever had. Thank you for listening to me and trying to make my wishes come true."

Our lips touch. "Thank you for being born. Thank you for crashing into my life. And thank you for letting me be a part of Scarlett's, too." He kisses me one more time and then leaps from the bed. "But I think there's one more gift I can give you tonight."

I sit up so I can see him. "Where are you going?" He doesn't answer me, but instead he locates his phone, clicking around on the screen before music starts to ring out, and I lose it, laughing hysterically. "Oh my God, Grant. Are you serious?"

Grant starts to swivel his hips, his naked ass on display while he faces away from me. He bends down to find his shirt, putting it back on but leaving it open, and continues to dance and lip-sync the words to "I'm Too Sexy" by Right Said Fred while wearing nothing but his dress shirt.

Holding my stomach as I laugh harder than I have in years, I watch him make a fool of himself for me. And I fall in love with him all over again, feeling like there's nothing we won't be able to survive together.

But little did we know, our world was about to be rocked just a week later, and the confidence I had in us would start to crumble as well.

Chapter 18

Noelle

Rubbing the side of my right breast, I groan. "Jesus. What's going on?" I stick my left hand inside the neck of my shirt and feel around, making sure nothing is poking me from inside my bra. And of course, that's the moment that my assistant enters my office, furrowing her brow at me.

"Everything okay?" Madison asks, shutting the door behind her and walking further into the room.

"Yeah, I think. I don't know. My boob just really hurts."

"Did you do something to it?"

"Not that I recall."

"Is your milk coming in? My sister always said she felt a burn when her milk would come down."

"No. I stopped nursing about six weeks ago."

"Hmm. Are you about to start your period?"

"Maybe. I haven't had one yet since I stopped nursing . . ."

She claps her hands together. "Then that must be it."

"Yeah, you're right." I wake up my computer by jostling my mouse. "Okay, what's on the agenda for today?" We slip into our usual routine, discussing my upcoming meetings and a flight I'm going to have to take to Chicago again in a few weeks. I'll meet with one of the executives of Larson Publishing and my client that lives out there, too, plus field a few new inquiries that have been sent in that Madison thinks are worth my time.

By the time we finish, it's almost lunchtime, and my stomach is growling with hunger.

"Want me to order in the usual?"

"Oh, yes. And don't forget my Coke?"

Madison rolls her eyes at me. "You act like I don't know you or something."

Laughing, I go back to the paperwork in front of me and knock a few things off my to-do list while I wait for my lunch.

By the end of the day, I'm exhausted but feel productive as I pick up Scarlett from daycare, knowing it's going to be just the two of us this evening since Grant is on an overnight flight. It's been a little over a week since my birthday, but things have been nothing but perfect when we're together. We've slipped into this routine of switching off between sleeping at his house and mine, talking on the phone on the nights when he's working out of town, and making time for each other on the days he has off. I'm tired but the happiest I've ever been in my life. The man has surpassed every expectation I could have in a partner, and every day that we're together, it just gets better.

As I'm getting Scarlett's dinner ready—some rice, green beans, and small pieces of chicken—a wave of nausea crashes through my stomach at the smell of it.

"Ugh." I shove the plate to the side as my stomach rolls. Breathing deeply through my nose, I wait for it to subside, but it doesn't. Instead, I brace myself on the counter, waiting for the inevitable—and then it hits me. I lunge for the trash can and puke up my lunch, heaving until I feel like there's nothing left in my stomach.

"Oh my God," I moan between breaths, trying to compose myself enough to stand up. Scarlett is fussing in her high chair, waiting on her dinner, but I hunch over the trash can until I feel the dizziness subside. When I stand up, she's crying, pissed that she doesn't have food in front of her, so I take her plate, put it on her tray and then move to wash my hands, filling my cupped hand with water and bringing it to my lips to rinse out my mouth.

"Well, that was unexpected." My stomach continues to roll as I hurry to the bathroom to grab my toothbrush, bringing it out to the kitchen to brush my teeth so I can still keep an eye on Scarlett. And even though I feel better, especially since my stomach has been kind of queasy since I ate lunch, apparently my body was not done extracting that meal from my system because I get sick two more times before I put Scarlett to bed.

By the time I lay down, I am so tired that I pass out and miss Grant's call.

In the morning, my stomach feels better though still slightly uneasy, but my lower back is killing me, and that's when it hits me—the last time I felt that type of lower back pain and nausea was when I found out I was pregnant. I gasp as I contemplate the possibility.

Grant and I haven't been using condoms since I stopped nursing. I was so caught up in him and the way he makes me feel that I didn't think about the likelihood of getting pregnant. But then again, with his history, I didn't even know if that was an option. And I would have if we had talked about it, but we still haven't. Even though I knew we needed to have that conversation, we've both been avoiding it ever since he told me about his cancer diagnosis, and I haven't been back to see my OB-GYN about birth control.

Oh my God. Could I be pregnant with Grant's baby?

Needing someone to go through this with me, someone who has experienced postpartum and how it affects your cycle, I reach for my cell phone and dial my sister's number.

"Hey. What's going on?" she asks as soon as she answers. I don't call my sister out of the blue normally, so I'm sure she thinks something's wrong.

I'm not sure if it is or isn't yet.

"I have a question for you. Do you have a minute?"

"Yeah, let me lock myself in the bathroom really quick." And then she scares me with her outburst. "Oh, wait! Let me grab my coffee and a few frozen Kit Kats first."

"You eat frozen Kit Kats this early in the morning?" I

glance at the clock on my nightstand, noting it's just after seven.

"Um, yes. There is no time constraint on when it's appropriate to eat chocolate." I hear the crinkle of candy wrappers and then a door shut. "Okay, I'm alone and have sustenance. What's going on?"

"So this may seem out of left field, but when you were nursing and then you stopped, how long did it take for your period to come back?"

"Usually within the month. With Nicholas, though, it took almost two." Her answer both reassures and scares me. "Why? What's going on?"

"Well, you know I stopped nursing about six weeks ago, but I haven't had a period yet."

"Okay . . ."

"So yesterday, my boobs were killing me, and then I got sick several times last night."

"Oh, shit. Do you think you're pregnant?"

"I don't know," I whisper, almost afraid to admit it's an option.

"Well, how does the possibility make you feel?"

"Both terrified and excited. I mean, I would love nothing more than to have a child with Grant."

"Have you guys been doing anything to prevent it from happening?"

"Not really."

She laughs. "I'm impressed. I didn't know you could be so reckless."

"It didn't dawn on me until now. We've just been so wrapped up in each other." I do feel reckless and irresponsible right now, but in the same breath, I can't be mad, either. I love him.

"Must be nice. Do you think he'll be upset? Have you called him?"

"I haven't talked to him about it yet. He's working, and this all happened last night. It just hit me moments ago that me being pregnant was an option. My lower back is killing me, too."

"I never got lower back pain until further along in my pregnancies."

"It was one of the first symptoms I experienced with Scarlett, which is why I'm thinking this is a possibility."

"Well, there's only one way to find out, Noelle. Take a test."

"Should I wait for Grant?"

"When will he be home?"

"Tomorrow. He's coming over tomorrow night."

"Can you wait that long?"

"I-I don't know. But part of me wants to do it with him. I never got to do that last time—that moment when you're both waiting together for the results. It's one of those moments I had to mourn that I would never experience."

"That's understandable. So wait for him. And who knows? It could just be your period coming back. Our bodies do strange things after we have a kid."

"But what about the throwing up?"

"Did you eat something that didn't agree with you yesterday?"

"It wasn't anything I haven't eaten before . . ."

"Well, like I said, there's only one way to find out."

I take a deep breath and blow it out. "Okay, thank you for talking to me."

"Of course. I feel honored that you called."

"I needed someone to talk to who's been through this. Charlotte just had Ivy, so she doesn't know yet, you know?"

"I know, but it means a lot to hear from you regardless."

"I love you, Holly. I always have. You and I just don't see eye-to-eye on everything—but that's okay. We're very different people."

"I called a marriage counselor yesterday."

"You did?"

"Yup. And I told Seth that I want him to go with me. He fought me on it, but then I laid everything out there for him— told him how I've been feeling, what I need from him. By the time I was done, he looked at me like I'd grown two heads. I told him that if we don't go talk to someone, I would rather parent by myself."

"And what did he say?"

"He kissed me and said he would be there, to just let him know when the appointment was."

My heart beats so hard for my sister. "I'm so glad, Holly."

"Thank you. There's still a lot to unpack, but it felt really good to know that he wants to fix things. He really wants to keep our family together."

"Then that's what you focus on." Scarlett's mumbles come through the monitor on my nightstand, letting me know she's awake and ready to go for the day. And I'd better get going as well. At least it's Saturday and I don't have to worry about going to work today, although the distraction would be welcome right about now. Instead, I have to wait all weekend to talk to Grant about our situation, because that is definitely something I do not want to discuss over the phone. "Hey, Scarlett just woke up, so I need to go."

"All right. Keep me posted."

"I will. Love you, Holly."

"Love you, too."

I end the call and get out of bed, preparing myself to take on the day even though there are problems in my life that I can't solve right now. But whatever happens, I want Grant beside me when I find out. So I'll wait for him. I'd wait for him forever.

Chapter 19

Grant

Two Days Earlier

"I'm sorry, Grant. I wish I had better news, but the tests don't lie. The numbers are low, even for what we would deem a low sperm count, which is less than fifteen million per milliliter, but yours was around one million."

My stomach plummets. This is exactly what I was afraid of. "Fuck. So what does that mean?"

Sitting in Dr. Anivan's office, I'm hit with news that I've been avoiding for weeks. After I requested to have my sperm tested, life kind of got in the way, and things progressed with Noelle to the point that avoidance became the name of the game. The more I slipped into my life with her, the more I didn't want to know what the outcome of the tests I sought out was, especially if it was a poor one. And I guess my gut was right, because the results that my doctor just delivered have me grinding my teeth together while an onslaught of emotions barrels into me.

The doctor's office has been calling me, trying to get me to come in to talk about the results, but I didn't return their calls until this week, when Dr. Anivan called me himself.

"Not all hope is lost. You still could potentially father a child naturally, but I'm not going to lie, the chances are low. Studies have shown that while your count is down, there are men with those same numbers who have fathered children the good, old-fashioned way. And you still have your deposit from ten years ago. You can still be a father, it just won't necessarily be through common means."

"Is my deposit even still viable?"

"It should be. We can always assess that, too, but the process for freezing and storing sperm is highly clinical and proven to be very effective." Clenching my hands together, I stare down at the floor. "I can tell this isn't the news you were hoping for, but there are still options, Grant. You just need to have a conversation with your partner to decide on which ones you may want to proceed with. Were you trying to conceive?"

Fuck. How do I answer that?

Were we actively trying? No. But was I trying to prevent it? Also no. Was I playing a game of Russian roulette just to see if I could land on the number I bet on? Perhaps on a subconscious level I was, but now I know that my choices—or efforts, if you will—were for nothing.

"I would also recommend testosterone therapy."

"Therapy?"

He nods. "Weekly injections. Your levels were low for your age, but that's not uncommon, given your history."

"Great."

"Grant, look at me." I force my eyes up to meet his, both hating the man sitting in front of me for being the bearer of bad news and grateful to him as well for saving my life over ten years ago. "Please, don't let this defeat you. I know it can be hard to accept, but if the woman you're with loves you, this is just a speed bump you'll have to get over."

"Thanks, Doc."

"Come in next week to start your injections. And you can email me with any questions you may have."

I leave the office feeling defeated and angry—resentful for a diagnosis I thought I came to terms with all those years ago and fearful for a situation I'm in now, where I have to have this conversation with Noelle. I already knew it would need to happen eventually, but now that I know the truth, I feel like she needs to know as well.

Closing my eyes and resting my head against the back of my seat, I sit in my truck as all of these emotions run through me. I have to be at the airport in three hours for an overnight flight to Seattle. I won't be back until late tomorrow, so Noelle and I agreed that I would come over Sunday evening. At least that gives me a few days to get my head on straight, to process what I'm feeling right now, which I think can only be described as rage mixed with uncertainty.

Maybe I need to take my aggression out on a punching bag later. That may be the only possible cure to wake me up from this black hole I feel I'm being sucked into.

And the shitty thing about black holes? Once something enters them, it gets lost forever.

Sunday evening comes faster than I wanted it to, which is why I'm currently standing on the front porch of Noelle's house, refusing to knock on her door just yet. I tried calling her for the past two nights to talk, but she didn't pick up either time. She said she passed out early on Friday, and then last night, she texted me about an hour after my call, stating that she was at her mom's house and would call me later.

But that call never came.

I don't know why, but my intuition is rearing its ugly head again, and my gut is telling me that I'm about to walk into her home and into a situation that I might not like the outcome of.

"Hey." Startling me from my thoughts, the door opens, and Noelle is standing on the other side, brow pinched, with Scarlett on her hip. "How long were you planning on standing out here? I was watching you on the doorbell camera, waiting for you to knock, but you looked deep in thought. Are you okay?"

Scarlett squeals at that exact moment, reaching out for me. Without any hesitation, I grab the little girl who's stolen my heart, cradle her in my arms, and kiss the top of her head. "Hey, sweet girl. I missed you."

She lunges for my mouth, pressing hers to it to give me a kiss. It's her new favorite thing to do.

"She missed you, too, babe. Come inside, yeah?" Noelle holds the door open wider, allowing me to step through. The smell of a fall-scented candle hits my nose—apple and spice. "You sure you're okay?"

"Yeah, it was just a long trip," I reply, which isn't a total lie. But I'm not about to unload all the information I need to on her the second I walk through the door.

"It was." She closes the gap between us, presses up on her toes, and kisses me softly. "I missed you, too."

"Same, baby." Holding her to me, I draw in a shaky breath and let it out slowly. "So much."

"Come sit down at the table. Dinner is almost ready."

"You didn't have to cook. I could have grabbed something on my way over." Carrying Scarlett to her high chair, I buckle her in and then sit across from her, handing her toys to play with as we wait for our food. Her minion is on the floor next to her chair, so I pick it up, put it in front of my face, and make the "Bah!" noise. She falls apart laughing.

"I know, but I figured you'd be sick of takeout and would appreciate a home-cooked meal. Besides, I made chicken and dumplings in the crockpot. It was one of the only things that sounded good, and it was easy, so it's not a big deal."

"Thank you." I stare at the little girl in front of me, knowing that her DNA has no effect on how much I care for her, but there's a part of me that will always wonder what it's like to look at another person and see your features in them. When I look at Scarlett, I see so much of Noelle—her eyes, lips, and light hair. But there's someone else in there, too, and for a short while there, I thought maybe I would get to experience that as well.

Now, I know the chances are slim, and it's eating away at me. No matter how much I internalized it while I was away, the news I received from my doctor on Friday is all that I've been thinking about. The last thing I want to do is disappoint the woman I love.

Noelle sits a heaping bowl of chicken and dumplings in front of me and then grabs one for herself. She places a small plate with bite-size pieces of food on it on Scarlett's high chair before taking the seat next to me.

We eat in silence until she finally looks over at me, a pinch in her brow so deep that I can't help but feel irritated by the way she's staring.

"What?"

"Grant, I feel like something's wrong."

Sighing, I lean back in my chair. "Fuck, Noelle. I'm sorry. I'm just . . . all up in my head right now."

"Did something happen while you were away?"

"No. Well, kind of. I-I do need to talk to you about something. I'm just not sure how to bring it up."

Huffing out a laugh, she takes a deep breath and blows it out slowly. "Well, I need to talk to you about something, too."

"Why don't you go first?" I suggest, hoping that what she

has to say is less dire than what I have to divulge. But then she hits me with something that feels like getting shot with a bullet and then stabbed in the same spot where the bullet pierced my skin.

"I think I might be pregnant."

All I can do is blow out a breath. I close my eyes on instinct, grinding my molars together as I debate what to say. Unfortunately, I land on, "You're not pregnant, Noelle."

That has her brows drawing together. "What? How do you know that? I haven't even taken a test."

"Because I just know."

"Grant," she says, reaching for my hand and placing hers on top of it. "We've been having unprotected sex for weeks, I haven't had a period since I stopped nursing almost two months ago, and I got sick the other night. My boobs are sore, my lower back is killing me, and the last time I felt this way was when I found out I was pregnant with Scarlett."

I stand from the chair and start pacing the floor, running my hands through my hair. "Noelle, the chances that you are pregnant are so fucking slim that it makes my chest ache. But I'm telling you, if you take a test, it's going to be negative."

"Why are you acting this way?" She looks like I just slapped her across the face, and I don't blame her. The tone I'm taking with her isn't one she's used to, but in my heart, I know she's not pregnant. She can't be. "Do you—do you not want to have a baby with me?"

I spin around to face her, clenching my jaw and fists together. "Of course I do, and that's the problem."

She shakes her head at me. "I'm so confused, Grant. This is . . . this is not how I thought this conversation was going to go." Tears fill her eyes. "I think I need to take a test—"

"You're not fucking pregnant, Noelle!" I shout so loudly that it startles Scarlett to the point her eyes bug out and then she cries. "Fuck!"

"Grant!" Noelle launches herself from her seat. "Calm down!"

"I can't, Noelle. I can't calm down, and I can't fucking get you pregnant!" I finally say. "It's virtually impossible."

"How do you know that?"

"I had cancer, remember?"

Her eyes bounce back and forth between mine. "I know, but most men can still have children after that."

"Well, I'm not one of them. I have so little sperm, Noelle, that the odds are monumentally stacked against us. I just went to the doctor on Friday, and he gave me the results of my sperm count test. Less than one million, Noelle! A normal man is shooting fifteen million per milliliter at a minimum! I barely had one!"

She inhales a shaky breath. "When did you get this test done?"

"About a month ago."

Her eyes narrow as a tear slips free. But the confusion from before has morphed into frustration and hurt. "And you didn't think to tell me? What happened to honesty, Grant? What happened to you saying you would always be honest with me?"

"I'm being honest now, aren't I? You're not fucking pregnant, Noelle. I'm almost positive."

"I still think I should take a test."

"And I know it's a waste of time. I can't give you a baby that way, Noelle, and it fucking kills me," I choke out, watching her suck in her lips as she fights her desire to cry.

"Grant . . ."

Shaking my head, I realize I can't look at her anymore. I can't deal with this conversation at the moment. It's still too fucking raw. I should have waited, talked to my brother or something before I spoke to her about it. That way, I could have been more levelheaded. But then she dropped this bomb on me about being pregnant, and I just . . . *can't*.

"I need to go."

Heading for the door, I feel her on my heels, Scarlett still screaming in the background. "So you're just going to run away? You're not going to stay here and talk about this? You're not going to wait with me while I take a pregnancy test?"

"I can't. I just . . . I need some space."

"How long do you need this space, Grant? How long are you going to leave me here, heartbroken and angry that the first time we encounter an obstacle in our relationship, you're headed for the door?"

"I don't know." Gripping the door handle, I whisper, "I don't know how long I'm going to need to get over this." I don't wait to hear her response, I just leave.

I hop in my truck, peel out of her driveway, and head for the first liquor store I can find. I buy a bottle of Jack Daniels and a thirty-six pack of beer and head for my house, ready to drown these feelings in alcohol. Maybe I just need to numb them for a little while, although leaving Noelle the way I did already has me halfway there.

A loud pounding on my door startles me from my perch on the couch. Groaning, I open my eyes as sunlight burns my retinas and a man with a jackhammer starts getting to work inside my skull.

"Grant! Open the door!" Gavin's voice is too sharp to ignore, so I wipe the drool from the corner of my mouth, slowly stand from the couch—which only makes my stomach turn—head for the door, and let him inside. "Jesus Christ. You look like shit."

"I feel like shit, too." I let out a burp, but that was a mistake as bile and last night's dinner decide to evacuate when I do. I run to the bathroom just in time to empty the contents of my stomach, heaving until I feel like there's nothing left. But the worst headache I've had in ages beats to the tune of its own drum with every step I take back toward my brother, who's staring around my living room.

"Tied one on last night, did ya?"

"What do you think?" I glare at him as I move into my kitchen to fetch a glass of water.

"Well, I was pretty sure that's what was happening, but your voicemails left much to be deciphered because I could only make out every few words. I definitely heard Noelle's name about a hundred times, and now that I see the damage, I'm guessing something happened." He picks up too many beer cans to count from my coffee table and deposits them in the recycling. I plop myself back on my couch and cover my eyes with my forearm. "Wanna talk about it?"

"I'm a fucking idiot."

"I kind of got that, but I need more details as to why." The couch dips beside me. "The last I saw, you two were headed down the aisle. What on earth could have possibly ruined that?"

I twist my head toward him, opening only one eye because it hurts too much to do both. "I got my sperm count results on Friday."

His eyebrows shoot up. "Oh."

"And it wasn't good."

"Well, I gathered that. What did the doctor say?" I relay the information that I can remember right now with the hangover from hell, and Gavin just stares at me, his brow furrowed. "Okay, so that's not too bad."

"I know it's not, but that's not the point." I point a finger at my chest. "It's how it makes me feel as a man, Gav. The one thing I'm supposed to be able to do, I can't."

His face softens. "Fuck, Grant. I'm sorry. I am, but you knew this was a possibility. We knew this back when you were diagnosed. They told you the odds. They told you that your treatment could lower your count, and it could happen over time."

"It just matters more now because of Noelle."

"Did she not take the news well?"

I growl. "No, but that's because she told me she thinks she might be pregnant, and I went off on her about how I know she isn't."

Gavin slaps his forehead. "Jesus Christ, Grant. Really?"

With my hand, I gesture toward the half-empty bottle of Jack Daniels and empty beer cans. "Hence my binge last night."

He blows out a breath and leans back on the couch. "Okay, so now what?"

"I told her I needed a few days. I need to get my head on straight."

"About what, Grant? The facts are there. Do you think she's pregnant? I mean, it's not impossible, right?"

"It's very unlikely," I say, glaring at him.

"But you didn't stick around to find out?"

"No. I had to get away. The way she was looking at me, it's been my worst fear since I met her. My past and my future have collided, and I just . . ." I pinch the bridge of my nose. "I need a minute."

"Okay, but I will tell you this. I have never seen you this happy with someone, not even Denise before she left you after your diagnosis. You love that woman and her daughter, and even though your life didn't go as planned, this is where you are now. So the question is: Are you going to let this knowledge fester and infect your soul like a pimple that needs to be popped? Or are you going to accept your circumstances and be grateful for the life you have now, a relationship and future that you never thought you'd have in the first place?" He rests a hand on my shoulder as I feel my eyes well with tears. I fought them all last night, but now, in the aftermath, perhaps I just need to let the suckers out. "You beat something that could have killed you, Grant, and then you shut yourself off from love because one woman left you when you were vulnerable. Do you realize that on some level, you did the same thing to Noelle last night?"

"Fuck, Gav. Make me feel worse about it."

"I'm going to, because if you thought you hit rock bottom back then, I'm here to let you know that losing the woman you love because you've got your head up your ass will be a million times worse. You finally opened yourself up again, and because you're having to face shit you never dealt with back then, you might lose the best thing that has ever happened to you. Don't be that guy, Grant. That guy will be a miserable son of a bitch, and I don't want to see what that might turn you into. Just talk to her—or at least let her know that you need a few days and *then* talk to her. But don't shut her out. You're no less of a man because you're shooting low numbers. Franklin taught us what it means to be a man, brother: loyalty, honesty, and reliability. That's what a woman needs. The rest you can figure out later."

I lean forward and brace myself on my knees, hanging my head low as I draw in a shaky breath. "Fuck, Gav. I hear you, okay?"

He rubs my back. "That's all I want you to think about. I'll let you go. Lord knows, you're going to be in pain all day.

You're thirty-eight now, brother. Hangovers last for, like, three days now, don't they?" he jokes.

"Yeah, sounds about right."

I feel him stand from the couch, patting my back one last time. "Take a shower, get something to eat if you can stomach it, and then write some shit down or go to a place that will allow you to think. But don't make her wait too long. She doesn't deserve that."

"I know. Thank you."

I don't look up when I hear the door open and shut, but now that I'm alone, I let it all out. I let the tears run free as I imagine myself without Noelle and Scarlett in my life. If they are all I get, I know I'd die a happy man, but having choices taken from you isn't an easy pill to swallow, either.

By the end of the day, I feel halfway normal, but I still don't know what to say to Noelle, so I text her the next morning, hoping she'll respond.

Me: *I'm sorry.*

It takes her about twenty minutes to text me back, which feel like the longest twenty minutes of my life.

Noelle: *We need to talk.*

Me: *I just need a few days, please.*

Noelle: *Two? Three?*

Me: *I have Thursday off. Can we talk then?*

Noelle: *Yes. Your place or mine?*

Me: *Doesn't matter.*

Noelle: *You choose.*

Me: *Yours, I guess.*

Noelle: *See you then.*

And that's all I get. By the shortness of her texts, I can tell that I've hurt her, but I just know that my headspace is clouded right now, and until those clouds part, I need to be alone. Future me will thank me for this later.

Chapter 20

Noelle

"Oh my God! What happened?"

I'm a blubbering mess. I couldn't even make it up the driveway without falling apart, knowing I was going to see the girls tonight. It's Monday night, which means football is on, and since we couldn't have brunch yesterday, Amelia invited us all over to watch the game this evening. The team is away tonight, so Penelope is here, too, and as soon as Amelia opened the door, I lost it.

I contemplated texting them yesterday, but I was hoping that Grant would reach out to me and this would be resolved quickly. Unfortunately, he didn't text me until about ten o'clock this morning, and our conversation was dismal, at best.

"Here. Give me Scarlett," Penelope declares as I wipe the

snot from my nose on the sleeve of my shirt, the same shirt I've had on for two days. I called into work today, knowing I wouldn't possess the mental capacity to deal with it, and luckily Madison was able to reschedule meetings and push things around for me. I owe her big time.

"Thank you."

Amelia wraps her arm around me and leads me into her kitchen, placing me on a stool at her island and handing me a box of Kleenex. Penelope follows us, holding Scarlett, while Charlotte rounds the corner with Ivy sleeping in her arms. "What the hell happened?"

"Grant and I . . . we . . ."

Charlotte gasps. "Did you break up?"

"No. I mean, I don't know. We just kind of had a fight, and it was bad, you guys. Like, really bad." I dab a tissue under my eyes. "I just hope this isn't going to turn into the end."

"Disagreements are normal," Amelia explains, stroking my arm. "Every couple has them. I mean, look at the three of us. You were there for all of the big ones, especially in the beginning of each of our relationships."

Penelope shakes her head as she hands Scarlett a cracker. "Damn, Grant. I thought I wasn't going to have to threaten him. And Maddox is out of town, so I can't get him to do it. I need to send Grant three hundred of something, ladies. What should it be?"

I roll my eyes. "No need for that."

"Tell us what happened," Amelia says, setting a glass of water in front of me, which I'm grateful is not wine because I still don't know if I'm pregnant or not. I couldn't make myself take a test. I wanted to do it with Grant, but who knows if that will happen at this rate. The entire vision I had in my head of how that conversation would go blew right out the window when he raised his voice and told me he knew I wasn't pregnant, like the man knew my body better than me. I think that's the part that pisses me off the most.

I spend the next few minutes relaying everything I was feeling on Friday that leads me to believe I am pregnant.

"Are you?" Charlotte whispers.

"I still don't know. I couldn't bring myself to take a test, but I have yet to have a period."

"We can be there for you," Penelope says with a nod of her head. "It will be like when Monica and Phoebe were there for Rachel when she took her pregnancy test on *Friends*. You didn't let us be a part of that the first time, so I know we can be the support you need this time. Just say the word, and I'll run out and get you one."

I huff out a laugh, the first one that's felt natural in days. "It's okay. I'm gonna wait for him to come around. That is, if he does."

Charlotte shakes her head while adjusting Ivy in her arms. "I'm still confused. How did this turn into a fight?"

"Because the moment I told him I thought I was pregnant, he told me he knew I wasn't, which led him to admitting that he recently had his sperm count tested and it's not good. The chances of us conceiving a child naturally are very small."

"Oh God," Amelia whispers. "That had to be tough for him to share."

"I'm sure it was, but he shouted it at me before storming off, refusing to let us talk about it."

Amelia softens her gaze. "He's hurting, Noelle. That couldn't have been an easy thing for him to admit to you."

"I know." More tears fall, tears for the man I love who I know is struggling but also tears for my heart that never got the chance to tell him that the information he shared doesn't matter to me. I already made up my mind a long time ago that whatever future I got with Grant was the one that I wanted, as long as it included him. "But I want him to know how I feel about the whole thing, and he didn't give me the chance to tell him."

"Seems to me that he's still trying to figure out how it's making him feel," Charlotte interjects. "Have you heard from him at all?"

"He finally texted me this morning, telling me he was sorry. I told him that we need to talk, and he asked to wait until Thursday. He said he needed some time."

"Then that's what you need to give him, Noelle." Amelia places her hand on mine. "He deserves your patience, even though he was harsh about the entire thing."

"He yelled so loud it scared Scarlett."

Penelope winces. "I'm sure he feels terrible about that. But I can kick him in the balls for you if you really want me to teach him a lesson."

"That's not necessary, but thank you."

"Hey, girls." Damien comes around the corner, kissing

Charlotte's temple before stealing their daughter from her. He nestles Ivy into his chest and then directs his gaze to me. "Don't be upset, but the guys and I were kind of eavesdropping and wanted to offer our two cents."

Jeffrey pops his head around Damien, waving enthusiastically. "Hello, ladies." He clears his throat dramatically. "So as my friend here was saying, I think we might be able to offer the male perspective on this situation, if you're interested."

I shrug, kind of nervous that they heard as much as they did but desperate to see if they can offer some insight that will give me a little clarity. I just feel so hurt and lost right now.

"Excellent. So if I were a guy—" Jeffrey begins but gets cut off almost immediately.

"You're not a guy?" Damien and Ethan ask at the same time, giving each other a high five as they cackle.

"Fuck you both. You know what I mean."

"Just wanted to clarify." Damien snickers.

Jeffrey rolls his eyes. "No one takes me seriously around here."

Damien slaps him on the back. "Sorry, friend. Sometimes you just make it too easy." Then he looks down at his daughter in his arms and sighs. "Noelle, I know that we don't know Grant that well yet, but I don't know how *I* would handle finding out something like that. I'd probably react very similarly to how he did. Men—we are programmed to procreate. It's in our DNA. Not being able to do that would be a hard pill to swallow and would definitely affect how I feel about relationships. I mean, if I couldn't have given a baby to Charlotte, that would've been really tough to deal with. I don't blame Grant for feeling some sort of way right now."

I wipe under my eyes. "But we can still have kids. He froze his sperm before his cancer treatment."

Damien tilts his head at me and shrugs. "It's still not the same. I'm not sure how else to explain it to you."

Jeffrey jumps back in to the conversation. "Maybe like if you wanted to breastfeed more than anything but realized you couldn't. Like your supply never comes in or you never got your period. That would suck, right?"

Penelope cackles. "Um, threatening a woman with never having a period is *not* an appropriate comparison. Don't threaten us with a good time. If I never had to use a tampon again, I'd be happy."

"Yeah, but then you'd never be able to have children," he counters, arching his brow.

"Okay, I see your point, but still—not the best example."

Ethan wraps his arms around Amelia. "Noelle, part of what makes us feel manly is our ability to reproduce, and when we meet a woman we love, this innate need to make babies with her can possess our minds. Grant's probably feeling that need but knows he can't make it happen, and that would be extremely frustrating." He kisses Amelia's shoulder. "If I can't give Amelia a baby, it'd kill me. I know several alternatives exist, but it would be a difficult truth to accept. Even if past experience with cancer is a factor in that—maybe *especially* because of that."

I look around at the other men in my life, trying to grasp

what they're saying. And it's resonating with me, but I still know that none of that matters for us.

"I appreciate the insight. I do. I just need to talk to Grant about it. I think he needs to hear from me how I feel about the situation, and then he might feel better."

Amelia turns to Ethan. "She's right. You men might feel one way about it, but us women deserve to be heard about our feelings on the matter, too. Male infertility can be just as daunting for a couple as female infertility. Hell, *any* infertility is a difficult obstacle to navigate, but it's important that a couple does it together."

"Exactly. And ultimately, I just want Grant, any way I can have him."

Ethan smiles. "Then he's a lucky man who will eventually pull his head out of his ass. We all do at some point for the women we love."

"Let's hope you're right about that. I don't think my heart can take the aftermath if he doesn't. This can't be the end."

"Everything will be okay, Noelle," Charlotte speaks up. "If it's not okay, then it's not the end."

By Wednesday night, I'm just numb. I'm lonely and tired and have cried so much that the bags under my eyes have their own designer bags.

I'm anxious to see and talk to Grant tomorrow but also ready for this to be over, one way or the other. If he says he doesn't want to be with me anymore, I know it will feel like a thousand knives stabbing me all over my body. But I also know that I will survive. I've survived every heartbreak before—I can survive this one, too.

I hope.

I just put Scarlett to bed. She'd wrapped her arms around the stuffed elephant that Grant bought her all those months ago and wouldn't let go. I can tell she misses him. She's had that elephant in her arms for the past three days. Even though this isn't the longest stretch we've gone without seeing him, they're so attached to each other now that I feel as if she knows something is wrong. She's been fussy and more irritated than normal about certain things, too. Even the minion movies haven't helped quell her frustrations about life.

Seems she's already moody at her age. I have so much fun to look forward to when she's a teenager.

I move into my closet, throwing my dirty clothes in the hamper on my way after just getting out of the shower, when I glance up and notice a box I haven't opened in years. Something about it calls to me, so I pull it down from its spot on the shelf and bring it to my bed, taking a seat before I lift the lid. And I'm instantly assaulted with memories from my childhood.

Old birthday cards, notes from friends in high school, and pictures from Polaroid cameras lay before me, memories that transport me back to a lifetime ago. And as I sort through the papers, one appears that has me gasping as I unfold it and read the words in my hands.

It's my life plan, the same list I wrote over and over again, reordering and adjusting it so many times, thinking that a list was going to make everything work out the way I wanted it to. But now as I stare at these words, I just laugh. I laugh deeply until those laughs turn to sobs, looking at a life I thought I wanted, a life I thought would make me happy.

If I've learned anything in the last five years, it's that happiness isn't a destination—it's a choice. And I've made a few choices that have led me to where I am today, things I never thought I'd do, but I wouldn't change a thing.

I wouldn't have my friends. I wouldn't have a better relationship with my sister now. I wouldn't have my daughter if I hadn't gone after what I wanted for myself. Instead, I took control of my life and started living. And you know what? I'm happier now than I ever thought I could be.

Well, happy and exhausted, but I guess that's a small price to pay.

I spent my entire childhood planning my life out, and nothing went the way I thought. And I think it's because I was waiting for my life to happen instead of living it. For the first time ever, I just want to *be*—be present, be thankful, and be content. And that may mean that life is going to throw me some curveballs along the way, but I know that how I react to them is what's going to make the difference about how I feel about my life.

Meeting Grant was a curveball. Realizing his mom was my client was a plot twist. And now realizing that having children together may never happen or at least will be far more complicated than I imagined is a speed bump that we can get over as long as we're together. I'm not going to let this man shut me out. Not when we finally found one another, not when I know that no matter what I envision in the future, it's his face I see next to mine. All the other details? We can figure those out along the way.

I just want *him*. And I plan on letting him know that.

The doorbell rings, and my stomach drops just as my pulse skyrockets. I asked Amelia to watch Scarlett tonight so Grant and I could speak alone. Ultimately, if this reconciliation goes well, I know he'll want to see her, too, but I thought it would be easier for us to talk without her as a distraction.

When I open the door, the man I can't imagine my life without stands there looking rough. His face is sullen and his shoulders are hunched, but he's holding a bouquet of red roses. That has to be a good sign, right?

"Noelle," he breathes, moving toward me as I brace myself for him. But as soon as his body is in my vicinity, I melt, just like I always do. I shut the door behind him as he leans down to kiss me on the cheek. "Hi, baby."

"Hello."

"These are for you." He hands me the flowers, which I bring to my nose instantly and take a deep inhale.

"Thank you. Let me put these in a vase, and then we can talk." I walk into the kitchen, finding a vase and filling it up as my entire body vibrates with nerves. He seems quiet and reserved, but who knows what may come out of his mouth next? "How were your days you needed?" I ask with a pinch of saltiness in my words. Part of me would love nothing more than to chastise this man for what he's put me through over the last four days, but I know he's also been through hell, so that makes me feel slightly better.

"Awful. Long. I have so much I need to say."

I spin to face him, and his haunted blue eyes stare back at me. "Yeah, I do, too."

"Can we sit, please? I don't want to waste another minute."

I follow him over to the couch, and we take a seat next to each other, leaving space between us. And that little bit of space might as well be a crack in the earth.

"Noelle," he starts, staring down at his hands in his lap before lifting his eyes to mine. "I'm so fucking sorry for running out on you."

"Thank you." My eyes start to well, but I'm trying to hold it together.

"I shouldn't have reacted that way, but in that moment, I just needed some space."

"And did it give you the perspective you needed?"

He nods. "Yes, baby. It did."

"Why didn't you just tell me what you were doing?"

His brow furrows. "What do you mean?"

"I mean about the tests, Grant. You never told me that you wanted to find out the answers to those questions. I could have been there *for you*, been there *with you*. I wouldn't have let you go through that alone."

"I did those tests over a month ago, Noelle. So much has happened and changed since then, that, for a moment, I wasn't sure I wanted to know the results."

"What hurts the most is that you kept this from me and were suffering alone. I thought we were at the point in our relationship where we could tell each other anything, where we could be the person the other could lean on." I think that's what hurts the most, that he felt he couldn't lean on me when I've done nothing but lean on him for months. He's been there for me in so many ways, but he didn't give me the chance to do the same for him. "I just don't get why you couldn't have just told me?"

"Because I was scared! I'm fucking scared, Noelle." His eyes fill with moisture behind the lenses of his glasses, and it makes my heart ache even more. "I love you, and the last thing I wanted was to lose you. I know I would have told you eventually, but at that moment in time, I just wanted to be with you and Scarlett and enjoy the life we were living together. I never thought I'd have that. And I love that little girl as if she's my own."

"I know you do."

"You're the one woman I want to give everything to, and *I can't*. I can't fucking give you everything that a man is supposed to. No one talks about male infertility. No one discusses how emasculating it feels to know you can't give the woman you love kids—"

I cut him off. "You had cancer, Grant. You survived an illness that could have killed you. That is completely the opposite of emasculating. That is strength and courage on a level that most people never possess. And there are other ways to have a family." I cast my eyes to the side, wondering if he's questioning the choice I made to have Scarlett now.

"But it made me feel weak. Back then, I was only concerned about surviving, and I did it. In retrospect, I know I never dealt with the emotional damage that whole period of my life inflicted on me. My brother helped me see that, though, and I think maybe I need to speak with someone about it."

"I think that might help you a lot."

He reaches for my hand. "And I want to do that for you. And I don't want this to be a burden for us, something that keeps rearing its ugly head at the wrong time." He drops his head and sighs. "And I'm so fucking sorry for reacting to your news the way that I did. That's what kills me the most. I know you may not be pregnant, but you did not deserve that reaction from me, and I'm so fucking sorry."

A tear falls down my cheek as he lifts his head again and looks at me, waiting for my response. "Thank you."

"Did you ever take a test?"

I slowly shake my head as his brows lift. "No. I wanted to wait for you. I was hoping you'd come around eventually."

Scooting closer to me on the couch, he reaches up to cup my face. "I did. I'm here, and I'm not going anywhere. I'm sorry that I walked out on you, because that's not the man I want to be for you. I made a mistake, and I'm not saying I won't ever make another, but the last thing I want to do is make you question how I feel about you." He leans his forehead against mine. "I love you, Noelle. I love you so fucking much, and I'm so sorry."

"I love you, too. I just wish you would have let me explain something to you, how your news made me feel."

"I'm listening now."

Drawing in a deep breath, I prepare to tell him what I need him to know. "Grant, I don't want to drag this out. I've read enough romance novels to know that the third-act breakup is something that's necessary but doesn't have to be dramatic. Sometimes all two people need to do is talk, say what they're feeling, and let the other person know that one fight doesn't mean it's the end. So let me talk before you try to tell me what I'm thinking or how I should be feeling again, okay?"

He chuckles. "Okay."

"I've spent most of my twenties looking for my guy, and I never found him. But I also never settled. Growing up, I was so terrified that I would never have children. It's something I've always imagined for myself. So I set out to have a child on my own because I was tired of waiting. Was it harder than I ever thought it could be? Absolutely. But then I met *you*. And lo and behold, you were under my nose the entire time. I think this was how it was supposed to work out because now I have Scarlett *and* you. That wouldn't have happened if I met you first. I didn't get what I wanted because I deserved better. I deserved *you*."

"Babe . . ."

"Let me finish." He nods, his hand still cupping my face. "I know that having kids together may never happen for us or will take many steps, but ultimately, I would rather have *you* in my life. I have a child, and I love her dearly. But with you? I have my family. It may be unconventional and completely backward from how society has deemed it should work, but fuck that. I'm tired of trying to live my life by a checklist and a plan. Nothing worked out the way I planned it, and you know what? I'm glad —because I finally found you, and you have enriched my life in a way I never knew was possible."

I draw in a breath. "For the longest time, I lived my life according to this idea that *when* this happened or *if* this happened, I would be happy. *If* I lost twenty pounds, or *when* I found the perfect man . . ." I shake my head, realizing how crazy that sounds. "But you helped me realize that the *if* and *when* is trivial. Maybe it is the *who* I was waiting for, because with you, I'm happy, truly happy for the first time in my life.

"And that doesn't mean that my happiness depends on you. It means that having you by my side has shown me what life can be: fulfilling, rich, and full of love, joy, little moments that steal my breath away, and experiences with the three of us that literally make my heart hurt because I'm so overwhelmed by the love I feel with you in my—and Scarlett's—life."

I take out my list from my pocket and show it to him. Every line is crossed out, and only two words are written legibly on the paper now. *Be happy.* "This is the only thing on my plan now, Grant. To be happy. And that can't happen without you. The only thing that matters in this moment is us together, the three of us as a family. We love you, *all* of you, and everything you have to offer us. And we want to give you the same thing in return."

With tears in his eyes, he leans over and kisses my lips. "God, I'm the one who doesn't deserve you. I don't deserve your forgiveness and heart after keeping this from you and running away when I was hurting."

"Yes, you do. You deserve happiness, too, Grant. You deserve love. We both do. We've waited long enough."

"You are the end of my new beginning, Noelle. I never thought I'd have one, but I know you're the one I want at the end of whatever journey awaits us. You're the only thing that matters to me, too. I will die a happy man with you and Scarlett in my life. You two are my whole world now, and I promise I won't let you down again."

"I love you, Grant."

We waste no more time talking. Instead, Grant kisses me with so much intensity that I feel like I'm floating, almost as if a weight has been lifted from my shoulders and I can finally breathe again.

"I need you, Noelle. Please," he mumbles against my lips as he lays me back on the couch and begins to undress me.

"Yes."

We claw at each other's clothes, Grant rips off his glasses in that Clark Kent way that makes my libido spike every time, and before I can get comfortable, Grant slides home between my legs.

"Fuck, I love you," he growls in my ear, setting a relentless pace as he makes love to me, frantic and hard but full of emotion.

"I love you, too."

Our lips move over each other's, our hands roam and grasp for flesh, and electricity sparks between us, setting our bodies on fire. And in record time, we come apart in each other's arms.

Once we're sated yet still naked on the couch, Grant brushes the hair from my face. "We just had our first fight."

"Yeah, and it was a big one."

"It won't be the last," he counters.

"I know. But that's okay as long as we figure it out together."

"Speaking of figuring things out." He draws a lazy circle around my belly button before placing his palm flat against my skin there. "What do you say we find out if there's really a baby in there?"

I gasp. "Are you sure?"

"Yes. I know you waited for me, so let's figure it out together now, baby. Okay?" He rests his forehead on mine. "I'm here now."

"Thank God."

We get dressed and then head for my bathroom where the box of pregnancy tests has been haunting me all week.

"I'll wait out here," Grant announces as he takes a seat on the edge of my bed. I close the door, do my business, and then open it up to join him on the bed as we wait.

"What if it's positive, Grant?"

"Then I'll truly believe in miracles and be the happiest man on the face of the planet."

I smile and lean my head on his shoulder. "And if it's negative?"

"Then we keep doing what we're doing and make a plan for how and when we want to try to grow our family." He takes my hand in his. "I would love to have more kids with you, Noelle, so we will figure that out."

"I know. At least we'll have each other."

"And Scarlett," he adds. "And one day, I'd like to adopt her. Make her my own in the eyes of the law."

"Really?" I pop my head up to look at him.

"Absolutely. You'll be mine in the eyes of the law soon enough, too, but I want both of my girls to have my last name."

"I want that, too." Grant kisses me just as the timer on my phone goes off. "Shall we?"

He nods. "Yeah."

Holding my hand, we go into the bathroom and look down at the test on the counter, the test that displays only one pink line in the window.

"What does that mean?" he asks.

"It's negative," I reply, feeling sad even though I knew the chances were small. And even though I don't want to, I break down in his arms.

"It's okay, baby. That just means we get more time to enjoy each other. That's how we have to look at it."

"I know. I'm just sad. I'll get over it."

"I wanted it to be positive, too, Noelle. And one day, it will be. But if not, then you, me, and Scarlett is enough."

"*You're* enough for us," I mumble against his chest.

He lifts my chin so that our eyes meet. "I will always try to be the man you deserve, okay? But even then, you deserve the entire world, and I might not be able to give that to you."

I shake my head. "You don't get it, Grant. You already are my whole world. And knowing I found you is everything to me. You're the love of my life, Mr. I'm-too-sexy-for-my-shirt."

His laugh covers me like a warm blanket. "Don't make me play the song again."

"Maybe not tonight. How about tonight you just be Grant and I'll just be me?"

"No playing pretend? No wanting to escape?"

"Nope. Tonight, I just want us to be real. To be us. Not as planned, but perfect, nonetheless."

Epilogue

Grant

Two Years Later

"You're doing great, Noelle." I brush the sweat-matted hair from her forehead to place a kiss there. "Are you sure you don't want the epidural?"

"I'm sure. I did it last time with no drugs. I can do it again."

"There's no badge for that," one of the nurses in the delivery room teases. "And we don't judge. Childbirth is a bitch, and medicine is a gift from God."

My wife laughs and then looks up to me. "It's okay. I have my husband here with me this time. That makes a world of difference, believe me."

Standing in a delivery room waiting for our son to be born is a moment I've been looking forward to my entire life.

I proposed to Noelle on Scarlett's first birthday, just two short months after our fight. She was shocked but eagerly accepted. I told her I wasn't getting any younger, and we love each other, so why wait? We were married on Valentine's Day the following year. And then we got to work on expanding our family, but not before I legally adopted Scarlett as mine. That little girl is my daughter, no matter what her DNA might say.

We never used protection after our discussion about kids because we knew the chances of us conceiving naturally were low, so we figured we'd take our chances with that route. Unfortunately, nothing stuck, so after six months, we decided to try IVF using my deposit I'm glad I was smart enough to hold on to. The process took a lot longer than I thought and a ton of money, so we agreed we'd give it one shot.

When the test came up negative, Noelle and I both lost it. It took a toll on us, and we both slipped into a dark place for a little while. We sought out counseling and then debated trying one more time, but my mother actually approached us with an idea. She suggested we try using the same sperm donor that Noelle chose for Scarlett's dad, that way our children would be biological siblings with the same parents.

With hope in her eyes, Noelle turned to me and asked me if I would be okay with that. It was a cheaper route to go versus IVF, and we both liked the idea of them being related completely. But I wanted one more shot. I desperately wanted to see if I could have a child of my own, so we gave IVF another round, and miraculously, it worked.

Noelle turns and looks at me. "You're about to be a daddy, Grant. How does that make you feel?"

"I'm already a father, Noelle. Scarlett is mine, too."

"I know, but you weren't here to witness her being born. You are about to experience an entirely different realm of love."

I rest my forehead on hers. "I'll take all the love I can get. You can never have too much of that."

Noelle's face scrunches up as another contraction hits her, so I hold her hand, place a cool cloth on her neck, and watch the strongest woman I know labor my son into the world—even though the process is slow going, I will say that.

She sighs and lets her head drop back to the bed once the contraction lets up. "I'm so happy that you're here this time. Not that I don't love my girls, but Penelope kept making comments last time about how my vagina would never look the same. She wasn't exactly supportive."

I chuckle at the mention of Penelope. Out of all of Noelle's friends, she's the one I definitely find the most entertaining. Although a few months back, Amelia brought out some new prototypes of sex toys at a dinner party, and Charlotte basically took her bra off from under her shirt one night that we were all hanging out together since it was bothering her. She'd just found out she was pregnant again, and her boobs were sore, so she declared there was no way she could keep it on any longer.

I've never met a group of women like these four, but I can't help but love them all and their friendship.

"Don't worry, baby. I'll love your pussy no matter what. And I'm sure it will be just fine since it was after the last time." I wink at her just as another contraction hits, and we slip back into labor mode.

Fortunately, things progress rather quickly from there, and soon, Noelle is pushing my son into the world.

"One more push, baby. He's almost here." I keep her leg pressed back as I lean over and see my son's head sticking out of my wife. I'll never forget the sight for a multitude of reasons, but mostly because in a moment, I'll finally be able to hold him.

Noelle bears down, and then he's out, crying and covered in blood but one of the most beautiful things I've ever seen.

Moisture flows freely from my eyes before I lean down and press my lips to Noelle's. "He's fucking perfect, baby. You did so good."

"*We* did, Grant. I love you so much."

"I love you, too."

"Here you go, Mom," the doctor says as she places Asher on her chest. The name means "happy" in Hebrew, and that's exactly what Noelle and I have endeavored to be —happy and content with our life just the way it is.

"Hello, my beautiful boy," Noelle coos as she strokes his head. The doctors are still doing their business between her legs, but the two of us are completely oblivious to anything but our son.

"Hey, Asher. Daddy's here, too." Just saying those words make more tears fall. I rest my head against Noelle's and sob. "Thank you, baby. Thank you for giving me the greatest gift I've ever received." I can't even see right now, but the love that's pouring out of me feels like a light that's setting my soul on fire.

"You, Asher, and Scarlett are mine, Grant. I love you all."

One of the nurses comes over and reaches for our baby. "Let's get this little guy cleaned up so Daddy can hold him."

I grab the box of tissues from the table beside us and begin cleaning myself up, helping Noelle do the same. But when the nurse hands me my son, I lose it all over again.

An hour later, I'm sitting in a chair, holding Asher close to my chest while Noelle sleeps soundly in the bed. Her mom will be here shortly with Scarlett so that she can meet her baby brother, but this little slice of silence is one I don't want to waste.

I stare down at my son, at his lips that look like mine, at his dark hair that I know he got from me, and that's when the most contented sigh I can manage slips out. But then Noelle's voice pulls me from the moment.

"You okay over there?"

"Yeah, I'm more than okay." I reach up and brush the tear from my cheek. "I can't stop fucking crying though."

She laughs at me. "It's okay. There's no other feeling like holding your baby for the first time."

"This is unreal, Noelle."

"No, Grant. This is love."

Her words sink in. "It's overwhelming."

"The real kind always is."

"Thank you for giving me the life I never thought I'd have," I say as I stand and move over to her, settling on the edge of the bed right next to her side.

"Right back at you, baby."

"Who needs a life plan, anyway?"

She smiles. "Not us, apparently."

"Nope. I'd say we did good without one."

"I agree. Because you and me, we were destined to be from the beginning."

"All because of a wet shirt, a beautiful baby girl, and these stunning green eyes." I draw my finger down her cheek. "I didn't stand a chance."

"Yes, you did, Grant. But when you got your chance, you took it. And that's what made all the difference."

THE END

Thank you so much for reading! If you enjoyed the book, PLEASE consider leaving a review on Amazon and/or Goodreads.

And if you want one last glimpse of our Ladies Who Brunch, you can download a SERIES EPILOGUE here! Ten years later, what are our girls up to? Find out by clicking the link.

But wait . . .

You know I couldn't end the series without giving you a story for a character that everyone just loved and readers begged for.

That's right!

Jeffrey gets his own story! And you can read it here in Nice Guys Still Finish.

Acknowledgments

This book was a rollercoaster of emotions and a tad cathartic, if I'm being honest. But I knew that in a series that focused on women and the obstacles we face in life, there had to be a book about becoming a mom and how incredible yet life-altering it is. And therefore, Noelle's story was born.

Motherhood is the roughest hood you'll ever go through, and it felt therapeutic to put into words some of the hardest moments of raising children while simultaneously loving it. Noelle's thoughts were raw, unfiltered, and honest. And many moms will tell you they've thought the same things a time or two. More importantly, it's okay that we share those things. No one should feel like they can't. Transparency is so important nowadays, and so I hope that all of the moms can see themselves in Noelle at some point throughout her book.

Growing up, I always wanted kids and was terrified that someday I wouldn't be able to have them. Thankfully, I found an incredible man and we made two beautiful, healthy children, but I know that doesn't happen for everyone. Infertility—both female and male—is very real, and my heart goes out to any couple who has been affected by it.

Finishing this book was rough, I'm not going to lie. My life was extremely chaotic while trying to tell Noelle's story. But every time I sat down to write, it helped me escape from the chaos, and I'm very proud of it. I hope that you've enjoyed this series, and choose to read Jeffrey's book, Nice Guys Still Finish, which will tie into my next series coming later this year.

Don't forget to download the series epilogue to get a glimpse into the gang's future 10 years down the road! And don't worry—you'll get more of them in my new series too.

To my husband: Thank you for cheering me on and celebrating my success with me as I release each book. Thank you for understanding how much joy this hobby brings me. And thank you for being my real life book husband and giving me my own true love story to brag about.

To Keely: One of the best things that has come out of this author journey is my friendship with you. I cherish our friendship so much! Thank you for always being there to chat and cheer me on. I love ya!

To Melissa: I am SO grateful for our working relationship. Your attention to detail and thoughtfulness shined throughout the process. Thank you for your dedication to my stories and I look forward to working together again.

To Melanie: As always, your expertise and friendship has made this author journey even more rewarding. I'm so grateful for our connection and honest discussions about this author gig. So thankful to have you in my corner.

And to my beta readers, ARC readers, and every reader (both old and new): Thank you for taking a chance on a self-published author. Thank you for sharing my books with others. Thank you for allowing me to share my creativity with people who love the romance genre as much as I do.

And thank you for supporting a wife and mom who found a hobby that she loves.

About the Author

Harlow James is a wife and mom who fell in love with romance novels, so she decided to write her own.

Her books are the perfect blend of emotional, addictive, and steamy romance. If you love stories with a guaranteed Happily Ever After, then Harlow is your new best friend.

When she's not writing, she can be found working her day job, reading every romance novel she can find time for, laughing with her husband and kids, watching re-runs of FRIENDS, and spending time cooking for her friends and family while drinking White Claws and Margaritas.

 facebook.com/HarlowJamesAuthor
instagram.com/harlowjamesauthor

More Books by Harlow James

More Books by Harlow James

The Ladies Who Brunch

Never Say Never (Charlotte and Damien)

No One Else (Amelia and Ethan)

Now's The Time (Penelope and Maddox)

Not As Planned (Noelle and Grant)

Nice Guys Still Finish (Jeffrey and Ariel)

The California Billionaires Series

My Unexpected Serenity (Wes and Shayla)

My Unexpected Vow (Hayes and Waverly)

My Unexpected Family (Silas and Chloe)

The Emerson Falls Series

Tangled (Kane & Olivia)

Enticed (Cooper & Clara)

Captivated (Cash and Piper)

Revived (Luke and Rachel)

Devoted (Brooks and Jess)

Lost and Found in Copper Ridge

A holiday romance in which two people book a stay in a cabin for the same amount of time thanks to a serendipitous $5 bill.

One Look, A Baseball Romance Standalone (you can get this for FREE if you sign up for my newsletter)

Guilty as Charged

An intense opposites attract standalone that will melt your kindle. He's an ex-con construction worker. She's a lawyer looking for passion.

McKenzie's Turn to Fall

A holiday romance where a romance author falls for her neighborhood butcher.

Made in the USA
Middletown, DE
06 March 2025

72139398R00233